#noescape
A #murdertrending novel

Gretchen McNeil

FREEFORM BOOKS

Los Angeles   New York

First Edition, September 2020
10 9 8 7 6 5 4 3 2 1
FAC-021131-20213
Printed in the United States of America

This book is set in Adobe Garamond Pro
Designed by Marci Senders

Library of Congress Cataloging-in-Publication Control Number:
2019050709
ISBN 978-1-368-02626-0

Reinforced binding
Visit www.freeform.com/books

For John Flynn,
who forced me to type most of this novel with one hand

"Our puzzle will be your undoing."
—DERRICK AND MELINDA BROWNE,
FOUNDERS OF ESCAPE-CAPADES, LLC

ONE

"FOUR MINUTES."

Persey tried to ignore the voice booming through the loudspeaker, but it was impossible with three people crowded in behind, desperately waiting for her answer. She could feel their dank breaths against her neck in a claustrophobic (creepy) way and fought the urge to start throwing elbows to get them to back off.

You don't have time for that.

Which was true. Instead of starting a fight, she concentrated on not internalizing their tension. But between the ticking clock, the stress of the moment, and the physical proximity of their bodies, Persey could feel herself absorbing the anxiety that dripped off her teammates in heavy, saplike beads, which made it super freaking difficult to focus on the image before her.

Persey swallowed, her eyes darting around the touch screen at the sixteen cryptic squares filled with color and lines and shadows. Each depicted a snippet of a larger image, but they had been scrambled, rotated. Lines and curves no longer met neatly at the seams, and it was Persey's job to rearrange them into something that made sense before time ran out.

Okay, well, technically it was a puzzle all four of them should have

1

been unraveling together. But her "teammates" had all thrown up their hands in confusion and so the responsibility (stress) of completing this final task had fallen squarely on Persey's shoulders.

"Hurry up!" a shrill female voice chirped from behind. "We've only got three minutes left."

Persey didn't even need to turn around to know the look on the woman's face. Her beady brown eyes, flanked with creases as if they'd spent the better part of their five decades on this planet pinched in a scowl, were burned into Persey's memory. Ms. Middle-Age Stress Case had been on edge since they met in the lobby before even entering the library-themed escape room, as if the whole thing was a matter of life and death instead of a silly competition with some prize money on the line.

And my dad called me *the idiot.*

"Maybe we should let someone else try," the woman continued, her voice increasing in pitch as her anxiety swelled. "She's what, like nineteen?"

Seventeen.

"Maybe an adult should do this."

"Calm down, Sheryl," her husband countered. The tall Black man with the distinguished gray hair. He exuded the kind of cool, professorial calm that Persey found comforting (intimidating). "She's nailed everything else so far. Let her have at it."

"Yeah, *Sheryl.*" The young, tanned guy in cargo shorts and flip-flops— with a surprisingly pristine pedicure—emphasized Sheryl's name as if they were old friends, even though he had no connection to her and her husband. His pretend familiarity reeked of sarcasm. "Why don't you just pipe down and let, uh . . ." He paused, and Persey felt his warm breath move from her neck to her cheek as he leaned closer. "What did you say your name was?"

I didn't. "Persey."

"Whoa!" He sounded (pretended to be) impressed. "I have a cousin named Percival."

"Per-ci-val," Mr. Sheryl mused, drawing out each syllable as if he was evaluating how they felt in his mouth. "You have an odd name." He didn't elaborate and seemed to be waiting for Persey to chime in with her thoughts on a name that wasn't hers, had no connection to hers. Like, who the hell would name their daughter Percival? And why were either of them wasting even five seconds thinking about her name at a time like this?

Persey was fourteen when she decided to go by her middle name of Persephone instead of the one her parents had christened her. It felt more comfortable, somehow, even though her family refused to use it. And though she loved the nickname Persey, she hated explaining what it was short for. The moment "Persephone" left her lips, everyone within earshot chimed in with some little factoid about the name, gleaned from their eighth-grade Greek-mythology modules. As if Persey didn't know exactly who her namesake was.

"The reason I say that," Mr. Sheryl said, displaying a penchant for pontification, "is because Percival is generally viewed as a male name, from the Chrétien de Troyes epic poem *Perceval, the Story of the Grail*, set during the—"

"It's short for Persephone," she said with a heavy sigh.

"Fascinating!"

Here we go.

Mr. Sheryl cleared his throat. "You know, she was the queen of the underworld in Greek myth, destined to spend six months a year there due to the identical number of persimmon seeds she ate—"

"Pomegranate," Pretty Pedicure said, correcting Mr. Sheryl.

"Eh?"

"Persephone ate pomegranate seeds in Hades."

"As a *professor* of English literature," Mr. Sheryl began, "I'm relatively sure I can distinguish between my fruits, young man."

Persey retracted her previous assessment of Mr. Sheryl: although she'd nailed the professorial vibe, there was nothing comforting about his personality—he was as pompous as his wife was tense.

"Two minutes!" Sheryl squealed. "She hasn't moved a single tile yet. We'll never win that prize money now."

As if you actually need it.

"It's not about the prize, Sher . . ." her husband said, trying to placate her. Persey wondered if that ever worked.

"Don't you 'Sher' me. I'm going to ask for our money back the second we get out of here. I don't care if this is supposed to be the only unbeatable escape room in the world. We spent months on the waiting list for this spot and she's been hogging all the challenges!"

Whose fault is that? It wasn't so much that she was hogging the challenges as she was the only one who'd offered a solution to them. Or at least, offered the correct one. After the first two puzzles, the other three participants had informally abdicated leadership of the team to Persey, and it was pretty much understood that it was now her responsibility to solve this final puzzle.

The unbeatable one. According to the propaganda in the lobby, several people had made it to this final challenge of the Hidden Library before time ran out, but no one had managed to solve it and claim the thirty-thousand-dollar prize. This escape room had been installed all over the world, and yet in its four months of operation, not one single person had unscrambled this tangled mess of images on a touch screen embedded in a narrow, old-fashioned secretary desk in the corner of the faux library.

What makes you think that you can, huh? You can't even pass algebra.

The voice in her head was right. This was her first ever escape room, and it was crazy to think that she could succeed when literally thousands of Escape-Capades aficionados from around the world had already failed. Sure, she'd learned a fair amount about how these things worked—the challenges that built one upon the next, the red herrings and misleading clues, the attempts by the room designers to create a claustrophobic atmosphere—but that was a far cry from *actually* participating in one of these games. And now here she was, on the brink of solving the impossible. Was she delusional to think she could win this?

Persey closed her eyes and took a deep breath. If she refused to be bullied into action by Sheryl, she needed to be equally as stubborn in resisting her overwhelming (ever-present) sense of self-doubt. Neither would help her, and giving in to either would probably result in a wrong move. She was so close.

According to the counter beside the scrambled image, she could move or rotate only eight tiles in her quest to re-create an image, which would have proved difficult (impossible) even if she had the original in front of her to compare it to. Which she didn't. She had no idea what the muted browns and reds, diagonal lines and sharp edges, were supposed to represent, but the clues they'd picked up over the course of the last hour *should* have helped her figure it out by now:

1. The large mural painting of skeletons and peasants dancing in a circle behind which Persey had found a key to the rare bookcase.

2. The eighteenth-century rhyming dictionary on said bookcase in which the word "saucer" had directed them to the half-consumed cup of tea on the librarian's desk.

3. The tea-leaf motif around the border of the librarian's framed certificate of completion in a language course on Old English, but written backward in a florid scroll so it looked merely decorative when viewed head-on, but became readable while viewing it in a mirror.

4. The pin on the lapel of the librarian's tweed coat, slung lazily across the arm of his desk chair, which depicted a medieval cathedral.

They had all led Persey and her co-participants to this secret screen, hidden away in the back of a research cubicle behind a stack of books about the Black Death in Europe. They had to unscramble the image in eight moves or less. . . .

She had missed something. Some connection between the previous clues and the jumbled mess before her.

Danse macabre. A cathedral. Old English.

"Sixty seconds!" Sheryl cried.

And what did a teacup and saucer have to do with anything?

"We're gonna have to agree to disagree here, Prof," Pedicure said, still arguing the persimmon-versus-pomegranate point. "But, hey, maybe you can answer me this—any idea what 'Persephone' means? Like in ancient Greek and shit?"

"None," Mr. Sheryl said drily.

Persey froze, her brain fixated on the question. Mr. Sheryl may not have known the answer, but she did.

"Bringer of death," she said, turning to face them.

Mr. Sheryl's brows shot up. "Pardon?"

"Persephone means 'a bringer of death.'" A slow smile spread across her lips as her eyes drifted to Pretty Pedicure's face: he'd just given her the key to this puzzle. "And I know how to solve this."

"Seriously?" he said.

"We don't have time." Sheryl grabbed her husband's arm. "THIRTY SECONDS!"

Persey spun back to the screen, flanked by the research volumes on the plague in fourteenth-century Europe. A bringer of death. A bringer of *Black Death.* How could she have been so blind? She swept her fingers across the screen, swapping and rotating the image tiles as she went.

"A mirror to see the image in reverse, and saucer because it rhymes with 'Chaucer'!" One more tile swap, then with a single pass of her palm across the screen, all the tiles flipped to their mirror images.

A photograph appeared. It was an old leather-bound tome, medieval in appearance, open to a weathered page with an elegant scroll of handwritten words beside an illustration of a red-robed man on horseback holding a cross. Embellishments of leaves and vines peppered the margins and the first letter of text had been given an elaborate treatment of interlocking scrolls and ribbons. The instant the image came together, the countdown froze and a bookcase on the far wall swung open, revealing the secret exit from the room.

With just three seconds to spare.

TWO

MR. SHERYL, THE ENGLISH LIT PROFESSOR, LEANED OVER Persey's arm for a better view of the screen. "'The Pardoner's Tale.' From *The Canterbury Tales*." His voice was breathless, disbelieving. "*You've* read Chaucer?"

Persey wasn't about to admit that reading was not her strong point, or that audiobooks were the only reason she hadn't failed out of high school yet. Mr. English Lit Professor would 100 percent turn up his nose at her for having listened to *The Canterbury Tales* instead of reading the words on the page. And she wasn't about to give him that satisfaction.

"Yes."

"'If that ye be so leef to fynde Deeth, turne up this croked wey,'" he quoted in a strange accent. "I should have known."

You really should have.

"You really should have," Pretty Pedicure said. His voice was a smirk.

Sheryl embraced her husband. "We did it! We just beat the unbeatable challenge. And not like that Internet debacle last year with the Prison Break escape room. We did this on our own."

Our own?

"Our names will go down in history!"

Our names?

Pretty Pedicure smiled. "My name *does* have an historic ring to it."

"Which is?" Persey realized he'd never said it.

"Kevin Lima."

"What an incredibly uncommon surname," the professor said. "Are you of Portuguese decent?"

Kevin opened his mouth to reply, but before he could say a word, applause rang through the room. Persey turned to find a tall young woman with a severe black bob and red-lacquered lips entering the Hidden Library through the secret exit, clapping her elegant, well-manicured hands. She was professionally dressed in a cream pantsuit, which seemed out of place for a Saturday morning, and she was followed by a dozen people, all clad in matching lime-green polo shirts. The entourage beamed from ear to ear, twittering about like a flock of ravenous twentysomething geese, fresh out of college if not still students, and though they didn't look much younger than their leader, she exuded maturity and authority.

"Congratulations!" the woman cried. Her impossibly high, pointy-toed stilettos clicked in discordant syncopation with her slow clapping as she crossed the library. "You've beaten the Hidden Library escape room!"

"Thank you so much!" Sheryl squealed, rushing forward. "Are you from the *Five O'Clock News*? Do you want to interview us? No one's ever escaped the Hidden Library before, you know."

No mention of the prize money, which she'd seemed so intent upon just moments ago—Sheryl was only focused on claiming her fifteen minutes of fame.

"My name is Leah," the newcomer said, extending her hand to Persey. An intricately carved gold-and-diamond ring glittered in the overhead lights. "And I represent the parent company of the Hidden Library—Escape-Capades."

The lime-green-polo brigade behind her cheered dutifully at the mention of their employer as one of them scooted out from the pack, holding a large camera. Its shutter snapped rapidly, mimicking the escalating excitement from the Escape-Capades employees, but while Sheryl turned toward the camera and smiled, hand planted on her right hip, Persey flinched away.

They're taking photos? Seriously?

Persey shielded her face from the camera, desperately hoping her picture wouldn't turn up on Escape-Capades' array of social media platforms.

"It's just for our social media," Leah said, reading Persey's body language as she attempted to avoid the camera's lens. "Don't you want the world to know about your accomplishment here today?"

No.

Sheryl grabbed her husband's arm and pulled him to her side. "Take one of Clay and me. And the cash prize! I almost forgot."

I didn't.

"It should be split evenly four ways."

Leah ignored Sheryl for the second time in as many minutes and kept her focus on Persey. "It was impressive to watch you solve that final puzzle despite . . . distractions."

Persey smirked at the idea that Sheryl and her husband, two highly educated adults who probably could have run intellectual laps around the academically challenged Persey, had been categorized as distractions. "Thanks."

"I suppose you're quite the connoisseur of escape rooms."

"Obviously," Kevin said, answering for her. "Persephone here is a champion."

Leah's eyes drifted toward Kevin; her smile softened. "Funny you should use that word."

"Persephone?"

"Champion."

"Champion*s*," Sheryl said correcting her with the plural. "We're a team."

For the first time since she walked into the room, Leah addressed the other two contestants. "Mr. and Mrs. Rohner, I sincerely hope that you've enjoyed your escape room experience at Escape-Capades. If you'd give your information to the cashier on your way out, your prize money will be mailed to you."

Sheryl's face dropped. "That's it?"

"Were you expecting something else?"

"Well, yeah," Sheryl said, sounding thrown. "Ten Hidden Library escape rooms in five countries, and my husband and I are one-half of the first team to ever beat it. Shouldn't we be on CNN? TMZ? Oprah?"

"It's possible Persephone might find herself on the news." Leah's permasmile deepened, though her flawless skin showed no creases or wrinkles, as if the shiny red lips were merely painted on the canvas of her skin. "Her victory today might—"

"'*Her* victory'?" Sheryl said, eyes wide with shock. "You mean '*our* victory.'"

Leah was having none of it, and her tone, while firm, was dismissive. "Persey is the one who figured out every single clue and put them together for the final puzzle."

"But we're a team," Sheryl whined. "We were in this together."

Kevin laughed. "Like five minutes ago, weren't you threatening to ask for your money back because she was 'hogging' the challenges?"

"I didn't mean it like that."

Persey cocked her head. *Seriously?* "How *did* you mean it?" She should have let the comment go—there was no reason to argue with this woman—but for some reason, Sheryl rubbed her all kinds of wrong.

"How do you know it was all her?" Sheryl pressed. "How do you know my husband and I weren't instrumental in—"

"We were regulating the game," Leah said, intervening before the argument could escalate further. "Via hidden cameras. All Escape-Capades rooms are monitored this way. That's how we know exactly what happened here today, and might I just add that we were all really impressed with your problem-solving ability, Persephone."

Persey's eyes dropped to the floor. She was unaccustomed to praise of any kind.

"So while the prize money will be split four ways," Leah continued, "we do have something special just for you."

"Special?" the professor asked.

Leah folded her arms across her chest. "I'm sure you're aware of the Escape-Capades All-Star Competition taking place next month in Las Vegas?"

The lime-green posse's energy exploded as soon as Leah mentioned the all-star competition. As the Escape-Capades employees' whispers and fidgeting doubled, Persey caught stray phrases like "last spots" and "totally secret."

"Never heard of it," Professor Rohner answered, even though Persey was pretty (totally) sure the question had been meant for her. "Is it a new escape room?"

Leah's eyes were cold as she turned to him. "Perhaps you don't frequent the online communities where we promote this kind of information. Geektacle definitely caters to a . . . younger crowd."

"I've heard of Geektacle," Sheryl snapped.

No, you haven't.

Leah sighed, resigning herself to an explanation. "Positions in the

All-Stars are only offered to the best and brightest in the escape room community. And beating the unbeatable? That scores you an invitation."

"Oh," Persey began, "I don't—"

"The All-Stars?" Professor Rohner said, leaning forward in excitement. "Us?"

Sheryl grabbed his arm. "We're in!"

"I'm terribly sorry," Leah said. Her voice was smooth and even, and dripped with sincerity even though Persey suspected (knew) she felt none. "But I only have two slots left for the All-Stars and I'm offering one of them to Persey."

"Me?"

Kevin snorted again. "No, the other puzzle-solving genius in the room."

Genius was possibly (definitely) the least likely word to be used to describe Persey. "Failure" or "lazy" would have been her dad's choices. But genius? No way.

It wasn't that she was necessarily stupid—she knew, deep down, that she wasn't—but tests in school were so long. Excruciating. It was difficult (impossible) to focus on the questions, the letters and words swirling together before her eyes, so even though she usually knew the material backward and forward, she'd never finished an exam in her entire life.

"What do you say, Persephone?" Leah prompted.

Persey's head snapped up from where her eyes had unconsciously drifted to the floor. The guy with the camera had it pointed directly at her face. There was nowhere to hide, no time to turn away, and she flinched when she heard the shutter sound effect indicating that he'd taken her picture at close range.

"I . . ." *I don't want to do this.*

"You're not really going to say no, are you?" Kevin said. "I mean, you're here because you wanted this, right?"

Persey pressed her lips together. "I guess."

"You guess?" Kevin snorted again. "So it's just about the money, huh?"

Persey flinched again. The camera was still fixed on her, as were the eyes of everyone in the room, and she desperately wanted to crawl into a cave, pull a giant boulder across the opening, and hide from the entire world. "I really appreciate the offer," she began, "but—"

"Are you insane?" Sheryl said, eyes wide while the lime-green brigade gasped in unison. "This is like the greatest honor. Ever."

Persey was tired of the Rohners interrupting her. "I can't."

"Can't?" Kevin said. "Or won't?"

That was inappropriate. "What are you, my dad?"

"Ouch." Kevin cringed. "Maybe, like, an older brother or something."

"I already have one of those."

"Yeah?" Kevin laughed, but Persey could tell it was forced. "I bet he's a cool dude."

He's definitely cold. "You're a lot like him."

"Handsome?" Kevin smiled. "Wicked smart? Life of the party?"

"Smug," Persey replied, matching his grin.

Sheryl cleared her throat. "Get a room, you two."

Ew. "I should be getting home." *Yeah, like you have a home anymore . . .*

"Hold on, Persephone," Leah said, stepping in front of her as Persey started for the secret door. "You haven't even heard what the grand prize is."

Persey sighed. *I don't want to do this.* "Yeah, okay. What is it?"

"The grand winner will receive a cash prize of ten million dollars."

Kevin's jaw dropped. "Holy shit."

"That's ten times what they offered for the Prison Break escape room last year," Sheryl said. "And *that* bankrupted the company." She side-eyed Leah. "Do you even *have* that kind of money anymore? The Hidden Library hasn't been *that* popular."

Leah stiffened. Clearly Persey wasn't the only one who was weary of the Rohners. "Escape-Capades has rebounded nicely since the tragic events of last year, due to our new private investors. . . ."

Professor Rohner cleared his throat. "Two spots left," he said, directing Leah back to her offer. "If she doesn't want one of them, my wife and I would be more than happy to fill out your roster."

Leah caught her breath, as if she'd just had a brilliant, groundbreaking idea. "Actually . . . Persephone—"

"Persey." The nickname was easier.

"Persey, what if I offered you *both* of the last two spots?"

"Both?"

Leah nodded, casting her eyes at Kevin. "One for you and one for your friend."

"Oh, we're not friends," Kevin said quickly. "At least not yet."

Ugh.

"I'm in," Kevin said, extending his hand to Leah. "All in."

"That's nice," Leah said, "but you're only in if Persey is too."

"Oh, so *he* gets special treatment but we don't?" Sheryl huffed, then grabbed her husband's arm. "That's it. CNN is going to hear about this!"

Persey eyed the Rohners as they stormed out through the bookcase door, but Leah ignored them. She was focused on Persey. "Well?"

Persey sighed. Ten million dollars. She'd never have to worry about where she'd sleep or how she'd feed herself. She could get her own place or . . . Persey pressed her lips together to keep them from quivering. *I could disappear.*

Unconsciously, her eyes drifted to Kevin's face. His blond hair flopped over one eye and his hazel eyes practically twinkled as he beamed at her, willing an answer.

"I really don't want to do this," she said softly, finally voicing the refrain that had been running endlessly through her mind all day.

"Please?" Kevin took a step toward her, a devil's grin on his face. "I mean, who the hell turns down a chance to win ten million bucks, huh? You'll never get this opportunity again."

Ugh, again. "Fine."

"Wonderful!" Leah cried. Behind her, the gathered Escape-Capades employees burst into cheers and applause. Persey wished she could share their enthusiasm.

Kevin held his hand up for a high five, which Persey half-heartedly returned. "Sweet! This is going to be so awesome! You're the best, Perse."

The best. Persey seriously doubted it.

THREE

PERSEY WATCHED HER DAD'S FACE AS HE READ THE PIECE OF paper on the dining table. His fingers were in constant motion, spinning his ornate wedding ring over and over on his finger as he processed what he was reading. She could almost pinpoint the moment his temper went from slow roll to out-of-control freight train, all by the color of his face. His pale skin was like the worst poker tell ever: a flush of pink when his anger sparked, then a deep rose as it grew, and finally a purplish red like an angry zit as he crossed the point of no return.

"WHAT THE FUCK?"

She should apologize. Say she was sorry. Try to believe it. That's what her twelve-year-old self would have done, but she was thirteen now, and knew better than to try and argue with her father. It only made things worse. Instead, she just stared defensively (tactically) at the floor.

"A sixty-one percent on your algebra test? How is it even possible that you could be this stupid?"

She wasn't sure why she thought high school would be any different from middle school, where her bad grades had always been a surefire way of igniting her dad's rage. Especially since he'd insisted she attend the same fancy prep school as her brother, even paying someone smarter than her to take the entry exam on her behalf. But once she was admitted to the Allen Academy, Persey was way out of her league, and only two months into freshman year, her academic situation already had her teetering on the brink of expulsion.

"Absolutely UN. AC. CEP. TA. BLE." He pounded his flattened palm on the table with each syllable, as if he needed to make his point any clearer. Then he waited, staring at her, unblinking.

What did he want her to say? She'd never been good at math, and the anxiety she'd feel creeping up from somewhere deep in her stomach as she sat down to take each and every exam certainly didn't help.

"Well?"

"I thought I knew the answers," she began, carefully choosing her words. "But . . . but then I panicked. I just . . . Tests just aren't my strong point, Dad."

His steely eyes burned into hers. "That implies you're good at something. That you *have* a strong point. Which you don't," he added before Persey could answer.

That's not true. Okay, so tests and reading were a struggle. But she wasn't lying when she said she knew the answers beforehand. She'd listened to an audiobook that covered all the material on the exam. She could have recited every formula verbatim if the teacher had asked her, but once she saw the questions on the page, it was as if her mind went blank.

Persey was savvy enough to know that her difficulty might actually be a form of learning disability and that there was probably medication that could help her, but her father didn't believe in learning disabilities. Or mental health maintenance. Or weakness of any kind.

Which didn't stop her from bringing it up again.

"Dad, I think I have, like, an actual learning disability. Maybe if I saw a doctor or—"

"Laziness isn't a learning disability," he said, cutting her off. Like a king issuing a decree.

"I'm not lazy," she protested, unable to stop herself.

"Read my lips." He rocketed to his feet. "Lay. Zee. And no child of mine is lazy, get it? You've got two, three years tops to get your shit together before no college in the world will touch you. No child of mine doesn't go to college. No child of mine doesn't *try*."

"I did try!"

"A D-minus is trying? Are you kidding me?" He wrinkled his nose and angled his face away from her, as if his daughter smelled like rotting flesh. "This is basic algebra. A third grader should be able to get a D-minus on this exam. Or were you *trying* to get this grade?"

"N-no, sir."

"Three *x* minus five equals seven," he said, reading from the page. "Solve for *x*. How did you come up with seven? Literally, seven is part of the equation. It's not even a factor of three!"

"Four." She didn't even hesitate. Standing there in front of her father, picturing the numbers and letter in her mind, she knew the answer. Quickly. Easily. But in a classroom with a ticking clock and numbers on a stark-white page staring up her at her? Panic. Mistakes. It was as if her brain couldn't function normally in such circumstances. Everything fell apart.

"Honey . . ." Persey's mom's voice drawled from the living room, where she sat on the sofa, scrolling through her phone. There was a pause, which usually meant she was taking a sip from her wineglass, then a gentle clank as she placed it (temporarily) on the coffee table and leaned back so she could see her husband and daughter. "Honey, why don't we get her a tutor?"

"No!" her dad snapped. "We tried that once, and it did nothing. Just an embarrassing waste of money. She has to learn to do this on her own."

"But you have this same argument every time she brings a test home," her mom persisted. Which was a rare occurrence. Usually her defense of her daughter was withdrawn as soon as her husband swatted her opinions down. "Maybe it's time to try something else?"

"Yes," her dad said, catching them both off guard. Was he really going to agree with his wife? "Yes, she needs to pay attention in class for a change."

Persey knew it was futile to try to reason with him—he was the kind of man who always got his way, either through coercion, force, or the large amounts of money he'd throw at a problem—but she was thirteen now. Not a child anymore. She should be allowed to advocate for her own needs.

"I can't focus," she said, staring at the packet of pages on the table in front of her dad, the "D-minus" in red ink jabbing at her insides. "When I'm taking a test, it's like I can't remember anything."

Her dad arched an eyebrow. "Can't or won't?"

Did he really think she was getting mediocre grades on purpose?

"I . . ."

His phone vibrated against the table, mercifully interrupting the conversation, and the screen lit up with a photo. It was a familiar one—a young guy with unkempt hair holding up the MVP trophy from last year's varsity regionals soccer championships. Her older brother.

"You're on speakerphone," he said, answering the call.

"Hey, Dad. Everything okay?" Their father was so predictable: Persey's brother knew from just three words that Dad was in a mood.

"It's nothing."

Just another Tuesday night of Dad tearing me to pieces.

"Ooooh-kay."

"What can I do you for, Boss?" He always called her bother "Boss." Grooming him to take over the family business.

"Just wanted to let you and Mom know that I won't be home for dinner. I've got study group after practice, and it may go late." In the background, Persey could clearly hear a girl giggling. Anatomy study group, apparently.

"Is that my beautiful boy?" Persey's mom called from the living room.

"Hi, Mom! How's that chardonnay I recommended?"

"The butteriest!" she cooed, as if wine suggestions from your seventeen-year-old son were the most normal and delightful things in the world.

"Knew you'd love it!"

Her mom raised a glass, silently toasting the phone, and Persey fought to keep from rolling her eyes.

"Anyway," he continued, his voice more serious. It was the tone he took when addressing their dad, as if matching the gravity of Dad's tone would make him take his son more seriously. And it seemed to work. "I might miss curfew tonight. *Might.* I'll do everything I can not to, but tomorrow's exam—"

"Don't worry about it, Boss," her dad said. "Do what you need to do. Senior year, after all! I'll have Esme leave a plate of food out for you."

"Thanks, Dad. You're the best!"

Her dad stared at the phone until the portrait of her brother blipped off the screen. "I wish you were more like him," he said without looking up.

Of course you do.

He was perfect; she was a mess. He got straight A's; she struggled not to flunk. He was senior-class president; she was a nobody.

That's what her parents saw, what they believed to be true.

But they didn't know their son at all.

FOUR

PERSEY'S INTESTINAL TRACT HAD TWISTED ITSELF INTO SOME kind of Eagle-Scout-merit-badge-worthy knot during her flight to Las Vegas. She didn't love flying—she'd watched one too many runway disaster shows on the Weather Channel late at night when she couldn't sleep to make air travel a totally relaxing experience—but that wasn't the real reason for her anxiety. She was less stressed about the flying than about what she was flying *toward.*

Escape-Capades World Headquarters.

Why did I agree to do this?

It was a stupid question to ask, since she knew the answer already. All ten million of them. When you're seventeen with no money and no future ahead of you, ten million dollars can make you do a lot of things. Even things you really, *really* don't want to do.

It's going to be fine.

Fine. Right. Sure.

The commuter jet bounced gently as the wheels screeched against the runway, signaling their arrival in Sin City, and while Persey's stomach troubles should have escalated as the aircraft taxied to its gate, she instead felt a wave of relief wash over her. She was here. The decision had been made. This was happening. Her body unclenched, the dampness on the back of her neck began to evaporate, and Persey practically smiled as she watched the gleaming towers of Las Vegas casinos pass her small window.

She'd (half) expected to find Kevin Lima on her flight from Los Angeles, since that was where she'd seen him last at the Hidden Library escape room, but though she clandestinely cast her eyes around the terminal before the plane boarded, she didn't spot his scruffy blond hair or well-maintained feet. Whatever. She'd see him soon enough.

Persey dragged her ancient black carry-on with its broken zipper and lazy wheel up the aisle and onto the gangway while she checked her phone. She'd read the confirmation e-mail from Leah about fifty bajillion times in the last two weeks, but she carefully parsed through each word of it again, just in case she'd missed anything.

A car will pick you up at the airport. Look for the driver at arrivals near baggage claim. Accommodations and all meals will be provided during your stay.

The words were exactly as Persey remembered them—simple logistical information, lacking in specifics. Nothing about the competition itself.

Maybe that was part of it? Part of the game? Withholding information might just have been another way the escape room designers tried to throw everyone off-balance and instill a sense of confusion. In fact, the competition might have started the moment Persey agreed to participate, and every detail from Leah's bare-bones e-mail to Persey's flight number, departure time, and seat assignment might be valuable puzzle-solving elements for a later challenge.

Persey sighed, tucking her phone back into the hip pocket of her cargo pants. She had no idea what to expect, a situation that did not sit well with her, and she'd have to pay close attention to everything and everyone from now on if she was going to get that money.

The smell of Vegas hit Persey the moment she stepped into the terminal: a nose-wrinkling mix of stale air, body odor, and desperation. If the sparkling casino façades and red-hued desert plateaus hadn't clued her in to her location, the familiar stench of McCarran Airport would have, and when mixed with the cacophony of sound and lights, Persey felt slightly dizzy as she turned toward baggage claim. Not to waste a square inch of gambling real estate, slot machines littered the terminal, greeting visitors with bells and beeps and swirling lights as they exited their aircraft.

Gambling seemed so sad to her. Mindless. Pathetic. Money was such a precious commodity—why would anyone throw it away? Las Vegas was all show and no tell, all surface with no substance, and it was a place where she'd never felt like she belonged. She felt like she should be exiting the terminal in a sequined halter dress and five-inch clear Lucite heels instead of the olive-green cargo pants, layered long- and short-sleeve tees, jean jacket, and Toms she'd chosen for her journey. She was like the anti-Vegas—always had been and always would be.

She shook her head, casting off dark memories of this place, that threatened to derail her, and focused on the crowd gathered at the bottom of her escalator. It was a mix of locals greeting family and friends, and livery drivers holding signs with the names of their passengers, and it took Persey approximately .2 seconds to find hers among them.

Because unlike all the other drivers in their near uniform boxy black suit jackets and matching neckties, the driver holding Persey's name on a dry-erase board was dressed head to toe in an eye-numbing lime green.

He wore a bright green polo shirt, just like the Escape-Capades employees at the Hidden Library, paired with matching track pants and athletic sneakers. On his head, a lime-green baseball cap had the Escape-Capades logo emblazoned across it, and as if that wasn't enough, the poor guy had a fanny pack strapped around his waist overflowing with flyers advertising the premier Las Vegas escape room experience. He was a walking billboard advertisement.

"Persephone?" he asked, stepping forward as she slipped off the escalator. Leah's probable description of Persey—medium height, medium build, medium brown hair and eyes—could have matched two-thirds of the females in the terminal, and Persey realized with a start that this driver must have seen her before.

"Persey," she said, once again beating back the fear that she'd made a terrible, horrible mistake. There was something familiar about this guy. Not just the lime-green getup . . . his face.

"You were taking pictures at the Hidden Library." She didn't mean it to sound like an accusation.

"I'm Greg," he said, neither confirming nor denying her statement. His voice was flat, eyes dull and focused at a spot over her head. "If you could wait here? It'll just be a minute."

Wait?

Greg flipped his sign around and instead of Persey's name, it now read NEELA CHATTERJEE.

She was going to have to share a ride to Escape-Capades? Persey hadn't been prepared for that. She'd just assumed (hoped) she'd have the entire car ride from the airport to compose herself and get her head in the game—or whatever other sports cliché seemed appropriate—before the competition began. Now, once again, she was struck by how off-balance she felt with this new turn of events. Her challenges had already begun.

Greg was true to his word: it was only a few minutes before the driver, barely registering the amused looks as people streamed by, perked up. Persey followed his gaze to the escalator where a girl clad entirely in black descended. She wore her dark hair long and heavy, swept forward over each shoulder, which gave the impression that her small heart-shaped face was being eaten alive. Her hair flowed seamlessly into her clothes, all in the same hue—black long-sleeve Henley tee with a three-button collar over black jeans and black Converse, the white rubber siding the only other "color" in her outfit. Enormous square-rimmed black glasses stretched the width of her face, and even her backpack was black, slung over both shoulders like a hiker about to attack the Pacific Crest Trail, though her black eyeliner, plum lips, and mascara-clad lashes made her look like she was heading for a night out.

"Neela Chatterjee?" Greg asked as she stepped off the escalator.

Neela froze, causing the Tommy Bahama–wearing tourist behind her to stutter-step so he didn't smash into her as the escalator deposited him on the ground floor. He shot her a dirty look as he shouldered by, but she didn't notice. She just stared at Greg, her eyes slowly scanning him from head to toe before she answered. "It is I."

"Awesome. Glad you're here." He sounded anything but. "I'll take you guys to HQ now."

Neela's eyebrows shot up. "Guys?" She seemed as surprised (disappointed) as Persey had been to discover that she'd be sharing a ride, but as Neela tilted her head to the side, her heavy mane of hair shifting across her monochrome outfit, she looked more intrigued than annoyed by Greg's announcement. "Do you mean 'guys' in the colloquial sense referring to all members of a gathered party regardless of gender, or are there one or more male members of our party whom I don't see standing behind you?"

She spoke quickly, the words practically falling upon one another in the race to get out of her mouth, but her tone lacked even a trace of sarcasm, and her energy, despite her black on black on black exterior, was perky and buoyant.

"Um . . ." Greg faltered, dropping his sign. He was having difficulty understanding the question. "I'm Greg." Or if he'd even been asked one.

"I'm Neela," she said good-naturedly. "But since you already know that, I'll assume the colloquialism was intended, and though I don't love genderism, I understand your meaning exactly."

Persey usually (always) disliked strangers. Or, more accurately, assumed that every single person she met disliked *her*, if not immediately, then eventually, and so it was just easier to get a jump on the mutual dislike-atude. Between that propensity and the natural distrust of a rival contestant, Persey should have instantly disliked Neela. But she didn't. In fact, her reaction was the exact opposite. Which was a first.

"I'm Persey," she said, smiling. "The other *guy* he's taking to Escape-Capades."

Neela's heavy fringe of spidery black lashes quivered as her big, inquisitive eyes appraised Persey. The glass lenses were thick, distorting her pupils so they looked enormous, like some kind of Snapchat filter gone awry as she took in every detail of her new acquaintance. Just like Persey, Neela assumed the competition had already begun.

"Pleased to meet you," Neela said, matching Persey's smile with one of her own. It felt genuinely warm, and Persey fought against the (unfamiliar) sensation of friendliness bubbling up from within. Maybe in another time, at another place, she and Neela could have been friends?

But not here.

FIVE

"THIS WAY."

Lime-colored Greg turned abruptly and strode toward the exit, exhibiting all the joy of a prison guard escorting the new inmates to their cells. Not that Persey could blame him for his lack of enthusiasm. She'd be sullen, too, if her job were to pick people up from the airport looking like the Grinch who stole Christmas.

She followed him in silence, Neela falling into step beside her, not-so-silently.

"So where did you fly in from?" Neela began, though she didn't actually wait for an answer. "I was on flight four-twenty-two from Nashville, which was supposed to be three hours and thirty minutes of flight time, but ended up at three hours and forty-seven minutes due to a heavy headwind. Not that I'm one of those people who obsessively check to see how long their flight is but I *am* interested in the effects of weather on aircraft, so I was doing some calculations in my head based on that flight info they show you on the screen at your seat to see if I could pinpoint our exact time of arrival. I'm kind of a math person and I always love a good 'one train leaves the station at four o'clock traveling at fifty miles per hour with a steady acceleration of one mile per hour per minute and another train leaves a station thirty-five miles away traveling half that speed with twice the acceleration, et cetera, et cetera' kind of equation." She paused for a quick breath. "I was three minutes off."

"Wow." Persey wasn't sure if she was more impressed (terrified) by Neela's math skills—those narrative problems always left Persey's head spinning, her brain paralyzed—or if she was more awed by the fact that Neela got all those words out in one single exhalation.

"I know," Neela said with a sad shake of her head. "I can't believe I fudged it up that badly."

If Neela had been a different sort of person, that comment would have rubbed Persey the wrong way: false modesty was one of her major pet peeves. But in casting a quick glance at her travel companion, she realized that Neela was being 100 percent genuine. Which Persey appreciated.

Neela had just opened her mouth to start another monologue when the words converted into a gasp. A monstrous lime-green Hummer was parked on the ground floor of the lot, straddling two spots, as fugly as it was unfunctional. Despite its size, the sport utility vehicle had almost no trunk space for their bags, and it was so high off the ground that Persey had to step up on a platform, balancing herself on Greg's outstretched arm, in order to climb into the back seat behind Neela, doing so with about as much grace as a sumo wrestler trying out ballet.

"Interesting," Neela said, latching the safety harness over her lap. The interior was decked out in soft black leather, muted by tinted windows, and though it wasn't a limousine, the driver and passenger areas were separated by a glass panel for total privacy. "I didn't realize Hummers came in this color. Was this customized in-house? Or was it a special order? Or is it—"

"No," Greg said sullenly as he slid into the driver's seat. It seemed his response was meant not so much to answer any specific one of Neela's rapid-fire questions, but to end the conversation, as he punctuated it by yanking the privacy window closed.

Sorry, Neela mouthed, rolling her eyes up to the ceiling.

Traffic was slow going as they edged out of the airport and onto the I-15, the massive hulks of Vegas's casinos flanking both sides of the freeway, each sporting their own thematic ambiance from the Old West to the Far East and everything in between. The older, less ritzy offerings stood more sparsely on the west side of the interstate while the gleaming gold-and-jewel-toned behemoths of "new" Vegas hugged the east side, packed in so densely it was sometimes impossible to tell where one casino ended and the next began.

Neela had pulled out her phone, which should have been a welcome sight to Persey, who wanted to avoid conversation in the world's most awkward ride share, but something about Neela's stream-of-consciousness style was oddly soothing, and as they crawled down the freeway, Persey realized that she would prefer being monologued to the oppressive silence that currently existed in the back of the Hummer.

That said, establishing lines of communication was not her forte. Half a dozen times she wanted to open her mouth and say, *Where are you from? How did you get invited to the tournament? So black's your favorite "color," huh?* Each time, she'd steal a glance at her ride-mate, who maintained a laser-sharp focus on her smartphone, and the words would dry up on her tongue.

The Hummer began to pick up steam once they made it through downtown Las Vegas. Casinos and shopping malls transitioned into tract housing developments and mini malls, from urban to suburban, and finally both fell away so suddenly it was as if they'd crossed an invisible barrier into no-man's-land.

Which wasn't too far off the mark. Before long, Persey caught sight of a bullet-shaped white object out of the corner of her eye, pacing the green

Hummer. She turned and saw what appeared to be a remote-controlled jet plane landing on an air strip that ran parallel to the highway.

"Whoa," she said, hardly even aware the syllable had come out of her mouth.

The word seemed to snap Neela to attention. "Cool, right? It's a drone landing at the air force base. I've never seen one in person, but I researched this whole area before I got on the plane and saw that they run a lot of drone training missions from here. I also studied the demography, topography, and climatography of this region." Neela snorted. "All the 'aphies,' really. That's a joke."

"I laughed on the inside," Persey said, hoping as the words left her mouth that she didn't sound too much like an asshole.

"You did? Oh, nice! Thank you." Then Neela quickly typed something into her phone. "Sorry to be rude, but I have to write down what I just said. I, um, like to keep track of what I do that makes people laugh because I don't always understand why they do it. I didn't want you to think that I was ignoring your very kind overtures of camaraderie by escaping into my phone even though it is my safety mechanism when I'm not quite sure of social cues."

Persey could only imagine Neela in high school, where snooty bitches would make fun of her mercilessly behind her back. Shit, to her face. Humans were brutal.

"You think it'll come in handy?" Persey asked, hoping to steer the conversation away from anything personal. "I mean all your studies. Like for solving one of the puzzles?"

"Maybe," Neela said with a shrug. "Who knows? My ex-girlfriend always told me I go overboard with stuff like this. Thinking of every possible outcome. I can't not overprepare, you know? It would make me bonkers. I'm the kind of person who needs a concrete sense of all contingencies in order to weigh my decision-making efficiently. It helps me cut down on my anxiety."

Persey understood completely. She could count on one hand the number of times in her life that she'd done something—from picking out clothes to asking her parents for, well, anything—without reasoning out (agonizing over) the possible outcomes first. She'd try to consider all aspects of the decision, all possibilities, before taking any kind of action, fearing not only the negative outcomes of her decisions, but the positives as well. Basically, anything that put her in the spotlight. Persey's number one goal in life was not to be noticed at all.

Neela cocked her head to the side. "You said your name is Persey?"

"Yep."

"For Persephone?"

Please don't say it. Please don't say it. "Yep."

"I like it. I had a girlfriend named Penelope once, which I know isn't exactly the same as Persephone, though they're from sort of the same source material and people were always telling her where her name came from as if she wouldn't have known that information already from every stupid genealogy project she'd been forced to do in elementary school. I would get irritated when someone tried to mansplain her name because I hate it when people share their knowledge with total strangers to make themselves feel superior, but she always told me to ignore it."

"I'm more Penelope there," Persey said. "I let it go." *Do you?*

"Yeah, I thought you might be. But that's why you need friends to—" She stopped mid-sentence, her attention caught by something outside the heavily tinted windows. "Holy cow babies!"

Persey stared out the window, though at first she couldn't tell what had elicited the closest thing to a swear word Neela had used since they'd met. Desert surrounded them: yellowish-brown dirt and scrub brush as far as she could see, flanked by imposing mountains on all sides, and she was just about to ask Neela if she was feeling okay when she spotted a neon-green building sticking out against the monotonous rocky landscape.

"Is that it?"

Neela sucked in a breath as if she were looking at the most beautiful sight in the world. "Yes," she said reverentially.

It was the first time she replied to anything with a single word.

SIX

THE PARKING LOT IN FRONT OF THE ESCAPE-CAPADES HQ WAS mostly empty when Greg pulled the Hummer around to the main entrance. Neela had gone quiet again—her two modes apparently being word vomit and total silence—as Greg unloaded their bags and ushered them into the green monstrosity through a set of double doors. The lobby, thankfully, was not such an eyesore: shiny white surfaces were accented with chrome-and-leather furniture, with mere pops of the signature green hue in picture frames and potted plants. Without a word, Greg escorted them through the empty lobby into a separate room, and Persey felt as if she'd been transported to another time and place.

Gone were the shiny tile floors, chrome-footed chairs, and light streaming in through floor-to-ceiling windows. Gone were any hints of lime green. This room, which was so dark it took Persey a few moments for her eyes to adjust, was the polar opposite of the lobby, with brocade curtains obscuring the windows, wood paneling, and muted, artificial light filtered through vintage stained-glass lampshades.

At first, Persey thought her initial assumption—that the competition had already started somehow—seemed to bear out: this room looked so eerily similar to the Hidden Library that Persey did a double take. From the dark inlaid wood flooring, which stretched from wall to wall, to the bookcases that ringed the room, towering ten feet above her and requiring a ladder to access the upper shelves, this space could have been the model for the famously unbeatable escape room. Heavily polished mahogany furniture was scattered throughout the expansive space—desks and coffee tables, clusters of leather-backed chairs neatly arranged, and a long claw-foot sofa positioned in front of a brick fireplace.

The room felt simultaneously comfortable and staged, as if every element within was meant to evoke a certain mood or memory, and as Persey glanced around at the people who inhabited the space, she felt very much like she'd just seen the curtain go up on the opening scene of a play.

The "actors" were sprinkled around the lounge in little groupings: some clumped together like bits of dust under the sofa, attached by proximity but ignoring one another as much as was humanly possible, while others had intentionally self-segregated in lonely corners. Everyone was very busy with something or other. Their phones mostly. Just like Neela in the car ride over. One guy sporting a Mohawk with dyed-red tips perused the book shelves slowly, as if intently searching for a specific volume, and an Asian guy dozed on the tufted claw-foot sofa before the empty fireplace, long hair obscuring his face, while his Teva-clad feet were propped up on a coffee table.

Persey mentally catalogued all the details she could, convinced that she would need them later, and though each contestant took great pains to pretend like they weren't paying attention, Persey noticed that everyone glanced up at Neela and her within seconds of their entrance. Even Sir-Sleeps-a-Lot, who wasn't quite as out of it as he appeared.

The competition was sizing them up.

"Welcome!" Leah cried, crossing the room. Other than Greg, she was the only Escape-Capades employee Persey had seen since their arrival. "I hope your flights and transportation were adequate?"

Not pleasant, not comfortable, but adequate. Persey kind of liked her no-bullshit approach. "Yep."

"I found the flight time passed quite pleasantly," Neela said, readjusting her huge glasses. "Despite the lack of decent entertainment options. I don't understand why the American air-travel industry can't come up with a uniform means of—"

"Excellent," Leah said, cutting her off. "May I take your bags?" Without waiting for an answer, she deftly caught the handle of Persey's carry-on, then firmly slipped Neela's backpack from her shoulders, sweeping both across the room to a closet. "You won't be needing these for a bit."

"Why not?" someone asked. Persey's eyes shot toward a burgundy leather easy chair where a Black guy wearing a pin-striped short-sleeve shirt sat stiff and tight, knees pinned together, while he frantically thumb typed on his iPhone. He didn't even look up as he asked the question.

"Patience!" Leah cooed. "All will be explained soon."

Persey was relatively (positively) sure she'd watched this scene in an old movie: a group of strangers gathered for some reason, but none of them 100 percent sure what was going on. *In the movies, this would end with a bunch of dead bodies. . . .*

A girl about Persey's and Neela's age stepped forward, meeting Leah's bright, practiced smile with one of her own. She had flawless pale skin, deep brown eyes, and impossibly long lashes. "I'd *really* like to check into my hotel room first. To freshen up, change my clothes." She leaned forward as if conspiring with their hostess. "I want to look my best for the press, you know?"

Persey *didn't* know, but the girl's outfit—skinny jeans tucked into buttery tan suede knee boots, a cream-colored one-shoulder tee, and an enormous turquoise cuff bracelet on her upper arm—hinted that this was a girl who didn't leave the house without being camera-ready.

"There won't be any press, Mackenzie," Leah said with a shake of her head.

Mackenzie's face fell. "No press? For the biggest All-Star competition ever? With a ten-million-dollar prize?"

"None."

"Are you seriously telling me that no one's going to interview me for the nightly news?" It was Sheryl Rohnor all over again.

"I'm afraid not."

"You're missing a built-in marketing opportunity," the Black guy said, leaning back in his chair but still not looking up.

"Thank you, Shaun," Leah began. "But our media team is more than capable of—"

"What he said," Mackenzie interrupted. She arched a filled-in brow. "Especially considering what happened to your company last year, I'd think you could use all the positive media coverage you can get."

Leah pursed her lips. The invocation of "last year" clearly irritated her. "I'm sure there will be plenty of media interest for whoever wins today's competition."

"Today?" An Asian girl in a T-shirt that read IT'S NOT A PARTY TILL I SLYTHERIN looked up from her phone. "So this is happening now? The competition has already started?"

Just for a moment, Slytherin's eyes drifted to Persey, covering her from head to toe, sizing her up. She pursed her lips, looking wholly disappointed, then, without even waiting for Leah to answer, she dropped her head back to her phone.

What the hell was that all about?

Leah's smile was fixed and bright. "I'll explain everything in detail as soon as—"

"Wussup, bitches!"

Persey recognized the voice before she saw the head of mussed-up blond hair enter the room. Kevin looked almost exactly the same as the last time she'd seen him, down to the cargo shorts, having only exchanged his flip-flops for an old-school pair of checked Vans. He certainly hadn't changed his wardrobe much for the competition.

"That's incredibly offensive," Slytherin said, staring daggers at him. "Misogynistic and antiquated."

"Cool." Kevin grinned, winking at Persey in a way that made her want to simultaneously laugh out loud and smack him across the face. "Offensive is what I do best."

Meanwhile, Mackenzie didn't miss a beat. "You two know each other?" she asked, looking back and forth between Persey and Kevin. "That sounds like collusion to me."

"Do you even know what 'collusion' means?" Slytherin asked. She was taking nobody's side.

"Do you know what 'mind your own business' means?" Mackenzie snapped.

Slytherin rolled her eyes. "Um, yeah. Cuz that's literally a definition. Like you *literally* just defined the concept you were asking me about."

"Whatever," Mackenzie said. The last defense of someone who knows they've been bested.

"Okay, everyone," Leah said, with a clap of her hands. She seemed ready to get down to business. "Now that we're all here, I'd like to welcome you to the first annual Escape-Capades All-Star Competition!"

SEVEN

AS SOON AS LEAH MADE THE OFFICIAL ANNOUNCEMENT, the lights in the library dimmed and a flat screen descended from the ceiling above the fireplace. When it clicked into place, a video began to play, the audio piped into the room from unseen speakers.

Persey recognized the Escape-Capades façade immediately. Not that it was difficult. There wasn't exactly an overabundance of bright green five-story campuses in the middle of the high desert.

"Welcome to Escape-Capades World Headquarters." The female voice-over was warm and friendly, and sounded a lot like Leah. "We are honored to host you for the first annual All-Star Competition."

The image faded into a slide show of laughing, cheerful Escape-Capades employees going about their daily tasks, both at the headquarters building and at escape room installations across the world.

"Since coming under new management," the voice-over continued, "after the unfortunate events of last year, Escape-Capades has grown to become the single largest purveyor of elaborate, intricate, and downright diabolical escape room experiences in the world. And with its initial public offering last month, Escape-Capades is now valued at well over five hundred million dollars."

Holy shit, really? Persey had never paid much (any) attention to business matters. She knew Escape-Capades had been the hot new thing at one time, but she had no idea that the corporation was such a big deal. Such a big *money* deal.

"Now, in memory of our founders, Derrick and Melinda Browne, we have initiated a yearly All-Star Competition, featuring the best and brightest escape room fans from around the world."

Persey cast a furtive look at the group. *The best and brightest.* The faces reflected a mix of confidence and smugness. And, in Neela's case, abject wonder. She watched the video with wide eyes behind her thick lenses, lips parted in an unconscious smile, like a kid going to Disneyland for the first time, staring up at Sleeping Beauty's castle as if a fairy tale had really and truly come to life.

"And so, as you embark on this adventure," the voice concluded, sounding very much like she was giving some kind of farewell speech, "we wish you all good luck. You're going to need it."

The music swelled as the establishing shot of the HQ exterior faded into and out of view before the video ended.

"Well, that wasn't helpful," Slytherin said as the lights resumed their normal brightness. Her skeptical face wrinkled into a frown. "You explained exactly nothing."

"Maybe that's part of the game," Mohawk suggested, leaning back against a bookcase.

"Maybe we *all* are," Mackenzie added.

Leah stepped in front of the fireplace and spread her arms wide. Like the voice on the video, she seemed a little stiff, an android following her programming or a bad actor reading from a script. "How about I start by introducing you to each other."

"Why bother?" Kevin said. "We're going to smoke you all. Names will just get in our way."

"'We'?" Mackenzie sauntered forward. "'Us'?" She threw a withering glance at Persey. "You sure you want to throw in with *that*? There are better options here."

"There is no 'we,'" Persey replied. For the second time that afternoon, she wanted to smack Kevin upside the head for drawing everyone's attention to her.

Kevin winked. "You sure about that?"

Yes.

"You'll *all* be working together," Leah said by way of an explanation, "and also be in competition with one another, so it might be nice if you at least knew each other's names."

Kevin shrugged, then hoisted himself up on a heavy table. "Fine. I'm Kevin." He turned back to Mackenzie as if he knew he was facing a friendly audience. "But *you* can call me Kevin."

Mackenzie giggled.

"That isn't actually a joke, Kevin," Shaun said, turning his head stiffly. "So I'm not sure why it would cause anyone to laugh." His flat, even tone of voice reminded Persey of a computer-generated telemarketing call.

Leah laughed impulsively, then seemed to catch herself, suppressing the instinct and resuming her poised, professional demeanor. "Shaun"— she gestured to him—"is a computer science and history double major at Notre Dame, where he serves as captain of the university's History Masters chapter. He won their annual escape room competition."

"Notre Dame?" Slytherin said, head tilted to the side. "My little brother goes there. Small world."

"There are approximately eight thousand, five hundred undergraduates at Notre Dame," Shaun replied coldly. "It could only be considered a 'small world' if your brother was my roommate or something to that effect."

Slytherin squared her hips, combative. "I don't know. He's also a computer science major, about your age. Kind of a prig. I bet a hundred bucks you know Atticus."

Shaun's right eyebrow raised a centimeter, displaying more motion than he'd shown since Persey walked in the room. "Atticus?" He cleared his throat. "Never heard of him."

Persey was pretty sure he was lying.

Before Slytherin could follow up, Sir Sleeps-a-Lot yawned from his sofa. "ND is cool. I mean, it's no Yale. But cool."

Kevin turned to him. "Guessing you went to Yale, huh?"

He shrugged. "I don't like to brag."

"So what you're saying," Kevin said coolly, "is that you're a douchebag."

"Right?" Mackenzie said. She batted her heavy lashes at Kevin, and Persey wondered what she was up to. "Why is it that people who go to Harvard or Yale always seem to let you know it in the first few moments of meeting them?"

Mohawk raised his hand. "Just for the record, I went to Harvard and I don't usually tell people that I went to Harvard."

Mackenzie rolled her eyes. "Except, like, right now."

"And Mackenzie," Leah said, quickly stepping between them, "is currently studying abroad."

"At the Royal College of Music in London," Mackenzie added. She shot Mr. Yale a withering glance. "That's in England."

"As opposed to the one in the Bronx?" Slytherin quipped.

Mackenzie tilted her head. "There's a London in the Bronx?"

"Um, no. I just meant, like, where the fuck else would the Royal College of Music in London be?"

"Are you making fun of me?" Mackenzie whirled on her, nostrils flared. Slytherin had hit Mackenzie's insecure spot. "Because I'm not the kind of person who ever gets made fun of, okay? I'm hot as fuck, charming, and fun. I'm a classically trained opera singer, so I'm, like, totally cultured, and I speak four languages, plus Latin."

Latin isn't a language?

"*Plus*, I've solved escape rooms in France, Spain, Latvia, Sweden, and Germany," Mackenzie continued. "Where have *you* solved them?"

Slytherin's face never flinched, her eyes never faltered. It was like watching two alpha wolves stalk each other for dominance. "I won't wait for our hostess to out me. I'm Arlo Wu. I live in Brooklyn, where I run a pop-culture lifestyle website, and I'm really into Harry Potter."

"Arlo was invited due to her renowned encyclopedic knowledge of pop culture, focusing on the latter half of the twentieth century," Leah added. "You might have seen her appearances on the *Today* show?"

"Third hour."

Everyone turned to the back of the room where Harvard Mohawk still perused the shelves. The comment had clearly come from him, despite the fact that he appeared not to be paying attention.

"Excuse me?" Arlo said.

"You made five guest spots on the third hour of the *Today* show," he said. "That's the one they reserve for C-level guests."

"Sounds about right," Mackenzie said with a laugh.

"C-level or not," Arlo said with a shrug, "my website gets over two million unique hits a month, and I have paid advertisers from twelve different countries. And you have . . . ?"

"Meet Riot Ramirez," Leah said. Her grin was beginning to look strained.

"Riot?" Shaun asked. "Your parents named you Riot?"

"'My name engrav'd herein,'" Riot said, his tone elevated. "'Doth contribute my firmnesse to this glasse.'" He reminded Persey of Professor

Rohner, who quoted Chaucer lovingly, reverently, as if he'd written it himself.

"Philip Sidney?" Neela asked. "Spenser? Not Jonson, he's more lyrical, I think."

Riot glanced over his shoulder. He'd shown a decided lack of interest in the conversation taking place behind him, but his eyes found Neela immediately, as if he knew exactly who had spoken.

"Close," he said, seeming to appreciate her knowledge. "John Donne."

Leah crossed the room to the bookcase he was examining and pulled out a leather-bound volume from the shelf above his head. "Riot's getting his master's degree now, but as an undergrad, he was known as something of a savant when it came to English literature, the Elizabethan period especially." She glanced at the cover. "I believe this will interest you?"

When Riot's eyes met the cover, they grew wide. "Is this the Voynich manuscript?"

"A rare copy," Leah said, handing the book to him.

"Holy shit." Riot stroked the cover lovingly. "I've never even seen one in person."

Leah grinned. "Once a librarian, always a librarian."

Neela cleared her throat while Riot gaped at the book in his hands. "I'm also not going to wait for an introduction, because anticipation makes me nervous and besides even though I'm an INTP heavy on the introvert, also known as the 'thinkers' of the personality portrait world, I'm not exactly shy and I'm perfectly capable of introducing myself and my accomplishments, which mainly involve math, math puzzles, math theory, and tactile puzzle solving, as well as a few published articles on the human brain's innate problem-solving ability in regard to patterns and yes, I know you're thinking, *Oh my God, she's way too young to do all of that!* Well, yes and no . . ."

She paused and took a deep breath, replenishing her lungs. Persey half expected someone to jump in with a question, but silence hung heavy in the room as everyone stared at Neela in dumbfounded awe. Not that Neela noticed (cared). As soon as her breath was noisily inhaled, she started again.

". . . because age is merely an arbitrary delineation of the physical being and has nothing whatsoever to do with the human mind's ability to learn and develop and grow, beyond the obvious neonatal period, so even though I've just finished my freshman year at Vanderbilt—and yes, I know, it's not Yale or Harvard or the freaking Royal Music whatever but it's *in-fi-nite-ly* superior to any of them in my not-so-humble opinion—I feel I'm already significantly more accomplished than your average nineteen-year-old."

The silence continued after she finished; the rest of the room appeared to be waiting, as if the faucet of words might be turned back on full blast at any second.

"I'm done," Neela said. "You can talk now."

Kevin, shockingly, was the first to break the silence. "I don't know what the fuck you just said, but I think I love you."

"I'm also a lesbian," Neela added quickly. "For the record. And I'm not just saying that because you expressed an emotional connection to me, even if it was only used for comic effect."

"Duly noted."

"Right," Leah said, exhaling slightly as she turned to Mr. Yale, who still lounged on the sofa, nodding in and out of sleep. "Would you care to introduce yourself, Wes?"

"Nah," he said with a yawn, too tired (or lazy) to bother covering his mouth. "You'll do it better."

Leah arched an eyebrow. "Wesley Song comes to us from right here in Las Vegas, by way of Yale. . . ."

Wes laughed as if he were in slow motion, a grumbling noise that reminded Persey of an outboard motor sputtering to life, and she wondered just how much weed this guy smoked. "Not anymore. Institutionalized education is such a . . ."

"Necessity?" Shaun suggested.

"Privilège," Mackenzie said on top of him, with perfect French pronunciation.

"Drag," Wes said heavily. "I'm getting an advanced degree in life now, man."

"What the hell does that mean?" Arlo asked. Her words, as always, sounded confrontational.

Wes sat up, and Persey could see that his eyelids were pink and puffy. "You know. *Living?* Do you even know how to do that? Like *really* do that?"

Arlo stared at him, unblinking. "Yeah, I'm sure you're really 'living.' Your parents must be rich as fuck to facilitate your first-world male-privilege bullshit." She turned to Leah. "How the hell did he get invited?"

"Now look," Leah said, clapping her hands again like a schoolteacher to gather everyone's attention. "You all have one thing in common. One reason why you deserve this invitation." Leah folded her arms across her chest. "You scored the highest of all participants in the Hidden Library escape room."

Grumbling rippled through the group, and Persey caught snippets and words: "audition," "not real," "now it makes sense."

"The Hidden Library was the most difficult escape room ever created, an update of last year's Prison Break challenge, which was supposed to be the first unbeatable room." She paused, lips pressed together as if remembering something horrible. "Updated and improved with one purpose in mind: to find the most talented code breakers, pattern identifiers, and puzzle solvers in the world."

"I.e., us," Wes added.

Leah's poise never faltered. "Exactly. Which is why *most* of you received invitations to participate. We wanted to ensure that the brightest minds got a crack at this room, and we were not disappointed. You all scored the highest aptitudes in your attempts to solve the Hidden Library."

Riot whistled through parted lips. "That thing was tough."

"Thank you," Leah said, accepting Riot's words as a compliment. "It was designed to be unbeatable, and it almost was."

"Almost?" Shaun asked. "It was my understanding no one had actually beaten it."

"No one had. Until two weeks ago." The explanation should have come from Leah, but it was Arlo who had spoken the words. She looked (glared) right at Persey. "By her."

EIGHT

MACKENZIE SPUN TOWARD KEVIN, WHO STOOD BEHIND PERSEY. "You mean *him*."

Seriously?

Kevin was (too) quick to make sure he wasn't getting any undo credit. "Man, I wish."

"How did you know?" Shaun asked Arlo. Persey was wondering the same thing.

Arlo rolled her eyes. "Don't you guys follow the Escape-Capades feed? There's a photo of her win."

Persey sucked in a breath. *I shouldn't have agreed to do this.* "There is?"

"Yep," Arlo said. "I mean, your hands are up in front of your face all hiding-from-the-paparazzi style, but I recognized you."

"*She* solved the Hidden Library?" Mackenzie said, eyebrows knitted together. "I don't believe it."

"Totes true!" Kevin said. "I was there to see it. Lemme tell you, that thing was impossible. The freaking 'Pardoner's Tale'? That's a deep-ass cut."

Riot sucked in a breath. "Fuuuuck. 'The Pardoner's Tale.' 'If that ye be so leef to fynde Deeth, turne up this croked wey,'" he said, quoting the same passage as Professor Rohner. It was like the *Canterbury Tales* sound bite. "I'm a freaking idiot."

"'And gladly wolde he lerne,'" Neela said, "'and gladly teche.'"

Riot held up his hand to her for a high five. "Nice."

"'No empty-handed man can lure a bird,'" Mackenzie said, not to be outdone.

"Not the Middle English," Riot said, wiggling his hand from side to side to denote he thought her quote was iffy. "But I'll allow it."

Can everyone on the planet quote Chaucer but me?

"But the images in the final scramble," Shaun said, refusing to be derailed by a Chaucer quote-off. "They were nonsensical." His brows knitted together, wrinkling the area above his nose ever so slightly. It was the first hint of emotion he'd shown since Persey arrived. "Even unscrambled, there was no way they would form a cohesive picture."

"You had to use the mirror," Kevin explained. "They were all backward."

"I see." Shaun clearly didn't.

"Are you serious?" Wes sat up, staring at Kevin as if he didn't quite believe him. "How is that even possible to solve?"

Kevin shrugged. "I dunno. Ask her."

Persey groaned, the weight of eight sets of eyes boring into her as everyone in the room focused on her. She tried not to blush, to let her eyes drop to the floor, to flee in abject terror—all of which were signs of weakness. If she was going to do this thing, *really* do this thing, she needed to project strength. Confidence. Even if it wasn't real.

Fake it till you make it.

"You just had to see the whole thing in reverse, I guess."

"Wow," Neela said under her breath. Which made Persey smile despite her extreme discomfort.

"Then what's he doing here?" Shaun asked, nodding toward Kevin without actually looking at him.

Kevin held his hands up before him, palms out—the universal symbol for *I didn't do it.* "I'm just a lucky loser, my man."

Arlo looked skeptical. "Loser, maybe. But lucky?"

"Wow. You are charming," Kevin said. "I'm just here because of her. We were randomly paired up as teammates, and she wouldn't agree to participate unless I did, too."

That is not *how it went down.*

"Well, isn't that precious?" Mackenzie sneered.

"So she *did* have help," Arlo said with a smile.

"No, she didn't." Leah meandered around the room as she spoke, snaking through the different contestants. "Persey is the only person out of one-point-four million participants who has been able to solve the Hidden Library. And she did it single-handedly."

Arlo and Mackenzie closed in on Persey immediately, shooting rapid-fire questions at her with such ferocity that she couldn't even tell which of them was talking.

"How many escape rooms have you done?"

"You got lucky, didn't you?"

"Did you talk to someone who'd done the room before?"

"How many times did you try it?"

"Did you get some insider information?"

Persey's head whipped around toward Mackenzie, who had asked that last one. "Why would you think that?"

"Pretty sure she's referencing the scandal from last year," Kevin said. "She doesn't think you could actually solve it yourself unless you stole the secrets from someone at Escape-Capades."

Wes sat up straight, his sleepiness either forgotten or discarded, depending upon whether it was real or feigned. Persey wasn't sure which. "Is that what they think? That someone bought info on Prison Break?"

Bought? Persey was pretty sure that wasn't what Kevin said. "Prison Break? I don't understand what you're talking about."

"The. Fuck." Mackenzie threw up her hands. "You can't be for real."

Riot, still gripping the copy of the Voynich manuscript Leah had pulled for him, joined the half circle that had formed around Persey. "You've never heard of the Prison Break escape room scandal? The prize money. The secret that was leaked and ended up all over the Internet . . ."

"The owners of this company," Kevin added, "who went bankrupt because of it and decided to take their own lives rather than deal with the consequences?"

"It was covered on the national news approximately twenty-three times between May and July of last year," Shaun added. "You must have seen it."

Kevin blinked at him. "Did you actually have that statistic at the tip of your tongue, or did you make it up?"

Shaun's gaze was as flat and emotionless as ever. He would have made an amazing poker player. "I do not make up statistics."

"You're a weird dude," Kevin said after a pause. "Like an android with less personality. Gonna call you Shaun-bot."

"Please, don't," Shaun said, sounding very much as if he didn't really care either way.

"Too late, Shaun-bot!"

Meanwhile, Mackenzie and Arlo were still circling Persey, like a pair of mean-girl sharks swarming before a kill. "How is it that you solved the single most impossible puzzle in the world," Mackenzie began, "and yet you've never heard of Derrick and Melinda Browne?"

Persey wasn't entirely sure what those two things had to do with each other. "I'm not online much."

"If you're into escape rooms *at all*," Arlo continued, "you must have heard of Prison Break. My blog covered it extensively."

Right. Because it was just a given that everyone in the room followed Arlo's blog. And though her first instinct was to apologize, Persey once again reminded herself that she needed to project strength and confidence, especially in this moment, at the very beginning. Persey knew from experience that if she didn't assert herself right here, right now, she'd be prey to these bullies for the rest of the day.

She'd learned that lesson the hard way. With her dad.

So Persey decided to say the one thing that was sure to piss off Arlo, Mackenzie, and pretty much everyone else. Or at the very least, unbalance them.

She'd tell them the truth.

"Hidden Library was my first escape room."

Arlo raised her hand. "I call bullshit."

"Are you still in high school?" Shaun asked. "I bet she's still in high school." He was assessing her again, only somewhat less dismissively than before.

Wasn't he only, like, two years older than her? "I graduate this June."

"Where from?"

"And where do you start college this fall?" Riot added.

"I'm . . ." The words "not going to college" were on the tip of her tongue when she realized she was oversharing. That was a mistake in a game like this, especially since Leah hadn't outted any of her educational information as she'd done with the others. Best to leave them guessing. "I'm pretty sure that's none of your business."

Wes rolled off the sofa, suddenly alert. "You beat the unbeatable. Mensa members, renowned PhDs, cryptographers, and mathematicians from all over the world have tried to solve that thing. So, yeah, if you tell us you're at Exeter or Harvard-Westlake, or that you've got a full-ride scholarship at Oxford next year, it's going to make more sense than if you're a nobody from some local public school in Bumfuck, Nowhere."

I'm a nobody at some local public school.

Mackenzie eyed Wes closely. "Somebody woke up on the wrong side of his diamond-encrusted bed this morning."

"You were thinking the same thing," Wes snapped.

If she was, Mackenzie wasn't about to admit it. "Not everyone gets to go to boarding school, then drop out of Yale."

How does she know he went to boarding school?

"Um, I believe the bias toward private school education in America is not founded on actual statistics." Neela spoke even more rapidly than usual. "Based on a recent study of college preparatory test scores, there is very little evidence to suggest significantly higher achievements among the top ten percent of students in either environment, suggesting that intelligence, in an academic sense at least, is independent of the grade— no pun—of one's education."

"I still think it's sketchy," Wes said.

"Maybe her win was accidental," Shaun suggested. Clearly that was the only thing that made sense to Shaun-bot, who could not compute that a nobody like Persey could do what he could not.

"Shaun, I can assure you that Persey's win was legitimate, intentional, and not in the least bit accidental," Leah said, attempting to regain control of the room. "As were all of your scores."

"Fine," Shaun said. His face was so unreadable Persey couldn't tell if he bought the explanation or not, but Wes was more obvious (disdainful) in his disbelief.

"Sure it was."

Leah turned to him. "If you would like to review Persey's win, I have the full video footage of it upstairs in my office."

Persey cringed at the reminder that video footage from the Hidden Library existed.

"And after the All-Star Competition is complete," Leah continued, "you are more than welcome to see it."

"Just might." Wes turned away, flicking his black hair out of his face as he mouthed, *Watching you*, in Persey's direction. For creepy emphasis.

That's when something inside Persey snapped. All these privileged, egotistical assholes were judging her, doubting her. They couldn't believe that she, an escape room newbie, a social media nobody, who had flunked out of private school and was definitely not going to college, had managed to solve something they could not. They weren't any better than she was—just contestants in this game, there for the ten-million-dollar prize.

They were all the same. Even playing field. And she wasn't about to let this douche make her feel inferior even for a second. She squared her shoulders and met his stare with narrowed eyes.

Oh yeah? Well, I'm watching you too.

NINE

PERSEY HUNG BACK FROM HER PARENTS AS THEY SEARCHED
the quad for her brother. It was a dizzying sea of blue graduation gowns—
most still creased as if they'd been taken out of their plastic packaging just
moments before the ceremony—and matching square hats, yellow tassels
dancing around the faces of the 125 former Allen Academy seniors as they
cried and hugged and laughed their way through the throng of family and
friends flooding out of the auditorium.

She'd spent only one semester at the Allen Academy before the lofty
tuition no longer made up for her poor academic achievement and the
headmaster suggested she transfer to the local public school to finish
out her freshman year, as it would be "more appropriate" for her level.
No donations from her dad, no promises of improvement, not even her
brother's status as star athlete and valedictorian candidate could save her,
and so Persey had started as a transfer freshman at West Valley High School,
where she knew no one and her last name meant nothing to anyone.

Entering the West Valley campus that first day, Persey had smiled
voluntarily for the first time in months.

Her dad had refused to speak to her during the drive to school, which
was actually pretty perfect. They'd barely exchanged a dozen words since
midterms, so she was used to the silent treatment. Besides, it gave Persey a

chance to compose her thoughts. After months of being the stupidest girl at her fancy private school—population five hundred—she was looking forward to just being the stupidest girl amongst the twenty-five hundred West Valleyians. Where no one would notice.

She didn't mind the loneliness: being at school with no one to talk to was actually a helluva lot easier than being at home with no one to talk to, because at least at school there was a practical reason for it—no one knew her. At home it was just her dad's pettiness, her mom's drunkenness, and her brother's absence that accounted for the silence. There had been a two-week stretch over Christmas break while her brother was off skiing with friends in Gstaad where Persey had gone fifty-seven hours without saying a single word.

There was no way West Valley could be that bad.

Being back in the Allen Academy quad, even under completely different circumstances, was enough to heighten Persey's stress level, but as much as the buildings and the outdoor spaces and the perfectly poised students themselves reminded her of the misery earlier that year, she clearly didn't jar anyone's memory. No one's eyes flashed in her direction or lingered confusedly on her face as if trying to place her. She was a nameless nobody today, and that was just the way she wanted it.

Unlike her brother, who she finally spotted in a large circle of friends, all congratulating one another as if they'd just won the championship game. He, as always, was in the middle. The most popular of the popular.

He had everybody wrapped around his finger. It was tough to watch.

"Hey, Boss! How does it feel to be a high school graduate?" Persey's dad asked, slapping her brother on the back in a display of machismo that felt appropriately staged. A *this is how guys act, right?* kind of gesture that was just 100 percent her dad.

Her brother immediately turned on the charm. "It feels like the beginning of the rest of my life." He flashed his thousand-kilowatt smile.

"You're going to *love* Columbia," Dad continued. "And I'm not just saying that because you chose my alma mater. Being in the New York financial community will give you so many business contacts. I'm glad you picked it over Harvard."

"Picked it?" Persey couldn't help herself. They were the first words she'd spoken all day and they came flying out of her mouth on instinct. *They think* he *turned Harvard down?*

Her brother smiled at her. Not the cold, fake kind he used on their parents, but a genuinely warm one. He'd always had a soft spot for her, even now, when she had almost blown his cover, and it was a sentimentality he believed that she returned.

Not so much.

"Yeah, don't you remember? I told you about all my acceptances: Harvard, Columbia, Stanford, Cornell, Penn, Georgetown as a safety." He nodded for each one as if willing (demanding) Persey to remember. Remember the lie.

"Sorry," she said. "Yes, you did."

"That's what a fourteen eighty SAT score will get you, Boss." Her dad beamed as he said it, as if those numbers could somehow encompass all his paternal pride. "Acceptance anywhere you want."

Of course he believed anything his star son told him. Maybe if Persey hadn't scored so dismally on her PSAT test, he'd give her the benefit of the doubt once in a while too. Like when she swore she studied for a test but "only" got a B-minus.

"If your sister paid better attention, she wouldn't have been kicked out of Allen." Her dad pretty much took every opportunity to cut her down, even though he was still not addressing her directly.

One of her brother's buddies bounded up from behind, punching him lightly in the arm. "Dude! You ready for tonight? Party bus picks us up at eight."

Her dad gave them a knowing wink. "You boys letting loose tonight?" His face was at once conspiratorial and envious.

"Yes, sir," her brother said. "Just going to blow off some steam."

"That's my boy! I remember back in my day . . ." Then he started to tell some story about his own drunken antics—something about a toga party and a bathtub full of ice that was supposed to be cool and relevant—but Persey's brother wasn't listening. Though the permasmile never left his face, his buddy was whispering something excitedly in his ear. Something that made her brother's eyes widen with excitement. His lips parted, and she saw his tongue pass gently over them as if he was mentally savoring the five-star meal he'd enjoy later that night.

But it wasn't pan-seared pork belly or Royal Kaluga caviar that elicited such a response in her brother.

A cold chill rocketed down Persey's spine, numbing her hands and feet. She remembered that day last year when she'd walked into the seldom-used guesthouse and found her brother with the corpses of several animals: possums, squirrels, even a raccoon. Their mutilated bodies had been arranged in a little scene, and her brother stood above them, taking photos with his phone. When he'd turned toward the door where she stood rooted to the ground, stomach roiling with disgust and horror at what she was seeing, he'd had that same look in his eyes. Desire. Hunger. Need.

As she watched his buddy snickering now, Persey wondered what they were up to, then quickly forced any speculation from her mind.

She wasn't sure she wanted to know.

TEN

"SHALL WE BEGIN THIS APTITUDE TEST?"

Leah threw open the main doors of the library's reception room, and Greg entered the lounge. He approached Persey while Leah took up a position near the closet that housed everyone's luggage.

"Arms out, please," Greg said, in his now-familiar deadpan voice. "Legs shoulder width apart."

She complied, assuming this was just part of the first challenge, since Leah had signaled as much, though "aptitude test" seemed like a weirdly academic (don't panic) way to describe this pat-down. "Is this the beginning of the escape room?"

"Looks more like a first date," Arlo snarked.

"You're searching her?" Shaun asked. Only, the questioning inflection was barely present in his voice, like it had started out as a statement and morphed into a question mid-thought. "So you *do* think she cheated at the Hidden Library."

"You're *all* being searched," Leah explained, "before I take you to the first challenge."

First?

Wes jolted off the sofa. "You're treating us like common criminals."

"Like *suspects*," Kevin corrected him. "They search you *before* you're booked."

"You know that firsthand?" Wes said, curling his lip.

"He's right," Riot said, "and you're tried before you're a criminal. Innocent until proven guilty."

"I don't mind being searched," Arlo said, though her body language contradicted her words. With arms folded over her chest, her subtext practically screamed *I DON'T LIKE THIS.* "But I'd like to know why."

"We want to make sure you don't have any devices that could aid you in this competition," Leah explained. "No books. No reference materials. And most importantly, no cell phones."

On cue, Greg pulled Persey's smartphone from the pocket of her cargo pants and shoved it in the bag he had slung over his shoulder; then he yanked a device from his own pocket. It looked like a walkie-talkie with some kind of meter readout on its face that blipped back and forth as he swept her body head to toe.

"That's an electromagnetic scanner," Leah explained. "To make sure you don't have any devices hidden on your person."

"Whoa," Riot said, taking a step away. "Keep that cancer-causing shit away from me."

"It's perfectly safe," Leah said. "No different than going through a TSA scanner."

"Which I don't do. Full pat-down for me. No way I'm letting the government collect a DNA readout of my body."

Kevin looked at him curiously. "Um, even if that's true—"

"It is," Riot said.

"Okay, but why would they want to collect your DNA?"

Riot rolled his eyes. "Organ harvesting, human cloning. You think these genealogy testing kits advertised on TV are just so you can find out if your great-grandparents came over from Ireland versus Scotland? Fuck no. It's to round out the government's collection of our genetic codes."

Kevin stared at him for a moment, then turned to Neela. "Sorry, but I think I love him more."

"Clean!" Greg cried, stepping away from Persey to stand in front of Neela. Whatever he'd been looking for, Persey didn't have it.

"Why would anyone want to cheat at an escape room competition?" Persey asked as Greg patted Neela down.

Kevin laughed. "I can think of about ten million reasons."

"Egomaniacs," Neela suggested. "Or I suppose anyone suffering from an acute personality disorder. Probably from the cluster B or cluster C groups—histrionic, narcissistic, avoidant, dependent, even perhaps obsessive-compulsive. I could see arguments as to why any of these disorders would drive a person to cheat on a seemingly irrelevant game like this."

"True." Persey had personal experience with enough egomaniacs and narcissists to see Neela's point.

"True," Neela repeated, then laughed good-naturedly. She was totally unfazed by Greg, who added her phone to the collection in his shoulder bag. "I like your style. Tell it like it is. Use three words instead of twenty. The opposite of me, right? A veritable Zelda Fitzgerald of understatement."

Persey had no idea what she was talking about, but she was relatively sure Neela meant it as a compliment. Her energy gave Persey a headache, and yet she couldn't help but smile. Neela was right: they were complementary opposites.

"Clean!" Greg said, backing away from Neela with his electro-whatever detector as he moved to Kevin.

"Excuse me," Arlo said, holding her hands up in defense. "But what if we don't want Lime Boy's hands all over us, huh?"

"The. Fuck." Mackenzie snorted. "Not used to having a man's hands on you?"

Arlo scowled but didn't respond to the taunt. "I didn't sign a consent form. It is wholly within my rights to request some other form of a search. An X-ray machine. Or . . . or a female agent."

"This isn't the TSA, Ms. Wu," Leah said. "You don't have an option. Unless you'd rather leave now and forfeit your spot in the competition?" Leah gestured toward the main door. "It's not too late."

Arlo eyed the door, then Greg, then Leah, weighing her options. "Fine," she said. "But I'm going to lodge a formal complaint with the owners when this is over."

"Duly noted," Leah said, smiling with everything but her voice.

"Bee tee dubs," Wes said, arms stretched out to his side as Greg moved to him. "Who *are* the owners of Escape-Capades these days? Since, you know, what happened . . ."

"Escape-Capades is controlled by an LLC," Leah responded coolly, "registered with the state of Nevada. All board members are part of the public record."

"Okay, but . . . Hey!" Wes jumped as Greg, removed something from the former's hoodie pocket. "That's mine."

"Sir, no electronics." Greg wrenched his arm away as Wes attempted to wrestle the item out of his hand.

"What is it?" Leah asked.

Wes finally managed to extricate his property from Greg, then held the item up between two fingers for her to see. "It's a fucking vape pen."

"Electronic or mechanical?" Leah asked.

Wes's brows scrunched together. "Um . . ."

An imperceptible sigh left Leah's lips. "Does it use a battery?"

"Yes, but—"

"Then I'm terribly sorry, but you can either relinquish the device or thank you very much for your time, Mr. Song."

Wes looked as if he was going to punch Greg in the face as he dropped the e-cigarette into the driver's open hand, kicking the leg of a nearby table as he turned away, sulking.

A taut, tense silence settled over the room as one by one, Greg searched the remaining contestants, confiscating possible devices and clearing them of additional electronics. The competition had started, and everyone's game face was in full effect.

"Wonderful," Leah said as Greg deposited his backpack full of contraband at her feet like an offering to the queen. She glanced into the open bag, making a summary account of its contents, then nodded swiftly to Greg, dismissing him. As he exited, Leah stood before the large bookcase. "Will you please follow me?" Then she pulled a leather-bound volume from the middle shelf, releasing a lock. With a heavy creak that felt like it came directly from a haunted-house movie, the entire bookcase swung inward, exposing a secret passageway.

"Just like the exit from the Hidden Library!" Kevin said.

"I knew it was behind one of the bookcases," Riot said, peeling himself away from the wall. "Point for me."

Arlo clicked her tongue. "Of course the exit was behind a bookcase." She scowled at him, as if his very presence was somehow an insult. "The room was literally one big bookcase. How could it not be?"

Riot glanced up at the ceiling. "Trapdoor. False ceiling. One of those ladders that drops from the attic."

"Please silence yourselves," Shaun-bot said, stilted and weird, as if piping down was like turning your cellphone to mute. "It's starting."

Leah stepped through the bookcase as Shaun and Arlo hurriedly crossed the room, following close on her heels. Neela grabbed Persey's arm and dragged her forward behind them with Wes, Mackenzie, Riot, and Kevin packing in behind.

Persey blinked as they stepped from the wood-and-leather-and-Tiffany-lamp reception room to the blinding light of the corridor. It was lit from above and below, with fluorescents running the length of both the ceiling and the translucent floor, and Persey winced from the brightness, squinting her eyes as her pupils fought to dilate. A far cry from the old-school library, the hallway made Persey feel like she was walking through a spaceship, and she half expected to pass a window with a panoramic view of stars and galaxies.

"Where are we going?" Mackenzie asked, her voice close behind. Persey glanced over her shoulder and saw that Mackenzie walked at Kevin's side, as near to him as she could get without actually holding his hand. Persey had zero interest in who Kevin chose to spend his time with, but for some reason, the idea that it might be Mackenzie was irritating.

Leah ignored the question, sticking to her script. She was really good at that. "From the moment the competition begins, there will be no stopping it." She pivoted mid-stride so she was walking backward as she addressed them. "You have to keep moving forward, never back."

"Why would she say that?" Neela chattered anxiously. Without waiting for an answer, she turned her questioning from Persey to Leah. "Why would you say that? Why would we want to go backward? Is there something dangerous in there? Do we need a safe word? What could we possibly be doing where we'd need a safe word and what would it be? Linoleum? Amoxicillin? Has to be a word you wouldn't say in everyday life but I don't remember signing a waiver before we started, so if there's going to be anything potentially dangerous involved I feel like we should be adequately informed beforehand so we can make an educated decision about our further participation."

Persey marveled at her lung capacity.

"Does she have an off button?" Arlo asked.

"Do you?" Persey may have only known Neela for like an hour, but she already preferred her harmless prattle to Arlo's constant negativity and targeted condescension.

Leah paused at the end of the hallway before a door, laying her fingertips on the handle with a dramatic flourish. "Keep your eye on the clock. If it ever reaches zero, you will lose. You will *all* lose. Which means you need to work together. Do you understand?"

"Don't go for the buzzer beater," Wes said. "Check."

"How utterly cliché," Arlo added.

Mackenzie smiled. "Him or the game?"

"As you move further through the challenges," Leah continued, "it might help to remember why you're here in the first place. This is a test of your aptitude." Persey wasn't entirely sure why Leah used that word again, but something in the back of her brain suggested it might be important later, so she made a mental note. "Some of your strengths are tactile, others *scholastic*, but whatever your talent, I wish you good luck."

Leah paused as she opened the door with a flick of her wrist.

"You're going to need it."

ELEVEN

THE ROOM LEAH USHERED THEM INTO WAS DARK—SHOCKINGLY so, after the blinding white lights of the hallway—and as they shuffled through the doorway single file, Persey unconsciously reached out her hand and touched Neela's shoulder, using her as a guide so she didn't bump into anything. The lights from the hall hardly penetrated the new space; the darkness seemed to repel the light, pushing its beams away. She could vaguely discern the outline of an object right in front of her—a low, elongated structure that looked like some kind of shelf or wall—and though she could sense rather than see a smattering of large furniture pieces staged nearby, she couldn't make out any details.

Persey fought the urge to flee back into the hallway. She really, really, *really* didn't want to be there. She could feel a restless fluttering in her extremities, and the telltale tightness in her chest, as if someone was lacing a corset too tight, crushing her ribs and her diaphragm and her lungs in the process. A panic attack was lurking in the depths of her belly, ready to take over her entire body.

You shouldn't be here, she argued with herself. *Tell them you made a mistake.*

She was just about to leave (flee) through the still-open door when she heard it click into place, simultaneously cutting off even the slightest glow of light from the outside.

Calm down, she told herself, fighting back the spreading anxiety. *You just have to get through this. Eyes on the prize.*

"Now what?" Arlo twittered nervously. "Are we just supposed to stand here?"

In an instant, Persey's anxiety vanished. It was comforting to think that the self-confident Slytherin found this experience as off-putting as Persey did, and it reminded her that she wasn't alone.

"I don't see a countdown clock," Shaun replied. "The game must not have started yet."

"Maybe we have to turn the lights on?" Neela suggested. "Find the mechanism and—"

Without warning, overhead lights flickered, then buzzed to life, flooding the room.

"Oh," Neela said, almost disappointed that there wasn't an immediate puzzle to solve. "Well, that works too."

Meanwhile, for the second time in as many minutes, Persey's eyes needed to adjust to harsh, blue-hued fluorescents. Only, unlike the futuristic feel of the hallway, Persey now found herself in the most depressing-looking space she'd ever seen: an office full of cubicles.

The ceiling was low, paneled, and lined with said fluorescents. The walls were gray, the high-endurance industrial carpeting picked to match, and all the common office-place necessities had been included, like a water cooler, complete with a dispenser for teensy paper cups, and two side-by-side coffee machines, each with half-filled carafes resting on their hot plates. The walls on either side of them were blank, just textured wallpaper that looked as if a rake had been scraped through wet plaster, and in each corner of the room sat an indoor office plant—ficus, if Persey wasn't mistaken. Mounted on the far wall at the end of the room was a whiteboard covered in handwritten notes in red, blue, and black ink.

Two rows of desks stretched before them, each with a low wall around it on three sides, creating individual cubicles, the nearest of which had been decorated as if someone actually worked in it. The details were impeccable, the ambiance suitably drab—it was as if Leah had ushered them onto the research-and-development floor by accident instead of starting the game.

BZZZZ!

The sound of a buzzer pierced the tense silence and made Persey jump. Beside her, Neela let out a muffled yelp. Mackenzie seemed to find that incredibly funny: she snorted and buried her face in Kevin's bicep to prevent herself from laughing out loud, while Arlo rolled her eyes, but whether it was at Mackenzie, Neela, or both, Persey wasn't entirely sure.

"Thirty minutes." The voice was feminine and almost sarcastic in its sweetness, a far cry from the monotone announcer in the Hidden Library, who counted down the minutes near the end of that challenge, and as with the narration in the introductory video, Persey wondered if this voice also belonged to Leah.

"Shaun, your countdown clock." Arlo had turned around and was facing the door they'd come through, her chin raised toward the ceiling. Following her gaze, Persey found a digital clock face, which read twenty-nine minutes and forty-three seconds in blazing red numbers.

"Okay, then," Wes said, and without a further word, he started to perv through the nearest cubicle.

Spurred into action, the rest of the contestants scurried away from the entrance, each taking a different part of the room in a form of self-segregation that seemed tacitly agreed upon. Mackenzie gave Kevin a wink before dashing off to the water cooler, pulling out the paper cups one by one and checking their surfaces. Kevin gave a sigh as he watched her, but Persey was pretty sure it was a *what a hot mess she is* kind of sigh as opposed to a *what a hottie* kind of sigh. Then he half-heartedly headed for the end of the cubicles, glancing over each wall as he passed.

Riot headed straight for the whiteboard while Shaun-bot 2.0 spun around, like a Terminator running a search-and-destroy program. After a few seconds, he turned toward the nearest potted plant and meticulously combed through its copious leaves. Arlo hesitated a moment, which seemed strangely uncharacteristic for someone who presented nothing but snark and confidence, then marched up to the whiteboard, stood squarely beside Riot, feet shoulder-width apart and hands planted on her hips.

"It's a flowchart," Riot explained. "For an elaborate Escape-Capades escape room build."

Arlo shushed him. "You want to just share that with everyone?"

Wes cupped his hand to his mouth. "Works for me!"

"Leah said we'd have to work together." Riot shrugged. "I'm just following directions."

Rather than jumping right into action, Neela watched everyone else stake out a claim in the room before she moved, letting out another anxiety *meep* as she assessed her surroundings, verbalizing her thought process. "The whiteboard is too obvious, but the water cooler, yes, that's a good idea. Seems innocuous, but innocuous places are usually where the best clues are found. The cubicles are interesting. Lots of drawers and decoration, plus the computers themselves. I'm editing my valuation: the cubicles are *very* interesting. Don't you think?"

Persey had known her long enough to realize that an answer was not expected.

"One, two, three . . ." Neela counted under her breath. "Eight. Just like us."

Persey tilted her head to the side. Now that *was* interesting. "Let's check them out."

"Together?"

"Why not?" Leah *did* say that they'd have to work together, and she liked Neela, whose mindless chatter calmed Persey's nerves.

Neela's not-very poker face reflected skepticism, then suspicion, and finally relief. "Sure!"

Wes was making his way down the right aisle, so Persey and Neela took the left one, sticking their heads inside the first cubicle. It was pretty standard: leather chair, desktop computer, file holders and stacked binders, plus a "Sights of Old Las Vegas" calendar pinned to the cubicle wall.

Neela read the label on a white binder leaning against the computer monitor. "Escape-Capades Employee Manual." She snorted. "I guess it was easy to gather props for this one."

Too easy.

"But why last year's calendar?" Neela said, more serious than before. "Nothing on it but this one day circled. What's the significance of—" She cut off mid-sentence, her eyes growing even wider behind the thick-framed lenses as she stared at the artistically rendered photo of the Stratosphere hotel and casino above the month of May.

"What?"

Neela swallowed. "May twenty-second of last year."

"What about it?"

"The murder-suicide of Derrick and Melinda Browne. The founders of Escape-Capades."

"Oh, right."

Neela leaned forward eagerly as she took a deep breath. Girl really loved a long-winded explanation. "The Brownes did this promotion with massive prize money for anyone who could beat the unbeatable escape room but someone leaked the secret to the final challenge and somehow it ended up on the DaringDebunker website and I'm just going to assume that you have no idea what that is either, so I'm not going to wait for you to ask. It's like the WikiLeaks of escape room, gaming, and RPG secrets where insiders and enthusiasts alike can post spoilers, secret codes, et cetera, et cetera, but Escape-Capades had never, *ever* had a leak in the history of their company because they were family-owned and everyone loved the Brownes, et cetera and so forth, but suddenly there's this rumor that's leaked and supposedly it's a clue to the big final secret to solving the room and . . . and . . ."

Neela paused. Not to take a breath, but because she was suddenly flustered.

"You okay?'

"Yeah." Her face scrunched up as she continued, but the words came more slowly now. As if she was choosing them carefully. "It wasn't the solution per se, but a schematic of the final challenge. I mean, I'm sure the person who posted the solution didn't actually realize what they were doing. Or—or what it might be used for. The anonymous owner of DaringDebunker just promoted the puzzle as like the ultimate challenge. A bragging-rights thing. So the one person who finally *did* figure out that the whole chamber was a Baguenaudier with a solution that corresponded to a specific binary code . . ." She paused, panting. "Well, I don't think *that person* realized what it would do."

That person. "What did it do?"

Neela shrugged. "Like two thousand people solved the Prison Break escape room on the first day. All over the world. They all tried to claim the prize money. But Escape-Capades didn't have two hundred and fifty million dollars lying around and then . . ." She grimaced, glancing away from Persey. "And then, two days later, on May twenty-second, the bodies of Derrick and Melinda were found. Right here in this building."

Persey's eyes drifted to the calendar, where May 22 was circled in thick red ink. "What do you think that has to do with this challenge?"

"Not sure." Neela scrunched up her face again. "Maybe we should search the desk."

Persey pulled open a drawer and rummaged through the contents. "Stapler, Post-its, pens, ruler. Seems pretty normal for an office drone."

As Persey worked her way down through the desk drawers, Neela flipped through folders neatly lodged in a desktop file organizer. "Accounts payable," she said, perusing the contents. "Vendors, employee expense reports, monthly statements. If these are even remotely accurate, Escape-Capades was rolling in dough last year before . . . before the Prison Break fiasco."

"Find anything intriguing?" Wes tried to sound casual as he asked the question, but his intonation was too high. He stood in the cubicle next to them, and though he pretended to be interested in something, Persey noticed that he stood very close to the wall, as if trying to catch a glimpse of whatever she and Neela were looking at.

"Not really," Neela answered.

Shaun walked by, heading for the next potted plant. "Just that whoever works at this desk had the date of the Brownes' suicide circled on a calendar." Had he heard that from the opposite corner of the room? Maybe he really was an android.

"I'm sure that has nothing to do with us," Wes said quickly, then exited the adjacent cubicle and went to join Mackenzie at the water cooler.

"Which of course," Neela said, dropping her voice to little more than a whisper, "means that it does."

Persey liked the way she thought.

The second drawer had more personal items from its supposed occupant. A movie stub for the latest Fast and Furious franchise offering. Scattered packets of fake sweetener in pastel paper packages of yellow, pink, and blue. A singer-dancer audition notice for one of the casino floor shows. Several receipts, all from a bar called Shangri-La at the Lotus Hotel. A Halloween photo of two guys and two girls dressed up as members of the band Kiss, and on the back were written the names "Antonia, Jessica, Todd, and Brian."

"Now this is interesting," Neela said, a file folder spread open between her palms. "Credit card statements. Personal, not business. Five different cards, all maxed out. This person does not understand the usefulness and inherent pitfalls of extended credit."

"Is there a name on the bills?"

Neela shook her head as she flipped back through the pages. "The top of each statement has been cut off."

"Seems super sketch to me," Kevin said as he whizzed by their cubicle. "Keep searching."

"Like we need his permission," Persey grumbled as she began to search the bottom drawer, wondering who the statements might belong to—Antonia, Jessica, Todd, or Brian—and how that information might be relevant to the challenge.

"Twenty minutes."

"Same voice from the video presentation," Neela mused, still rifling through files. So Persey wasn't the only one who noticed. "Empty parking lot, only one other employee here. Doesn't it feel like Leah put this whole thing together herself?"

Doesn't it? "You make it sounds so ominous."

"Silly, I know," Neela continued, "because even though it's Sunday, there must be people working here somewhere, especially since the average Escape-Capades room requires at least three or four people to control and supervise, so it feels a little weird that so far the only people we've seen are Leah and—"

"What's this?" Persey straightened up as she removed a leather case from the back of the bottom drawer. It was a medium-size zip pouch, like the kind Persey's dad would have packed his toiletries in for a business trip, and it felt so out of place in the office drawer that it immediately drew her attention.

"Should we open it?" Neela asked, excitement growing in her voice.

Persey grinned in response and slowly pulled the zipper open.

"What did you find?" Mackenzie appeared from nowhere, hand outstretched toward the pouch like a teacher taking possession of classroom contraband. "Let me see."

"You see with your eyes," Arlo said from the whiteboard. Could everyone hear them? "Not with your hands."

Persey turned her back on Mackenzie. "We've got this. Thanks."

"But we're supposed to work together," Mackenzie whined. She wasn't used to not getting her own way. "Leah said—"

"Someone is *really* into newspaper clippings," Persey said, cutting her off as she carefully lifted a stack of crinkly paper from the pouch, clipped together at the center. "And . . ." This time she pulled out a tangled knot of four small metal hoops and held it up to Neela.

"Looks like a key chain," Neela said. "Or an elaborate bracelet maybe."

"Lame," Mackenzie said, stomping off. "All yours."

Neela shook her head as she fingered through the clippings. When she spoke again, she dropped her voice. "This one's an article about the death of the Brownes." The paper crinkled at her touch, rigidity setting into the material even though it was barely a year old. "Looks like it's the first report, from the same day their bodies were discovered. 'Derrick and Melinda Browne found dead in the Escape-Capades Headquarters building in northwestern Clark County Thursday, in what police are calling an apparent murder-suicide.'"

"And the rest?" Persey whispered quickly. She didn't need a full rehashing of those events.

Neela, thankfully, took the hint and skimmed through the pack. "It's basically everything the *Review-Journal* wrote about this case." She thumbed through, then paused at the last page. "This one's from three months later. The official investigation had finished. Mentions corporate espionage in the Prison Break scandal. I guess there was some evidence to suggest that they had been murdered, but the official verdict was murder-suicide."

Official.

"And then all business inquiries should be directed to an L. Browne."

Kevin's head popped up over the wall from where he'd been searching the adjacent cubicle. "Must be a son or daughter who inherited."

Persey sighed. "Don't you ever knock?"

"I thought there was an open door— Hey! A puzzle ring!"

Neela pointed to the tangled key-chain-looking thing on the desk. "Is that what it is?"

"Hell yeah. My parents' wedding rings are puzzles like this." He snapped his fingers and pointed at the ring, which Persey dutifully handed to him. "Watch this."

In Kevin's nimble hands, what Neela had identified as a key chain or bracelet went from four separate metal rings—gleaming white gray like platinum—to an intricate knot of a ring. He turned and aligned the bands, threading the curved parts of the metal between each other until their loops and dips lay perfectly flat with each other. He held up the finished product after just a minute's work—a man's ring in the pattern of a Celtic knot.

"Holy cow babies!" Neela cried. "I should have known what that was."

Kevin pushed the ring in Persey's face. "Beautiful, right?"

She couldn't deny it. "Yes."

"Think it might fit me, too," Kevin said. And before Persey could stop him, he'd slipped the ring onto the fourth finger of his left hand.

The instant the ring was in place, Persey heard a swooshing sound. Something had moved behind her.

She spun around to find an open door in the wall, where nothing had been before.

TWELVE

THE DOOR OPENED ONTO A SLIM CORRIDOR, HARDLY WIDE enough for a single person to squeeze through sideways. It reminded Persey of an aisle in a cramped airplane, complete with dull red LED lighting strips embedded into the floor. Before the corridor disappeared into darkness, Persey saw a single name stenciled onto the black wall with stark white paint: "KEVIN."

"Why just *his* name?" Wes asked as everyone gathered around the newly opened door. "He doesn't deserve to win. He didn't even discover that thing. Fuck, he doesn't even deserve to be here! This competition is fucking rigged."

"I don't think this is the end of the game," Arlo said. "I think it's just the beginning. Look." She pointed to the top of the flowchart, where a large box encompassed the words "Individual Challenge." It came directly after a section entitled "Office Drones," which must have been the room they were currently exploring.

"What else is on that board?" Shaun asked, although the question was merely perfunctory as he was already in motion toward the whiteboard to examine it for himself. "From the Individual Challenge it goes to Boyz Distrikt. That must be the big escape room."

"I don't think so," Persey said, peering around his shoulder. "Look down there." Below the first phase of the flowchart were several more boxes, each labeled with a name. "Collectibles. Cavethedral. Iron Maiden. Recess. High Tea. True North."

"They must all be separate rooms," Neela said. "One after another."

"Eight rooms?" Mackenzie groaned.

"Nine," Kevin said, "if you count this one."

"This is going to take forever."

Arlo rolled her eyes at Mackenzie. "You got somewhere else to be?"

"Unlike the rest of you, I happen to have a life."

"I wonder what 'Individual Challenge' means," Riot said, checking on the structural integrity of his Mohawk with his fingertips.

Arlo took command, turning to face everyone like a general addressing her troops. "How did this door open?"

"Sir!" Kevin saluted her, clicking the heels of his Vans together and squaring his shoulders. "I put on this puzzle ring, sir. Er, ma'am."

"His parents had ones just like it, he said," Neela added. "And we, I mean Persey and I, were thinking that with eight cubicles and eight of us, it might mean that there is—"

"Spread out!" Arlo barked, interrupting Neela. "Each of these cubicles must have a puzzle that is personal to one of us. Solve it, and we open the door."

"Or," Wes countered, "everyone can just find their own shit."

Arlo pointed to the clock, which continued its steady countdown. "We don't really have time for that. We need to work together."

"Why do you have such a hard-on for this collaboration shit?" Wes asked. He stepped (too) close to her. Close enough that it was either meant as a come-on or a threat. "Is it because you won't have anyone to boss around if we're all working on our own?"

"It's because Leah told us to. Those are the rules."

"Your rules. Not mine."

Shaun laughed, a calculated approximation of a laugh, which of course made it creepy and unnerving, and it was so mechanical that Persey almost believed Kevin's android joke. "Inability to follow the rules. In an escape room competition. That's funny."

Persey was pretty (definitely) sure it wasn't.

"Is that what got you kicked out of Yale?" Kevin asked. "Rule breaking?"

"I *dropped* out. Big difference."

Kevin folded his arms across his chest. "How much do you want to bet that old Wes here dropped out just seconds before they were about to boot his ass?"

Wes clenched his fists, his laid-back-stoner vibe abandoned. "You think I'd want to come back to this shithole town?"

Kevin grinned at him, obviously pleased with himself. "Touchy, touchy. Must've hit pretty close to the mark."

"Fuck you," Wes muttered. But despite his protests, Wes's sunken shoulders and faltering eyes revealed the truth in Kevin's theory.

"Okay, kids," Kevin said, turning away from the defeated Wes. "My door is open, and I think we all know I'm not going to be of any use to you here, so . . . see ya!" With another salute, more casual this time, he stepped through the door into the darkness.

"Ten minutes."

"Everybody report in," Arlo ordered even though they'd barely had five seconds' worth of search time. It was a good thing she ran a website for a living: dealing with breathing, emoting humans in the flesh clearly wasn't her strong suit.

Shaun pointed to the two nearest cubicles. "That one is almost entirely empty, and the only out-of-place items in this work domicile are a poker chip and a toy slot machine."

"Any clues on either?" Arlo asked.

Shaun held the chip up to the light. "Lotus Hotel and Casino," he read. "Las Vegas, Nevada."

Same casino as the receipts in the drawer Persey had been searching. Coincidence? Probably not. She was about to bring it up when Wes stormed into the cubicle and snatched the chip from Shaun-bot's hand. "Gimme that."

Arlo approached the desk. "You gonna tell us how you're related to the Lotus Hotel, or shall we guess?"

But Wes ignored her, jaw clenched, body suddenly tense and awkward. Whatever the connection he had to that casino, it wasn't a pleasant one.

Wes turned the poker chip over in his hands a few times while he stared fixedly at the miniature replica of the one-armed bandit mounted on the desktop beside an inkjet printer. It stood about a foot high, and unlike the modern electronic equivalents that populated other Las Vegas casinos, this one was old-school: the arm attached to its side looked as if it might move, the three reels on its face sported classic symbols like cherries, a lemon, and the number seven, and a large opening in the side could fit a full-size poker chip.

"There's a coin slot in the side, you know," Arlo said, prompting him. "That's probably where—"

"I know how to work a fucking slot machine," Wes said. Then, with a glance at the ticking clock and an expression that Persey could only describe as constipated, he dropped the poker chip into the coin slot on the machine.

The chip thunked against the metal interior as it fell to the bottom, then another door opened on the far wall.

"Finally," Wes said as he ambled across the room. "Anything is better than being stuck in here with you assholes. Out."

Persey was pretty (positively) sure no one was sorry to see him go.

The remaining contestants spread out again, digging through items in the six remaining cubicles. While Neela busied herself with the drawers, Persey noticed that Mackenzie, Arlo, and Shaun kept glancing in their direction. Keeping an eye on the competition.

"I found this," Neela said, holding up an old-fashioned brass key, the kind that Victorian housekeepers would have dangling from their pockets by a large chain, used for opening the mistress's chamber, the good parlor, and the wine vault. "And there's a set of locks in one of the drawers."

"Seriously?" Arlo asked. As if Neela was going to lie to her.

"Yeah. Different sizes and shapes. And each has a number. Like in a hotel or an apartment building."

"Ring any bells for anyone?" Arlo asked.

Everyone shook their heads, whereupon Neela began to recite the numbers out loud. "Twenty-seven. Four hundred and twelve. Two-B. One Eighty West A."

Mackenzie sucked in a breath. "What?"

"Two-B?" Neela repeated. "One Eighty West A?"

"What does it mean?" Shaun asked.

"It's the address of—"Mackenzie caught herself in time. Whatever information she'd been about to divulge in her dumbstruck state froze on her tongue and was lost as she recalled where she was and who she was with. "Address of a friend," she said confidently. "Just an old friend."

Persey knew what a lie looked like when she saw it on someone's face. Mackenzie's hand trembled as she took the key from Neela and approached the lock labeled "One Eighty West A." She turned it slowly, chest completely still as she held her breath, and in the near silence, Persey could hear a soft click and, once again, another door opened on the far wall. Mackenzie didn't wait to be asked about her "old friend"; she was across the room and down the narrow passageway before anyone could ask a follow-up.

THIRTEEN

"THREE DOWN, FIVE TO GO," ARLO SAID; THEN SHE HELD UP AN item from inside her cubicle so they could all see it. "This Rubik's Cube on steroids . . . any takers?"

As much as Persey hated to admit it, Arlo's description was appropriate. In the palm of her hand sat a multisided ball-shaped thing with pentagonal faces made up of little shapes, all in different colors. Brown, green, blue, red, yellow . . . There had to be a dozen at least, and Persey saw that they were all mixed up on each of the faces.

"A Magic Dodecahedron!" Neela cried out, like a child on her birthday who just discovered that Mom and Dad *finally* brought that pony she'd been asking for. "Also known as the Megaminx. And you are correct, Arlo. It is a Rubik's Cube on steroids."

"Anyone else know what it is?" Arlo asked.

Everyone shook their heads. Persey couldn't even solve a regular Rubik's cube, let alone this monster.

"Then this must be for you." Arlo tossed the Megaminx over the wall. Neela caught it one-handed and eagerly began to examine the faces. "Twelve colors, probably looking for a standard solving pattern. I was Megaminx champion for the greater Philadelphia area three years running when I was in high school." She smiled sheepishly at Persey.

"Puzzles like this are kind of my thing."

"I thought math was your thing?" Shaun asked.

"My *other* thing."

"Can you solve it?" Persey asked.

"Oh yes," Neela said with a slight laugh. Then she glanced at the clock. "Eight minutes, but this should only take me about four. Keep looking while I take care of this."

"Looks like this cubby has its own library," Riot said, rounding the corner at the end of the aisle. "That must be for me."

"Librarian?" Persey asked, remembering Leah's comment from the introductions: *Once a librarian, always a librarian.*

Riot nodded. His Mohawk didn't budge. "Part-time, ever since high school. And I've been putting myself through grad school working as a shelver at . . ." His voice trailed off as he scanned the row of books on the desk. "Huh."

"What?"

"N-nothing," he stuttered, his face turning a sickly shade of yellow. "I just . . . It's weird that they're all books from the same section. Six five two point eight. Filed correctly."

Persey hadn't brushed up on the Dewey decimal system lately (ever), and she couldn't fathom what genre of books would make the color drain from Riot's face. "What section?"

"Cryptography." He pulled one book from the shelf, and immediately another door slid open. Instead of rushing in like Wes did, Riot stared at the opening, shaken.

"You okay?" Persey asked.

Riot nodded. "Yeah. Yeah, I'm fine." Then he smiled at her over his shoulder. It was genuine, not like Kevin's smirks, which always made Persey feel like he was a step ahead of her, and there was something else—the way he glanced down at the rest of her before his eyes focused on her face. Persey didn't know why, but she felt her chest heat up.

Riot's smile deepened. "I'll see you on the other side, okay?"

Persey nodded, confused and betrayed by her body's reaction. "Yeah. Of course."

"Done!" Neela cried, sparing Persey a moment of much-feared introspection. She held up the dodecra-thingy in victory. Each side was now a solid color. "Less than three minutes! It was easier than I anticipated. An amateur must have set it, and unlike the standard three-by-three of a Rubik's or similar puzzle, the solving of a Megaminx is really *all* about who sets it up."

"If it's solved," Shaun said slowly, "then why isn't your door open?"

Neela's face fell, confidence shaken. "I . . . I don't know."

"I've got a weird old-fashioned typewriter over here," Arlo called out from the far side of the room. She was like a well-oiled machine when it came to rummaging through other people's stuff. "Ring a bell for anyone?"

Shaun stood on tiptoes to peer over the wall into the cubicle. "That's an original SIGABA, also known as an ECM Mark II encryption device, circa 1944. Standard-issue Allied electric cipher machine." He sounded neither excited nor impressed.

"Then Ima guess this is for you," Arlo said, stepping aside.

"Riot's books were on cryptography, and Shaun's thing is an encryption device?" Neela muttered at Persey's side, the solved puzzle toy still firmly clasped in her hands as they rounded the wall to where Arlo had discovered it. "That can't be a coincidence, can it?"

Persey seriously doubted it. "Let's figure out what to do with your mega-thingy."

The cubicle she and Neela were currently in was the least decorated workplace Persey had seen in the room, other than the one Shaun described as being mostly empty, making the appearance of the brightly hued puzzle toy that much more striking among the drab, impersonal interior. And it also meant that the solution to Neela's challenge should be easy to spot.

Except not so much. "Arlo," Persey asked. "Where did you find that thing?"

"In a drawer," Arlo replied from the last cubicle in the row.

So (not) helpful. "Which one?"

Instead of answering, Arlo verbalized her search process as she went. "This desk is cluttered with tchotchkes, collectible toys, novelty paperweights, a mouse pad designed like a Pac-Man maze. I think this one is mine."

"Thank God," Neela muttered under her breath. "Maybe she'll stop talking now."

As much as Persey had to acknowledge the irony of Neela's words, she also had to laugh. Cuz yeah.

"I believe my door is open," Shaun announced. Persey hadn't seen what he'd done, but he was right. One more section of the wall had slid open, revealing a dark passageway beyond. "I shall be leaving now."

"Okay, Shaun-bot," Arlo laughed dryly. "Don't let the door swat your metal ass on the way out." She was fixated on something, which probably meant she too was just moments away from opening her door.

Meanwhile, Persey and Neela were getting nowhere.

"Let's list everything we see," Persey suggested. "Sometimes it helps to say it out loud."

"Computer," Neela began, starting with the obvious. "Keyboard, mouse, external speakers, stapler, empty document caddy, pen holder with exactly one pen in it, and a coffee mug warmer."

Persey's eye was immediately drawn to the black-and-white tray meant to keep one's coffee cup from getting cold. Everything else on the desk would have been standard-issue office supplies, except that. *That* was something the company wouldn't have supplied. Something the employee would have brought from home. As she stared at the generic device, its white plastic shell and circular black metal base began to take on a familiar pattern. Leaning closer, Persey could see that someone had drawn a shape in black marker, almost imperceptible except for the fact that the dried ink reflected the lights in a different way. There were five lines drawn inside the circle, creating a pentagon.

Just like one of the faces of the Megaminx.

"Put it on the coffee warmer," Persey said, pointing.

"You think?"

Persey nodded quickly. "Look close. There's a pentagon drawn on—"

"There's a pentagon drawn on here!" Neela squealed. "Jinx, one, two, three, four, five, six, seven, eight, nine, ten," she said, rattling off the numbers so quickly as she tried to undo the bad luck created when the two of them said the same thing at the same time, that she sounded like an auctioneer on cheap trucker speed. Then, with a flourish, she lined a face of the Megaminx up with the shape drawn on the coffee warmer and placed it delicately on the surface.

Something on the desk clicked, then another door opened.

"Holy cow babies!" Neela cried, throwing her arms around Persey's neck. "Thank you so much. I never would have seen that myself. I get a little, um, crazed when my adrenaline is up."

"A little?"

Neela blushed. "Right."

"There!" Arlo cried. The door beside Neela's opened with a thud. "The IP address for Geektacle? Too easy, Escape-Capades!"

"Arlo's pop culture website," Neela explained, without waiting for Persey to ask. "For gamers and puzzle solvers, sci-fi and comic book and fantasy fans. It's like our happy place." Her eyes followed Arlo as she disappeared through her door, which sealed itself behind her.

"Our?"

"I have an account and I peruse quite a bit." Neela laughed uncomfortably. "Like, I'm kind of an Arlo fangirl, but don't tell her. I mean, I'd die."

"I won't." Especially since it would only increase Arlo's ego.

"But I also like the content. Arlo posts a lot of puzzles, and there's some healthy competition to solve them first. That's my favorite part. Keeps me sharp."

"Like the Megaminx?"

"Ha, yes! I don't like to brag, but I can generally solve a level-eight puzzle box in under an hour, which is top ten percentile. Like last year when DaringDebunker posted specs to this one top secret puzzle that no one could solve and I was able to—"

"Five minutes."

"Son of a Shatner!" Neela said, rated G even in a time of extreme stress. "We still need to figure out your door mechanism."

Persey waved her off. "Oh, it's over there."

Neela tilted her head to the side. "You already found it?"

"Well, there's only one cubicle left."

"Good point! You need help?"

She didn't want anyone to see what her special "thing" might be. Even (especially) Neela. "I'll be okay. They don't want us to fail this early, so I bet it's pretty easy."

"You sure?"

"Totally."

"Okay," Neela said, heading toward her door. "Here goes nothing!"

Persey waited until Neela had completely disappeared down the hallway before she entered the last cubicle. As soon as Shaun had mentioned that one of the cubicles was mostly empty, she knew it was meant for her.

With three minutes remaining, Persey stepped through the low wall into the barren space. Not even a standard-issue desktop computer and wheelie chair had been added, and all that stared back at her were the items that couldn't be removed: the built-in L-shaped desk and an office telephone.

She picked up the handset, registering the old-fashioned dial tone coming through the speaker, and quickly typed in a phone number. She'd barely released the last digit when one final door in the wall swung open.

FOURTEEN

THE PADDED CORRIDOR ENDED WITH YET ANOTHER DOOR, which Persey pushed open, stepping into the chamber beyond. The moment she entered, the door swung closed and locked behind her.

To say that the room was dark was a total understatement. It was completely freaking black; not even a hint of the red lights from the hallway. Can't-see-your-hand-in-front-of-your-face kind of dark. Persey knew because she tried.

There's no need to panic. Nothing to be afraid of. Focus on why you're here.

The prize money. That was enough to calm her down.

She reached her hands to either side in an attempt to get a feeling, literally, for the room. Her palms steadied as they landed on smooth, hard walls just inches beyond her shoulders. So less a room and more a closet. Hands held up in front so she didn't smack into anything, she took several tentative steps forward before she was stopped by the fourth wall.

In the darkness, she felt around for something that might denote the kind of challenge she was up against. A puzzle. A maze. Something visual or something tactile? No clue.

"Hello?" she said out loud, testing the acoustics. Her voice sounded dead and flat, which meant the closet was probably soundproof, or heavily insulated at the very least. She could barely hear the sound of her own breath as she struggled (failed) to keep her heart rate at bay.

She knew the darkness and the muted quality of the room were tactics meant to instill panic, to inflame her desperate need to escape, which would inevitably lead to her inability to think clearly. She'd read about how escape room designers used things like claustrophobia, peer pressure, and misdirection to make their challenges more difficult, and at Escape-Capades, they had that shit down. Persey could feel her heart thumping in her chest, her breaths coming shorter and shorter, which would eventually lead to light-headedness, and it took every ounce of her emotional strength not to turn back toward the door and pound on it with her fists, demanding to be released.

The lights will come on soon. They'll have to. Stay calm. Be patient. Everyone else is in the same boat.

Maybe, but Persey seriously doubted if super-cool Mackenzie or tough-as-nails Arlo were freaking out. She closed her eyes—wondering if it even mattered since it was as dark with her lids down as with them up—and counted. *One. Two. Three. Four. Five . . .*

"Ten minutes."

The lights inside the chamber flared to life with such ferocity that a searing pain ripped through Persey's eyeballs, like a dagger driving straight to her brain. *Seriously, again?* Even with her lids closed, she let out a groan as her heavily dilated pupils screamed against the onslaught. She peeled one corner of her left eye open, exposing it to a piercing white-yellow glow, then snapped it shut again.

Another tactic to keep her unbalanced, the utter darkness and the blinding light in alternation. She had to do it like a Band-Aid. Rip it off in one swift pull. With a deep breath, Persey opened her eyes.

The wall in front of her appeared blurry at first, but as her eyes focused, and her pupils raced to resize themselves, the panel came into view. There was a number pad embedded in the wall, angled at forty-five degrees with an old LCD screen beside it. Pixelated white letters scrolled across the blue background, spelling out "Welcome to the Bank of Persephone" and above it were two stationary readouts in each corner of the screen: on the left, a countdown clock, starting at ten minutes, and on the right, a bar graph like the battery indicator on her phone, but labeled O2.

The Individual Challenge had begun.

Unfortunately, it was a stressful start. Persey groaned as she registered what the O2 bar graph must mean. She was about as good at chemistry as she was at math, so if this test involved some kind of reaction calculation, she was pretty much screwed. Puzzles and patterns? Those seemed to come naturally to Persey, but the academic stuff triggered her anxiety. She knew enough to identify the O2 as a measure of oxygen, but other than that, she had no idea. Was the required code the atomic number of oxygen? That seemed too easy. . . .

Persey tried to picture the periodic table of elements with its distinctive rainbow-hued squares and U shape. She'd stared at that table for hours, trying to memorize the letters and numbers in each square before her chemistry final last year. Which she (barely) passed. Oxygen was one of the basic elements. Lighter. Near the top. What was that saying her chemistry teacher had drilled into them to help the class remember the order?

Henry Helps Little Betty Brown Crack Nuts On Friday Nights.

Her inner eight-year-old always snickered when she got to "crack nuts," but the potentially dirty mnemonic had done its job. O for oxygen, which was eighth in line, so that meant an atomic weight of eight.

Persey's hand hovered over the keypad. Eight seemed too easy. Too simple. This was the All-Stars for Chrissakes. The rest of the competitors wouldn't need a stupid mnemonic device to remember what order the elements were in. They probably could recite every number in each of those little periodic squares as easily as Persey could say the alphabet. No, there had to be something else.

"Nine minutes." The sickly-sweet female voice filled the room. As in Office Drones, there were speakers somewhere in her tiny prison, but Persey didn't have time to search for them. *Don't let the clock get to zero.* Part of Leah's instructions. Persey had to figure this out in nine minutes or less.

Okay, the design had to be the first clue. It was an ATM machine, and the keypad was where you'd enter your PIN. Your four-digit PIN. Great! So she needed four numbers.

Next, her eyes drifted up to the O2 bar. What did that mean? Oxygen. But two atoms of oxygen. Right, so that would be twice the weight, or sixteen.

Still, Persey hesitated. She only had two digits. 0-0-1-6? That seemed stupid. But it wasn't as if she had any other options. Besides, maybe typing in the wrong answer would give her a clue about the right one? It was worth a try.

Persey quickly typed in the digits.

A short buzzer blared through the speakers, indicating that Persey's answer was incorrect. On the screen, the O2 bar shortened a notch.

What did that mean?

Think, Persey.

The words continued to scroll across the screen, catching Persey's eye. The Bank of Persephone. That had to be a clue. The bank was her. The PIN to withdraw funds had to be related, in some way, to her. But how?

Persey's face felt damp with perspiration. Was the temperature in the room rising?

Okay, ignore the temperature. The most logical four-digit code she could think of was her birthday—two-digit month, two-digit day. Feeling that this was too simple but unable to come up with an alternative, she typed in the numbers.

BZZZZZ.

Once again, the O2 bar shortened.

Damn it. Last four digits of her social security number?

BZZZZZ.

The O2 indicator was at the halfway point now, and Persey definitely felt as if the room was hotter. Her back and chest were damp as she peeled off her denim jacket, letting it drop to the floor beside her, and her breaths were getting shallower by the second. The air was heavy and hot, forcing her lungs to work overtime, and she felt dizzy. Like she wanted to lie down on the floor. Just for a minute (forever).

That's when it hit her: the O2 bar? It indicated the oxygen level in the room. Every time she inputted the wrong answer, the game cut off some of her breathable air.

It had taken three missteps to get to the halfway point. What would happen when the bar dropped to zero?

Persey wasn't sure she wanted to know. This was just a game, right? *No one is supposed to get hurt.*

She wasn't going to think about that. The faux danger was just a distraction, something to prevent her from figuring out this puzzle. She needed to focus.

"Seven minutes."

Seven? Where had eight gone? Crap, she was losing track of time already. There had to be a clue she was missing. Somehow. Her initial feeling that the competition began the moment she stepped off the plane came back to her, and as the beads of sweat on her forehead began to trickle down her face, she attempted to remember every detail from the moment she saw Greg at the bottom of the escalator until the lights came on in her closet-like ATM room. Had Greg said anything? Or Leah?

This is a test of your aptitude. Some of your strengths are tactile, others scholastic, *but whatever your talent, I wish you good luck.*

Leah's last words before they all entered Office Drones. It had felt weird at the time, and the words "test," "aptitude," and "scholastic" jumped out at her. Were they the key to the solution?

Test. Aptitude. Scholastic.

Scholastic. Aptitude. Test.

Persey's eyes grew wide. *How could they even have that information?* Was the key to getting out of that suffocation closet her freaking SAT score?

A new panic washed over her. Unlike the rest of the contestants, who probably had their super-high SAT scores proudly tattooed on their bodies somewhere, Persey had taken the test under duress—a devil's bargain— and had hardly registered what her crappy score had been, she cared so little about it. Had she even broken four digits? Yes, she vaguely recalled that it was one thousand and something. . . . Her dad had repeated her score over and over, not out of pride but because he couldn't believe how low it was.

What had he said? That a fourth grader could have managed that score just by filling out the name and address portions correctly.

Persey had wanted to tell him that *he* should sit through an SAT exam and see how well he did, but instead she'd just stared at the pattern on the marble countertop, the little gray smudges and squiggles arranging themselves into familiar shapes. An eagle in flight. Bunny slippers. A space shuttle.

Not the quartz, Persey. What was the score her dad kept repeating?

Numbers swirled before her eyes, mocking her, as her oxygen-deprived brain desperately tried to remember. She leaned against the wall to keep her body steady and upright—all she wanted to do was lie down and take a nap instead of being forced to recall unpleasant events from her past.

One thousand and . . . sixty? No, that wasn't right. One thousand and eighty?

One thousand and eighty? Are you kidding me? Did you manage to misspell your name on the test?

There was only one way to find out.

With a trembling hand, Persey managed to type in 1-0-8-0 Enter.

Instead of the dreaded buzz, the ATM swung away from her into the next room.

FIFTEEN

PERSEY STARED AT THE NEON-PINK FLYER FOR A FULL TWO minutes, fluttering in the hot afternoon breeze of the West Valley quad. As she read the text for the fortieth time, the tingles of excitement at the tips of her fingers were tempered somewhat by the gurgling of anxiety deep in the pit of her stomach.

He'll never let you.

Why her father cared what she did was a mystery. When he wasn't obsessed with work, practically living at the office for large stretches of time as they developed some new project, he was wholly focused on her brother. Ever the dutiful son, he checked in from Columbia weekly, sharing anecdotes from the dorms and character sketches of new friends, all of which allowed their dad to live vicariously.

Persey had only picked up snippets of those video calls, unintentionally eavesdropped as she was going to and from the kitchen. She'd been half-afraid her dad would insist that Persey be present at the weekly calls—an audience for the greatness of her older brother—but her dad had spared her that torture. But not out of mercy. He just wanted his son all to himself.

Though Persey had been exempted from those calls, she certainly hadn't been able to fly under her dad's radar in any other facet of her life. He was still fuming at her expulsion from the Allen Academy a year earlier, and his silent treatment had morphed into a nightly teardown session over dinner, where no matter what topic of conversation began the evening, it always dissolved into a litany of Persey's faults.

UNLV made the Final Four? *Persey wouldn't know—she can't count that high.*

The latest electorate manipulation scandal? *Don't use any big words—Persey won't be able to follow.*

Unemployment rates up in the metro area? *Persey will be joining them as soon as she graduates.*

It was like a game her father played with himself, attempting to make even the most banal bit of information, like the weather report, into a dig at his daughter. Only eighty-five tomorrow? *Still higher than Persey's IQ!*

Most (all) of the time, Persey just grinned and bore it. There wasn't really a point in fighting back. Her dad's tactics were childish, and there was no arguing with children. They just doubled down. So she kept her mouth shut, eyes glued to her dinner plate, wondering if her mother would ever (never) sober up long enough to realize that her husband was an emotionally abusive dickwad.

And even though Persey knew her father was just trying to punish her for some imaginary crime, the constant barrage wore on her, until she'd begun to contemplate skipping dinner altogether just to avoid the deluge of insults. Going to bed hungry might have been worth it.

But this flyer, this garishly colored piece of paper taped up to the door of the school theater, it was a lifeline.

THEATER DEPARTMENT NEEDS:
STAGE CREW
ORGANIZE PROPS, MOVE SETS, ETC.

MUST BE AVAILABLE FOR EVENING AND WEEKEND
REHEARSALS AND PERFORMANCES
SEE MR. BECK IF INTERESTED

Evenings and weekends? That was exactly when Persey didn't want to be home. But was there any chance in hell her dad would let her do it?

This was an extracurricular activity, a thing much coveted by students targeting college, as she'd learned from listening to her brother and his friends. They'd been obsessed with appearing "well-rounded" on applications. Maybe she could spin it that way? Her dad was constantly pestering her about college—perhaps he'd see it as Persey finally "getting serious" about her future?

Persey snapped a picture of the flyer with her phone and hurried off to fourth period, the hint of an elusive smile cracking the corners of her mouth.

It was worth a shot.

Persey was almost halfway through the nightly forty-five-minute dinner with her parents and she still hadn't brought up her stage crew plan. It should have been a simple conversation starter, as easy as *So I think I'm going to work on the spring musical at school,* but nothing was ever easy with her dad. He'd spent most of the meal on his tablet in a furious back-and-forth with the tech department at the office over some glitches in the new product.

Which, of course, meant her dad was in a fouler mood than usual.

He'd been grumbling to himself for the better part of twenty minutes while typing so vehemently that Persey thought he might crack the glass on his device. Every third word was a poorly muffled curse, and every few moments, he'd glance up at the chandelier, thinking about his response, before diving back in.

Twice he'd laid the tablet aside, heaving something between a sigh and a growl, and leaned back in his chair, daring his wife or his daughter to ask what was wrong. But neither took the bait. Persey's mom, who usually placated her husband by facilitating his airing of grievances, had retreated into a second bottle of chardonnay, and since Persey hadn't initiated conversation around the dinner table in years, the oppressive silence remained.

Persey had been going back and forth in her mind about shelving the idea. Was it worth bringing up, worth opening herself up to her dad's ridicule? Persey wasn't sure. Weirdly, it was the tension at the table that kept her from abandoning her plans altogether. She couldn't live like this indefinitely.

So when her mom broke the silence with a muffled sneeze, Persey pounced on the opportunity.

"Bless you," she said, then quickly followed with "And I'm going to join the stage crew for the spring musical at school. You know, for an extracurricular."

The words came pouring out so quickly, Persey wasn't even sure if her dad had heard them all. He sat there, tablet still in hand, staring at the blue-lit screen. His face was immovable, and the only proof that Persey had spoken the words at all came from her mom, who almost spit a mouthful of wine across the tablecloth, followed by a sputtering cough as she tried to swallow her gulp.

Ten seconds. Twenty. Should Persey say it again? Maybe he was lost in work thoughts? She was about to repeat herself when her dad spoke.

"Why?"

So I can stay as far away from you as possible. "I thought it would look good on my college applications," she lied.

That elicited a dry laugh from her dad. "There won't be any college applications with your grades. Besides, you haven't even taken the SATs yet."

Persey grimaced. Nothing intimidated her more than the thought of three straight hours of standardized tests. The PSAT last year had been torture, and so far, despite his pestering, Persey had refused to sign up for the real thing.

"And why should I allow you more time away from studying?" he continued. "So your grades can get worse?"

This wasn't going the way she'd hoped. "But I—"

"Give me one good reason." He laced his fingers together in front of him, the company CEO confronting a troublesome employee. "One good reason why I should let you. Just one. Can you do it?"

Persey's mind raced. He was laying a trap: no matter what excuse she gave, he'd have a comeback ready, a biting criticism. She looked to her mom for support, but she was at least three glasses into bottle number two, which meant her mom's mind was dulled into nothingness. Persey wanted to cry—from anger, frustration, resentment. She couldn't take two more years of this strain. She wouldn't turn eighteen until after graduation, so there was no escape from her father before then. This plan to join the stage crew had offered her a glimmer of hope, a crutch that could help her get through the next two-plus years, but it was on the verge of defeat. She didn't know what she could offer up that would convince her dad to . . .

The answer came to her in a flash, a gift from her subconscious, and she smiled, despite knowing that it would piss off her dad.

"If you let me do stage crew, I'll take the SAT."

It was replacing one evil with another, but even though test taking was an anxiety-inducing clusterfuck, it was better than the extended pain of endless hours in this house. It was worth the gamble.

Her dad's hard stare faltered for just a moment, and Persey held her breath. Would he go for it? Had she won?

"Fine," he said. "But if you score under one thousand, the deal is off."

Persey had no idea whether or not she could actually break one thousand on that test, but as she bused her plate to the sink, she couldn't help feeling as if she'd finally won a battle.

SIXTEEN

PERSEY STUMBLED THROUGH THE OPENING AND GULPED down a cool breath of fresh, fully oxygenated air. She leaned forward, hands on her knees, panting. That oxygen thing—had it been an illusion? Were her elevated heart rate, sweaty face, and shortness of breath merely results of the power of suggestion?

No way. She'd felt the heavy air, the burn of her lungs as breathing became more and more difficult. The oxygen deprivation had been real.

But was it meant to scare us or to kill us?

The answer might be scarier than the question. She stood up, worried that this test was some kind of preview for what the rest of the day had in store, and looked around. She was in a large, airy room with hardwood floors and a lofty ceiling. Brightly painted walls—one electric blue, one pumpkin orange, one a neon shade of plum—were dotted with open shelves displaying a variety of framed records, and spaced on the wall she'd come through were posters of musicians and their songs, all of whom Persey kinda sorta recognized. She stepped back, taking them all in. The cartoon world of Green Day's "Basket Case." A dapper trio called Bell Biv DeVoe posed on a graffiti-covered concrete wall to promote their song "Poison." A movie poster from something called *The Bodyguard* featuring the Whitney Houston song "I Will Always Love You." Radiohead's

"Creep," "Sabotage" by the Beastie Boys, LL Cool J's "Mama Said Knock You Out," and "Wannabe" by the Spice Girls, which took Persey back to the early days of her childhood when she (secretly) wanted to be Sporty Spice.

Which probably said more about her personality than she'd ever be willing to admit.

In addition to the music-themed decor, sleek black-leather sofas were clustered together, facing an old-fashioned tube TV that had some kind of antiquated video game system hooked up to it. At the other end of the loft, three wide stairs led to a double door with impossibly shiny brass knobs, while an oversize desk stood facing the steps, supporting an iMac desktop with dual monitors with both a regular and piano keyboard attached. Massive speakers stood on elevated stands facing the desk, which, along with a huge mixing board and microphone, signaled that this might be some kind of musician's studio.

Boyz Distrikt, if she recalled the whiteboard flowchart correctly, though she had no idea what the name meant. Probably set in the '90s, judging by the choice of music posters, which made sense because the loft was hyper modern in an utterly dated kind of way—the ancient iMac, tube television, even the leather sofas screamed of a decade long past.

But more important than the dated decor and pop music references was the fact that Persey was totally and completely alone.

Did that mean she was the first one who had figured out the PIN? Seemed unlikely that Persey, who had only taken the SAT as a bargaining chip with her dad, would have been the first person out. Maybe this was still part of the Individual Challenge, and each of their ATM booths opened into a different room? *That must have been expensive.*

"Five minutes."

Persey snapped back to reality. Was the countdown still going? Was she supposed to find another exit in just five minutes? That wasn't enough time. She spun around, searching the loft. Mounted in the middle of the brick wall at the far end of the room was a digital timer—the kind Persey would expect to see on the scoreboard at a high school basketball game— which very clearly showed that the clock was still ticking from the same place she'd just left it in the ATM booth.

Keep your eye on the clock, Leah had said. *If it ever reaches zero, you will lose.*

The clock had continued its countdown, which meant the last challenge wasn't completed.

She turned back to look at the door through which she'd entered, which still hung open on its hinges, exposing the dark closet beyond. Circling to the other side, she saw that the door contained a poster mounted in such a way that the edges of the black wooden frame were flush with the edge of the door itself. Sinéad O'Connor's brooding "Nothing Compares 2 U," a song about a woman mourning the loss of a relationship. Was that supposed to represent her in some way?

When pushed, the door swung noiselessly closed, locking into place with the faintest of metallic clicks, and the only sign that a door even existed was a thin line, camouflaged by the poster frame, which delineated the wall from the door itself.

Persey scanned the room. There were eight framed posters on the wall. She had to assume that behind each of them, another contestant was sequestered in front of an ATM machine, trying to figure out the PIN while the oxygen was slowly sucked away. Which meant she had been the first to solve the puzzle. Crazy.

"Four minutes."

Almost immediately, the Green Day poster swung open and Wes stumbled into the loft, wheezing as he gasped for breath.

Persey wanted to laugh. "Basket Case" seemed like the perfect theme song for this guy, but she decided not to antagonize him since he was currently her only ally.

"You okay?" she asked, eying him closely as he slowly straightened up. His face was slick with perspiration, his eyes wide, pupils dilated.

"Yeah." Like Persey, he looked around the room. "You're the only one?"

She nodded.

"Sweet." A slow smile spread across his face. "That narrows down the competition quite a bit."

Only Persey wasn't so sure. "The clock is still going," she said, pointing at the digital readout on the brick wall.

Wes shrugged. "Yeah, for them."

"For all of us."

"I understand that you haven't done many escape rooms," Wes said, strolling along the far wall as he examined the display of gold records, "so you don't get it. We already solved the challenge. We smart. Them stupid. If they don't make it out, they don't move on. End. Of. Story."

He spoke to her like he was explaining a complicated concept to a young child—overarticulating, tone as condescending as was humanly possible. For all his happy-go-lucky stoner vibe, Wes was actually an asshole.

"There won't be a next challenge if we don't help them figure this out in time."

"Whatever." Wes arrived at the desk, pulled out the ergonomic leather chair, and plopped into it, kicking his gross sandals up onto the desk beside the computer. "You be you, kid. I'm just going to wait for the next challenge to start."

Kid?

"I will." Persey turned to the nearest song poster. "Hey!" she cried, pounding her fists against the lead singer of Radiohead's face. "It's your SAT score! S. A. T!"

From across the room, Wes snorted. "They can't hear you. Pretty sure that shit is soundproof."

She hated to admit that he was right, but he was right. Even if the person inside could feel the impact of her fists against the wall, they wouldn't be able to hear what she was saying. And the door itself had no release mechanism.

Another door swung open, the Beastie Boys this time, and Neela bolted into the music loft, glasses knocked askew in her rush.

"Son. Of. A. Shatner!" she cried between breaths. Even near asphyxiation didn't curb her need to talk. "That was. So crazy." She caught sight of Persey, and a huge smile spread across her face. "Knew you'd. Beat me."

Neela was apparently the only person other than Kevin that had any faith in Persey's problem-solving abilities.

"The countdown's still going."

Neela straightened her glasses as she checked the clock. "All of us or none of us. We have to help them before time runs out."

"Exactly." Persey was relieved to have an *actual* ally. Even if they were, technically, competitors. "The posters conceal the doors, but the booths are soundproof and there's no way to open them from our side."

"Maybe the trick is oral?" Neela spun around and pushed the Beastie Boys closed. When the lock clicked into place, she stood back a couple of feet and raised her chin. "Fifteen fifty!"

"You scored fifteen fifty on your SAT?" Persey asked, wide-eyed. She'd never met anyone who'd scored that high. Not even her brother.

Neela flushed, embarrassed. She might have been the only other person in the competition with a sense of modesty. "I know. My dad didn't understand it either. Why I didn't get a perfect score, I mean."

That was pretty much the opposite of what Persey was thinking. She really was surrounded by a bunch of geniuses.

A spicy, dank scent wafted into the loft. It was equal parts skunk, wet newspaper, and aftershave, and it was a stink Persey recognized right away. Turning to the computer, she found that despite the confiscation of his e-cigs, Wes had blazed up a giant blunt and was proceeding to suck it down, filling the loft with the pungent aroma of grade-A ganja.

What the actual fuck?

Wes registered Persey's reaction. "It's medicinal," he said while holding his breath. Then he tilted back his head as he blew smoke up over the piano keyboard.

He was completely useless.

"Did you transport that over state lines?" Neela asked with a gasp. "I realize Leah said you were from Vegas, but I was unclear as to whether or not you still live here, but I asked about interstate transportation because that is considered trafficking due to current federal statutes, and if you are caught they could charge you with possession with intent to sell, which is a felony instead of a possession misdemeanor, which carries a minimum sentence of—"

"Two minutes."

The voice came from a speaker mounted in the corner of the loft, and as Persey's eyes bounced between it and the desk at which Wes sat, she suddenly had an amazing idea.

"There was a speaker in my room."

"Mine too," Neela said, abandoning her previous monologue. Her brows knitted together, unclear of Persey's point, but then, all of a sudden, her forehead smoothed out, her eyes grew wide, and her jaw gaped open. "The speakers must connect to something."

There was literally nothing else in the room but . . . Persey's eyes met

Neela's. "The microphone!" they said in unison.

The girls sprinted across the room to where Wes continued to lounge and toke.

"Um, Wes," Neela said politely. "Would it be possible for you to relocate to the—"

Only, Persey wasn't waiting for him. While Neela was mid-sentence, she yanked Wes's wheelie chair away from the desk and spun him out of the way.

Wes's feet crashed to the floor, stopping the momentum of the chair. "What the hell?"

Persey didn't give two shits about him. With a swipe of the mouse, she woke the computer screen from its sleep state. "There must be some kind of program that runs the mic."

"Judging by the blue translucent body and matching mouse, I believe this to be an iMac G3, launched in 1998 and probably running Mac OS 8.1. Standard QuickTime 3.0 software for recording through internal or external microphones."

Another door popped open, but Persey didn't even turn from the computer. "Arlo," Neela said. "Four left."

"What the fuck was that?" Arlo panted. She staggered over to the desk, bracing herself against it. "Are you fuckers trying to kill me?"

"Wasn't us." Persey clicked the mouse rapidly, double clicking the "Q" icon on the desktop. "Got it!"

"Excellent." Neela grinned. "We make quite a team."

"Check to see if it's working."

Neela leaned over the piano keyboard to the microphone. "Um, check one. Check two."

"This isn't funny!" Arlo screamed.

Persey jumped. She turned, expecting to see Arlo yelling at her and

Neela, but instead, she had found a camera mounted in the corner of the room. Arlo was pointing at it as she screamed, her face red, eyes watery. For the snarky, self-controlled Slytherin, it seemed totally out of character.

"How did you even know it was me, huh? Did you hack into my computer? Steal my password?" Her voice cracked. "That's illegal. I'll press charges. You can't prove I run it!"

"Chill out," Wes said, blowing another cloud of weed into the air. "You sound like a nutjob."

"Fuck you!" Arlo cried.

"One minute."

"Your SAT score!" Persey shouted into the microphone. She didn't have time to worry about Arlo's weird behavior. "Type in your score!"

"Your *final* score," Neela added. Right. Because there were people in the world who took it more than once. The idea made Persey's skin crawl.

"Leah, I know you can see us!" Arlo yelled as she pointed at the camera again, only slightly less ragey than before. "I want out of here right now, do you understand? I want this door open or I'm calling my attorney."

"Type your SAT score," Persey repeated more slowly, pausing after each letter of SAT. Riot, Shaun, Mackenzie, and Kevin might be having difficulty understanding her, especially if the oxygen level in their rooms had dropped too low. Of course, that was only if her and Neela's plan with the speakers had worked at all in the first place. If not, they needed to—

Four soft clicks emanated from the back of the room. Persey spun around and saw that the final doors had opened.

The clock stopped.

SEVENTEEN

RIOT SPUTTERED AS HE SLUMPED AGAINST THE OPEN DOOR, tweed vest unbuttoned, his eyes only half-open as if he'd just emerged from a deep sleep. "That's . . . the Man," he panted. "Test scores. Inside job."

Even that close to passing out, Riot was formulating a conspiracy theory.

Mackenzie had the opposite reaction: she rushed into the loft and collapsed onto the nearest sofa, arm draped dramatically over her head like a swooning 1930s Hollywood starlet. "The. Fuck."

Shaun was in the worst shape—he crawled out of the room practically on his belly. Red-faced, sweating profusely, he looked to be on the edge of passing out, and the abject fear on his face was the closest thing to an emotion Shaun-bot had shown all day.

All of them looked shaken. Except for Kevin. He sauntered out of his prison cell, smiling, calm, and showing absolutely no signs of distress. No sheen of perspiration or pallor of panic. And it wasn't the first time that his carefree attitude intrigued (annoyed) Persey.

"Is everyone okay?" Neela asked, her hands clasped before her as she stood up on the balls of her feet, swaying lightly back and forth. "I detect some complexion aberrations, heightened respiratory response.

And I'm just worried because the symptoms of cerebral hypoxia due to oxygen deprivation include memory problems, decreased dexterity and fine motor skills, increased heart rate, and blueness of the lips and skin."

"Save it," Mackenzie said, pink overtones beginning to ebb from her cheeks. "I can memorize the cerebral hypoxia Wikipedia entry too."

Neela dropped her hands. "Sorry."

"You should be less of an asshole," Persey said, overcoming her usual (permanent) reticence to speak up. "Since she helped get you out of there."

Mackenzie just rolled her eyes. "Whatever."

"I would have figured it out eventually." Shaun's face was once again stony and devoid of emotion as he pushed himself to his knees. Shaun-bot had rebooted. He looked Kevin up and down, then tilted his head to the side as if discovering something for the first time. "Why aren't you suffering from oxygen deprivation like the rest of us?"

Kevin's smile deepened. "Because the O2 never dropped in my coffin."

"That's not fair."

"Totally fair," Kevin replied. "I never typed in a code. That's what made it drop, right?"

Shaun looked confused. "You mean, you never even tried to escape the room?" Lack of effort did not compute.

"I figured someone else would do it for me." He gave Persey a thumbs-up. "Thanks."

"Well, *I* thought I was going to *die*," Mackenzie said, still reclining on the sofa. "Which is impressive."

"Impressive?" Riot asked.

"Yeah. That's one crazy effect! To make us think we're *actually* asphyxiating?"

Was she trying to convince herself that it was just an illusion, or everyone else? "I don't think that was a special effect," Persey said slowly.

"Oh, come on!" Mackenzie laughed with practiced charm. "Do you think that was *real*?"

Persey shrugged. She wasn't sure if that's what she was saying, but the whole episode had left her uneasy.

"We didn't *actually* almost die," Mackenzie continued. "This is just a game. No one *actually* wants to kill us."

You sure about that?

"I mean, they couldn't *actually*." She laughed again. "We'd sue." Mackenzie swung her right leg over her left, bouncing it jauntily. "I still might. Sue, that is. But it would be worse if someone was *actually* trying to suffocate us, so that means it had to be staged."

"*Actually* staged?" Riot asked, with a wink in Persey's direction. Heat rose from her neck to her cheeks again, despite her best effort to suppress it.

Mackenzie narrowed her eyes at him. "Yes. Also, who's smoking weed?"

"Who do you think?" Kevin replied, but his eyes were fixed on Persey.

Mackenzie marched over to Wes and whipped the blunt out of his hand. "Gimme that." She took a long pull.

"There needs to be a serious investigation into this when the competition is over," Riot said as he rebuttoned his vest. "Our SAT scores aren't something you can just download from the dark web. Who released this information without our permission? Or, more accurately, who stole it?" His near-death experience seemed to have less of an effect on him than the possibility that "the Man" had somehow infringed on his sovereign rights.

"The most important question," Shaun began, "is who was out first?"

"Not me!" Neela cried, her buoyant mood recovered. "Persey and Wes were here when I arrived."

"It was just a lucky guess," Wes said, retrieving his weed from

Mackenzie's outstretched hand. "Leah's repeated use of the word 'scholastic' caught my notice. I'd been waiting to put that clue to good use."

Persey stiffened. Did Wes just imply that he solved the puzzle first? "Um . . ."

"What was yours?" Shaun asked him.

"Fifteen twenty, but I don't like to brag," Wes said without the kind of hesitation with which an actual humble person might speak.

"Not bad for the *lesser* Ivy," Riot said. "But fifteen forty gets you into Harvard."

Persey wanted to point out that Neela scored higher than either of them, and that her own was probably the lowest of the group and yet she was the first one to figure out the puzzle, but it wasn't worth it: letting these privileged egomaniacs underestimate her was for the best. She had to win this competition, had to get the prize money. Without it, her future looked bleak.

Arlo tugged absently at the hem of her Slytherin shirt. She'd been uncharacteristically quiet since the challenge ended. "What the hell are you guys talking about?"

"Their SAT scores," Neela answered. "In relation to the challenge we just faced."

"What?"

"The code to get out of the room." Riot eyed her closely. "It was your SAT score."

"No, it wasn't."

"Um . . ." Riot turned to face the rest of the group. "Anyone *not* use their SAT score to open the door?"

No one raised a hand, and as Arlo scanned their faces, slowly turning from one to the next, Persey watched all the color drain out of her face until her skin was a sickly shade of green.

"What. The. FUCK!" Arlo screamed through clenched teeth. "What the fuck? What the fuck? *What the fuck?*"

"Um, are you okay?" Persey asked, stepping forward. Arlo clearly hadn't used her SAT score to defeat the challenge, so what code had opened her door? She'd been screaming about something when Persey and Neela were trying to use the microphone . . . a password. That must have been it. But a password to what?

Persey's politeness backfired as Arlo whirled on her. "You're supposed to be some problem-solving savant, so you tell me. Do I look okay?"

"No."

"Good eyes, Sherlock." Then she turned to the camera. "What the hell are you trying to prove, huh? I had nothing to do with it, okay? NOTHING."

Girl was losing her shit. "Arlo, what are you talking about?"

"It wasn't my fucking SAT score, okay? That wasn't my challenge."

Duh. "What was it?"

Arlo shook her head. "Something isn't right here. The competition, the prize. It's all wrong."

"We got different challenges. So what?" Wes leaned back in his chair, his eyes half-closed and sleepy. "Doesn't mean the check for the prize money won't clear the bank."

"Don't you have a trust fund?" Kevin asked.

"I never said that." Wes's voice was instantly serious, despite the weed.

"This is just part of the game," Mackenzie said, giggling. "Like that fake-suffocation thing. So clever!"

She sounded calmer now, like the weed had helped her to fully accept her own theory about their experience in the ATM booth being nothing but an illusion. Not that Persey blamed her. Because if it *wasn't* all an illusion, then what were they supposed to believe? As much as she hated to admit it even to herself, Mackenzie was right. The whole near-suffocation thing was just a fancy hoax.

"I think you need to reevaluate your definition of the word 'fake,'" Riot said. "The lack of oxygen in that room was real."

"You think someone tried to kill us?" Persey asked. Her voice sounded small and frail, despite her efforts to present a strong façade.

"I think . . ." Riot paused, lips pressed together as if deep in thought. He was choosing his words carefully. "I think Arlo's right: something about this competition feels off."

"Look," Kevin said, his arms thrown wide in supplication, "we got through the challenge, right? We're all still here. No one's dead. Let's just assume that everything that's happened so far is just part of the competition."

Persey pictured the whiteboard in Office Drones. If it was accurate—and so far it had proven so—that meant they had seven more escape rooms, including the one that they were in. If the Individual Challenge had proved nearly fatal, what the hell did that say for Boyz Distrikt? Or the rest? Would the challenges escalate in both complexity and danger?

That was a terrifying thought.

"Guys!"

Persey looked up at Neela, who was pointing to the clock on the wall. It had been frozen at thirty-three seconds since Shaun, Riot, Mackenzie, and Kevin had escaped from their ATM booths, but now the red digital numbers had reset themselves to thirty minutes. As Persey watched, the seconds began to count down.

"Another puzzle!" Mackenzie squealed, clapping her hands together like an elated five-year-old watching a magic show. Her dramatic exit from the Individual Challenge was all but forgotten. "I'm so excited!"

Without a word, everyone jumped into action. Shaun strode over to the closest wall and began examining the mounted records while Riot got up close and personal with the collection of posters. Mackenzie strolled aimlessly around the room, gazing here and there like a Realtor assessing the loft for the marketplace, and Neela focused on the computer, clicking through folders and files. Even Wes wheeled his desk chair back up behind Neela, peering somewhat aimlessly at the mixing board beside the desktop.

But Arlo just continued to stare at the backside of the door that had released her—the same Spice Girls poster that Persey had in her bedroom once upon a time—and didn't move.

Kevin watched her for a moment as if trying to puzzle something out, then got bored. "Any idea what we're supposed to be looking for?"

No one answered.

Shaun picked the nearest record off the shelf and checked its label, front and back, then turned coldly to Mackenzie, as if she was invading his personal space. "Do you mind?"

"So 'people person' isn't on your dating profile, huh, Shaun-bot?" Kevin said.

Shaun continued to examine the records. "I don't date."

"Shocking," Kevin muttered as he sat down on one of the sofas and picked up a video game controller. "Nintendo 64? Sweet! I haven't seen one of these since I was a kid."

Persey crouched down beside him, reading the label of the game cartridge in the machine. *"Mortal Kombat Trilogy."*

"I love this game." Kevin fired up the machine. "It has the Star Bridge and you can unlock new characters if you have the hidden code, plus there are these secret menus. All kinds of crazy shit. Way better than the PlayStation version."

"Isn't there supposed to be a guide or something in these escape rooms?"

Persey asked, recalling the actor from the Hidden Library, dressed as the ghost of a Cistercian monk, who explained what the group's goal should be and helped corral them toward the initial clues. "So we know what we're looking—"

Before she could finish, a singing voice rang out strong and clear.

"Welcome to the Boyz Distrikt!"

EIGHTEEN

AT FIRST, PERSEY THOUGHT THE SINGING MUST BE coming through the loudspeakers, like the voice of the countdown, but out of the corner of her eye, she saw movement at the top of the stairs. Someone new had joined them.

He was young, Persey was pretty sure: even though he wore aviator glasses that hid his eyes, his baby face was clean-shaven and wrinkle-free. But despite his youthful appearance, his outfit, just like the room they were in, was painfully dated. His spiky hair was frosted at the tips, and he wore baggy acid-wash jeans that were at least one size too big, cinched at the waist with a leather belt. He'd paired those jeans with a "Hollister, CA" T-shirt beneath a dark denim jacket with the confusing addition of a tweed men's suit vest—similar to the one Riot wore—over both, and peeking out from the hem of his jeans was a distinctive yellow-beige pair of Timberlands.

"Where did he come from?" Riot asked.

"He's on your side of the room," Shaun said. "Didn't you see?"

"I believe our visitor entered through the main set of doors," Neela said. "Though I neither saw nor heard them open. Most likely some ingenious design made so that he would seem to appear out of thin air."

"Do you narrate the world with every single thought that pops into your head?" Mackenzie asked. "Or are you some kind of witch just making shit up as you go?"

"Aha!" Neela said, forcing a laugh before Persey could jump to her defense. "The black arts! I do not partake of them, good madam."

"Don't you want to know what the Boyz Distrikt is?" the newcomer sang, sounding confused by their lack of immediate interest.

"I suppose you're going to tell us!" Kevin warbled in an off-key response, his voice crackling with suppressed laughter.

"My name is Beeeee Jaaaaay," he sang, stretching out the syllables of "B.J." *"And I'm a member of . . ."* He paused, swinging down to one knee and cupping his chin with his hand like he was posing for a photo shoot. *"Boyz Distrikt!"*

"I think we're supposed to ask what Boyz Distrikt is," Arlo said flatly, her former bossiness returning.

"Ab-so-lute-ly!" B.J. sang. This wasn't going to be annoying (torture) or anything. . . .

But Shaun answered for him, pointing to one of the framed records on the wall. "They're a band. 'Distrikt' with a *k*."

B.J. leaped back to his feet. *"Because everything spelled with a* K *is"*—he took a breath—*"special."* He let out a melismatic R&B vocal run on the first syllable that made Persey's head spin.

"Swoon," Mackenzie said, approaching B.J. with one of her signature smiles. "I *actually* love boy bands. For reals. And your voice is *en pointe*." As if flirting with the paid Escape-Capades employee was going to help her in any way. "Now can you tell us what we're supposed to be looking for?"

It was the cue B.J. had been waiting for. He pulled a handheld remote from the pocket of his jeans, pointed it at the computer Neela had been poring over, and clicked a button. Immediately, a techno beat filled the room's speakers, and B.J., using the top of the stairs like a stage, launched into a carefully choreographed dance routine while he sang along to a familiar tune.

"Everybody,
Listen to me.
Together,
You must find the key.
Boyz Distrikt knows what's right!"

"Sweet baby Jesus," Riot said. "Is he doing Backstreet Boys?"

Kevin kicked his legs up on the sofa. "I wish I had some popcorn. This show is epic."

"Shh!" Shaun hissed. "Some of us are trying to listen."

Persey had gotten half-lost in the song-and-dance number. B.J. was actually pretty talented. His dance moves were sharp, his singing voice on key, and she wondered if he'd moved to Vegas to try to get a job in one of the many Broadway shows installed in various casinos.

"Oh my God, you're back again.
Brothers, sisters, you should listen.
I'm gonna tease the exit, show you how.
I've got some questions for you, better answer now."

She perked up, sensing that important clues were forthcoming. "Can someone write this down?"

"On it!" Neela opened a text document on the computer and typed quickly while B.J. sang.

"Am I unlocked by code?
Am I a song you know?
Am I the hidden choice?
Am I twelve tones that you need?
You better play your song right now!
Everybody . . ."

Then he looped back to the opening chorus and struck a dramatic spread-eagle pose as the music ended.

"Bravo! Encore!" Kevin rocketed to his feet, applauding enthusiastically.

But Mackenzie looked disappointed. "That didn't even rhyme."

"Not really the point." Arlo began pacing back and forth, her anger with Leah and Escape-Capades forgotten when there was a situation where she could take control. "Something unlocked by a code. I think that's where we start."

"The ATMs?" Riot suggested.

"Maybe," Wes said. "But we already solved that, so why give it to us again?"

"It could be a starting point," Neela suggested. "The next line refers to a hidden choice. So what could be a hidden choice in this room?"

It was the word "hidden" that triggered Persey's memory. "Hey," she said, tapping Kevin on the arm. "When you were talking about this video game, what did you say about it?"

Kevin scrunched up his face. "I don't remember."

"Then clearly it wasn't important," Wes sneered.

Persey ignored him. "Something about unlocking characters with a hidden code?"

"DUDE!" Kevin said, his eyes wide. "Yes!"

Wes stiffened, unwilling to admit that Persey might be onto something. "That's ridiculous."

"Why would it be ridiculous?" Neela asked, joining Persey and Kevin at the television. "B.J., what did you say about things spelled with the letter *K*?"

B.J. shifted his pose, dropping one hand to his side and laying the other on his heart as he took a deep breath. *"They're speh-eh-eh-eh-eh-eh-eh-shul!"* he sang.

"Right." Persey smiled. *"Mortal Kombat* with a *K*."

"Shit," Arlo said, rushing over. "I think this is it."

"Twenty minutes."

"Fuck this," Wes said, and wandered off toward the back of the loft. Which was fine. Persey was pretty (completely) sure he was useless in the face of a challenge anyway.

Mackenzie elbowed past Persey and sat down on the sofa next to Kevin, leaning possessively on his arm. "Do you know how to do it?"

He winked at her. "I know how to do a lot of things."

"Ew." Persey couldn't help herself.

"Jealous?" Kevin asked.

Double ew.

Shaun snatched the controller out of Kevin's hand. "We don't have time for flirting," he said, firing up the game. "We need to figure this out."

"You sure you know how to use that thing?" Kevin asked, eying Shaun skeptically. "You gonna plug it directly into your USB port?"

Neela snorted. "There were no USB game controllers in 1998!"

"I know my way around a Nintendo," Shaun said.

Persey was getting tired of the posturing. It didn't matter who solved the puzzle—it only mattered that they did. "Yeah, but do you know how to get to the screen where you can unlock the secret characters?"

Shaun pursed his lips, wavered, then handed the controller to Kevin.

"That's what I thought," Mackenzie said, leaning on Kevin possessively.

With an impressively deft sequence of clicks and joystick swivels, Kevin eventually brought up a fighting challenge. The game announcer laughed ominously as play began, and Persey quickly found *Mortal Kombat* to be true to its name: two combatants fought to the death in a vaguely Asian-inspired setting. Kevin had obviously invested (wasted) many hours of his life in this game, or one like it, and in less than five minutes, his character—a guy in a big white hat who could apparently harness the power of lightning—beat his reptilian ninja opponent by electrocuting him until his entire body exploded and rained down around the victor as severed limbs and bone.

"That's disgusting," Mackenzie said, wrinkling her nose.

Kevin's character was celebrating his victory on the screen. "Be thankful I didn't pull his spine out. Now watch this." Pressing a series of buttons, the voice on the video game said, "Outstanding," before Kevin opened up a secret menu. "These are the new characters," he said, highlighting them one at a time. "Human Smoke and Khameleon." He turned both of their options from off to on, then returned to the regular game play.

"Is that it?" Shaun asked.

Kevin shrugged. "I guess."

"Great," Arlo said, turning her back on the screen as Kevin continued to play, weighing in with his own commentary. "We opened new characters. Now what? We watch numbnuts play until the clock bottoms out?"

"Remind you of your average Friday night?" Kevin asked, his eyes still locked onto the TV screen as he used his body to mimic the moves he was trying to make with the controller, leaning left, then zigging right.

They'd revealed the new characters, which was hopefully the first part of the puzzle. "Neela, what's the next line?"

"'Am I a song you know?'" she quoted, repeating it from memory.

"Human Smoke and Khameleon," Riot mused. His hand crept to his Mohawk and patted the tips to make sure it was still standing at pointy attention. "Can anyone name that tune?"

Neela rushed back to the wall of records. "Maybe it references one of these." She picked the closest record off the shelf. "'Tearin' Up My Heart,'" she read.

"'NSYNC," Mackenzie replied.

Riot joined her at the wall, starting from the other end. "'Step by Step.'"

Mackenzie knew that one too. "New Kids on the Block."

"'Because of You,'" Riot asked, as if testing her.

Mackenzie never hesitated. "Ninety-Eight Degrees."

"'I Wanna Sex You Up.'"

Kevin sucked in a breath. "So. Many. Jokes."

"Color Me Badd."

"'End of the Road'?"

"Oh my fuck!" Arlo cried, rolling her eyes. "We get it. She's a nineties-boy-band savant. Woo-fucking-hoo."

"Boyz II Men," Mackenzie whispered.

Neela paused with a record in her hand. "'Chameleon'?"

"I said, Boyz II Men," Mackenzie repeated, raising her voice.

"No, this record. It's called 'Karma Chameleon.' One of the characters we unlocked was named Khameleon."

Persey was pretty sure that song was not by a nineties boy band. "Can't be a coincidence."

"It's nah-ah-ah-ah-aht!" B.J. yanked off his aviator glasses and winked at them; in the far corner of the room, Persey saw Wes flinch.

"That is an old song by Culture Club," Shaun said.

Neela shook her head, examining the album. "This says it's by Boyz Distrikt."

"Really?"

"From the album . . ." Neela's voice trailed off as she stared at the record.

"From the album what?" Persey asked.

"*Distrikt by Numbers.* I think I saw that file name on the computer."

As Neela rushed back to the computer, B.J. danced toward the back of the loft, where Wes was sulking, using a series of boy band moves as he slid and shimmied his way around the desk, sofas, and television set. *"You think ri-ri-right. Right right."*

"Ten minutes."

They weren't close enough to a solution. They weren't going to make it. *What will happen then?*

"Here it is!" Neela cried, opening the folder. An "enter password" box came up and Persey felt the press of bodies behind her as people gathered around the computer screen.

"Password protected," Mackenzie said with a defeated sigh. "We're screwed."

Riot wasn't about to give up. He pointed at Kevin. "What's the key sequence? To open the new characters in *Mortal Kombat*?"

"Uh . . ." Kevin glanced at the ceiling, thinking. "Left, right, A, B, B. Pretty sure."

Neela didn't need to be told what to do. She was already typing it in. "L, R, A, B, B." Persey held her breath as the folder popped open, revealing a single song file inside labeled "No Escape." When Neela clicked on it, a music player opened and loaded the file, starting the song immediately.

It had a techno beat similar to the Backstreet Boys tune B.J. had sung earlier, but the melody and lyrics were different, and though Persey wasn't a musician, it sounded as if this song was made up entirely of a simple chorus, looped over and over again.

"Sound familiar at all, Mack?" Wes asked, rejoining the group. He seemed way too comfortable using a nickname for someone he'd just met.

Mackenzie shook her head. "No. This one's an original."

"'Am I twelve tones that you need?'" Neela said, quoting B.J.'s introductory song. "'You better play your song right now.'"

Persey's eyes drifted to the Casio keyboard beside the mixing board. "I think we're supposed to play the first twelve notes of this song." She spun toward the back of room, where B.J. had ended up after dancing his way across the loft. "Is that—"

Persey froze. She'd intended to ask their guide if they were on the right track since she didn't believe Leah really wanted anyone to fail this competition just yet, but instead of seeing the melodious boy band member leaning against the brick wall in some kind of character-appropriate pose, she saw his pair of Timberlands sticking out from behind the sofa, toes pointed at the ceiling, motionless.

"Anyone know how to play the piano?" Kevin said.

"Guitar," Riot said.

"Flute," Neela added.

Mackenzie elbowed him aside and stood before the keyboard. "Um, hello! Royal College of Music."

"Guys," Persey said, taking a few tentative steps toward the brick wall. She didn't like the way B.J.'s body appeared totally and utterly still. "I think something's wrong."

No one responded. With the clock ticking down, Persey heard Mackenzie trying to plunk out the melody on the keyboard, but her brain was only half registering the noise. She was completely focused on the immobile form of the boy band singer.

Persey didn't know why she felt the need to discover why B.J. was lying on the ground, but she did. Logically, his role in the escape room completed, he was just staying out of the way until they either opened the door or failed miserably. But then why lie on his back? Why not crouch down behind the sofa, where he'd be completely out of sight? Or better yet, just duck inside one of the still-open ATM booths? Either of those choices made more sense.

But as she rounded the leather sofa, she knew exactly why B.J. was on the floor. He lay on his back, his pale face turned toward her at a sharp, unnatural angle with open, unseeing eyes. His frost-tipped hair was slick and matted, blood pooled around his cheek and nose, oozing outward as if in slow motion, and on the ground beside him lay one of the framed records, the plastic corner of which was cracked and caked with skin and blond-tipped hair.

B.J. was dead.

NINETEEN

PERSEY WANTED TO BELIEVE THAT B.J.'S BODY WAS A FAKE, A masterful illusion meant to up their panic and anxiety levels as they continued through the competition, but she couldn't tear her eyes away, and as the seconds turned into a minute, she noted that his chest never moved. He wasn't breathing.

B.J. was dead. There was no doubt. His eyes never blinked, his neck was crimped at an unnatural angle, and as she peered down at his body, she could even see the jagged wound peeking out through the blood-matted hair where the plastic corner of the framed record had made contact with his skull.

Not just dead. Murdered.

There was no way he could have slipped and landed unluckily on the framed record—it had been on a shelf at shoulder height, which also meant that it couldn't have fallen from the shelf and hit him. From that height, it might have broken his big toe, but the kind of force required to crush his skull and possibly break his neck . . . No. Someone did that to him. Someone—perhaps one of the other competitors—picked up that record and struck B.J. down from behind.

Panic hit her like a bucket of ice water to the face. The anxiety Persey had felt in the airplane as it approached Las Vegas and the claustrophobia she'd fought against in the ATM booth were nothing compared to the terror that descended upon her as she stared fixedly at B.J.'s corpse. He had died right there in the room with eight other people and no one heard a sound. Had they been so absorbed in solving a puzzle that they didn't even notice a man dying on the other side of the freaking room?

"Guys!" she cried, forcing her eyes away from the body. At the keyboard, Mackenzie was plucking out a tune on the keyboard, with more wrong notes than right ones.

"Aren't you supposed to be a music major?" Arlo asked, wincing as Mackenzie hit another wrong note.

"I am," Mackenzie said through clenched teeth. "But I'm a voice major."

"So?"

Mackenzie sighed. "So if they asked me to sing that stupid tune, we'd be out of here by now, but transcribing by ear isn't exactly the opera singer's forte."

"No kidding," Wes said.

"Guys!" Persey yelled louder. Her voice felt raw, strangled. "You need to see this."

"Yeah, well, your superweed didn't help." Mackenzie shook her head as if trying to clear it.

"Guys?"

"Kosher Kush," Wes said reverently. "So good."

If anyone heard Persey, they paid her no attention. They were all focused on Mackenzie and the piano keyboard and the relentlessly ticking clock.

"*Guys!*" Persey yelled. She hated yelling. "Something happened—"

"Shh!" Arlo hissed, holding her hand up for silence. Mackenzie, shoulders hunched over the keyboard, was starting again.

"B, A, G," she sang out the note names as she played them. *"E, F-sharp, Geeeee!"* Quick breath. *"B, B, Deeeeeee, G, F-sharp, G."*

Persey heard a loud thud, as if a huge bolt had been thrown, and the double doors at the top of the stairs slowly swung open, revealing a brightly lit room faced in shiny, silvery steel.

"You did it!" Neela cried. But her excitement was short-lived. "The clock is still ticking, though, which leads one to believe that the challenge is not completed. Maybe we need to vacate this room entirely?"

Persey staggered toward the desk. Her legs felt like limp spaghetti. "Neela . . ."

"Agreed," Arlo said. "Let's move."

"Yes, I concur," Shaun said. As if his robot opinion mattered. Mackenzie, Wes, and Neela had already dashed up the wide staircase toward the open doors.

"Stop!" Persey screamed. The sound coming out of her own mouth was jarring, disconnected. She was pretty (positively) sure she hadn't screamed since she was in diapers.

At least not where people could hear.

"Two minutes," Neela said, her eyes shifting back and forth between the countdown clock and Persey so quickly Persey was afraid she might give herself motion sickness. "I think we all have to be out of the room to pass the challenge."

Persey shook her head. As much as she didn't want to hang around with a dead body all day, she certainly wasn't going to just leave him there. "It's B.J."

"He probably disappeared into one of those booths," Kevin said. He jogged across the room and took her hand. "Let's go."

"All the doors are locked." She yanked her hand away, pointing to the floor. "Look!"

"Holy shit." Kevin's eyes grew wide as his voice dropped to a whisper. "Is that real?"

Are you joking? "Of course it's *real*. He's dead!"

Neela sucked in a breath. "What?"

"I think this is an elevator," Mackenzie mused. She stepped through the double doors into the giant metal box. "Oooh, I wonder where it goes?"

"Um, didn't you hear me?" Persey asked. These people were unbelievably self-involved.

"Yeah, yeah," Wes said. "Dead body. Sure."

"You have ninety seconds to get into the elevator," Shaun said, "or this competition goes on without you."

"Or we all fail . . ." Neela's voice trailed off. "Persey, please. We have to go!" She stepped into the elevator with the others, leaving just Kevin and Persey at the far end of the room.

"He's dead," she said again, as if repeating it made it more real.

Kevin was noncommittal. "He looks dead, but we have to go."

"But—"

"Don't make me carry you."

Persey narrowed her eyes. He wouldn't.

For a moment, Kevin looked as if he was going to throw her over his shoulder and drag her kicking and screaming into the elevator, but then his body relaxed. "It's just part of the game," he said, repeating Mackenzie's line from before. Regardless of whether or not he believed it. "Are you willing to risk everything to stay here with him?"

The prize money. *Damn it.*

Kevin smiled, sensing victory, then grabbed her hand again. "Come on!"

Reluctantly putting one foot in front of the other, Persey followed Kevin into the elevator.

Persey glared at Kevin as the elevator doors closed, angrier at herself than at him. She shouldn't have let him talk her into continuing. B.J. was dead, and this competition needed to end, but she'd allowed the promise of money to sway her. What kind of a horrible human being was she?

Just like your dad. Just like your brother.

"Are we even moving?" Neela asked, her voice higher pitched than before. She must have sensed the tension in the cramped elevator, and it heightened her nervousness.

Riot shook his head. In contrast to Neela, he seemed cool and calm. "Not yet."

"It's all part of the game," Kevin said dismissively, off Persey's look.

"You saw him!" Persey cried. "How can you say that wasn't real?"

Mackenzie jumped in immediately, taking Kevin's side. Shocking. "Totally a setup. Like Kev said—this happens all the time in Escape-Capades rooms."

Kev? Ew. "He was dead."

"*Looked* dead," Mackenzie said, correcting her. She was going to cling to her "none of it is real" routine to the bloody end. "It's amazing what they can do with special effects and makeup."

Persey was relatively (unfortunately) sure that she'd had more up-close experience with dead bodies than Little Miss Royal Academy, and she was not about to let herself be lectured on what she did or didn't see. Not even Hollywood's biggest and brightest could replicate that glassy, open-eyed look of death. No matter how much you wanted it not to be real.

"When we get out of here, I bet Leah will show you how they did it," Mackenzie continued. She liked the sound of her own voice almost as much as Arlo did. "Like a magician exposing her tricks. You'll see!"

"There was a camera in the room," Shaun said. "It might have the proof."

Persey sucked in a sharp breath. That's right! Arlo had been threatening Leah through the camera when she was released from the ATM booth. Somewhere in the Escape-Capades HQ, Leah was watching the proceedings.

"Do you think they caught Brian's death?" Wes asked.

"Who?" Kevin asked.

"The . . . the singing dude," Wes stuttered.

"His name is B.J." Mackenzie clicked her tongue in annoyance. "How you made it into this competition with your inability to remember details is totally beyond me."

Wes scowled at her. "His name doesn't fucking matter to that camera."

Persey pictured Arlo shouting at the wall. She'd been standing just inches away from where Persey had later discovered the body. If the camera had caught her antics, then it had caught the killer as well. Whoever was monitoring them must have seen B.J.'s murder.

Without warning, the elevator began to move. They were going up, and rather quickly, judging by the way her stomach sunk to her knees, and Persey just hoped that Leah and a dozen 911 first responders were there to meet them when the door opened. Prize money or not, this competition needed to end before someone else got hurt.

No such luck.

The first thing that struck Persey about the new room was its height: twenty-foot ceilings soared above her, dotted with skylights through which blue halogens streamed semi-realistic sunlight. The room was two stories with a banistered second floor hugging three of the four walls while an open staircase climbed the fourth, and a fire station–style pole had been installed at the far end for quick escapes from the upper level.

But while the room was technically spacious, it squandered that breadth with a claustrophobia-inducing assortment of shelving and display cases, all of which were stuffed to bursting with toys.

Action figures, lunch boxes, Pez dispensers, Hot Wheels cars, posable dolls, Lego constructions, spaceships hanging from the ceiling, and everything was sorted and displayed by genre: superheroes on one side, horror on the other, anime in the middle, sci-fi upstairs. Mannequins dressed in everything from Wonder Woman's costume to a human-size Rocket Raccoon were posed throughout—some staged in the corners, others facing the bookcases, which housed their matching memorabilia, and special items such as signed comic books and personalized letters were mounted on the support beams that held the upper balcony in place. It was a dizzying hoarder's delight of collectible junk.

"Hello?" Persey called into the pop culture chaos, unwilling to leave the elevator. She needed to raise the alarm, demand that Leah end this competition and bring in the authorities. "Is anyone listening? There's been an . . ." A what? It wasn't an accident.

"There's been an incident," Kevin said for her.

"A *murder.*" He was technically correct, but Persey didn't think he was adequately relaying the gravity of the situation. "Someone needs to call nine-one-one."

"Murder?" Neela squeaked.

"Um, no! You don't!" Mackenzie elbowed past her, dragging Kevin by the hand. "Everyone but Miss Crazy Pants knows that it's all part of the competition. Right, Kev?"

Kevin gave Persey a look of encouragement as he followed behind Mackenzie. "Right."

Shit.

"Shit!" Arlo's voice was as elated as Persey's mood was depressed. "Is that an original *The Incredible Hulk* number one eighty-one?" She dashed to the nearest display case and crouched before it, pressing her hands against the glass. "First appearance of Wolverine. Pristine. That thing is worth like fifteen grand. Easy."

Mackenzie wrapped her arms around her waist, Kevin's hand still firmly clasped in hers, as if she was afraid of touching something icky and was using Kevin as a human shield. "I doubt Escape-Capades would have anything that valuable in here. Gotta assume it's fake."

"Just like Persey's dead body." Wes laughed. He'd seemed tense in the elevator, but now his stoner happy-go-luckiness had returned.

"You mean the dead body I saw," Persey said coldly. "Not *my* body, which is not dead."

Wes shrugged. His signature move. "Whatever."

"Look," Riot said as he scanned the walls for the ever-present cameras. "We have to assume that if B.J. really died back there, Leah would have ended the game and the police would have met us the second we stepped out of the elevator."

You'd think. "Okay, then if his death is *supposed* to be fake, what does it mean? You'd think a dead body would be a pretty big clue, but we didn't even search him."

"I bet we'll find out in the next room," Arlo said. "Try to remember every detail of the 'crime scene,'" she added, using air quotes.

Persey shuddered. B.J.'s battered skull certainly wasn't an image she wanted to dwell on.

"See?" Riot's tone was light. Was the conspiracy guy really buying this theory? "Logically, it was just a part of the competition like Mackenzie suggested."

Mackenzie flashed him a smile, sparkly brown eyes crinkling at the corner. "Thank you!"

Persey understood right away why Mackenzie was so used to getting her own way. When you were that pretty, everyone gave you what you wanted.

But Riot seemed unaffected, turning away from Mackenzie's flirtation to lay a hand on Persey's shoulder. "I'm not saying you're wrong," he said, his voice hardly above a whisper. "But if he was murdered, then we have to assume Escape-Capades is involved. . . ."

Persey stiffened. "You think this was planned?"

He nodded. "Which means no one is going to call the police."

No police. No help. And they were completely cut off from the outside world. Persey felt the bottom of her stomach fall away as the realization sunk in. *We're at the mercy of Escape-Capades.*

"And if someone from Escape-Capades killed him," Riot continued, dropping his voice even further, "we have much bigger problems."

We sure the hell do.

Riot placed his other hand on her opposite shoulder. "Because they may not want any witnesses."

You're right.

The tingling of panic returned to Persey's hands as she looked up at Riot. His soft eyes were a stark contrast to his firmly set jaw, lips pressed tightly together. She saw kindness in him, but also fear, and she wasn't sure which of them scared her more.

She turned away, unwilling to let him see the wave of emotions cycling through her. The others were never going to listen—they had spread out around the room, searching for clues, blissfully (pathetically) unaware of what was happening.

But maybe they were right? Despite Riot's willingness to believe her—or maybe because of it since he was a conspiracy-theory kinda guy—perhaps she'd been mistaken in what she'd seen. Riot probably wanted to believe that there was something nefarious at work. No police *could* mean that Escape-Capades was involved, but it could also mean that there was no reason to call them. No actual murder.

Persey forced a laugh. "Maybe I'm just seeing things," she said, shaking free of Riot. "We're not exactly superspies. No one could have killed him in that room without someone else seeing." It sounded like a good rationale, and she wanted to believe it.

"If you say so," Riot said, retreating to the stairs that led to the balcony. "But I'm going to keep my eyes open, and I suggest you do the same."

I always do.

TWENTY

"FIND ANYTHING INTERESTING?" WES ASKED, STROLLING through the aisles, staring aimlessly at all the collectibles.

"Like I'd tell you if I did." Mackenzie leaned against the wall, yawning. The weed hadn't worn off yet.

Arlo glared over her shoulder. "You could, like, pretend you're trying."

"Why?" Kevin laughed by Mackenzie's side. "We're not even on the clock yet."

A chime dinged as if in answer. *As if someone was listening.* Above the elevator door, the countdown clock had just blipped to life ushering in another forty-five minutes of puzzle-solving fun. In addition to the digital face, the clock was ringed by eight lightbulbs, screwed directly into the wall, lending the room an old-timey fun-house vibe.

"I wonder what those are for?" Persey asked to no one in particular.

"Eight of them," Shaun replied. "Eight of us. Just like the cubicles." Not that his observation explained anything, but it was certainly something to keep in mind.

"An original *Greatest American Hero* costume," Arlo said, gawking at a mannequin wearing a heinous long-sleeve suit and cape with a curly blond wig on its head.

"Looks like Harpo Marx and Mrs. Claus had a love child," Kevin mused.

Arlo slowly circled the mannequin. "There are only two of these left in existence." Then her eyes caught something else. "That must be a Batarang set," she said pointing to a case with metal-tipped bat-shaped plastic boomerangs, "from one of the films. *Batman Returns*, if I were pressed to make a guess."

"You're not," Wes said.

"And *that* appears to be an original-issue Captain America action figure. From 1973, I believe." The smugness in her voice signaled that she knew damn well which year the little red-white-and-blue toy had been issued. She practically could have designed this room herself. "This collector is into everything. DC *and* Marvel. Jason Voorhees *and* Freddy Krueger. I'd pretty much kill for most of this stuff."

Mackenzie clicked her tongue. "Careful what you wish for."

"Pop culture is amusing," Shaun said, "for a distraction." Persey was confident he'd never been amused or distracted in his entire life.

Wes chortled, his laugh dripping with condescension. "It *used* to be. Now every hipster with an eBay account can claim some piece of media history."

Arlo bristled. "I'm *not* a hipster. I unironically listen to the Monkees, okay?"

"How could someone ironically listen to the Monkees?" Persey was genuinely confused.

Before Arlo could formulate an answer, Neela grabbed her arm, pointing to a framed envelope mounted on the wall. "Arlo, look! It's a No-Prize!"

Arlo bolted across the room toward the spot Neela had pointed out.

"Holy shit! From 1964. And it's not even opened."

"A what-what?" Kevin asked.

The question had been addressed to Arlo, but Neela jumped in immediately with a long-winded answer. "It was a system instituted by Stan Lee at Marvel Comics in response to fans who wanted the company to issue rewards for readers who pointed out continuity problems in the comics. The prize is a non-prize—a letter from Stan Lee himself explaining that the letter writer had won exactly nothing."

Arlo arched an eyebrow. "So you read my blog?"

"I . . ." Neela's face flushed a bright shade of magenta and, for the first time since they'd met, she seemed to be lost for words. "I'm a member of the Geektacle community."

"Really? What's your screen name?"

Neela paused before answering. "TaraMehta91."

"Ohhhhh," Kevin said. "You two know each other?"

Arlo faltered. Just like when she emerged from the ATM booth, her sarcastic, worldly air slipped, the ever-present scowl widened into something more akin to confusion. But it hardly lasted long enough for Persey to notice, before the ballsy, combative Arlo had returned.

"Nope" was all she said, then stepped away, supposedly to examine the next set of collectibles. "We should spread out. Look for something weird or unusual."

"How are we supposed to know?" Shaun asked. "Everything is weird."

"Shaun-bot's right," Kevin said. "It's like the contents of two children's bedrooms were consumed by a goat and we've just arrived in its stomach."

"I know you're only here because of Persey," Arlo said. "But even *you* should be able to tell if something looks odd or suspicious." She sounded chipper again, the momentary alarm vanished. She loved being in charge, loved putting Kevin—and everyone else—in their place.

With a shrug, Kevin followed Mackenzie, Shaun, and Wes, who had fanned out on the ground floor with Arlo, scanning the contents of every book and display case in minute detail, hoping to come across a certain something that might signal the crux of this challenge. And since they were all downstairs, Persey immediately did the opposite. She quietly backed toward the staircase, then tiptoed up to the second floor.

Despite her proximity to the ceiling, the upper story of the Collectibles room felt less oppressive than downstairs. Even with Riot poking around at the far end, she felt like she could breathe more easily, move more freely. Probably the skylights and their fake-but-almost-kinda-real glow. If she forced herself to, she could pretend she was outdoors, alone, rather than cooped up in the Escape-Capades headquarters.

I shouldn't have come. I shouldn't be here.

She laughed out loud. Shouldn't have come? Like you had a choice. Ten million dollars . . .

Even a fraction of that would make a huge difference in her life. She'd be able to get her own place, pay her own bills. Her future would be limitless instead of her current reality: frothing lattes after school and on weekends for people (assholes) who thought that six dollars for a cup of coffee was totally reasonable, trying to make enough extra cash to get by until she graduated from high school and had to not only find a real job but a real place to live.

She paused, leaned forward on a low glass case tucked into a corner and let her head hang down, stretching her back. On the other side of the glass, a half dozen or so toys had been arranged in little clumps.

At first, Persey didn't know why the case seemed weird. Its contents—toys and action figures—looked identical to every other bookshelf and display case, both downstairs and up on the balcony, so there shouldn't have been any reason for this one in particular to grab her attention. But as she continued to stare, she realized that this case *was* different.

First, the case was drastically (suspiciously) underpopulated. All the other displays were packed with similarly thematic dolls and toys, but this case had only a handful. Second, the figures were compiled from "mixed media"—the other areas of the room were all organized by character or character type, but this case had Legos and superheroes, movie characters and cartoons, all jumbled together.

"What did you find?" Kevin asked, Mackenzie glued to his side. She hadn't heard them come up the stairs. "Anything interesting?"

"Maybe."

"Maybe?" Kevin smiled, generating the same warm, comforting sensation that had bolstered her in the Hidden Library, and she cursed herself for being susceptible to his charm. "Looks to me like you've hit the jackpot."

But Mackenzie was more dismissive. "It's just a bunch of toys like everything else up here."

"These are definitely out of place." Arlo squeezed in between Kevin and Mackenzie. Of course Arlo would want to take control, especially in this room, which was so perfectly tailored to her strengths. But Persey wasn't interested in the power struggle. She stepped aside, abdicating leadership, just as Shaun and Wes slid in to take her place.

"Definitely anachronistic." Shaun's eyes slowly scanned the contents from character to character.

Arlo scowled. "I literally just said that."

"You *literally* said 'out of place,'" Shaun corrected her.

"Which means the same thing. Literally."

Wes groaned. "And I figuratively wish you'd both shut the hell up."

The power struggle was in full effect.

Riot crouched down at the side of the case. "Marvel, Star Wars, Scooby-Doo . . . And is that a wrestler?"

Persey stood on her tiptoes to see over his spiky hair. He was right. Shirtless and ripped, the figurine wore the usual black Speedo bottoms, kneepads, and lace-up boots that indicated he was a professional wrestler. He was a redhead, the plastic beard molded onto his face painted a deep auburn, which matched the hair on his head—shaved on both sides and sticking straight up in the middle. A Mohawk.

"Like you," she murmured out loud.

"Huh?" Riot said, looking up at her.

Kevin hit him on the arm. "She said this dude looks like you. Or maybe she's just picturing you shirtless in manties."

Persey gritted her teeth. She wanted to smack him.

"Jealous?" Riot asked.

"As if," Mackenzie answered for him. She couldn't fathom why Kevin might be interested in anyone else while she was around.

"I can see the resemblance in the hair," Kevin continued, unperturbed. "The rest? I don't know—you don't look yoked up under all that tweed."

Riot blinked. "I understand the individual words coming out of your mouth, but when you attempt to string them together into a sentence, I'm just completely lost."

"If you're done participating in the hetero mating ritual," Neela said, sounding somewhat irritated, "I believe this collectible doll *is* meant to be a representation of Riot." Then she pointed at a different part of the case. "Because that Lego figure? She's dressed in Slytherin house robes."

Arlo tilted her head. "You're right. That's Pansy Parkinson."

"Slytherin," Persey said. "Like Arlo."

Neela smiled. "Exactly."

"I think . . ." Persey crouched in front of the case so she could see the figures straight on, the similarities coming into focus as she scanned them from left to right. *Eight figures . . .*

"You think what?" Kevin asked, prompting her. As always.

"I think these are meant to represent each of us."

TWENTY-ONE

"HUH." ARLO KNELT DOWN BESIDE HER. "PANSY PARKINSON and the redheaded wrestler, check. Then we have Lando Calrissian. Judging by the rubber cape and unarticulated elbow and knee joints, I'd say that's from the original 1980 *Empire Strikes Back* collection, and I'm assuming it's meant to represent Shaun."

"The Lando system?" Kevin said.

Shaun tilted his head. "What are you talking about?"

"Dude," Kevin laughed, "funny."

"I don't understand."

Kevin's laughter switched from amused to nervous. "It's a quote. From *Empire Strikes Back*. Leia says, 'Lando system?' and Han replies, 'Lando's not a system; he's a man.'"

Only Shaun wasn't being funny. He was missing that upgrade. "I've never seen a Star Wars movie."

Kevin teetered backward as if he'd been kicked in the chest. "I'm sorry, what?"

"Lando Calrissian, as originally portrayed by American actor Billy Dee Williams," Neela explained rapidly, "is an old friend of Han Solo's, who at the time of *Episode Five* is serving as the baron administrator at the mining colony on the planet Bespin."

"So he's middle management from the seventies?" Shaun asked.

"Eighties," Kevin said.

"Well, technically the character is from a long time ago, in a galaxy far, far away," Neela said, laughing at her own joke, "but by way of 1980, yes."

"Could be worse," Mackenzie said, nodding to the other end of the case. "You could have been Velma."

The big-headed Funko POP! doll of Velma from Scooby-Doo had massively exaggerated square-rimmed glasses that reminded Persey of . . .

"Is that me?" Neela squeaked.

Mackenzie wrinkled her mouth in fake sympathy. "'Fraid so."

"But . . . but isn't she the frumpy one?"

"Well, she's not the hot one," Wes said, "that's for sure."

Neela's fuchsia blush was back, deeper and more intense than before. "I don't think . . . I mean, I know I'm not . . ."

Poor Neela. She should have known better than to put her insecurities on display in front of this bunch of jackals, just waiting for the smell of a rotting corpse to pounce on their dinner. But Persey wasn't going to let Neela fall prey to the likes of Wes and Mackenzie.

"She's the smart one," Persey said. "The one who solves every mystery."

"Yeah." Neela looked crestfallen. "Smart and frumpy."

"Which one am I?" Mackenzie said, angling past Neela. "Oooh, that retro-looking Barbie doll in the corner. Her hair is *so* on point."

Everyone's eyes shifted to the Barbie in question. Unlike the blond fashion doll that Persey's mom had bought her when she was younger, this version had darker hair—more honey than platinum—and instead of cutting-edge fashion or a runway-ready gown, she wore retro dark blue bell-bottom pants and a light blue blouse that had a strange tear through the left upper arm. She was posed in the corner of the case, alone, and though her plastic, painted-on smile was happy and demure, her body was crouched down as if she'd collapsed in exhaustion, face leaning against the glass, and beneath the tear on her blouse it looked as if someone had drawn a line on the doll's skin with a red marker.

The outfit and the pose were vaguely familiar; Persey couldn't quite put her finger on why. Until she noticed who was standing behind this Barbie. A tall male figure, dressed in a blue jumpsuit with a featureless white mask on his face and a long knife grasped in his hands.

Suddenly Persey knew exactly who the Barbie was supposed to be. "Laurie Strode."

"Was that one of Barbie's sisters?" Kevin asked.

She shot him a withering glance, weary of his sarcasm. "She's the final girl from *Halloween.*"

"The heroine!" Mackenzie squealed. "See? I knew it was supposed to be me."

"Actually . . ." Arlo tapped on the glass, talking to Mackenzie. "I think you're Sue Storm here, making out with . . ." She paused, mouth scrunched up to the side. "With the cigarette in his mouth, I think that's supposed to be Sanji from One Piece. But his hair is usually blond."

Persey pried herself away from the serial killer at her end of the case to look at the duo in question. The characters—the Fantastic Four's invisible woman and her smoking friend—were clearly in the throes of a make-out session. Though their sizes and genres didn't match, she was bent backward at the waist, supported by his arm, as he leaned down and kissed her.

"Oh, look!" Arlo cried. "You can see the yellow of his hair poking through. Someone's colored this in black with a Sharpie or something."

"Black like Wes's hair," Neela said. "Who is also a known smoker."

"Seriously?" Mackenzie said, turning pale. "Is someone suggesting that Wes and I are a thing?"

"Are or were?" Arlo asked quickly. "You two seem like you know each other."

Mackenzie folded her arms across her chest. "The. Fuck."

"You did know that he went to boarding school," Persey said quietly. "But Leah never mentioned that in her intro."

"And you accused Persey and me of colluding," Kevin said, faking offense. "Hilarious, since we just met at the Hidden Library escape room. But you two . . . you wanna share your history?"

"Back in high school," Mackenzie said. "We *hardly* knew each other."

Persey seriously doubted that.

"We've got twenty minutes to figure out what these stupid toys mean," Mackenzie said. She was definitely trying to change the subject. "So why don't we focus on that, huh?"

"Fine," Arlo said. "But don't think we're going to forget about this." She turned back to the case. "That leaves Persey and Kevin, who by process of elimination must be *Halloween* Barbie and Michael Myers there." She narrowed her eyes at Kevin. "Do I even want to know why you're the serial killer?"

Riot snorted. "The designer must have misplaced his Big Lebowski doll."

"Har-har." Kevin pointedly turned his back on the librarian. "Okay, we're each represented here, so what?"

Arlo pinched her chin between her thumb and forefinger. It looked like a well-rehearsed "thinking" pose. "Let's see if we can find where these figures all came from."

She led the way back downstairs, pontificating about the steps they should take to solve this challenge, while the rest of the competitors reluctantly followed. Persey lagged behind.

She leaned over the balcony, hoping for a better view of the collection below, but her eyes bounced from superheroes to My Little Ponies—seeing without seeing. There was so much crap in here, she could barely process it all. Even the floors were decorated; from upstairs, she could clearly discern a set of footprints painted on the tile below like one of those learn-to-dance mats only with significantly less feet.

Persey stood up, eyes glued to the footprints. Was that a clue?

She hurried downstairs to the footprints, and as she crouched down to get a better look, she saw that they had, in fact, been painted onto the white tile—matte paint on the glossy surface. Glancing up, she found a giant cage propped up on a counter above.

Not just a cage, a cage filled with muscly, half-naked wrestlers. A steel-cage wrestling match.

The costumed performers were from a variety of different eras—" minimalist seventies, Technicolor eighties, dark and Goth nineties—who were posed in a frenetic mix of wrestling moves, including one guy in a flying nelson, hung suspended from the roof of the cage by near-invisible wires.

She wasn't even sure what she was looking for, other than that a redheaded Mohawked wrestler had appeared in the case upstairs, and supposedly represented Riot. Maybe there would be another version of that wrestler down here that would clue them into the figure's purpose?

But as Persey stepped closer to the toy set, she realized that there was something out of place. Literally. The floor of the case was coated in a thin layer of dust, and right in the middle, there were two prints. Foot-shaped prints.

Was that where Mr. Mohawk had been before he was moved?

She shifted her focus to the floor: the painted footprints matched the configuration of the smaller version perfectly.

"Riot," she said, eyes still fixed on the wrestling cage.

He appeared at her shoulder immediately. "You rang?"

"What's happening?" Arlo said, close on his heels. God forbid anything transpire that she wasn't a part of. "What did you find?"

"N-nothing," Persey said, flustered. Why did she let Arlo get to her? She shook her head, pushing aside her momentary (permanent) self-doubt. "Riot, can you stand here, in front of the case?"

"Of course." Riot took up a position in front of the wrestling cage. "Now what?"

"I . . . I don't know." Persey wasn't sure what she'd been expecting. A door to swing open? A light to go on?

"Fifteen minutes."

"Fifteen minutes," Mackenzie repeated, as helpful as ever. "Do we need to start searching for some other puzzle to solve?"

"Maybe you just need better wrestling flair," Kevin joked. Then he struck a pose, reminiscent of the one in the display case upstairs. He flexed his right bicep toward his head, and rotated his left arm so it twisted away from his hip, looking very much like Pee-wee Herman doing the "Tequila" dance.

Riot rolled his eyes. "The figure upstairs was posed like this." Then he re-created the pose, but with more teeth gritting and neck vein popping. Like a real wrestler. "How do I look?"

But nobody answered. Their eyes were all fixed on the wall behind Riot, where one of the red lightbulbs that surrounded the countdown clock had just flickered to life.

TWENTY-TWO

"THAT'S IT!" NEELA SQUEALED. "YOU DID IT!"

"Persey did it," Riot said, dropping the pose in his amazement. "I can't take credit."

The moment he let his arms fall back into place by his side, the light went out.

Perplexed, Riot struck the pose again, trying to hold his arms in the exact same positions as before. The light went on. He dropped them, and again, it extinguished.

"Spread out," Arlo said, not waiting for anyone to comment. "Each of our totems must be represented by footprints somewhere in this room."

Gee, you think?

"If we can get all of those lightbulbs lit," she continued, "maybe we can figure out the rest of this challenge."

"Mackenzie and Wes are Sanji and Sue Storm," Neela said, ticking them both off on her fingers. She spun around, pointing. "And the Marvel collection is right next to the anime."

"Maybe Kevin's the anime guy?" Mackenzie whined. "We don't know for sure it's Wes."

Kevin tossed his hair out of his eyes as he descended from the balcony.

"If it was supposed to be me, they'd have kept the hair blond. Besides, I don't smoke."

Persey smiled. She was pretty sure that was bullshit, but she appreciated that he wasn't falling into Mackenzie's hands.

Neela rushed across the room. "Footprints! Two sets!"

"At the juncture between Marvel and anime," Arlo said, nodding her head in understanding. "No wonder I didn't see these. I was distracted by the amazing collectibles." Because there had to be a reason why she wasn't taking the lead.

Wes was unimpressed. "Okay, so what? We found some feet. What are we supposed to do with this information?"

"You two." Arlo pointed to Wes and Mackenzie. "Match your feet to those and see if it replicates the pose from upstairs."

"Why me?" Mackenzie whined even louder.

"Maybe Leah wants to watch you make out with Wes?" Kevin suggested.

Persey was pretty sure the comment was meant as a dig, not a compliment, but Mackenzie missed no opportunity to flirt. "Would *you* like to watch?"

Wes raised his hand. "Do I get a say in this?"

"Nope!" Kevin positioned himself beside the nearby display case that housed all the horror-related items. Visible against the white tile below were two sets of footprints. He pointed at the floor, then at Persey. "Now crouch down like Laurie so we can get this show on the road, will you?"

But Mackenzie was like spilled glitter: you couldn't get rid of her that easily. "Kev," she said, dialing up the sugary sweetness, "you did such a good job with Riot's pose. Could you demonstrate to Wes? He's not going to know how to hold me."

I seriously doubt that.

She leaned over Persey and grabbed Kevin's arm, leaning in. "Pwetty pwease?"

"Go," Persey said, shooing Kevin off. If she had to listen to Mackenzie's flirty voice for one more second she was going to vomit up her airplane pretzels. "Or we'll never get out of here."

With his back to Mackenzie, Kevin rolled his eyes, then plastered on a goofy grin and hurried off.

Persey perused the horror section while waiting for Kevin to return. Her brother loved horror movies, especially those by John Carpenter, and when she was little, he'd routinely tortured Persey by making her watch them. She'd spend most of the movies with her hands over her eyes, too scared to peek, even when her brother would crack jokes. She was never sure if he was trying to lighten the mood or lull her into a sense of security so she'd open her eyes and see something she could never unsee.

It was amazing she could identify Laurie Strode at all: she'd barely seen any of that movie. Just heard the screaming.

Meanwhile, Mackenzie led Kevin back to Marvel corner, where Wes waited, leaning lazily against the wall. She helped position Kevin, one arm behind her back, as she sunk into a dip, then placed her hand daintily behind his neck and brought his face to hers for a kiss. Just before their lips met, she shot Persey a triumphant glance.

Persey merely sighed. Everything was a competition for girls like that. Even when the other party couldn't have given less of a shit.

"Is everybody in position?" Arlo called from upstairs. "Ten minutes on the clock."

"Hold up!" Kevin said.

"Uh, Kevin," Neela said, leaning over the banister. There was laughter in her voice. "You need to make like Madonna and strike a pose."

Persey smiled as she crouched down, attempting to line her feet up to the prints on the floor. *If it wasn't for this competition, we might have been friends.*

One by one the lightbulbs flared to life. Wes's and Mackenzie's came on simultaneously as Wes bent her backward, but before his lips touched hers, thankfully. Wes still tried to kiss Mackenzie of course, and for a moment, Persey almost felt sorry for her.

"Save it," Mackenzie said, turning her face away from Wes.

Seven of the eight lights were on; only Kevin's remained dark as he sauntered back to Persey. "You ready for this?"

"The competition?"

He shook his head. "To see if you were right. Again." Then, without waiting for her to answer, he took his position behind her, like Michael Myers holding a knife.

The eighth light buzzed to life, and as it did, the floor beneath the fire pole slid open.

It was a circular hole around the metal post, which extended down into the darkness beneath, where the tile floor had split in the middle and slid away.

"Are we supposed to slide down?" Mackenzie pushed Wes off and stutter-stepped toward the fire pole, leaning forward when her toes met the lip of the hole, trying to catch a glimpse of what lay below. As she did, one of the lights on the wall went out. But the trapdoor, thankfully, stayed wide open.

Kevin eyed the light bulbs closely. "I think that's the plan."

"Looks kinda dangerous," Mackenzie replied. "Can't someone else go first?"

Not quite so ballsy as she wants everyone to believe.

"I'll go—" Riot began, following Mackenzie to the edge of the trap-door. But he never got to finish his sentence. The instant he broke his pose, another light went out and the round door slammed shut.

"What's happening?" Arlo's head appeared over the edge of the banister, as another light went dark. "Why are all the lights going out?"

"Don't break your pose!" Wes shouted. Arlo jumped, startled at being snapped at instead of being the snapper, but hurried back into place. "Fine. Now what?"

"Looks like the powers that be want us to go one at a time," Kevin said. "Single file down into the dark, scary pit."

"Well, I'm *definitely* not going first," Mackenzie said.

"Just slide down the damn pole," Wes said, retaking his place. "There's not going to be anything dangerous down there."

"Yeah, but . . ."

"Eight minutes."

"Um, guys?" Neela said. "Could we hurry this up?"

"Nothing to be afraid of, right?" Kevin said.

"Right." Mackenzie was quick to respond, though not as quick to act. As Kevin and Wes resumed their positions and the door slid open, she still just stood at the edge of the hole, frozen.

The threat of imminent failure might not have been able to spur Mackenzie into action, but Persey was pretty sure the threat of competition would. "If you're too afraid," she said, "I'll go first."

Kevin grinned down at her, his face upside down like an evil jack-o'-lantern. "You're so badass, Persey."

Mackenzie instantly stiffened. The idea that Kevin might heap praise on someone who wasn't her was enough to get her moving. She hooked one leg around the pole with the ease and fluidity of an exotic dancer about to launch into a routine. "No, I can do this." She blew Kevin a kiss. "See you downstairs!" Then she leaped onto the pole, grabbing it with both hands, and swirled down through the floor.

Persey heard a dull thud as Mackenzie hit the ground below. "You okay?"

Mackenzie's reply was slightly delayed. "Yeah." Seconds later, an orangish glow emerged from the hole. "But you guys aren't going to believe this."

"Next." Shaun didn't even wait for a discussion of who would go, but broke his pose from the Star Wars section and grabbed the pole with both hands. He shook it vigorously, testing its sturdiness, then hurled his body onto the pole, disappearing into the orangey darkness.

Riot was next, and as soon as he disappeared down the rabbit hole, Kevin reached his hand to Persey. "Your turn."

Persey eyed the fire pole. She wasn't entirely sure she wanted to see what was at the bottom. "I'll go last?"

Kevin shook his head. "You don't want Mackenzie to think that you're as scared as she was."

He had a point, but she still hesitated.

"I promise there won't be any dead bodies down there, okay?"

Persey pressed her lips together, irritated. "You sure about that?"

"Absolutely." His boyish grin spread across his face.

"Fine." Persey took his hand, and he yanked her up with more strength than she was prepared for. She went airborne for a split second before her feet touched the floor—the move might have looked balletic if she hadn't almost fallen over.

"You good?" Kevin asked.

Persey nodded. "I'm good."

"I'm glad you decided to come today."

The comment was so out of left field that Persey did a double take. "Um, yeah." *I'd be gladder if someone hadn't died.*

She felt her face burn up, and she turned her back so Kevin wouldn't see her confusion, then hurried across the floor, gripping the shiny brass bar with both hands before wrapping her legs around it and slipping into the unknown.

TWENTY-THREE

PERSEY'S GRADES WERE SLIPPING. IT SEEMED IMPOSSIBLE (not really) that after two years of mediocrity—one at private school, one at public—things could get any worse, but only two months into her junior year, Algebra II was already kicking her ass per (more than) usual and Chemistry was an albatross around her neck.

There had been a slight reprieve sophomore year, a momentary miracle where it looked as if Persey's academic performance might be improving. Geometry made more sense than algebra, biology was a friendly science, and American history certainly wasn't as rough as econ. Plus, the change in schools had given her a boost. By second semester, Persey managed to pull all Bs and B-minuses—a first in her academic career—and though her dad still spent much of that summer once again ignoring her presence, there were moments when he'd forget that he loathed his daughter, especially after she took that stupid SAT exam. Moments when, if she closed her eyes and imagined hard enough, Persey could almost pretend that she had a normal family.

But even that sad little glimmer of normalcy evaporated with the first progress report of junior year.

C-minuses across the board except for an A-minus (study hall) and a D (algebra, of course.) Her math failure was dragging everything else down, even affecting normally stress-free subjects like English and political science. It wasn't as if much had changed since sophomore year, either. She still had almost no friends, definitely no social life other than working on the stage crew, and studied just as hard.

Her grades were discouraging, and she vacillated between wanting to try harder or just giving up. The one bright spot was that her dad had somehow forgotten (ignored) the fact that she spent a lot of her spare time at the theater, because if he'd actually remembered, she was pretty sure he'd make her quit. Which might break her entirely. It was the only thing she looked forward to, the only time in her day when she felt like she was actually good at something. After working as the assistant prop mistress last spring she'd been promoted to spotlight operator for the fall play. It was the perfect job: she didn't have to talk to anyone, plus Persey got to hide in the shadows and watch every moment of every performance.

She even took pride in her role. The director, Mr. Beck, had told her that her new job was an essential part of the show because she would be directing the audience to the most important bits of action and dialogue onstage.

And she was good at it.

They were only two months into rehearsals for the fall play, but Persey already knew every word of Sheridan's *The School for Scandal*, which she'd mouth along with the actors during rehearsals while she helped build and paint the sets.

She'd made a real attempt to compensate for the hours spent in the theater by doubling up her studying time, which, in theory, should have helped her grades. But, apparently, not so much. This progress report would merely reinforce her dad's assessment that she was lazy and slow and stupid. All the names he'd been calling her since it became clear she'd never "live up" to her brother.

Now she was going to have to endure all the beratement again.

With a day off from rehearsal, Persey decided to walk home from school, rather than call for a ride. A short reprieve, but one she needed in order to come to terms with the shitshow that would be family dinner. The searingly hot sun baked the sidewalk, the heat radiating up through the soles of her shoes so it almost felt as if she was walking barefoot on the concrete. She yearned for some air-conditioning and comfy leather seats, and more than once she pulled out her phone, ready to call for a pickup. It wasn't as if her parents would even be home when she arrived. They were at the office for longer and longer stretches each day, preparing for the new product unveiling. So if she'd be alone at the house for hours anyway, why subject herself to the sweltering heat?

It's my punishment. Her odyssey home was self-inflicted hell. By the time she reached the gate outside her housing community, she was slick with sweat and red-faced with exhaustion.

Tyson, one of the security guards, poked his head through the window of the air-conditioned station, his eyes wide with worry. "Are you okay?"

She nodded, feeling her head spin a little as she did. "Yeah."

"No." He opened the door and beckoned her inside. "Get in here and have some water."

Too exhausted to refuse, Persey stumbled into the guards' shack. It was a tiny square, hardly bigger than a closet, with windows on all four sides, two of which slid open to accommodate conversations with cars that were both coming and going from the gated development. A desk and computer were built into the front of the shack, a row of high-tech monitors embedded in the console cycling through camera angles that Persey didn't even know existed, and a walkie-talkie stood charging in its base beside the screen where the guards logged all visitors. Two chairs were tucked beneath the desk, one of which Tyson wheeled out for her.

As she fell into it, he reached into a mini fridge, retrieving a small bottle of ice-cold water.

"Drink this," Tyson commanded. The bottle felt soothing in her hand, and before she cracked it open, she held the refreshing coolness up to her neck. The cold air plus the chilled plastic against her skin did its job, and within seconds, Persey was feeling more herself.

"Thank you," she said, taking a gulp. "I needed that."

"You looked like you were about to pass out in the middle of the road." Tyson pursed his lips. "Why were you walking home? You know you're not supposed to be unaccompanied."

Persey smiled. She liked Tyson, and somehow, it was easier to talk to him than to any single member of her family. "I needed the exercise."

"Your dad know about this?"

Persey shook her head, avoiding his eyes.

"Okay. Well, it's not my job to tell him, but could you please think twice before you do something boneheaded like walk home from West Valley again?" He grinned at her, eyes crinkling. "It'd mean a shit ton of paperwork for me if you'd passed out on my sidewalk."

Persey laughed. "Noted."

"I'm calling James to take you the rest of the way in the cart," Tyson said, reaching for the walkie. He didn't even give her time to protest. "And no, I don't want to hear it. If your brother sees you walking into the house like that, it'll be my ass."

Persey froze. "My brother?"

"Yeah, didn't you know? He got here an hour ago."

Persey's mind raced as the golf cart slowly dragged her and James up the hill toward her house, the last one on the block. It was a Wednesday, late

October. There were no school holidays, not even the excuse of a long three-day weekend to come home from college. So why had her brother flown all the way across the country from New York?

Whatever the reason, it's not good.

She thanked James as he deposited her at the apex of the long circular drive that curved up to the front of her house, then waited until his cart disappeared behind the tall shrubbery before punching her security code into the keypad and unlocking the door.

"Hello?" She stepped tentatively into the foyer. The lights were off; the sterile white tile and matching walls reflected the coldness that always existed in her house despite the desert heat outside, and her voice seemed to echo up the staircase to the floor above, tinkling through the ornate chandelier and pinging around in the emptiness. "Anyone home?"

She listened, hardly daring to breathe. If her brother or her parents were home, they should have been able to hear her if they were in the main house. It was large, but it wasn't *that* large. She waited for the telltale sound of footsteps, a muffled garble of voices, bumping or clanking or anything that might indicate life. But the house was silent.

Weird.

Maybe her brother had come and gone? Arrived just to change his clothes and then headed out to meet one of his buddies? She was pretty sure at least one of them had stayed in town for college. She'd just placed one foot on the bottom step, ready to head up to her room, when she heard a loud thud coming from the back of the house.

From her parents' room.

The master suite occupied the entire east wing of the ground floor, consisting of a bedroom, sitting area, dressing room, master bath, and two walk-in closets, all of which opened onto a private lanai beside the swimming pool. It was more "resort living" than "cozy family home," and

Persey hadn't actually been through those double doors since she was a kid. But the modern decor with Spanish-style accents was exactly as she remembered it—just as ostentatious now as it had been when she crept inside as a five-year-old after having a nightmare in the middle of the night—without a floral arrangement or a pleat of drapery out of place.

With one exception.

There was a light on in her father's closet.

Now that she was inside the suite, she could hear rustling noises: someone was going through drawers, rummaging quickly, then moving on. They were the sounds you'd expect from a cat burglar, but as she crept across the plush carpeting toward the open door, she knew she wasn't going to find a stranger dressed head-to-toe in black with a ski mask pulled over his face.

Her brother stood in front of a wall of built-in drawers, quickly but methodically searching through each before moving to the next one. Beside him on the floor lay an open suitcase into which he'd just dropped a pair of gold cuff links. She could see the glitter of a gemstone, the gleam of other jewelry, as well as a healthy stack of cash—Dad's emergency supply—piled haphazardly inside.

"Hey," she said, trying to sound casual and normal, like she hadn't just walked in on her brother stealing from their parents.

"Hey." He didn't jump or start. *He knew I was here.* "How was school?"

The question was so ludicrous, given the circumstances, that Persey actually laughed out loud. Second time that day.

"That good, huh?"

"I didn't know you were coming home this week," Persey said, refusing to be sidetracked.

"I wasn't."

"So . . ."

He finally turned to face her. Despite the happy-go-lucky smile, there were deep creases around his mouth and his eyes, which were sunken and ringed with a purplish hue. An ugly gash on his right cheekbone had been cinched together with butterfly bandages.

"Holy shit!" she cried. He looked as if he'd gotten into a bar fight with the entire Columbia crew team.

His smile never faltered. "I'm going away for a while."

"Away? You mean like back to Columbia?"

"Away like out of the country."

"Why?"

He waved her off. "Nothing big. Just a little bit of trouble at school." His smile deepened as a dreamy, faraway look swept over his face. It was the same smile she'd seen at his graduation, when he and his buddies were discussing their party plans, and it was the same smile that had been on his face when he was taking photos of the mutilated remains of a half dozen rodents in the family guesthouse.

Her voice hardened. "What did you do?"

"Nothing. Big," he repeated. "I'll be fine."

He wasn't the one she was worried about.

Her brother bent down and zipped up the suitcase. "Tell Mom I'll call her this weekend," he said. "When I'm settled."

"They won't believe me," Persey said. "When I tell them what happened here."

"They will eventually." He dragged the suitcase toward her and placed a hand on her shoulder. It was a paternal gesture, but one that made her whole body tense up. "I'll tell them the truth. You won't get blamed."

Don't be so sure about that.

"But look . . ." He leaned closer, and Persey fought the urge to back away. "If anyone comes looking for me, you didn't see any of this, okay?

As far as you know, I'm still in New York."

What did you do?

He squeezed her shoulder when she didn't respond. It wasn't gentle. "Okay?"

"Okay."

"You good?" His grip lessened, but his hand remained.

"I'm good."

Then he smiled and stepped around her. "Take care, little sis. Don't let Dad get to you. He'll leave you alone. Someday."

TWENTY-FOUR

THE BRIGHTNESS OF THE COLLECTIBLES ROOM DISAPPEARED above her head as Persey slid down into the abyss. She dropped for what felt like an eternity, and when she finally landed (crashed), she felt the floor beneath her feet give slightly with the force of her impact. Balancing against the pole, Persey wondered if she'd slid far enough to make it underground. Because this room—if you could even call it that—was more like a cave than a man-made structure.

The walls and ceiling were made of rock, dark and textured, and if Persey didn't know better, she'd have thought this room had been hewed into the side of a mountain. The orange glow she'd seen from upstairs came from a dozen torches mounted on wall sconces, their comforting light dancing off the textured walls. It almost looked as if the walls themselves were rippling, like a flag in a strong wind, and it made the room feel alive. Sentient. *Intelligent.*

The rock walls curved toward each other, creating an egg-like oval with the fire pole at one end and a massive marble structure at the other. It looked like a tall kitchen island made from gleaming white stone, like something on a home improvement show. *An altar.* Persey had only been to church once—for a funeral—but she had been entranced by the heavy, ornate table the priest spent most of his time standing behind. As if to hammer the church-like point home, a large wooden cross hung behind the altar, so dark it blended in with the granite walls, yet big enough that you couldn't miss it.

"Persey, be careful!" Riot waved at her from the front of the room, where he was examining the altar top. "Someone might land on you."

"Right. Thanks." She hobbled away from the base of the pole. The floor wiggled with each movement, and the soles of her Toms buckled against an uneven surface.

Once clear of the pole, Persey crouched down, examining the floor. The unevenness was the result of a composite surface made of what appeared at first glance to be large slabs of stone, irregular in shape, with thick gaps between pieces like oversize cobblestones. Persey grazed her fingers against floor, expecting to feel smooth, textured stone. Instead, she found that the floor was made of customized pieces of wood, porous and flimsy, painted to look like stone.

It was bizarre that someone would make a floor like this—the wooden slabs were huge, two feet wide at least, and the seams between them were deep, as if the faux stones themselves were pushing upward through mesh with no discernible material holding them in place. And Persey had no idea why the entire floor structure felt bouncy. Was it intended to absorb the shock from rocketing down that long fire pole? Or was the floor meant to give for some other purpose?

"What is this room supposed to be?" Persey asked, more to herself than to the others.

"It's like a cave *and* a cathedral," Riot said, circling around to the backside of the altar. He was antsy, fingers drumming against his thigh.

"A Cavethedral?" Persey suggested, reciting the name from the whiteboard in Office Drones.

Riot chuckled. "Right! I guess I didn't think that would be literal."

Mackenzie wrinkled her upper lip. "I think it's creepy."

"It poses an interesting challenge," Shaun-bot said, without elaborating on how it seemed any more or less interesting than the last four.

"This altar is fascinating," Riot said, hauling himself onto the large tabletop. "These engravings. Intricate and yet they don't seem to be connected in any way."

"Clear a path!" Kevin called from above just before sliding into the Cavethedral. "Whoa, this place is badass."

"Right?" Mackenzie said. "The design. The attention to detail." A complete 180 from ten seconds ago. *She'll say or do anything to get what she wants.*

"Son of a Shatner!" Neela cried, en route down the pole. She collapsed into a puddle of limbs and hair on the faux stones, unable to slow her momentum. The floor of the entire room rebounded from the impact. "That was the single scariest thing I've ever done in my entire life and I've been to a Taylor Swift concert, and can someone tell me why the floor is shaking and also, is that the seal of the Inquisition?" She pointed at the cross behind the altar.

"The what what?" Mackenzie asked.

Kevin wagged an index finger at her. "And don't you badmouth Tay Tay."

"The Tribunal of the Holy Office of the Inquisition," Shaun said, his voice a flat drone as he answered Mackenzie's question, "established in 1478 by Ferdinand II and Isabella I of Spain to maintain Catholic orthodoxy, believed to be a response to the multi-religious nature of Spanish society at the time, and the spread of both anti-Semitism and anti-Muslim sentiments across Europe."

"Thank you, Siri," Mackenzie said. "You can stop now."

"Where?" Riot asked, still focused on the altar. "I don't see anything."

Neela hurried across the uneven floor toward him, stumbling every few steps. "On the cross. Look at the center."

"First point to Neela," Persey joked, impressed by her sharp eyes.

"I *might* have noticed it earlier," Mackenzie said, folding her hands across her chest, peeved. "If I hadn't had to go first down the pole. I was slightly more worried about not dying. Or worse."

"What, exactly, is worse?" Persey asked.

"Shit," Riot said. "A Spanish Inquisition–themed room sounds ominous."

"If you're scared," Mackenzie said, "you can always give up. Just tell Leah you're out and they'll extract you, I'm sure."

"Right," Persey said. "Because help was so quick to arrive when someone murdered B.J."

"Just one more sign that your 'dead body'"—Mackenzie used air quotes to emphasize what she thought of Persey's theory—"was all part of the game."

"I'm going to check out the back wall," Neela said, scurrying from the altar and picking her way carefully across the uneven floor. "Maybe there are some other engravings."

"I'm coming down!" Arlo cried. "Wes will be right behind me."

Persey looked up at the roof of the Cavethedral, rather surprised that Wes would agree to be the last one out of the room. She could just see Arlo leaning onto the pole, her body blocking out the bright blue-white glare of the halogen bulbs from the Collectibles room.

"All clear!" Riot called back.

Persey had just shifted her gaze back to the darkened interior of the Cavethedral, when she heard a loud snap and the dim glow from the roof was extinguished.

She knew the sound immediately—the trapdoor that surrounded the fire pole clamping shut—and her first thought was that Wes had some-how been cut off from the rest of them, perhaps ending his participation in the competition. Which wouldn't be such a bad thing at all. She was officially over his shit.

There was a squishy thud, something heavy and wet crashed onto the floor, and then Persey heard a scream. When she turned toward the fire pole, she saw Neela holding her hands out in front of her face. Both them and the rest of her were splattered with blood.

In reality, it only took a split second for Persey to realize what she was looking at, but it felt like forever. Like she lived an entire lifetime in that moment. Like the life she had known before died in a single heartbeat.

Flickering torch flames danced across a wet stain that was rapidly set-tling into the cracks between wooden slabs, and on the ground next to Neela was a crumpled heap of arms and legs. The "It's Not a Party Till I Slytherin" T-shirt faced Persey, but she could barely discern the lettering across the torso because the shirt was soaked in blood below the neck.

Or at least Persey thought it was her neck.

Arlo's head was gone.

TWENTY-FIVE

IF B.J.'S DEAD BODY HAD (NOT) BEEN A FIGMENT OF PERSEY'S imagination, Arlo's decapitated corpse was a mass hallucination. Or at least Persey *wanted* it to be. Because if it was real, if that truly was Arlo's lifeless body with blood still spurting from its gaping neck, it meant the Escape-Capades All-Star Competition now had two deaths on its head.

Er, bad choice of words, Persey.

Neela had been the closest person to the body when it fell, confirmed by the Jackson Pollock–esque splattering of blood on her face, hands, and clothes, manifesting as a wet sheen across the black fabric of her shirt. She stood with arms outstretched, frozen in time at the moment she'd tried to break Arlo's fall, trembling.

"Oh my Gorn!" she cried. "Get it off. Get it off me!"

Persey wasn't sure if she meant the blood or the specter of death, but there was only one of those that she could solve. She raced to Neela's side, stripping off her top layer of T-shirts en route, and deftly began to wipe the blood from Neela's face and hands.

"Is she dead?" Tears streamed down Neela's face. "Do you think she's dead?"

"Her head is missing," Shaun said, stating the obvious. "The probability of surviving a complete decapitation is zero." Even through his robotic intonation, Persey could hear the flutter of emotion in his voice. Fear.

"It was an accident, right?" Mackenzie crouched down on the ground, arms wrapped around her body, and began to rock gently back and forth. "It was just an accident."

Not claiming it's fake now, huh?

"Leah!" Riot spun around, searching the Cavethedral for the camera they all knew was there. "You need to call an ambulance. Stat!"

It's a bit late for that.

Light suddenly flooded the space, illuminating Arlo's body like the spotlights Persey used to operate in the West Valley theater as the trapdoor in the ceiling flew open. A shadow leaned into view; then Wes's voice drifted down. "Holy shit, you guys. Arlo's dead!"

"We know," Kevin replied, sounding way too calm.

"Her head . . ." Wes's voice trailed off. "It . . . it rolled across the floor and then got wedged between Captain America's shield and a collectible *Space: 1999* Eagle. Her eyes are still open. She's . . . she's staring at me."

"What the hell happened up there?" Persey called out.

"I . . . I don't know. She insisted on going before me. And . . . and then the door just snapped shut and . . ."

"And then her head just snapped off," Shaun said, completing the thought.

"I can't stay up here with those eyes looking at me." Wes's voice shook. "I'm . . . I'm coming down."

"Dude!" Riot said, waving his arms to get Wes's attention. "Do not slide down that thing! Just stay put and wait for the cops to show—"

"Too late," Kevin said. Wes had already swung himself onto the pole and released his grip.

He fell like a stone, not slowing himself at all as he passed through the murderous trapdoor. Probably thought that the faster he moved, the safer he might be, which was smart, but as he rocketed down toward Arlo's corpse, Persey immediately identified a new problem.

"Watch out!" she cried as Wes's Tevas skidded on the uneven floor made slick by a heavy coating of Arlo's blood. He clawed at the pole, desperately trying not to lose his balance. Kevin and Persey grabbed each of his arms and heaved Wes away from the gore, tripping on the awkward floor gaps as they went.

"It must have been a malfunction," Shaun said, gazing up at the circle of light in the ceiling. "Software glitch or a structural weakness in the trapdoor mechanism."

"Did you hear anything?" Persey asked. "See anything?"

"Just Arlo's head rolling across the floor like a bowling ball," Wes said as he regained his footing, shaking her off. *You're welcome.*

"But it was an accident, right?" Mackenzie repeated.

Silence. Persey couldn't stop thinking about how upset Arlo was after she escaped her ATM booth. What had she yelled at the camera? Something about a password.

"This doesn't mean you're right." Mackenzie spat the words at Persey, her diction so vehement that Persey could practically feel their percussive force rippling through the empty space between them.

"Right about what?"

"That singer." Mackenzie scowled. "Arlo's death doesn't mean that you were right about him. *This* was an accident. *That* was part of the game."

There was zero point in arguing (talking) with her. "Whatever you say."

Persey hadn't exactly meant to piss Mackenzie off, but her response was like striking a match near a fuse. Mackenzie's anger ignited.

"Don't you 'whatever' me." She stomped across the uneven floor, which bounced unnervingly with every step. "I'm right and you know it."

"Why does it matter who's right?" Persey said. She'd only known this girl for a couple of hours and she was already exhausted by her. "Arlo is still going to be dead either way."

Mackenzie threw up her hands. "It matters because I'm tired of you looking down on me."

"What?"

"On *all* of us. You think you're so special because you solved the Hidden Library. Well, you know what? I don't believe you really did, and I haven't seen anything so far from you that would make me believe it's true."

Persey laughed out loud. Actual hysterical laughter. She couldn't help it. Of all the contestants in the Escape-Capades All-Star Competition, Persey was the least likely to believe that she was better than anyone else. She'd spent almost her entire life being told she was less than worthless, and here was this high-achieving, internationally educated chick who was smart and beautiful and not at all awkward with people, and who had probably spent *her* entire life getting exactly what she wanted, and yet somehow she was jealous of Persey. It was utterly ridiculous.

"The. Fuck?"

"Sorry," Persey said, trying to contain herself. And she meant it. "I've just never had anyone jealous of me before."

Mackenzie's eyes grew wide, fists clenched. "You think I'm *jealous?* Of *you?*"

Aren't you?

"Okay, okay." Kevin stepped between them. "No one's jealous of anyone. Except me. I'm the one who isn't supposed to be here, right? So I'm jealous of all of you."

But Mackenzie wouldn't be placated that easily. "You're trying to make me think that I'm the jealous one, when really *you're* the one who's envious."

"Um, why?" Persey could think of several reasons that she might be jealous of the accomplished singer, but she doubted that Mackenzie was thinking of any of them.

Mackenzie leaned on Kevin's arm possessively. "Because of the way Kev feels about me."

To steal a phrase from Mackenzie: The. Fuck.

"Holy cow balls, you guys!" Neela cried. She tossed Persey's blood-stained T-shirt aside in disgust. "Are you seriously arguing over a guy? Right now?"

Wes snorted. "I'm with the lesbian. This is ridiculous."

"I don't see how my sexuality has anything to do with it." Righteous indignation had calmed Neela down. "But I have to agree. Arlo is dead. *Dead* dead. Like really completely dead with her gore dripping down between the cracks of this wholly nonsensical floor and in no way can that be explained by special effects. It has been approximately three minutes since her headless body crash-landed and we're still here. No one's come to get us. No authorities. No EMTs. Has anyone else wondered why?"

"Ambulance response time from the nearest medical facility would be approximately twelve minutes," Shaun-bot said. How he knew, off the top of his head, where the nearest medical facility was located boggled the mind. "Though an Escape-Capades representative should have been in contact by now."

"Maybe no one's coming," Persey said. "Maybe we're on our own?" *No "maybe" about it.*

"Leah did say that once the competition began, she'd be unable to stop it," Wes said.

"Yeah, but I thought that meant, like, if we got stuck or something. Not . . ." Kevin winced as if in pain. "Not because somebody freaking died."

Persey remembered Leah's words only too well. They'd felt ominous at the time, but Persey had no idea how prescient that feeling would be. She didn't believe for a second that any of this was an accident. B.J. had been murdered, and Arlo's death conveniently came after she freaked out at Leah. Persey was sure that both deaths had been intentional, and she didn't want to wait around to be proven right by a third. "We need to get out of here. Now."

"Agreed," Riot said. "If no one's coming to get us, we need to find our own way out."

Shaun arched an eyebrow. "Isn't that the point of an escape room competition?"

"Screw the competition!" Riot threw his head back, exasperated. "I don't give a shit who wins this thing anymore. Do you?"

Shaun shrugged. "We all knew the risks."

"Knew the risks?" Persey said. The android had no soul. "We didn't enter a guillotine-dodging competition. We shouldn't have to worry about getting decapitated."

Neela, visibly weary of all the bickering and wisecracks, plopped down onto the floor, hugging her knees to her chest. "I want to go home."

Even though she was two years older than Persey, Neela seemed younger. Maybe because she was so enthusiastic about life and its possibilities— hope and joy hadn't been beaten out of her yet by the cruelty of the world—and Persey instantly wanted to make her feel like everything was going to be okay. Even if it wasn't.

"Hey," she said, crouching beside Neela. "You're going to get out of here, okay?"

"Of course she is." Kevin sat down cross-legged on the floor beside her. "We'll just wait here until the clock runs out. Then someone will have to show up."

"Clock?" Persey asked. She hadn't seen a countdown since they were upstairs.

"Yep." Kevin nodded and pointed to the back wall.

Persey turned and saw the red digital numbers on the wall, set for thirty minutes again. It hadn't been there before, and even weirder, it hadn't started moving yet.

"That's your plan?" Riot asked, jumping down from the altar. The floor rebounded from the force of his body mass. "Sit here and wait?"

"That's my plan," Kevin said.

"Wait for what, exactly?"

"Police?"

"Maybe they can't get to us," Mackenzie suggested. "Maybe, wherever we are, the doors won't open unless we do it ourselves."

"Do it ourselves?" Neela's voice went up almost a full octave as she spoke as her panic re-escalated. "We can't keep going. What if there's another accident? Or . . . or . . ." She swallowed, unwilling to finish the thought, but Persey knew exactly what she was going to say.

"Or what if it wasn't an accident?"

"The. Fuck," Mackenzie said, throwing her arms up. "This again?"

"Like I said, I'm not going anywhere until we get some answers." Kevin's carefree grin seemed out of place in the blood-splattered Cavethedral. "Whether that clock starts or not."

A loud buzzer tore through the room the instant Kevin stopped talking.

The countdown had begun.

TWENTY-SIX

PERSEY JUMPED AT THE BUZZER, GASPING IN SURPRISE. Someone *was* watching, cuing off of Kevin's words for dramatic effect. Why hadn't they called the police?

"Thirty minutes," Wes said, as if anyone needed to be told. "Now what?"

No one answered. In fact, no one moved. Unlike previous buzzers that had kicked off a flurry of motion and energy as the contestants began their search for clues, this time no one seemed to know what to do.

Persey didn't blame them. She didn't know what she was supposed to believe anymore. Her eyes trailed to Arlo's crumpled corpse. Somewhere, she had friends, a family. Her brother who went to Notre Dame . . . What was his name? Atticus. Persey imagined he would be devastated when he learned Arlo was dead. Heartbroken by the loss of his sister.

I wonder what that's like?

Riot approached Persey, touching her back lightly with his fingertips. "I'm sure she didn't feel anything."

I'm sure.

"You okay?"

Persey peeled her eyes away from the body. "I didn't like her, but I didn't want her dead."

"Not your fault!" Kevin called up from the floor. He'd leaned back on his elbows and stretched out his legs before him.

Isn't it?

Riot glared at Kevin. "Maybe if you'd listened to Persey about that Boyz Distrikt singer, we'd all be outside right now."

"Maybe if you two stopped flirting," Kevin countered, "I wouldn't feel like barfing right now."

"Us? Are you kidding?" Riot laughed. "You and that prep school groupie have been practically dry-humping since you met!"

Kevin wouldn't be derailed. "And your eyes have barely left Persey's face."

Once again, Persey felt the heat rising up from her neck. She spun away from Riot, picked up her bloodstained T-shirt that Neela had discarded, and gently draped it over Arlo's remains, obscuring the gaping neck hole from view. She hadn't been a very nice person, or even a very good person, and there had been no love lost between them, but Arlo didn't deserve this. None of the contestants did. And Persey wanted to make sure that no one else shared Arlo's fate.

"Sit there if you want," she said, without looking at Kevin. "I'm going to try to find a way out."

"Excellent!" Riot dashed across the room, mounting the steps to the altar in one leap. He hoisted himself back up onto the marble slab and stood facing the crucifix, examining the engraving Neela had spotted on her way down the pole. "*Exurge Domine et judica causam tuam*," he read.

Riot's energy spurred everyone else into motion. "'Arise, O Lord, and judge your cause,'" Shaun translated. "The motto of the Spanish Inquisition."

"I knew it," Neela said under her breath.

Riot continued to read. "Then in the middle, it says Psalm

Seventy-Three. Any chance you know that one, Shaun-bot?"

"One of the Wisdom Psalms, also known as the Psalms of Asaph." Shaun cleared his throat, eager to show off. If he'd felt any fear or remorse in the face of Arlo's death, it had quickly been forgotten. "'Therefore pride is their necklace; they clothe themselves with violence. From their callous hearts comes iniquity, their evil imaginations have no limits.'"

"I really shouldn't be surprised that Shaun-bot can quote the Bible," Kevin said, "but somehow I am."

"Bible cryptography, also known as a Bible cipher, is one of the earliest known means of encoded messaging in the Western world." Shaun sounded even more like a computer reading an encyclopedia entry out loud. "It's relatively common for cryptographers to have more than a working knowledge of its verses."

Wes clapped him on the shoulder. A weirdly intimate gesture from the guy who had treated them all like enemies from the beginning. "I knew your Catholic schooling would come in handy."

"Don't touch me," Shaun said coldly.

"I didn't know you were into Bible code," Riot said, nodding his head as if discovering a newfound appreciation for the Shaun-bot. "Did you know the King James version predicted the 1906 San Francisco earthquake?"

"Bible *cipher*," Shaun sighed wearily. "Bible *code* is for charlatans and idiots. There are no scientific facts to back up a single fake prediction."

"Yeah, that's what they want you to think."

A distant rumbling interrupted the conversation. It sounded like thunder, and Persey could feel the reverberations beneath her feet. "Is there a storm outside?"

"No," Neela said. She pressed her palms flat against the floor. "That's coming from below us."

Kevin gasped in mock fear. "The call! It's coming from inside the house!"

"I don't feel anything," Mackenzie said, unprompted.

"It's true," Wes said. "She really doesn't."

Persey was amazed by how easily distracted they all were. "The floor is shaking. Can you feel that?"

"Probably just the construction," Kevin said. "I doubt these wooden slabs are very thick. Maybe they're mounted on scaffolding or something. That would explain . . ." He swung his arms forward, launching his butt and legs off the floor for a moment. When he landed, the floor jiggled. "The bouncy room."

"Seems safe," Wes said, sarcasm dripping from each word.

"One more reason to get the fuck out of here," Riot said. "Anything else in that psalm that might help us?"

"Let me think." Shaun placed a hand over his eyes, while he accessed his memory banks.

Persey wasn't Catholic, hadn't gone to Catholic school, so as she watched Shaun silently mouth the verses of the psalm, she was amazed by its length. The Bible must be wordy.

"'Those who are far from you will perish,'" Shaun said at last. "'You will destroy all who are unfaithful to you. But as for me it is good to be near God. I have made the Sovereign Lord my refuge; I will tell of all your deeds.'"

Mackenzie stared at Shaun as if he'd just spoken one of the many languages she didn't know. "How does that help us?"

"That's the ending," Shaun said, dropping his hand from his eyes. "It's the crux of the verse."

"Destroy all who are unfaithful?" Neela hugged her knees tighter to her chest. "What the Helvetica does that mean?"

Persey wasn't really sure, but she didn't like it.

"Is it getting hot in here, or is it just me?" Wes asked, unbuttoning his flannel shirt.

As much as Persey wanted to disagree with just about everything Wes had to say, as she sat beside Neela, she felt sweat on the back of her neck, and her palms were damp. She swept her hand across the floor, and when it passed over one of the seams between the wooden "stones," she felt a jet of hot air against her palm.

"It's hot," she said, scrambling to her feet.

One by one, each of her fellow contestants dropped to the ground, testing the temperature of the air wafting up between the floorboards.

"Well, that's not good," Kevin said.

Shaun also tested the stone walls, pressing his palms against it in several different places. "Walls are still cool. Heat must be coming from below."

"From hell," Mackenzie said.

"You're not wrong." Riot, from his position on top of the altar, was staring at something in the back of the Cavethedral, eyes so wide Persey could see the torch flames dancing in them. Emblazoned on the stone wall, as if it had been carved in flames, were two lines of verse.

"'What a day for an auto-da-fé,'" Persey read.

"That's from *Candide*!" Mackenzie squealed, showing a disturbing amount of levity considering the decapitated body oozing gore just a few feet from her. "I sing 'Glitter and Be Gay' at auditions all the time."

Persey ignored her. "What's an auto-da-fé?"

"An act of faith," Riot said, his voice suddenly hoarse.

"During the Spanish and Portuguese Inquisitions, that usually meant a public execution . . ." Shaun said. A tremor had crept into his monotone.

Persey didn't like the sound of this. "Executed how?"

"By burning."

As soon as he said the words, Persey felt the entire floor shake beneath her. This time, there was no mistaking the jolt. Was it an earthquake? Those didn't happen much in Las Vegas. She crouched, lowering her center of gravity to keep her balance, and just as she was about to make a break for the wall and press herself against it, one of the floor sections dropped away.

"Holy shit!" Wes cried. He was nearest to the newly formed hole and scrambled away from it. Almost immediately, another section at the opposite side of the room also dislodged from the floor, opening a gaping wound in the ground. Then another. Another. Persey watched in horror as a dozen of the huge wooden slabs disappeared into the darkness below the room.

Except it wasn't really darkness that swallowed the missing floor-boards. The new gaps in the floor flooded the Cavethedral with an orangey-yellow light emanating from below. The peppered, hickory scent of a campfire wafted upward along with choking black smoke. There was a fire raging beneath their feet.

Persey leaned tentatively over the nearest hole, trying to get a look at what was down there. Heat seared her face as scorching air rushed upward, but in the split second before Persey had to pull away, she saw what appeared to be an industrial furnace with the top removed. The flames were fed by the wood from the floor that had already dropped away.

"Auto-da-fé," Persey said, her voice hardly above a whisper. Death by burning. *This can't be happening.*

"Nobody move!" Kevin cried. He was on his feet now, crouching to maintain his balance.

"Just stand by and wait to be dropped down there?" Wes said. "No thanks." He was about to step toward the wall when the wooden platform beside him, the one he was nanoseconds away from shifting his weight onto, released and fell away.

"Or not," Kevin said.

Persey, meanwhile, couldn't move if she wanted to. She was petrified.

"How did they work?" Persey said, forcing her brain to function even if her body wouldn't. "These auto-da-fé things?"

"They lit you on fire," Mackenzie replied. She was scared, but not too scared for a dig. "What's there to know?"

"Like, the process." *Smartass.* "It might give us a clue as to what we're supposed to do."

"It was a public ritual," Shaun said. His voice quivered, his eyes locked onto the empty hole in the ground beside him. Shaun-bot might have been terrified, but thankfully he could still access his memory banks. "The accused would be paraded through a public square, their crimes of heresy, usually confessed under torture, would be read out loud, and then the guilty would be executed."

Shit. Well, they couldn't parade around the room with half the floor gone, and the execution part was something Persey was hoping to avoid, so that left only one thing.

"Confession."

"Good call," Riot said. "But confess what?"

Persey wasn't sure, but there was only one place to start. "I cheated on a test," she said, her voice clear and strong. "The entry exam for a private school. It was my dad's idea, to make sure I got in, but I went along with it."

There was a pause while Persey's confession hung in the air. She held her breath, hoping that was the worst thing she'd have to confess that day; then with a metallic creaking from whatever mechanical contraption controlled the floor slabs, the nearest wooden section slid toward her, stopping flush against the one she was balanced on.

Mackenzie stared at the fake stone as if it was possessed. "The. Fuck."

"Step on it," Shaun said. "See if it will hold your weight."

Kevin snorted. "What if it plummets into the inferno?"

"Then we'll know it doesn't."

Gee, thanks.

Kevin laughed. "You step on it."

"If I was close enough to jump without the risk of falling, I would consider it." His words were confident, but Shaun's voice sounded strange, like his tongue wasn't working correctly. He lisped his *s*'s and his pronunciation was indistinct.

"Are you okay?" Neela asked.

"Fine." Shaun sounded like he had a mouthful of cotton balls. "I highly doubt the platform would have moved if it wasn't meant to be used." At least that's what Persey thought he said. He was getting difficult to understand.

Maybe that's how androids react to fear? Mush mouth.

Regardless, Shaun had a point, though Persey didn't relish the idea of testing his theory with her life. As she stared at the wooden disc painted to look like a stone paver, another piece of the floor gave way, crashing to the inferno below. This time it was right behind Persey, and the roar of the fire as it consumed more food made her mind up for her. She took a deep breath and leaped onto the new platform.

"Be careful!" Neela cried.

The stone wiggled a little, bouncing with the force of her arrival in the same way the entire floor had jolted when Persey landed at the bottom of the fire pole, but it felt steady. Firm.

"I'm okay!" she said, surprised. She looked around and saw that there were two platforms within jumping distance of her own: one toward the altar, the other toward an empty wall. The choice was easy.

"I'm going to try to make it to the altar," she said, pointing toward it. "The exit's got to be up—"

But whoever was controlling the room wasn't about to make it that easy. Before Persey even finished speaking, both of the platforms within leaping distance shuddered, dropped a few inches, then crashed down into the fire.

So much for that.

"Confess something else," Kevin suggested. He was the closest to the altar but hadn't attempted to jump onto it. "See if another one moves."

Easy for you to say. "I'm glad you think I have so many sins at my disposal," she said, glaring at him.

Mackenzie rolled her eyes. "Little Miss Perfect doesn't do anything wrong, huh? Except she's a cheater. I bet that's how you passed the Hidden Library."

"Is it possible to cheat on an escape room?" Kevin asked, head tilted to the side.

Mackenzie smiled at him wickedly. "Ab-so-fucking-lute-ly."

"Perhaps . . ." Neela started tentatively. "Perhaps if you had something, um, bigger."

"What do you mean?" Persey asked.

"Well, if cheating on a test moved one platform, maybe a bigger confession would move more of them?"

"Don't say anything else," Riot said, holding up his hands as if to prevent Persey from making any further confessions. "I'll do it."

He was trying to protect her, which was sweet. But Persey felt a sense of responsibility for this mess, for not being strong enough to stand her ground in Boyz Distrikt after she found B.J.'s body. If she'd let the clock drop to zero, Arlo might still be alive. She'd let herself be persuaded away from doing what she knew was the right thing, and now it was her job to fix it.

Persey squared her shoulders, faced the altar, and thought of the actual worst thing she'd ever done.

"Wait!" Riot cried. But Persey ignored him.

"I told my father I hated him and wanted him dead," she said in a strong clear voice. "And I meant it." *So much.*

This time there was no hesitation. Four slabs slid into place, creating a straight line from Persey to the altar.

TWENTY-SEVEN

"HONEY, WE'RE NOT ATTACKING YOU. I DON'T WANT YOU TO feel attacked."

Persey's mom held a stemmed, half-full glass of chardonnay, which she brought to her lips between the sentences. Maybe she was hoping her husband would pick up the thread and save her the effort of having to voice the second one, or maybe she needed the liquid courage to so openly defy him. Because saying "I don't want you to feel attacked" when Persey was having a come-to-Jesus conversation with her dad was sort of like telling a postal service employee that you don't want them to feel wet while they're delivering your mail in the middle of a rainstorm. It doesn't matter what *you* want: someone's getting drenched to the bone.

Which is what every conversation with her dad had been like lately. This was just more of the same, but Persey's mom was trying her best to play mediator between the two parties, even if she was probably (definitely) too drunk to be of any significant help.

She wanted to say all of this, or at least half of it, but if there was one thing Persey had learned in her sixteen years in this family, it was that when her dad was on a tirade, he didn't expect her to respond. Doing so only made it worse.

Instead, she kept her head down, mouth shut, and waited for the storm to pass.

"Why shouldn't she feel like she's being attacked, huh?" He paced back and forth between the kitchen island and the family room, arms gesticulating like an octopus mid-swim, literally unable to keep still. "Nothing else has worked to motivate her. Maybe *your daughter* needs a little attacking."

It was always "our son" but "your daughter" when he was talking to his wife. As if their children were fathered by different men.

We weren't.

"Sweetie," her mom drawled, reaching out to her husband as he approached the sofa. It sounded more like "Shweetie" due to the constant stream of chardonnay, which she'd just refilled from a bottle in a cooler sleeve on the coffee table. "Please, don't."

Persey cringed. She appreciated her mom's well-meaning intervention and realized it came from a place of real, though weak, kindness, but telling her dad what he could and couldn't do was a losing tactic.

"Don't what?" he roared. "Parent?"

Her mom took a slow sip and remained calm. "Sweetie, it's not like you haven't tried this before. I'm pretty sure we've all heard this conversation."

Only like a million and one times.

"Well, your daughter clearly isn't listening. Have you seen her grades?"

Three Bs, a B-minus, and a C. If her dad had spent even twenty seconds processing her grades in reference to what they were versus what he expected of her, he'd have realized that this was a huge improvement over her progress report a few months ago. Only algebra continued to thwart her. An engaged parent would have been encouraging. But Persey's dad just used grades as an excuse to remind her what a disappointment she was. A loser. Worthless.

"Why can't you be more like your brother?"

Persey let out a long, slow breath. It always came down to this.

Her dad stared out the kitchen window, the sharp, hard lines of his face softening as he thought longingly of his firstborn. "He understood the importance of grades, of what it meant to his future. Of what it meant to his parents. Of what he owed them."

Owed them? What her brother owed them was about a hundred grand so far in legal fees and spending money, all of which they'd handed over willingly, and that didn't even include what he'd stolen. One hundred thousand dollars. And counting. Which would have been fine, Persey was pretty sure, except her parents were heavily invested in a new project at work, so cash flow had been tight. Even her dad, who usually did whatever his son asked without question, had looked strained during their last call. Worried (disillusioned). Pinched.

Her brother was spending all that money wandering around Southeast Asia. On Daddy's dime. The official line Persey's parents used for their friends was that he was taking a gap year to explore and improve the world around him before returning to college. No mention of the police investigation at Columbia. No mention of the missing girl. The reports of violence. The civil lawsuit. It didn't matter that her brother was probably a sociopath. It only mattered that he'd gotten straight A's at Allen and gone to an Ivy League college.

Her dad's priorities were so fucked up.

"These grades are worthless," he was saying, pointing at his open laptop screen. "How is she possibly going to go to college with these?"

"I'm not going to college."

The words dropped like an A-bomb. There was a moment of silence, the instant of detonation when she thought maybe the fuse was a dud, the bomb was impotent, the words hadn't actually come out of her mouth.

Then the flash of light as a nuclear reaction was ignited, followed by the mushroom cloud of her dad's fury, billowing upward.

Her mom sucked in a sharp breath, understanding even in the dizzying haze of her alcohol that Persey had just started a war.

"WHAT?" Her dad's face was tomato red. Already.

"I'm not going to college."

"Who told you that was an option?"

If her dad had spent five minutes talking *to* her instead of *at* her, he'd know that she already had a plan post–high school. It just wasn't the plan he wanted.

"You're not pretty enough to find a rich husband if that's what you're thinking."

"What? No."

"You're not smart or charming, so the only thing you have to lure a decent man is my money. And don't think for one second that you're going to get your hands on it."

Money? He thought she gave two shits about his *money*? Years of neglect and emotional abuse, of being cut off from kindness, isolated from any expression of love . . . She'd have given up the money, the house, the private drivers and fancy cars for one heartfelt hug from her father, and instead, he accused her of being a money-grubbing parasite.

I hate you so much.

"So what do you expect to do with yourself, huh?"

I hate you.

"Live here?"

I wish you were dead.

"And freeload off me?"

"It's working for *your son*."

This time it was Persey who sucked in a breath. Had she really just said that out loud? Her self-control, usually so strong and well-honed when it came to dealing with her dad, had slipped.

"You're done!" he roared. "Do you hear me? The second you graduate from high school you are out of this house and dead to us, do you understand?"

"Sweetie, please." Her mom's protest was feeble, but at least it was a protest. "That's not fair."

"Oh, it's more than fair. She's lucky I'm not charging her rent now."

"But . . ."

"Don't defend her. You women are always defending each other."

"I never did that well in school," her mom continued, "and look where I am now!"

Her dad's laugh was biting and harsh. "Yeah, married to me."

"But she's *trying*," her mom pressed, undeterred. It was the most vehement she'd seen her mom in years. "She studies all the time. Tests just aren't as easy for her as they are for her brother." Actual tears from her mom now as she struggled to her feet, though she still didn't stray far from her wine bottle.

Persey's dad ignored his wife's emotional display, whirling on his daughter with an accusatory index finger. "If you don't go to college, you are cut off the moment you get your high school diploma. No money. No cell phone. No cushy bedroom. And most importantly, no inheritance. Understand? As of that day, you are dead to us."

Persey could have cried, begged, asked for a chance to prove herself after high school, but she knew such protestations would fall on deaf ears. Her father's rage and misogyny needed an outlet, and she was it. Though she had no idea where she'd go or what she'd do, Persey accepted her fate as an accomplished fact. There would be no reprieve.

Without another word, she trudged to her bedroom. Her mom was weeping, her dad already on the phone with his lawyer explaining that he and his wife were planning to change their will.

She was about to be an orphan.

TWENTY-EIGHT

HER FIRST FEW STEPS WERE SHAKY: PERSEY COULD FEEL HER knees wobbling as she tentatively moved from stone to stone, expecting at any moment to feel the ground drop out beneath her and to plummet to a hideous, fiery end. But the platforms held—springy with her shifting weight, but firm—and soon she moved with more confidence, her stomach less fluttery, her panic less palpable.

But she still let out a huge sigh of relief when her foot met the solid stone slab on which the altar stood. As soon as she landed, the path she'd been on shifted out of place to ensure that no one else had direct access to the altar.

"The. Fuck," Mackenzie said. Only, her voice contained less of a sneer than usual. "It worked."

Kevin clapped his hands and jumped up and down on his slab, tempting fate. "Okay, everybody! Start your confessions!"

"When I was seven, I broke three of my nani's Hummels," Neela began without hesitation. "And blamed my little brother for it."

A platform groaned across the gap and tapped against hers.

"And I lied to my parents about why I was coming to Vegas this weekend," she continued quickly, only she dropped her voice this time, as if afraid her parents might hear her. From Philadelphia. "I told them I was at a leadership conference."

Two more sections of wood slid in front of the first, giving Neela a clear shot to the altar. She quickly scrambled across them, landing beside Persey. She smiled, then threw her hands around Persey, hugging her tight. "We made it."

Persey wished she could feel as much relief. They'd made it to the altar, but as she coughed on the smoke that was rapidly filling the Cavethedral, she wasn't yet convinced that they were safe.

Another piece of the floor fell away, this one just behind Wes. He flinched as smoke wafted up from the new opening. "That's what counts as a confession around here?"

Neela looked hurt. "Placing blame on an innocent party, even for something as seemingly innocuous as a broken collectible figurine, is a heinous crime."

"Don't listen to him," Persey said. She wanted to make Neela feel more comfortable with her confession. "You don't really want to be the worst person in *this* room."

Meanwhile, Riot was staring up the fire pole to where the trapdoor still gaped open in the ceiling of the Cavethedral. "I bet I could shinny up the pole," he said, reaching across Arlo's covered corpse to try to reach it. Persey's discarded T-shirt was now completely soaked in blood. "Maybe backtrack from there to the library where we started and—"

The section of the floor that anchored the fire pole shuddered. Riot leaped back just in time: the platform he'd been standing on collapsed into the furnace, taking 80 percent of Arlo Wu, the pole, and Riot's escape plan with it.

"Or maybe not," he said.

"Just confess something, dude!" Kevin said. "I'm sure you got some deep, dark librarian secrets lying around."

"Funny."

As they continued to bicker, Neela was kneading her hands together, her mood darkening by the second. "I'm sorry about your dad."

"Hm?"

"That you hated him, I mean. Have you two made up?"

Persey had to fight to keep from laughing. The idea that she and her dad could have any sort of reconciliation was ridiculous. "No."

"Do you think you ever will?"

The urge to laugh vanished, replaced by a dull ache in the pit of Persey's stomach. "He's dead."

"Oh." Neela paused. "Oh, I get it. So telling your dad that you wanted him dead . . . before he died . . . that was the worst thing you've ever done?"

It was. "Yeah."

Two dull crashes from behind signaled that more of the floor was disappearing, a reminder of the excruciating demise that might await them if they didn't find the escape mechanism for this room. But instead of jumping into action, Neela merely stared off into the distance while she chewed at her upper lip.

"Because mine wasn't," Neela said at last. "I mean, it *was* the worst thing I've done consciously, so maybe that's what the litmus is for this test, but I still can't help feeling like I should have confessed that other thing."

Other thing . . . "You didn't do this other thing consciously?"

"I know that sounds like a total cop-out, but it's true. I was just solving a puzzle, you know? Or so I thought. I didn't know it would be—"

"Hey!" Kevin called out from his platform. "What are you two whispering about? Secret plots to win the game?" He was joking (accusing), and though Kevin was the closest to the altar, Persey doubted he could have actually overheard their conversation.

"We're just wondering why the hell we're the only ones with big enough balls to make a confession," she said, not about to give up Neela's confidence.

"Fine!" Wes stood up, hands on hips. "I'll whip it out."

Mackenzie grimaced. "Please don't."

"I stole a Snickers bar from the drugstore when I was twelve. Happy?"

"Seriously?" Persey had grown up rich herself, and while she would have turned in all of her family's wealth to have had a happier home life, she certainly never felt the need to steal anything. Especially a candy bar. "Boarding school kid can't afford a Snickers?"

"What?" Wes shrugged. "I was hungry."

"And you didn't have, like, a buck fifty to your name?"

"Oh, honey," Mackenzie said, simultaneously condescending and commiserating, "rich people don't carry cash."

That's not true.

"Hey," Wes said, scanning the room. "Why isn't the floor moving? I made my confession."

There was a groaning noise, and for a half a second, Persey thought this lame confession might actually have worked, but instead of moving toward him, another piece of the floor near Wes broke away and tumbled into the inferno.

"Your confession sucked, dude," Kevin said.

Wes pointed at Neela. "It was as good as hers."

"Different strokes for different folks." Then Kevin turned toward the altar and pressed the palms of his hands together as if he was praying. "When I was in college, I accidentally killed someone."

Accidentally?

Two sections of wood immediately created an easy pathway for him, and as Kevin gingerly picked his way toward them, Persey desperately wished he'd elaborate about what happened. Only, she didn't want to ask. And he clearly didn't want to share.

"How do you accidentally kill someone?" Wes asked, voicing the question in Persey's head. Well, one of them.

"I believe that is referred to as involuntary manslaughter," Neela said, shaking off her reflectiveness from moments ago, "and carries a federal sentencing guideline of ten to sixteen months."

Kevin flashed her a double thumbs-up as he stepped up to the altar. "Good to know."

"Twenty minutes."

Right. They weren't out of the woods yet. "The platforms led us to the altar for a reason," Persey said, arguing out loud. "So the exit must be here."

Neela rounded the sold marble slab. "These engravings are so weird. Intricate patterns, but none of them match up."

"The markings don't make sense!" Riot called out. He still hadn't made a move toward confessing, which made Persey wonder what he, and everyone else, was waiting for. "But maybe it's a code?"

A code. They might need their resident cryptographer for that. "Shaun! We need you over here."

"Yeah, Shaun-bot," Kevin added. "Let's hear that confession!"

Shaun stood near the wall, staring away from Persey toward the auto-da-fé quote, and made no effort to respond. He didn't even flinch as a nearby piece of the floor between himself and Mackenzie fell away.

"This isn't fair!" Mackenzie said, watching the flames shoot up through the now-open hole behind her. The platform on which she stood only had one intact piece of adjacent flooring, and Persey wondered if the imminent danger would inspire enough introspection (maybe) and humility (no way) for Mackenzie to be able to confess her greatest sins. "I've got nothing to confess because I've never done anything wrong!"

Ego: one. Introspection and humility: zero.

"What good are you, then?" Kevin teased.

None.

"I don't think this is a code per se." Neela had climbed on top of the altar, perched at one corner so she could get a good look at the entire top. "It's . . . I think . . ." She was lost for words, not from fear but from excitement. Her entire face glowed, her smile extending from ear to ear. "This entire altar is a himitsu-bako."

Kevin blinked. "A whatid what what?"

"A puzzle box!"

"A whatiddy what what?" Kevin repeated.

"Why are you here?" Wes asked, stepping onto the altar. Persey flinched. How had he made it over? She hadn't even heard what his confession had been.

"A puzzle box," Neela explained, "is a construction of hidden levers, releases, and, occasionally, booby traps that require external manipulation of certain elements in a specific sequence in order to open a secret compartment. In this case, I believe the exit to this room is through the altar."

"Down through the altar?" Kevin peered over the side of the platform into the raging inferno beneath them. "That seems like the opposite direction we want to go."

Persey didn't disagree, but since Neela offered the first glimpse of an escape from the Cavethedral, she had to hope that the exit was a safe one. "What do we do?"

Neela held up her hand, eyes wide and fixed on the top of the altar. "Give me one minute."

"Okay," Kevin said. "But we've only got eighteen left."

Two more sections of the floor crashed into the inferno. There was so little of it left that Shaun, Mackenzie, and Riot looked like they were completely surrounded by smoke and flames, leaving Persey to wonder if there were even enough slabs left to escort them to the altar. The roar of the inferno reverberated through the stone-lined room, and the air was thick, ash whizzing around in the updrafts. It was getting difficult to breathe, and though the clock said they had eighteen minutes left, Persey wasn't sure her lungs would last that long.

She cupped her hands around her mouth and shouted at the three stragglers. "Hurry up!" There was no doubt in her mind that a fall into those flames would actually be lethal. That furnace was no fake.

Mackenzie, despite her earlier insistences, appeared to agree. "I cheated." Her voice cut through the roar of the fire. "On . . . on something big." She paused, and Persey watched her carefully. Mackenzie bit her lower lip, sucking in a spot just inside her mouth as she appeared to wrestle with a decision. Stalling, perhaps, to see if what she'd admitted so far was enough. It wasn't.

She doesn't want to tell us what she cheated on.

"It was a contest," Mackenzie continued, somewhat reluctantly. "And a friend of mine knew part of its secret."

Still no movement. It was as if the controller knew that Mackenzie was holding something back.

"And the fucked-up part is that I didn't need the prize money. I just wanted to win."

That was the final piece of her puzzle. Quickly, a series of stones zig-zagged into place, offering Mackenzie a route to the altar.

"And I stole something," Riot said. His shoulders sagged in resignation. "Not a lame-ass candy bar. But something big. Like corporate-espionage style."

Kevin tilted his head to the side. "I thought he said he was a librarian?" *He did.*

Riot waited a moment, hoping that would be enough, but when the stones didn't move, he continued. "And I used that information to fuck some shit up royally. People . . . got hurt."

Again, the controller seemed satisfied with the level of vagueness, and Riot made his way across the room.

Meanwhile, Mackenzie had pushed herself up on the altar beside Neela, who was still perusing the intricate altar top. Patterns were striped across the slab in rows—one checkered like a chessboard, one a mess of swirls, another looked like vines—and split down the middle so that each row had two adjacent pattern mixes. They extended over the edge and down the side of the altar as well, making the whole giant tomb-like slab a garbled mess of lines and shapes. It was as if someone had tiled a bathroom shower pulling tiles blindly from a grab bag.

"I've got this," Mackenzie said, elbowing Neela out of the way. Kind of ballsy for someone who had judged Persey for being a cheater before admitting to the same. "You can get down and—"

"Got it!" Neela cried.

Persey rushed to her side as Riot picked his way toward them. "You do?"

"You do?" Mackenzie echoed.

Neela traced a pattern across the altar top with her index finger. "It's like the scrambled image puzzle from the Hidden Library, but instead of creating a picture from mixed-up tiles, we need to move sections of the altar itself. See this pattern along the right edge?" She pointed to a part of the marble slab with a fleur-de-lis pattern, then drew Persey's eye to the perpendicular part of the altar below it. "It doesn't match up with this one. Same on the other side. And if you look at the entire top portion of the altar, you might notice that there are six distinct patterns in play."

Persey scanned the altar from end to end. The seemingly random placement of tiles suddenly seemed to arrange themselves before her eyes. "Like that Megaminx puzzle!"

"Kinda. Only . . . bigger. And without a central pivot access."

"What do we do?" Riot asked. Tweed vest discarded, he'd rolled up the sleeves of his shirt, ready to work.

Neela slid off the corner of the altar and placed her hands on the edge. "Help me push?"

Riot scrambled to her side, and on Neela's cue, the two of them leaned into the altar, using strength and body weight against the seemingly solid slab of marble.

"That's ridiculous," Mackenzie said. "You can't possibly move that thing. It's gotta weigh two—"

Her thought was interrupted by a mechanical click as altar they were pushing against gave way, shifting so that an entire foot of that row hung off the altar on the opposite side.

"—tons." Mackenzie looked and sounded deflated as she finished her sentence.

The right side of Neela's mouth twitched into a half smile as she quickly pointed to Persey and Kevin on the opposite side of the altar. "You guys, same thing."

Without a word, they both fell against the other side, pushing the tiled row. Just as before, with a heavy click, the vibrations of which Persey could feel radiating up her arms, the section of tile moved.

For the next few minutes, Neela directed traffic, shouting to be heard over the roaring inferno as she scurried around the dais. A push here, a pull, twist, and pivot there—portions of the marble altar top slid around in a seeming progression. It was tough work, and everyone had a thin sheen of sweat coating their faces while the clock continued its relentless countdown. Persey knew she had to trust Neela—no one else had a clue about what to do with that puzzle—but as she eyed the clock through the smoke-filled Cavethedral, she wondered what would happen if they ran out of time.

As much as she wanted to end this competition, a fiery end wouldn't save anyone.

More pieces of the altar were shifted out of place, and it became clear that, far from being a solid piece, the altar was actually a wood-and-metal frame over which two-inch-thick strips of marble had been laid. An intricate pattern of springs and hinges allowed some portions to swing from horizontal to vertical, while other sections of the slab were released by a mechanical infrastructure after a pattern of shifts.

The whole thing kind of boggled Persey's mind. As successful as she had been so far in identifying challenges and piecing together solutions, the three-dimensional vision needed for a spatial puzzle of this kind was a little beyond her.

Neela, on the other hand, was in her element. Her decisions were swift, and her orders concise and to the point—a far cry from the verbose nervous word vomit with which she usually communicated—and after just a few minutes, they'd managed to get all the pieces into place. Or at least Neela seemed to think so. Aside from the new arrangement of patterns and the cool breeze of air she could feel wafting up through the gaps in the marble, Persey couldn't tell if they were succeeding or not.

"This should be it," Neela said, her ear pressed to one side of the altar. Everyone was lined up beside her, ready to put their shoulders against the lid. "I'm pretty sure that last click released the entire top of this thing."

Wes eyed the countdown clock, which had just passed the ten-minute mark. "You'd better hope so. If you're wrong, we're not going to have much time to try again."

"I'm not wrong." Persey loved Neela's confidence. "Everyone ready?"

A round of grunts signified assents, and Persey hoped, for everyone's sakes, that this worked.

"On three, then," Neela said. "One. Two."

They heaved simultaneously. Persey felt, rather than heard, a groan as if something ancient and rusted and barely functional inside the altar gave way. Then, without warning, the individual strips of the altar lid broke apart, one by one careening forward and toppling onto the dais.

The puzzle box was open.

TWENTY-NINE

"YOU DID IT!" PERSEY CRIED, DUST RISING FROM THE INTERIOR of the altar as the marble strips crashed to a stop.

"We did it." Neela paused, peering into the hollow altar. "But what did we do?"

Persey joined her at the lip of the now-topless altar. The interior appeared to be some kind of a chute angling away from the altar, but beyond that, she couldn't see.

"Are we supposed to slide down that thing?" Mackenzie asked.

Kevin whistled. "That didn't work out so well for Arlo."

Wes coughed, choking on the oppressive smoke that was filling the room. "We can't stay here."

"Okay, okay," Kevin said, grinning ear to ear. "Don't lose your head."

Neela gasped. "Oh, Kevin."

"Too soon?"

Persey wrinkled her upper lip. "It will *always* be too soon."

The platform the altar was on sat shuddered, a warning that it too might drop at any moment. Would it hold until all seven of them made it down the chute?

Seven . . .

Persey spun around, making a quick head count. *One, two, three, four, five, six . . .* "Where's Shaun?"

Everyone turned toward the back of the Cavethedral. Standing on his isolated platform halfway across the room, Shaun was angled away from them. His body appeared even more rigid and unmoving than usual, so utterly lifeless that for a moment Persey wondered if he'd had a heart attack. But then, he would have crumpled to the ground.

"Shaun-bot!" Kevin cried, waving his arms over his head to try to get Shaun's attention even though they could only see his profile. "Dude, you've got to get out of there."

No response.

"Confess something!" Neela shouted. "Anything."

"He's in a fear coma," Wes said.

"Shock, more likely." Riot cupped his hand around his mouth. "Shaun! Hey, *Shaun*!"

Still nothing.

If the stinging smoke, crackling flames, and fear of death by immolation weren't enough to jar him out of his state of shock, Persey seriously doubted that shouting his name would do the trick. They needed something else to get his attention. There was actually a path of intact platforms—some of the last in the room—that led to within arm's reach of him, but the nearest platform to the altar was ten feet away. Too far to jump and risk falling. If only they could get to it, they might have a chance to reach Shaun.

Persey's eyes fell onto a chunk of marble that had broken from the side of the altar. Maybe if she could hit him with it, it might startle him into action? *Worth a shot.*

Persey picked up the shiny white stone and hurled it with all of her strength.

She'd been worried that she couldn't throw it far enough, but instead of falling short, the projectile sailed past Shaun's head, narrowly missing his temple.

"Trying to get rid of the competition?" Kevin said with a snort. "I didn't think you had it in you."

"I was trying to wake him up," Persey said, still wondering what Kevin's confession had really meant. "*I'm* not a killer."

Kevin's hand flew to his heart. "Ouch. That hurt."

"Target practice!" Wes cried, following Persey's lead. His aim was better, and less potentially lethal, striking the platform right beside Shaun. Who didn't even flinch.

"This is ridiculous," Mackenzie said, eyes fixed on the countdown clock. "We should just leave him."

Persey cringed, horrified. "We can't *leave* him. That's practically murder."

"Not like we can reach him anyway. We'd need a helicopter. Or a bridge."

A bridge? "Good idea!" Persey raced around the backside of the altar, where sections of the lid lay against the wall. "Do you think this will reach that nearby platform?"

Neela was by her side instantly. "Yes, but if that platform goes, the bridge goes."

"Right." If the platform released into the flames, Shaun, and anyone who was trying to rescue him, would be cut off.

"Who'd be stupid enough to go out there?" Wes said, a nervous laugh in his voice. Like he thought he might get volunteered.

Persey sighed, realizing the answer. *He's my responsibility.* Shaun might have been a narcissist, but she couldn't let him die. "Me."

"Eight minutes." Mackenzie pointed at the countdown clock. "We don't have time."

"Then don't help," Riot snapped. It was nice to know that Persey wasn't the only one who'd had it with Mackenzie.

Despite, or perhaps because of, Riot's words, Mackenzie joined the effort to haul the heavy marble slab around the front of the altar and slide it out toward the last remaining platform anywhere near the dais. As the fulcrum point was pushed farther out over the abyss, it took all of their strength to keep the slab horizontal, and just when Persey was afraid they couldn't hold it any longer, the marble scraped across rugged wood. The bridge was set.

"You sure about this?" Neela asked, her hand on Persey's arm as she stepped up onto the marble.

No. "I'll be okay."

Neela looked as unconvinced as Persey felt. "We'll all stand on this end. Keep the slab out there like a plank in case the platform goes. That way, you might be able to reach it."

"All?" Wes said. "Speak for your—"

"ALL." Kevin collared him, roughly pulling him up onto the marble. "Or I swear to God I'll throw you over right now."

Persey was pretty sure he'd do it, too.

"We'll keep this thing out there as long as we can," Kevin said. "Just don't dawdle."

She smiled at him, tight and grim. "Noted."

Feeble exit strategy in place, Persey took a deep breath. She could have ended this competition before they got this far, and now Arlo was dead, Shaun in danger. She thought of the animals her brother used to mutilate, wondered what he'd done at Columbia that would force him to leave the country. More of the same? His victims were helpless, all of them. Just like Persey was with her dad. Only, she wasn't helpless now and she wasn't going to sit around and let anyone else die if she could help it.

This wasn't about the money anymore; it was about survival.

The heat of the flames, dry and smothering, hit her full in the face the moment she cleared the dais. She half expected the wood platform to give way before she reached it, tipping her forward into the flames, but it stayed put. Stable. She was able to walk to the next two, then just a quick jump to a third. Then a fourth.

"Shaun!" she called as she got closer. She was on his left, hardly an arm's length away, and she could see that his immobility wasn't complete. His eyes found Persey's face as she approached, and she could have sworn they were pleading with her. Asking for help.

She was as close to him as she could get without landing on his narrow platform, but leaping the distance onto it would probably knock him over and send them both careening into the furnace. If they both reached toward each other from where they were, though, they should have been able to touch. "Take my hand."

But Shaun stood still.

"SHAUN!" she yelled. "You have to take my hand or you're going to die. Do you understand?"

This time, she saw him twitch. The fingers on his left hand, which hung limply at his side, wiggled ever so slightly. Like a man who'd been paralyzed desperately attempting to move his limbs. Once again, she saw that pleading look in his eyes and his lips, slightly parted, quivered.

"Helf," he said, his voice more air than tone. "Helf!"

Helf? "Help? Do you need help?"

"HELF EE!"

Help me. It was as if he couldn't pronounce the *p* or the *m*. *Can't move his lips.*

"Shaun . . ." She inched as close to the edge of the stone as she dared to go. "Shaun, are you paralyzed?"

"Persey!" Neela cried. "Hurry up!"

Slowly, Shaun's eyelids closed and reopened.

"One blink for yes," Persey said. "Right?"

Again, Shaun blinked his eyes. Just once.

Paralyzed. Shaun was trying to move—his fingers twitched as if they were desperate to reach out to her, his eyelids communicating but only by an extreme effort, and the one word he could get out between his parted lips was "help." No, Shaun's physical situation wasn't psychosomatic. It actually looked as if he'd been drugged.

The floor beneath her rumbled. The orange flames appeared to consume the whole room, casting their capricious glow on the rough-hewn walls as if even the rocks around them were on fire. Persey's entire body was damp with sweat, fabric sticking to her skin, and her palms were so slick she wasn't sure she could maintain a hold on Shaun's hand even if she could reach him.

Which she couldn't. Stretching as far as she dared without losing her balance, she was still a foot or two away from the immobile Shaun.

"Perse!" Kevin yelled over the roar of the furnace. "We're almost out of time."

She glanced at the countdown clock. Three minutes. What happened at the end of three minutes? Did the rest of the room collapse into the flames? Persey sure the hell didn't want to find out.

"I can't reach him," she called over her shoulder.

"Why isn't he taking your hand?" Neela's voice sounded frantic. "Why aren't you taking her hand?"

Persey had few options. She could jump to his platform. There wasn't much room for the two of them, and even if she could manage to do it without toppling him over, she had no idea if it would hold both of their weights. Or if she'd even be able to get him to move.

Still, she couldn't let Shaun die. She was so close. "Shaun, I can't reach you," she pleaded. "You've got to try."

"Didn't. Know." Shaun's lips could move a little bit more. Was the paralysis wearing off?

"Grab my hand!" she cried, trying one last time to stretch toward him. "You can do it."

"Didn't. *Know*." More emphatic this time. He was trying to tell her something.

Persey couldn't imagine what was so important that he needed to tell her right at this moment, when his very life was on the line. "Didn't know what?"

"Killed. Rye. Rouns."

"Rye rounds?"

"Rouns!" he screamed. "The rouns!"

"Brownes," Persey said, realizing what he meant. She stared at him, impotent. "The Brownes who used to own Escape-Capades? But they're dead."

"Rownes!" Tears poured out from the corners of both eyes. "Killed. Cuz—"

Another rumble interrupted his confession, and Persey could only watch in dumb horror as Shaun's platform gave way and he disappeared into the sea of orange flames.

THIRTY

PERSEY WASN'T SURE WHICH WAS MORE DISTURBING: THE stifled, paralytic screams as Shaun was burned alive in the giant furnace or the stench of charred flesh that wafted up from its depths. One thing she did know for sure—both made her sick. She felt her abdominals convulse as the remains of her airplane pretzels finally came rocketing up the back of her throat and were added to Shaun's remains deep in the cavern below.

Heat seared her cheeks, bringing her to her senses. As her cheeks ballooned like a chipmunk's holding the rest of her own puke in, she was able to stumble backward from the edge of the platform, just barely maintaining her balance.

Another person had died, this time even more horrifically than Arlo's decapitation or the bludgeoning of their boy band guide. Shaun's dying shrieks would haunt Persey's dreams for the rest of her days, and she would always blame herself for his death.

This is beyond you. There's nothing you could have done.

"There's nothing you could have done!"

It was Kevin's voice, bellowing above the roar of the furnace. Persey turned toward the altar, where he, Neela, and Riot were frantically calling her name and waving their hands above their heads. How long had they been trying to get her attention? How long had she been standing out there since Shaun's death?

"Listen to me!" Kevin cried. His voice sounded closer, as if he was moving toward her. "There is *nothing* you could have done to save him, okay? Nothing."

I'm nothing.

"Kev!" Mackenzie shouted, sounding more annoyed than alarmed. "What are you doing? It's not safe!"

"Persey, please!" It was Neela, her voice nearly hysterical. They'd barely known each other a day, and yet Neela was already more concerned about Persey's well-being than almost anyone else on the planet. Which was both sweet and really, really sad.

"Two minutes."

Right, the clock was ticking down. What would happen then? Would the whole altar collapse into the furnace? Leah wouldn't let them all die. The game would be over.

Maybe that was how Persey could shut this down? By just refusing to play along. Could she call the bluff?

"Persey, come on." She felt Kevin's hand on her arm, spinning her around. His face was pink and slick with perspiration, but other than a physical reaction to the heat, he looked completely and utterly calm, like he wasn't precariously balanced on a thin wooden platform poised to fall at any moment into a raging inferno. "We have to keep going."

"Do we?"

Kevin sighed. "You don't know what's going to happen if that clock runs out. Maybe we all die."

The coolness in his voice made her stomach clench up again. *Maybe we all die.* She saw Neela over Kevin's shoulder, frantically waving her arms. Persey might have been willing to risk her own life, but she certainly wasn't going to put Neela's on the line if she could help it.

She took Kevin's outstretched hand without a word and allowed him to escort her back the way they came. The platforms didn't block their path, and the bridge of marble held steady until just after Persey set foot back on the dais. Almost instantly the section that had anchored the marble over the fire pit dropped away, taking the bridge with it.

"I guess we know which way we're supposed to go," Riot said, watching the marble tumble down into the flames.

"One minute."

"Let's get this over with." Wes climbed up to the open chute, and before anyone else could protest, he'd swung both of his legs over the side, crossed his hands over his chest, and disappeared into the darkness.

Mackenzie followed with uncharacteristic silence. Her bow lips were pressed together as she climbed over the altar, her brows knitted low over her eyes. She did *not* like the fact that Kevin had come to Persey's rescue.

Riot and Neela went next, leaving just Persey and Kevin as the clock ticked dangerously low. He still held her hand, refusing to let go.

"Are you sure you want to do this?" she asked.

Kevin's smile was grim. "Can't be worse than in here, right?"

Persey felt her face go cold as the image of Shaun's paralyzed body dropping into the flames flashed through her mind. "No. No, it can't."

"You're going to be okay," Kevin said, giving her hand a squeeze. "I promise."

Persey seriously doubted it.

Persey had expected the slide to feel warm as it passed through or at least near the raging furnace below them, but as she zoomed down the smooth, curved surface, the metal beneath her felt cool to the touch. She could no longer hear the roar of the flames or smell the acrid smoke that had filled the Cavethedral, but though her sense of direction was all turned around in the total darkness, she was pretty sure she'd made a sharp right about ten feet down, so perhaps the chute was actually carrying them away from the furnace altogether.

The end of the slide came abruptly. One moment the exit was a dot of light in the distance, and then, suddenly, it was a gaping hole Persey was shot through like a bullet leaving the muzzle of a gun.

She felt herself free-fall, arms flailing as she attempted to find something to grab on to. She half expected to have her fall broken by a concrete floor, which would have busted her arm, shattered her leg, or cracked open her skull, depending on which way she fell, but instead, after just a second or two airborne, her body collapsed onto a soft, cushiony surface.

Persey felt the layers of airy fabric closing in around her as they absorbed the impact of her fall, and she had just processed the fact that she'd landed on some kind of giant pillow, when she heard a voice cry out above her.

"Cowabunga!"

Kevin. Who was about to land right on her head.

She curled up into a ball, thrusting her arms over her face to protect herself, and felt the impact of Kevin's weight just inches from her left ear. The pillowy cushion pushed up beneath her, like a water bed shifting its mass when someone else sat down on it, and as she was propelled upward on the swell, she tumbled backward and landed right on him.

"Oof," Kevin grunted as her knee accidentally impacted with his chest.

She rolled away as walls of the cushion rose up around them, and Persey finally realized that they'd landed on a giant air mattress, the kind used by stuntpeople when they jumped off buildings. The thick vinyl fabric roiled beneath her on a cushion of air as she scooted forward on her butt, trying to find the edge. Suddenly her legs fell out from beneath her, and Persey pitched forward preparing to face-plant on the floor, but with a swoosh of black curly hair, Neela grabbed her arm and helped haul Persey to her feet.

"You made it!" Neela cried, sounding somewhat surprised. "I . . . I kinda thought maybe you were going to stay up there."

It's not like I had a choice.

Riot wrapped his arms around her from behind, a gesture that felt both comforting and presumptively intimate. "I'm glad you're okay."

She indulged in his embrace for half a heartbeat, then wiggled free. "If I'm going to die, getting burned alive seemed like the worst possible option."

"Careful what you say." Riot pointed at the sky as if indicating a god. "You have no idea what else they have planned for us."

"Are you hurt?" Mackenzie rushed toward them, and Persey was momentarily dumbstruck at the fleeting thought that Mackenzie was actually concerned about her well-being, a confusion that was remedied two seconds later when Mackenzie launched herself into Kevin's arms. So much for being pissed off at him.

"Nope." His smile shifted to Persey. "You?"

Kevin's eyes reflected genuine concern, and when coupled with the closeness of Riot's hug, Persey almost allowed herself to give in. It might have been nice to lean on someone. To trust again.

Stop. It.

"I'm fine." She shook herself, hardly able to look him in the eyes. "Just short of breath."

He smiled, unaffected by her brush-off, and rubbed the spot on his chest where she drop-kicked him. "I know how you feel."

She seriously doubted it.

They'd landed in a narrow slit of a room, designed to look like the interior of a warehouse. Behind the crash pad, a blank wall of corrugated steel stretched to the roof, while the wall opposite was a third the height, a temporary division meant to separate this antechamber from what lay beyond. The roof soared above their heads with just a few stark lightbulbs hanging from the rafters to illuminate the room below, and the floor beneath Persey's feet was cold, sterile concrete. The air felt dank. In fact, the whole space smelled like a swimming pool at the end of summer, and the only way out was a single door, set into the low wall, at once welcoming and menacing.

"Anyone try the door yet?" Persey asked, not even sure she wanted to know what was behind it.

"Really?" Mackenzie asked, her upper lip curling into a snarl of disgust. "That's your first question?"

Persey's patience was pretty much gone. "I have so many questions, I don't even know where to start, but since I doubt anyone here can answer them, I thought I'd start with something we might some have control over."

"The door's locked," Riot said. Unlike Kevin, his calmness had an edge to it. Less terrified, more pissed off. "And it appears to be the only way out."

Great.

"You want to tell us what happened out there with Shaun?" Wes said, eying her suspiciously. *He thinks I had something to do with Shaun's death.*

The question had been meant for Persey, but Mackenzie took the opportunity to answer. "His screams . . . the stench . . ." She was all terrified victim again as she clawed at Kevin's chest, still trying to wrestle back his attention. Right, because *that* was the important thing right now.

"Still think this is all faked?" Persey asked, unable to stop herself.

"I don't . . . I mean, it can't . . ." Tears overflowed Mackenzie's eyes, streaking her once-perfectly-pristine makeup as they trailed down her face. She looked confused and terrified all at the same time. It was a combination of emotions that Persey could relate to.

"What did Shaun say?" Neela asked. "Why didn't he move?"

"He couldn't." Best just to lay it all out for them.

"Fear-inducing paralysis." Wes nodded. "Just like I said."

Persey was really starting to loathe his cockiness. "It was definitely paralysis, but fear had nothing to do with it."

Wes arched an eyebrow. "You think he had a stroke or something? Pretty sure that's not how it works."

"Shaun had been drugged."

"Here we go again." Wes's head rolled forward, his hair hanging down over his face. "Do we really have to sit through more of your conspiracy crap?" He jabbed his thumb toward Riot. "You're sounding more like your crazy-pants boyfriend every minute."

"Why would somebody want to kill the Shaun-bot?" Riot asked, thankfully ignoring the "boyfriend" mention. "Why would they want any of us dead? What the fuck did we do?"

"Shaun said something to you, didn't he?" Kevin asked.

"Yes." *The screams . . .*

He stepped closer, his hand resting gently on Persey's shoulder. It was possessive, and before Persey could shake him off, Riot's eyes had zeroed in on Kevin's grip. "What was it?"

"Uh . . ."

"She'll tell us when she's ready," Riot said. Persey was so unused to people defending her, she didn't even know how to respond.

"Persey?" Neela's voice quivered in the face of Persey's silence. "What's going on?"

Persey's eyes drifted past the others' faces, which all stared at her wide-eyed. They were scared now, finally. *Already scared and they don't even know the truth.*

Should she tell them? Should Persey be the one to take them from scared to terrified? From "Will I accidentally be killed next?" to "Someone is trying to murder us!" Shaun's final words would do just that.

Her eyes scanned the roof, looking for the ever-present camera. By explaining her theory, would she set the killer off in the process? Wouldn't that just be a green light to get rid of all of them? *Then their deaths really would be my fault.*

But withholding the truth might be just as bad.

She felt Kevin's fingers twitch against her shoulder. He was tense, though trying to hide it, and as Persey took a slow breath, she felt his hand fall away. They deserved to know. Whatever the consequences.

"Shaun was murdered," Persey said. "Just like B.J. and Arlo. And I think it has something to do with the murders of Derrick and Melinda Browne."

THIRTY-ONE

WES WAS THE FIRST TO VOICE THE QUESTION PERSEY KNEW they all had on the tips of their tongues. "The owners of Escape-Capades?"

"*Former* owners," Kevin corrected him. "Kinda hard to run a company when you're dead."

"Um, Persey?" Neela asked, raising her hand like a schoolkid. "You said 'murder' not 'deaths.' I thought the Brownes died by suicide, and while I suppose since it was a *murder*-suicide that is still technically a murder, in the context that you presented it, I rather believed or at the very least inferred that their deaths were the result of an unlawful, premeditated act by a third party."

Persey wasn't going to quibble about her use of the word "murder." "I think what's happening to us is related to the Brownes. And so did Shaun."

"That's fucking ridiculous," Wes said. Always charming. "You might as well claim that aliens have abducted us, and this is one big rat-maze experiment to test our survival abilities."

"That's not as fucking ridiculous as you think," Riot said, his body instantly relaxing as he talked about a favorite subject. "The Hill case aside, evidence in both the Shaver mystery and the Ariel School encounter in Zimbabwe was pretty compelling in support of extraterrestrial

221

intelligences mandated to assess the human instinct to survive."

"Nobody asked you, freak show."

Riot laughed. "That's exactly the kind of witty put-down I'd expect from a spoiled Deerfield asshole."

Wes went rigid, neck so taut Persey could see the individual tendons articulated through his skin. "How did you know I went to Deerfield?"

"The same way that Mackenzie knew you went to boarding school," Persey said, not waiting for him to answer. "Or that Riot knew about Shaun's code-breaking skills. Or that Neela is a power user at Geektacle. Don't you see? He knows where you went to school because you're all connected."

Instead of contradicting her, Riot, Mackenzie, and even Wes fell silent. Deep down they all knew it was true.

"That's the first time all day the three of you have kept your god-damn mouths shut," Kevin said, annoyance creeping into his tone. "So I'm going to take it that you've already come to the same conclusion."

More silence. *At least they're not lying about it.*

Satisfied with their non-answers, Kevin turned to Persey. "Why do you think this has to do with the Brownes?"

"Before Shaun died, he was trying to tell me something, but he'd been—"

"Paralyzed," Wes laughed, his silent acquiescence forgotten. "You told us. Hate to break the news, but I'm pretty sure that's not even possible."

"He couldn't move," Persey said through clenched teeth. She much preferred stoned Wes to mouthy-asshole Wes.

"Fear paralysis?" Riot suggested. "Not that I want to agree with our resident dickhead, but it is a real thing."

Wes shrugged. "I've been called worse."

I'm sure you have. "I don't think so." Yes, Shaun had looked utterly terrified, but Persey had the impression that he was scared *because* of the paralysis, not the other way around.

"I believe you," Kevin said, looking directly at Wes as he said it. Any opportunity to contradict. "The question is, why would someone want to drug the Shaun-bot?"

Persey leveled her eyes at him. "To ensure he never made it out of that room."

Wes pointed at his temple with his index finger and whistled while rotating his wrist, implying she was nuts.

"I don't think Persey's suggestion warrants that type of derision," Neela said. "In fact, her theory makes a great deal of sense if you consider the strange series of coincidences in our personal overlaps plus the fact that three people have . . . have . . ." She swallowed. "Have died already. Whatever is going on, those deaths are real."

"I had nothing to do with the Brownes," Mackenzie said haughtily, though she hadn't been asked. "And anyone who says otherwise is a filthy, dirty liar."

"I'm sure you didn't," Riot said, sounding anything but sincere. "And your 'confession' up there about cheating on a competition . . . that had *nothing whatsoever* to do with the Prison Break escape room, I'm sure."

"It's a lie!" Mackenzie squealed, *actually* squealed like she was in pain. A pig recently branded.

"I didn't accuse you of anything." A sly grin danced about the corners of Riot's mouth. "But your reaction sure the fuck told me everything."

"Whether you're innocent or not doesn't mean shit," Kevin said. "Persey and I had nothing to do with Prison Break, and yet we're stuck here, in the line of fire like everyone else."

Mackenzie didn't miss his insinuation. "I *am* innocent. I never even met the Brownes."

"Come off it, Mack," Wes said. He was scratching his right arm above the elbow. Repeatedly, obsessively, like he was having some kind of skin reaction. "Everyone knows you're full of shit."

Her mood flipped in an instant from aloof to attack mode. "I don't see you volunteering information."

"That's right!" Neela cried. "I never heard your confession." Her eyes were bright with excitement, as if hearing other people confess their deep, dark sins was the highlight of any given day.

"None of your business," Wes said.

"If our lives are on the line," Neela countered, "I believe that makes it everyone's business."

Wes sneered at her. "Maybe I didn't confess anything, huh? Ever think of that?"

"He said he stole something," Kevin said, staring Wes down.

Wes rolled his eyes. "Yeah, a candy bar. Everyone heard that."

But while Wes assiduously avoided Kevin, shifting his gaze from the ceiling to the floor to the slightly deflated air cushion, Kevin hardly moved, his face deadpan. "No, your *second* confession was also about stealing. But this time, you bribed someone to get what you needed."

Neela held up her index finger. "Um, technically, bribing isn't stealing. I just wanted to—"

"You're a fucking liar," Wes said. The tremor in his voice and the deep shade of fuchsia flooding his cheeks said otherwise.

Kevin shrugged. "I'm just repeating what you said, dude."

"Bullshit!" Wes exploded. He charged Kevin and tried to grab the collar of his shirt. "You were too far away. You couldn't have heard me."

Kevin shrugged. "If you say so." Then he turned to Persey. "He's full of shit, you know."

"He doesn't need to tell us," Persey said, attempting (failing) to suppress her nerves and excitement. Kevin had shared the puzzle piece she needed to explain this tangled web to everyone. "I know why he's here."

"Oh yeah?" Wes arched an eyebrow.

"Monsieur Poirot," Kevin said, bowing at the waist as he swept his arm across his body, ushering Persey forward. She hadn't pegged him as an Agatha Christie fan. "The floor is yours."

Persey took a deep breath. Fine. They wanted to hear the truth about this "competition" out loud? She'd give it to them.

"Room number one," she began. "The Office. Neela noticed that one of the cubicles had last year's calendar on the wall with May twenty-second circled in red ink." She waited, letting the date sink in.

Kevin's brow wrinkled up in confusion. "I don't get it."

"That's the day the Brownes died," Neela said quietly.

"Oh."

"Their bodies were found right here in this building," she continued, lower lip quivering as he spoke. "After the secret of the Prison Break escape room went public."

Persey reached out and squeezed her hand. "Shared on Daring-Debunker, right?"

Neela nodded.

"Which, like Geektacle where you had a power user account, happened to be owned and operated by Arlo."

Neela's face remained unchanged: no gasp, no raised eyebrows, no sign that this information was a surprise to her in any way, shape, or form. If she hadn't been 100 percent sure that Arlo was the gossipmonger behind DaringDebunker, she'd at least speculated about it.

Riot, on the other hand, looked genuinely shocked. "Arlo ran that site? Are you sure?"

"When she stumbled out of the ATM booth, she was completely wigging." Persey pictured Arlo's face, drained of color, her eyes darting around in a paranoid frenzy. "Everyone else had to enter their SAT scores to get out, but not her. Arlo started yelling at the countdown clock, threatening to sue Escape-Capades because she thought they'd hacked into her computer and stolen her password. She yelled, 'You can't prove I run it!' and I think she was referring to DaringDebunker."

Wes groaned. "She didn't *say*, 'Oh Em Gee, Leah, you totes guessed I run DaringDebunker.' You're just making that part up to fit your theory."

Persey suppressed a smile. All day she'd been waiting for an opportunity to score at Wes's expense, knocking his smugness down a peg. And the time had finally arrived.

"Except you're forgetting her conversation with Neela in the Collectibles room."

Neela cocked her head. "What did I say?"

"What *didn't* you say," Mackenzie grumbled.

"Remember when you showed Arlo that non-prize thingy?" Persey said, trying to remember the conversation verbatim. "She said you must have followed her blog and you admitted you did, then shared your screen name."

"That's right!" Neela said with a gasp. "TaraMehta91."

"And is that the same screen name you use on DaringDebunker?"

Neela flushed a deep shade of raspberry. "Um . . . yeah." She paused, eyes downcast and shaded by her thickly mascaraed lashes. "You knew?"

"I guessed. Between what you told me about the Prison Break fiasco and your confession in the Cavethedral, I just put the pieces together."

"Knew what?" Riot asked.

"Whatever it is, I don't see how it relates to me." Wes's obstinacy was probably (actually) a reflection of his own fear.

"DaringDebunker was where the solution to the final Prison Break puzzle was posted after someone figured it out," Neela said. Tears streamed down her face. "Only, I didn't know. I swear I didn't. I just thought it was another puzzle challenge from the person who ran the site."

Mackenzie's jaw slackened. "You're the one who broke the code?"

Neela's childlike sob ceased abruptly as she turned toward Mackenzie. "How did you know about the code?"

"But she didn't break the code!" Riot said almost simultaneously, at which point Kevin, whose head had been swiveling back and forth like he was watching a tennis match, held up his hands to form a T and eased away from the group.

"Hold it, time-out, back the truck up. What the fuck is everyone talking about?"

"The scandal around Prison Break," Riot sighed. "Try to keep up."

Kevin leaned against the wall beside the locked door and folded his arms over his chest. "I'm going to need CliffsNotes or something."

Persey didn't have time to deal with him; she was focused on what Riot had just said. "How do you know that Neela didn't break the code?"

He hesitated an instant, trying to decide whether or not he should tell the truth, then judging by the way the lines around his mouth suddenly smoothed out, he appeared to make up his mind. "Because Shaun did."

Wes turned sharply at the name. "Shaun got ahold of that code?"

"Yes."

"And you know this because . . ."

Riot coolly met Wes's gaze. "Because I'm the one who gave it to him."

THIRTY-TWO

THERE WAS A MOMENT OF PRETERNATURAL CALM WHILE Riot's words hung in the air, his face hard-set as he stared at Wes, daring him to respond. Wes, on the other hand, showed the full range of human emotions in the blink of an eye, all cycling through his face like an acting audition reel in fast forward: confusion, disbelief, realization, acceptance, and, finally, an anger that turned to rage so quickly that Persey barely had time to move out of the way before Wes launched himself at the librarian.

"You *dick*!" he cried as he rushed forward, hands aiming for Riot's neck. "I'll fucking kill you, you goddamn thief!"

Riot had seen or at least sensed the attack coming and was able to get his arms up in front of his face to defend himself. He grabbed one of Wes's hands and wrenched it behind his back. "Really, hypocrite? You're calling *me* a thief?"

"I didn't steal anything!" Wes roared. He managed to free his pinned hand from Riot's grasp and clutched at the Mohawk, trying to grab a fistful of gelled hair.

"Kinda sounds like you did, dude," Kevin said, making no attempt to break up the fight.

"Then how did you get your hands on it, huh?" Riot punched at Wes's side, aiming for his kidneys. "Escape-Capades just handed you a heavily encoded blueprint for the final challenge because you asked nicely and said 'please'?"

They continued to whale on each other—headlocks and sucker punches and ill-timed swings that resulted in only minor contact between fist and face. It was like watching two drunk guys wearing blindfolds go at it.

"Are you really not going to break this up?" Persey asked Kevin at last.

"Do I have to? This is kind of the best thing ever."

"Agreed," Neela and Mackenzie said in unison.

Persey sighed. Time was not on their side . . . even if there wasn't an active countdown clock. Yet.

"Fine." Kevin, who despite being about Wes's size seemed to tower over him in both bulk and presence, wedged himself between the two assailants. "Cut it out, children. You're *both* pretty."

Panting, Wes and Riot gave in quickly to Kevin, separating almost as soon as he stepped between them. Wes spun away, bent forward, hands on knees, while Riot fell back against the side of the air cushion, slouching into its folds, gassed. Neither wanted to be the first to quit, but neither was interested in continuing.

Kevin clicked his tongue. "They sure the fuck don't teach you to fight at Ivy League schools."

"I fight . . ." Riot said, gasping, "with words . . . not hands."

"That's the lamest thing I've ever heard."

Meanwhile, Mackenzie, unfazed by her ex-whatever's fistfight, had been staring at Riot, eyes pinched, like a nearsighted person trying to read a sign on the other side of the room. Then, suddenly, she straightened up.

"The UMass library!"

Riot was silent as his panting gradually slowed. But if he thought that would throw Mackenzie off, he was gravely mistaken.

"You work there. Or at least you did, a year ago. I remember now. And we . . ." She let her voice trail off, remembering. "How did you know?"

"I overheard you in the stacks." Riot must have realized there was no point denying it. "You were in six fifty-two point eight. Looking for books on code breaking. I was shelving two rows away, but I heard you discussing Escape-Capades and the Prison Break challenge."

"I knew it," Wes said. "You're a thief."

"I didn't *steal* anything," Riot said. "But you two morons had set up your laptop with the encoded file and then disappeared to screw in the bathroom without even dimming the screen."

"Classy," Kevin said, nodding.

"I just took a few photos on my phone. Enough to realize that you hadn't exactly come by that information accidentally."

"I thought you said you went to Harvard?" Neela asked. She still sat on the floor, hugging her knees to her chest, but her misery from earlier seemed to have abated somewhat.

Riot nodded. "Undergrad. I'm at UMass for my master's."

"To recap . . ." Kevin pushed himself off the wall. "For those of us who have no fucking clue what's going on, Wes and Mackenzie—who were banging—got their hands on some secret code shit—"

"*I* didn't get my hands on anything," Mackenzie said, correcting him.

Riot snorted. "Except Wes."

"Jealous?" She sidled closer to Kevin as she addressed the question to Riot. It was as if her entire reason for being revolved around what men thought of her. Which was fine, if that was her thing. Just kinda sad.

"Not at all," Riot said. His eyes trailed to Persey. "I prefer smart girls."

No one had ever called Persey smart before. It felt . . . nice.

"One more time from the top." Kevin laughed. Persey wasn't exactly sure what was funny considering how many people had already died, but whatever. "Wes stole some secret code shit and—"

Wes erupted, throwing his hands in the air. "I didn't steal it! How many fucking times do I have to say it?"

"Right," Kevin said. "You bribed it." He turned to Neela. "Is that a verb?"

"Sure!"

"I didn't do that either," Wes snapped. But his anger, like his fight, was ebbing.

"Then how did those coded plans come to be in your possession?" Neela asked, genuinely confused. "It's not like you worked for Escape-Capades or something."

Worked for Escape-Capades . . . "Brian."

Wes shrunk back at the name, his shoulders hunching so severely they threatened to turn him inside out. "I don't know who you're talking about."

Bullshit. "The cubicle in the Office. The one with the outdated calendar. Neela and I found a photo in one of the drawers. Four people in Halloween costumes, one of whom was named Brian. And in the Boyz Distrikt, you slipped and called B.J. 'Brian.' Because you recognized him."

"You're insane."

You have no idea. "Neela, what else did we find in that desk?"

Neela piped up immediately, listing off items as if she was still in front of the desk, naming things as she saw them. "A movie stub for a Fast and Furious sequel, packets of generic sweetener, an audition notice for a casino floor show, some statements for credit cards maxed out from cash advances, and a bunch of receipts from the Shangri-La bar at the Lotus Hotel."

Wes shrugged. "See? Nothing to do with me."

"Oh, please," Mackenzie said with a snort. "That's your parents' casino!"

Kevin arched an eyebrow. "Wes's parents own a casino?"

"Yep," Mackenzie said, answering for the now-silent Wes.

"Holy fajita." Neela whistled low after her fake curse. "I knew you were rich, but I didn't realize it was 'my parents own a Vegas casino' kind of rich."

"What kind of rich did you think he was?" Kevin asked.

"I don't know." Neela thought about it for half a second. "Like, regular kind of rich."

"There is no regular kind of rich, honey," Mackenzie said. "Just assholes who think they can buy the world."

For once, Persey agreed with her.

"So what, this guy was in debt and you paid him cash in exchange for this secret code thing?" Kevin pressed. "Seems like making seven the hard way."

"Don't you have a trust fund?" Riot asked Wes, wrinkling his nose as if disgusted by the very idea of wealth.

"What does that have to do with it?" Wes snapped.

"I mean, if you're rich, why do you give two flying fucks about some stupid escape room competition? Is your ego so huge that you just get off on winning whether you earned it or not? Because the million-dollar prize couldn't have meant shit to you."

"Oh, yeah it did," Mackenzie said, smiling sweetly. A honey trap. "Because *he's* not rich. His parents have all the money, and they were about to cut him off."

Persey tensed, disgusted by the idea that she and Wes had anything in common. He was a cocky, spoiled rich kid who expected everyone to do for him and had absolutely no problem taking credit for it. He was vain, self-serving, and the least likely person on the planet to help anyone but himself. Persey, meanwhile, had self-esteem that was so low there were cockroaches who had a better self-image, and though she'd also been raised with wealth and privilege, she'd never taken any of it for granted. In fact, she viewed her privilege as more of a curse than a blessing: Her father had wielded his money like a (deadly) weapon, holding it over her head and using it to control every aspect of his children's lives. Her brother had been able to live (mostly) within the mold, but Persey had not, and because she'd never been taught to do anything by herself, when her father cut her out of the family will, she was basically cast out into a world she was unequipped to deal with.

But unlike Wes, or Persey's brother, who would do anything to maintain his access to free money, Persey would have given it all up—the big house, the pool, the private school, the on-call drivers—for a father who loved her unconditionally. Or at all.

Persey bit her lip, forcing the memory of her dad from her mind. He was gone. She'd been disinherited. And the only thing she could afford to worry about right now was her future, which, at the moment, wasn't feeling particularly long.

"If Wes didn't have any money, then how did he bribe Brian?" Neela asked. She looked pinched, as if defending Wes was physically painful.

"Receipts at the casino bar and cash advances on credit cards?" Kevin said. "Sounds like Brian had a gambling problem."

Persey nodded. "Of course. I should have realized. Wes couldn't bribe Brian with money, but he might have been able to wipe out his debts at the Shangri-La."

"And he thought he'd claim that Escape-Capades prize," Mackenzie said, "and not have to go back to school like his parents wanted."

"Yeah, I needed the money, so what? I'm not the only one." Wes narrowed his eyes at Mackenzie. "You weren't exactly fucking me because you thought I was poor."

"That's incredibly sexist," Neela said. "Not to mention in poor taste."

Persey seriously doubted that "poor taste" was a label Wes worried about.

Wes rolled his eyes. "Please. She's one of those townies who used to hang around Deerfield just looking for a trust fund to snag. Old Mack here was just pissed that she banged up the wrong tree. Why do you think she was so hot to join in when she found out about the Prison Break clue?"

"One Eighty West A," Neela said. "Let me guess: Wes's dorm room?"

"Yes." Mackenzie, far from being offended, merely looked irritated by the accusations. "And I am *not* a townie. I'm from Springfield, for fuck's sake."

"Really?" Persey said. "*That's* the part you want to dispute?"

Mackenzie raised her chin, defiant. "I'm not afraid of sex. Or having sex. Or using sex."

Persey wasn't about to let Mackenzie play the slut-shamed victim. "You're also not afraid of benefiting from idea theft, apparently."

"I wish I had some popcorn," Kevin said, clapping his hands with glee. "This is amazing theater. Wes uses Mommy's casino to coerce poor little career-gambler Brian into handing over trade secrets, which Mackenzie, always the opportunist, finds out about and insists on getting in on. Am I nailing this all so far?"

"So far," Riot said.

"Then you overhear them in the library and steal what Wes already stole," Kevin continued, the laugh gradually ebbing from his voice. "And you gave the code to Shaun-bot, who cracked it."

Riot shrugged, utterly unapologetic. "I didn't give it to Shaun exactly. We were both members of the American Cryptogram Association, and Shaun occasionally wrote for their e-magazine. He had a reputation as a badass with codes. But though I knew him by name, I'd never met him."

Neela, still crouched on the floor, rested her chin against her knees. "So when you arrived here this morning, you didn't recognize him?"

"I suspected after Leah's introduction—but Shaun's a pretty common name, no matter which way you spell it."

"And you'd already escaped Office Drones by the time we found the code-breaking machine that was Shaun's challenge."

Riot laughed. "Yeah, that would have tipped me off, but honestly, I should have guessed it earlier. Oh well." He placed his hands at either temple, fingers and thumbs pulled together, then fanned his digits, miming an explosion. "Mind blown."

Next, Persey pointed at Mackenzie and Wes. "You two definitely recognized each other—"

Mackenzie rolled her eyes. "Duh."

"—but you didn't remember Riot until just now."

"I'm not sure why that matters," Wes said, unimpressed. "But yeah."

"I knew who Arlo was," Neela said. "But like I said, I'd only guessed that she ran DaringDebunker. I didn't know for sure."

Riot crouched down beside her. "Impressive job with figuring out the decoded schematics. I never thought that once it was cracked there'd be yet another layer of puzzle."

Neela's misery rushed back over her in an instant. "Thanks, I guess. As soon as Arlo posted it, I recognized the blueprints to a Baguenaudier, also known as the Impossible Staircase puzzle. It's a mathematician's dream, with an equation based on binary Gray codes to find the minimum number of moves necessary to solve. That was the one part everyone else missed, I guess. Except me."

"What I want to know is how the plans got to DaringDebunker at all," Riot said. "What was the connection between Arlo and Shaun? Best I could tell from today, they hated each other."

"Notre Dame," Persey said. "Don't you remember from the introductions? Arlo's brother went there. And when she mentioned Atticus's name in the library, I was pretty sure that Shaun was caught by surprise."

"They must have been friends. Shaun mentioned he had this puzzle he couldn't solve, and Atticus thought of his sister." Riot nodded in understanding. "Then Arlo, realizing what her brother had shared with her, put it up on her website, hoping someone would solve it."

"I still say the Brownes did it for publicity," Wes said. In case Persey wasn't already completely convinced that he was a skeezeball.

"Really, genius?" Kevin said. "They'd literally bankrupt themselves and their company on purpose, then Melinda Browne would pump two bullets into the back of her husband's head, and one into her own, letting their only son find the bodies . . . all for some CNN coverage? That's the stupidest business move ever."

"Maybe they faked their own deaths." Wes had jumped the shark from tasteless to offensive. "I bet they could have absorbed that prize money hit."

Only the trust-fund kid would think that two hundred and fifty million was absorbable.

Kevin pointed at him, thumb and forefinger posed like a pistol. "You're an asshole."

Wes pushed off the wall and strode into the center of the group. "Look, this is all a cute academic exercise, figuring out how we're connected all Scooby-Doo–style and shit, but I don't see how it matters. We're stuck here, and we need to get out. End. Of. Story."

You wish it was the end of the story.

"I agree with Wes," Mackenzie said. Shocking. "And I don't appreciate my past being dragged up like I'm a politician running for office."

"Thirded," Riot added. Persey glanced at Neela, wondering if she'd protest as well. She did not.

"It matters," Persey said, not at all surprised that these people wouldn't want their lying, cheating, and stealing in the spotlight, "because three people are dead."

"Leah must be behind this," Neela said. "Maybe she was close to the Brownes? Or . . ." She sucked in a sharp breath. "That article we found in Office Drones! It mentioned an L. Browne as next of kin. Could L stand for Leah?"

"It could," Persey said. "But if Leah's involved, she's not doing it on her own, and if we don't figure out who's helping her pick us off, one of us is going to be next."

Now it was Neela's turn to protest Persey's logic. "I don't understand. Why can't Leah be doing all this alone?"

"Because while Arlo's death could have been controlled from the outside, there was no one else with us in Boyz Distrikt, or in the Cavethedral to drug Shaun." Persey hoped she sounded decisive and strong, just like her brother always did, because this next theory was a doozy. "Which means one of us is a killer."

THIRTY-THREE

THE FACETIME CALL RANG FOUR TIMES BEFORE PERSEY managed to silence it.

She'd forgotten to turn off her ringer, and so when the melodious bell sounded through the nearly empty theater, she panicked and ended the call without even looking to see who it was.

Not because she was worried about disturbing someone, but because she didn't want anyone to know she was there.

The West Valley High School theater, which had long been her refuge from a tense and uncomfortable home, had recently become her *actual* refuge. Or at least, it would be eventually. With just weeks until the end of her junior year, Persey had begun looking for a place to crash once her dad made good on his promise to kick her out next spring. By dumb luck, Persey had stumbled upon the old dressing rooms while searching for a different stool to use in her spotlight loft. She'd been poking around backstage, searching through storage spaces, when she found the long-abandoned rooms. They were half hidden behind the recently remodeled proscenium stage. For whatever reason, the remodel had left the suite of three rooms intact. Unused, forgotten.

Which was perfect. A little digging around after hours and some creative arrangements of extension cords, and Persey had created a half-decent crash pad, complete with a couple of desk lamps (props from the fall production of *Deathtrap*), a dusty but not uncomfortable chesterfield sofa (from a long-ago staging of *Noises Off*), and a mini fridge she'd found stashed away in the basement.

Tonight, for the first time, she was going to spend the night, just to see if anyone noticed. As long as she didn't exit the building once the security system was turned on, she was fine. Bathrooms, vending machines, even showers in the newer dressing rooms. She could do worse.

It wasn't a permanent solution, but it was better than the street.

But her carefully laid plans would come crashing down if anyone found out she was in the theater after hours. Like if they heard her phone ringing.

Silencing the call, Persey raced out of her hiding place, opening and closing the door to the suite of rooms as silently as she could. She paused, listening. Hoping no one had heard.

A voice in the dimly lit theater caused her stomach to fall out from beneath her. "Hello?"

It was Mr. Beck. The theater director.

Persey scanned the wings, work lights on, looking for something that could plausibly have kept her there long after the *Grand Hotel* rehearsals had ended. Footsteps in the back of the house indicated that Mr. Beck was coming to investigate from his office. She didn't have much time.

Spotting a box of old lighting gels stashed in the corner, she dragged it toward the nearest work light, then plopped down in front of it. She just had time to shove in her earbuds and redial the missed FaceTime call before Mr. Beck rounded the curtain.

"Hey, little sis!" her brother said, answering her callback instantly. "I thought you were avoiding me. This is the fourth time I've called this week."

Shit. She really should have looked before she dialed. "N-no," she stammered. "I've been at rehearsal and—"

"Hey!" Mr. Beck said, eyes wide in surprise. They were bloodshot, and Persey could smell the spicy odor of his favorite whiskey wafting toward her. "I didn't know you were still here."

"Hang on," Persey said to her brother, then pulled out one of her earbuds. "Sorry, Mr. Beck. There was a tear in one of the gels in the house right bank of lights. I forgot to tell Amanda before she left after rehearsal, so I thought I'd stay late and replace it myself."

"You're still at school?" her brother asked.

"Oh!" Mr. Beck stared at the box of old gels. "You didn't hear me calling?"

She held up her one removed earbud. "Music."

"Right. Well, that's very kind of you. But I'm about to lock up."

Shit. Persey forced a smile as she pushed herself to her feet. "Got it. I'll head out through the side door."

Mr. Beck nodded, though he looked confused. She wasn't sure if he bought her story, but he clearly wasn't going to argue with her at ten o'clock on a Tuesday night. "Okay. See you tomorrow."

Persey started toward the side door, pushing it open as Mr. Beck retreated from the wings. When she heard his footsteps growing fainter, she let the door close, then dashed to the hidden suite and made it back to her crash pad as silently as was humanly possible.

"You want to tell me what's going on?" her brother asked.

Persey pressed a finger to her lips, indicating silence, then waited until she heard the faint click of the main lights as Mr. Beck shut everything down. Then she let out a sigh.

Cover maintained. But she so didn't want to explain this to her brother.

"Sorry about that," she said, as if everything that had just occurred was perfectly natural and normal. "We have a tech dress tomorrow, so it's crazy here."

"Uh-huh." He didn't believe her.

Time to change the subject. "So . . . how are you?"

She focused on the face on the screen for the first time. Her brother sported a leathery tan, like he'd spent the better part of the last six months working outside under a hot sun, and his skin glistened with sweat. He flashed his usual impish smile, but Persey couldn't shake the feeling that it was forced.

For once in his life, her brother's confidence had been shaken.

"I like what you're doing with your hair."

"It's in a ponytail." *Like basically every single day of my life.*

"I like it."

Persey didn't know how she was supposed to respond. She hadn't spoken to him in months—since that day she found him stealing from their parents—and after all that time, he wanted to compliment her hair? "Where are you?"

"Vietnam!" His face lit up. "You really need to come here one day. The people are amazing. Friendly, open. The food . . ." He brought his fingers to his lips and kissed them.

He was acting like he was on vacation, not fleeing a missing-person investigation back home.

"Oh, and I've met someone," he continued.

"Someone?"

"Yeah." His smile deepened, and his eyes shifted away from the camera. *She's in the room with him.* "Genevieve Cooper." He pronounced her name as if it he was in a rhapsodic trance, his eyes soft and dreamy, a hint of color in his cheeks. Whatever Persey thought of her sociopathic brother and his inability to feel emotion for anyone but himself, it was clear that this Genevieve had bewitched him.

"She's absolutely amazing. Beautiful, smart, funny. She's from California, but she's been living in Vietnam with her parents and younger brother for a few years. Persey, her brother . . ." He leaned closer to the camera, eyes even brighter than before. "He's . . . he's like me!"

Oh shit.

"He also got into some trouble back home, and so Genevieve just gets me."

Then she should be running in the other direction.

"But she's not another one of those trust-fund kids. God, that's all I met at Columbia. Entitled skanks."

Persey bristled. How could his new girlfriend listen to him talk about other women like that and not have it set off alarm bells?

Her brother made a kissy face to the person off-screen, then shifted his focus back to the camera. "And I really hope you two get along like . . . sisters."

Sisters? Persey winced. She couldn't help herself. Her brother was thinking about getting married. Persey didn't know if she was terrified *of* this Genevieve or *for* her.

"I know the last couple of years have been rough with me gone," he continued, his monologue planned and rehearsed. "Sorry I'm not there to keep Dad off your back."

"It's okay." *Like you ever did before.*

He smiled and softened his voice. "I, uh, heard about what happened. With the will."

Mom. Persey was pretty sure their dad wouldn't have bothered filling in his now sole heir on the fact that he'd written his not-yet-eighteen-year-old daughter out of his will, but Mom might have hoped her son could talk him out of it.

"And I just want you to know that even though I'm supposed to get everything when they die, I'm going to make sure you're taken care of."

"Uh, thanks." It was such a weird statement, a bizarre thought. Their parents were neither old nor infirm. Aside from her mom's excessive drinking, they were both perfectly fit, and there was absolutely no reason to believe they both wouldn't live for another thirty years or more. The idea that Persey would be worried about her well-being thirty years from now was laughable. The day after she graduated from high school, she'd be completely on her own.

"I'm sure you think it's unfair," he continued, still on script, "that Dad's been so lenient on me. Especially since I'm not in school right now either."

The thought had crossed her mind. "It's not your fault."

He laughed. "Oh, I know *that*."

Man, his ego.

"Dad's being irrational. But I want you to know that it's not just with *you*."

Persey sat up straighter. *Not just with me?* Could it be that their father, who had been hero-worshipping his BMOC son since the day he was born, could possibly be at a breaking point with his antics?

"Yeah," her brother laughed dryly. "I know. Hell freezes over, right? Dad's cut me off until I go back to school."

BOOM. The reason he'd called Persey in the first place.

"He says he has a lot tied up in the new business, but I think he just wants to make sure I get that college degree he's always rambling about."

It all made sense now. He'd only called because he needed something from her.

"I don't know what you've got lying around in your account," he continued shamelessly. "But if you could just Venmo me like a couple grand . . ."

"A couple grand?" Persey blurted out. Was he serious? Her allowance was supposed to be twenty bucks a week, but as "punishment" for mediocre grades and perceived laziness, her dad hadn't paid her since she started at West Valley. Her spending money, such as it was, came from her mom, who remembered to slip twenty bucks into her sock drawer on Monday mornings while her dad was on his weekly conference call with the London office. Usually. There were some weeks when the money just wouldn't appear. Some weeks when it was only a ten.

Thankfully, Persey didn't have anything to spend it on. The housekeeper put her lunch together every day, so other than buying a bottle of water at the school vending machine, she didn't need to worry about food. She had her brother's hand-me-down MacBook, which, though a little slow, worked just fine, and her dad begrudgingly paid for her cell phone every month, if for no other reason than that she needed it to call the company car for a ride home. She had no friends, only saw movies when they made it to cable, and spent the bare minimum on clothes and personal items. Her spartan lifestyle had enabled her to save five hundred and twenty-five dollars over the last few years. Money she was, apparently, going to need to live on very soon.

But a couple thousand? She'd never had that much in her life. And it made her wonder about how much of an allowance her brother had been getting all these years.

The look of surprise on her face confused her brother. "What? What's wrong?"

"I . . . I don't have that kind of money. I only get twenty bucks a week."

His eyebrows shot up. "Really?"

"I'm sorry."

"It's okay." His surprise quickly morphed into disappointment.

She didn't even know why she was apologizing. It just came so naturally. And she hated herself for it.

"Is there anything you could sell?" he pressed. "I'll pay you back, I swear."

Persey shook her head slowly. She literally didn't own a thing of value, and she was pretty sure her brother had already stripped the house of everything else that would turn a decent profit.

His eyes shifted off-screen again, this time in the opposite direction, down and to the left. He stared hard at something or nothing, his mouth chewing around behind closed lips as if he were having a conversation with himself.

"Okay," he said after a moment. He was immediately energized. "Okay. No worries. I knew it was a long shot."

"I'm sorry," she said again, secretly hating herself.

He flashed that über-confident smile. If he'd had a moment of self-doubt or indecisiveness during that call, it was gone. "Don't you worry, little sis. I'm going to take care of it, okay? It's going to be fine."

Persey wasn't certain who that statement was meant for, but as she hung up the call, she was pretty sure she saw a familiar gleam in her brother's eyes, and it made her blood run cold.

THIRTY-FOUR

"WHAT THE FAJITA?" NEELA SAID. PERSEY ALMOST (NOT really) thought she'd been about to swear. "One of us?"

Wes groaned. "Not this again."

"There is no 'again,'" Neela said, using air quotes. "This is the first time anyone has suggested that one of us might be involved in these deaths."

"Murders," Kevin said, correcting her.

"Fine." Wes whirled on him. "You want to single out potential murderers? You get my vote."

"How do you figure?" Far from being horrified or offended, Kevin merely smirked at Wes in amusement. Which only pissed off his accuser more.

"What's your connection to Escape-Capades, huh? You and your little girlfriend are all hot and bothered to figure out how the rest of us are linked to this place, but I don't see you volunteering information about yourself."

Like you did?

Kevin held his hands up before him, palms out, a gesture of innocence. "I'm just collateral damage, remember? Along for the ride."

Which wasn't really a point Wes could argue, given the reason for

Kevin's inclusion in this competition in the first place. Not that he was willing to give up his side of the argument.

"What about her?" Wes jabbed his thumb over his shoulder in Persey's direction.

Persey had spent her entire life being spoken about as if she wasn't in the room. She'd been conditioned to remain quiet, to accept the degradation because it had come from her father. But she sure the fuck wasn't going to take the same treatment from Wes.

"I'm right here," she said. "And I can hear you. So if you want to know if I have any connection to the Brownes, why don't you sack up and ask me yourself?"

"Persey didn't even know who the Brownes were before today," Neela said, clambering to her feet. "I had to tell her the whole story." Persey appreciated Neela's desire to defend her.

Mackenzie, never one to stay silent for long when it meant getting in a dig at Persey, joined the fray. "And you believed that?"

"Yes, of course."

"Then why is she here, huh? Every single one of us had a connection to the Brownes—we're just supposed to believe it's a coincidence that she's here too?"

"The logical explanation—though I use that adjective loosely because literally nothing that's happened to us so far has been logical . . . but I digress—the *logical* explanation is that whoever invited us here never expected anyone to actually beat the Hidden Library. When Persey did, they had to invite her."

Kevin raised his hand. "And me."

"And Kevin by default," Neela concluded. "Maybe they're even here to throw the rest of us off. In case we recognized each other."

"I don't buy it," Wes said. "There's something strange going on."

That's an understatement.

"Why does it have to be one of us?" Riot asked. Neither his voice nor his body language was defensive or combative. His question was born of pure curiosity. "Doesn't it make more sense that someone from Escape-Capades is killing us off?"

"Leah." Mackenzie scowled as she said the name, jealousy practically (definitely) seeping out of her invisible pores. "If that's even her real name. I knew there was something fucked about her."

"I agree with Crazy Pants," Wes said, waving his hand vaguely in Riot's direction. "The trapdoor that killed Arlo, the platform that dropped Shaun into the fire. Those couldn't be controlled by one of us."

Couldn't they? But Persey didn't really need to argue that point. "B.J. was killed by someone in the room. There was nowhere for anyone else to hide. The killer must have been desperate to get rid of him, and did it while the rest of us were focused on solving the puzzle."

"When we were all gathered around the computer," Neela said. "Anyone could have slipped away."

"But why kill him at all?" Mackenzie asked.

Kevin snorted. "Yeah, his singing wasn't that bad."

Persey ignored the joke. "Because he knew about Wes and his connection to the Brownes. If someone is killing us off as a vendetta against them—"

"Someone?" Wes said. "Are you accusing me of murder?"

Maybe. "The killer might just be tying up loose ends."

"I didn't kill him." Mackenzie tossed her long blond hair out of her face. "*I* was busy at the keyboard solving the last puzzle."

"Depends when he died," Kevin said with a shrug. "Does anyone know for sure?"

Wes refolded his arms across his chest. "I still say it could have been an accident."

"Shaun's paralysis was no accident," Persey said. She'd never forget the panicked look in his eyes as he desperately tried to move. "Someone drugged him. Someone *in this room* drugged him."

Wes threw up his hands. "With what? We were all searched."

"For electronics," Riot said. "You managed to sneak your weed through."

"I think perhaps the intelligent thing to do would be to have everyone turn out their pockets," Neela began. She sounded tentative, like she really didn't want to do the very thing she was suggesting. "And then whoever has the . . . Well, a syringe, I suppose, is what we're looking for."

Persey was quick to comply. She pulled the pockets of her cargo pants inside out to show that they were completely empty, even though she recognized the futility of the gesture.

"Unfortunately, anyone smart enough to kill B.J., Arlo, *and* Shaun was probably smart enough to dump the murder weapon into the Great Fire of London back there," Kevin said, voicing the unspoken thought in Persey's head while also emptying his pockets, which contained a micro pack of Altoids and a bag of airline-branded peanuts.

Wes clenched his fists. "You want to see what's in my pockets? Come at me."

Ew.

Mackenzie was also noncompliant, her narrowed eyes fixed on Persey. "If the rest of us are all connected to the Brownes, then isn't *she* the most likely suspect? She could have been in on it with Leah all along, which would explain her impossible performance in the Hidden Library."

She just couldn't get over that.

"You know," Kevin said, "ol' Mack here has a point."

Persey opened her mouth to say something, then stopped. How was she going to convince them that she wasn't connected to the Brownes in any way?

"It's true," Neela said. "She could be lying." Persey's stomach dropped. She thought Neela trusted her.

Mackenzie beamed triumphantly. "See?"

But Neela wasn't done. "Then again, we all could be."

Persey let out a breath. *Thank you.*

"You only have my word for it that I'm the TaraMehta91 who solved the Prison Break Baguenaudier," Neela continued. "Anyone could put on a red Mohawk and pass as Riot, and Wes and Mackenzie could be in it together. So Persey's right. We're all suspects."

"Okay, so if we're all suspects, then let's narrow it down," Riot said, academic even in the face of a murder. "Who would want to kill us off? An Escape-Capades employee? Seems kind of extreme, even for a die-hard career type."

"And difficult," Kevin added. "Whoever's doing this has access to money and resources. A fucking incinerator underneath a collapsing floor? Joe Blow in accounting ain't pulling that off."

"L. Browne could be anyone," Persey said.

BZZZZZ.

"Shit." Persey spun around to face the sound of the buzzer and found that a clock had come to life on the wall above the door, red numbers cast from a hidden projector somewhere. Even more disturbing, the door that had once been locked now stood wide open.

They had thirty minutes.

"Fuck that," Riot said. "I'm not going anywhere."

"We tried that in the last room," Neela said. "It didn't work out so well."

Mackenzie tentatively leaned to her right, trying to get a glimpse inside the now-open door. "Too dark to see anything in there. I don't like it."

A heavy, metallic groan shook the room, rippling across the concrete floor like an earthquake. It sounded as if an enormous piece of machinery, rusted and inert with age, had suddenly sprung to life. Behind them, the wall of corrugated metal shuddered once, twice; then it lurched and began to slide toward them.

"The. Fuck." Mackenzie backed away from the wall.

"Well, that's one way to keep us moving," Kevin said.

Then, to make the situation even worse, as the wall continued to inch its way across the concrete floor, an army of sharp metal spikes emerged from its face, pointy ends of death glistening in the weak overhead lighting.

THIRTY-FIVE

"YOU HAVE GOT TO BE KIDDING ME," RIOT SAID.

The tips of the spiked wall reached the inflatable cushion that had broken their fall down the two-story slide. The thick vinyl was no match for the sharp spikes, and a series of hollow pops followed by the whoosh of air signaled its surrender. Not that the cushion itself was a significant impediment to the wall's progress, but as it quickly deflated, the wall pushed forward, impaling the remains, without so much as slowing down.

"This room is a giant iron maiden." Neela squeaked as she spoke, eyes open so wide Persey was afraid her eyeballs might pop out of her head. "Like the name on the whiteboard. I just didn't think it would be so literal."

The wall was just a few feet from them now, advancing steadily. As much as Persey hated the idea of being herded into compliance, if the choice was plunging blindly into the darkness beyond the open door or meeting the business end of Mr. Pointy, she knew which one she'd choose.

"What the fuck is this?" Wes asked no one in particular. His voice cracked and his eyes were so wide she could see the bloodshot veins creeping through them. "Are you trying to kill me?"

For a guy who just thirty seconds ago was still trying to convince everyone that the deaths were fakes and accidents, he sure seemed terrified for life and limb all of a sudden. What had changed?

"I'm getting the fuck out of here." Then he dashed through the door, without waiting for anyone else.

"For once," Kevin said, shaking his head, "I agree with the stoner."

Without another word, they packed into a dark corridor, and even though Persey was literally right behind Kevin, before they were ten feet from the door, the light was so feeble she could barely make out the plaid pattern on his T- shirt.

"What's up ahead?" Mackenzie asked as they continued to creep forward in the darkness.

"Another door," Wes answered, dejected. "Closed."

"Probably locked," Neela said. She had her hand on Persey's shoulder; it was trembling.

"There's something on the wall." Wes's voice perked up. "It looks like . . . goggles?"

The line stopped abruptly, and Kevin pushed forward through Riot and Mackenzie to reach the item Wes had just described. "Not just goggles," Kevin said. "Night-vision goggles."

"The door *is* locked," Riot said, tugging on the handle. "Just checking all the boxes."

Kevin lifted the goggles from the hook on which they hung. Immediately, the door swung open. "It can't be that easy."

The interior of the new room was darker, if that was possible, than the hallway they were in, and judging by the offering of night vision, Persey had to assume the rest of the challenge would take place in utter blackness.

Then the realization dawned on her. Only *one* pair of goggles.

This was a trust exercise.

Mackenzie held out her hand. "Give them to me."

"Why should you get to wear them?" Wes said. "I found them. They're mine." He reached for the goggles, which Kevin deftly shielded with his body.

"We've established that *I* didn't kill that lame singer guy," Mackenzie replied. "I'm the only one who's for sure innocent."

Neela's face was just barely visible in the darkness. "That's what the killer would say."

Riot ran his hands through his drooping Mohawk, trying to bring it back to life. "Whatever lies beyond that door in the darkness, only one of us will be able to see it. And guide the others through."

"A trust exercise where one of us is a killer?" Kevin said. "That's my kind of game."

"I'm not entirely convinced that you should be the one wearing the goggles," Neela said, eyeing Kevin.

"And you should?" Wes countered.

"Holy cow babies, no. It should be Persey."

"Oh, *hell* no," Wes said. "I don't trust any of you fucknuts. I'm taking those goddamn goggles and getting the fuck out of here!" He made another half-hearted grab for the goggles, but even in the dulled light of the hallway, Kevin was able to dodge the attempt.

"Persey is the only one who believed from the beginning that something awful was going on here." Neela's voice was calm: logic had overcome hysteria. "And she's been actively trying to help solve each and every challenge since this game began. In my humble opinion, she is the closest thing we have to an objective observer. And on a personal note, she's the only one of us eff-nuts I do trust."

"My vote is Persey too," Kevin said, then nodded toward Wes. "And if we're ranking us in terms of most to least trustworthy, I think Mr. Sticky Fingers over here lands at the bottom of the list."

Wes gritted his teeth. "I. Didn't. Steal. Anything."

"Semantics," Riot said. "You bribed someone else to steal them. Same diff. By the way, I also vote for Persey."

Before anyone else could agree or protest, a large crash reverberated through the corridor. Persey turned just in time to see the pointy spikes obliterate the wall with the door they'd just come through, advancing steadily toward them.

"Out of time!" Kevin strong-armed Wes and took Persey's hand, pulling her toward him. As she stumbled toward the open door, he pulled the goggles over her head. "Where you lead, we'll follow."

"But I didn't get a chance to vote!" Mackenzie whined.

Persey tuned her out. She didn't have time to think. Which scared her more than whatever danger lurked in this room. As she reached up toward the pair of goggles perched on her forehead, she fought back the panic that was gurgling in her stomach, the voice that sounded very much like her father's roaring in her ears that an idiot like her couldn't lead a kindergartener out of the playground let alone shepherd a group of people to safety. The now-familiar refrain of *You shouldn't be here . . .* echoed in her mind. This was all wrong. She didn't belong here. She shouldn't be doing this.

"You can do this," Kevin prompted. He was the kind of guy it was difficult to say no to, and she could see why, despite his lack of "breeding" and his total lack of seriousness, Mackenzie had been attracted to him. There was something infectious about his smile, his belief in her. And while every atom in her body was screaming at Persey to hand the goggles back, she slowly, deliberately, pulled them down over her eyes.

Persey had seen night-vision footage on television—she had a penchant for ghost hunter shows that sent a group of hardened true believers into a supposedly haunted location and let them film orbs and mist and pixelated shadow figures for a reality TV audience ready to take it all as hard evidence of the paranormal—but the green-hued footage on her screen had not prepared her brain for the weirdness of actually looking through one of those lenses.

The moment she pulled the goggles over her eyes, the entire corridor sprang to life. She could see every detail of Kevin, from the longish sandy-brown hair swept across his forehead to the faded emblem on his T-shirt. Even his facial features were easily discernible; his wide grin was normal and humanlike, but his eyes, disturbingly, shone like glowing white coals in his head.

Wes was behind him, scowling. His gaze was shifty, moving rapidly between Persey, Kevin, and the ceiling above them like he was searching for something. Mackenzie had wrapped her arms tightly around her body with her shoulders hunched forward in a full-body clench. She looked like she was scared to touch anything. Riot had shoved his hands in the pockets of his jeans and plastered a smile on his face, focused on Persey. She wasn't sure who he was trying to instill confidence in: her or himself. But Neela's encouraging smile was authentic. Persey couldn't even see her mouth—Neela's hands were clasped together in front of her face—but her eyes smiled. Neela trusted her. Persey had to pull them all through this.

The sharp metal spikes gleamed an eerie Matrix green as they tore through the wood, splintering it into a million pieces, some of which remained impaled on the spikes, the rest shattering before the onset, jagged shards of plywood precariously held together by plaster and stucco that tumbled into a mound before the encroaching wall swept it up, pushing it forward. She was glad no one else could see the iron maiden as clearly as she could. It was positively terrifying.

"Lead the way," Kevin said calmly.

"Right." She had to go first. Into the unknown. Persey lowered her chin, turned toward the doorway, and strode through with as much confidence as she could muster.

THIRTY-SIX

PERSEY WASN'T SURE WHAT SHE EXPECTED TO FIND ONCE SHE walked through that door—an Indiana Jones–style booby trap ready to drop on her head? *Labyrinth*-ine maze complete with a spandex-clad David Bowie? Clarice Starling stalking her with a drawn handgun? All of those might have been legitimate possibilities, but none of them even compared to what she saw.

Nothing.

Well, not totally nothing. In the distance, Persey could see another wall—low and long, just like the one behind her, and she could just make out a single door in its face, the metallic doorknob glowing in night vision. But between her and that door, it looked as if someone had dug out an Olympic-size swimming pool.

She edged closer to the pit and realized that her swimming-pool analogy was somewhat apt—the pit was maybe ten feet deep, uniform as far as she could see in either direction, but this certainly wasn't a pool you wanted to dive into. The bottom was lined with the same pointy, lethal spikes that were coming at them from behind.

This room truly was an iron maiden.

"What do you see?" Mackenzie said, impatience fluttering in her voice. "Why are we just standing here? That thing is still after us!"

Persey felt a gentle push as five people pressed in behind her. "Don't move!" she yelled, stutter-stepping away from the edge. If they accidentally (purposefully) knocked her and her night-vision goggles into the spikes, they'd all be dead meat.

She felt a strong hand on her arm, holding her steady. Kevin. "We can't stay here."

"I know," she snapped, instantly wishing she hadn't. He was right, of course. But they also couldn't go forward until she found a way across.

"Tell us what you see," he said. Again, cool and calm.

Right. "The floor drops away right in front of me. Ten feet, maybe twelve."

"We should be able to jump down without breaking anything," Riot said. "Drop and roll, parkour style."

"Only if you'd like to add a few dozen holes to your body," Persey said grimly.

"You're kidding."

"The entire floor is riddled with those spikes."

"Okay, so jumping is off the list," Kevin said.

"There's a door on the other side," Persey continued, "directly across. But I'm not sure how we get to . . ." She stopped as her eyes fell on something all the way down the room to her left. It was light green against the blackness of the pit, and Persey realized what she was staring at. "There's a bridge!"

"Really?" Wes said. "That seems too easy."

It *did* seem too easy. But what choice did they have?

"We'll cross that, er, *bridge*, when we get to it," Kevin said with a laugh.

Persey groaned. "So glad you've retained your sense of humor."

"If I can't laugh in the face of death," he replied, "when can I?"

Persey could think of like a million other times where bad puns were more appropriate, but she didn't have time to banter with him. "This way!" she said, then remembered that no one else could see her. "Sorry. To your left. Put a hand on the wall so you stay away from the edge. I'll go first."

Even with the night-vision goggles on, Persey followed her own advice and kept her left hand against the wall, tracing its smooth surface with her fingers as she led the group down the narrow ledge toward the bridge. She kept her eyes moving, half expecting to feel the moving wall of spikes crash through the stucco at any moment, but the wall never so much as shuddered from the grinding movement of the iron maiden, and as she carefully hugged the wall, she realized that the mechanical rumble of the engine had also ceased.

"How much farther?" Mackenzie whined like a kid in the back seat of the family minivan on a cross-country road trip.

"I warned you to use the potty before we left," Riot said, taking the joke right out of Persey's mouth. "Now you'll just have to hold it."

But Mackenzie's nerves were too frayed to see humor of any kind. "THE. FUCK!"

"It was just a joke."

"Not funny." Mackenzie choked down a sob.

"Everybody stay calm," Kevin said. He strode confidently behind Persey, despite the darkness. "Listen to Persey and we'll all get through this."

I really hope so.

"Perhaps everyone would feel better," Neela began, her voice higher pitched than usual from nerves and adrenaline, "if Persey narrated what she's seeing? I think the silence is more terrifying than the darkness."

"Yeah, for you," Wes grumbled.

"Okay." Persey swallowed. Listening to herself monologue was probably the least stress-reducing thing she could think of, but if it helped her get everyone through this room alive and in one piece, it would be worth it. "I can see the bridge clearly now. It's thin. Like the plank on a pirate ship and . . ."

Persey's throat closed up. Wes *had* been right. A bridge had seemed too easy but now that Persey was steps away, she realized that this thin piece of wood, only wide enough to allow one person to pass at a time, had no railing. One false step and impalement awaited on the floor below.

"And?" Wes prompted, impatient.

Persey sighed. The trust exercise just got a whole lot more trusting. "And there's no supports on either side. No handrail. Nothing. If you don't walk directly straight ahead, you'll fall."

Wes emitted a sound somewhere between a growl and a gasp. "I knew it seemed too easy."

"We're here," Persey said, stopping before the bridge. The shuffling of feet behind her ceased as she stared out at the bridge. It was a foot wide, if that—more than a gymnast's balance beam but narrow enough that they'd have to walk one foot in front of the other, further diminishing their stability. To make matters worse, unless the wooden beam had been crafted around a titanium core, it was going to sag in the middle as they crossed. There were no additional support beams.

"It's narrow," she said, trying not to understate the danger but unwilling to instill panic. "And I don't think it will hold the weight of more than one or two people at a time."

"This isn't fair!" Mackenzie stomped her foot, her voice nearing hysterical. "She's the only one who can get out of here. What the fuck are we supposed to do?"

"How long is the bridge?" Kevin asked.

Persey wasn't great at judging distances, but it didn't seem that far.

"About as wide as a swimming pool?"

"Anything on the other side?"

"Just the door."

Kevin sighed. "You'll guide us across one at a time. There doesn't seem to be a clock in here, so we have all the time in the world."

"For fuck's sake!" Wes cried. "Don't say that! Every time you say that something awful happens."

"Like what?" Kevin said. "How could this possibly get worse?"

A whoosh of air blew past them. Persey felt the breeze against her cheek and turned in time to see something green streak past her from right to left across the length of the room. A split second later, a thud. It sounded like an arrow hitting the bull's-eye.

"What the hell was that?" Riot asked.

The green streak had struck the wall on Persey's left. She could have guessed what it was without looking at it, but one glance confirmed her worst fears. "That was a spike. Like the ones on the floor. Only it was shot across the room."

"Okay, my bad." Kevin sounded sheepish. "It's worse."

Persey didn't look at him. She was still fixated on the spike on the wall. Beside it, glaring white in her night vision, a countdown clock.

"Can you guys see what's on the wall?" Persey asked. "On your left."

"We can't see anything!" Mackenzie scream-sobbed. "Not a single fucking thing."

She was going to have to get her shit together if she wanted to survive.

"How much time?" Riot asked.

That was the weirdest part of all. "I don't know."

"Huh?"

"It's not a clock face. It's just a number. Eight hundred and twenty-one point three."

"Huh," Riot repeated, this time without the inflection of a question. "Elizabethan poetry."

Now it was Persey's turn to be confused. "Huh?"

"The call numbers. Eight twenty-one is poetry, point three is Elizabethan. My specialty."

As he spoke, the numbers began to move. "Eight twenty, eight nineteen," Persey said. "It's still a countdown."

"Thirteen minutes and forty-two seconds," Neela said. "In seconds. Approximately."

Persey had no idea what the Dewey decimal number for poetry meant or how she was going to ferry five people across that spike-filled gap in under fourteen minutes even if they did manage to evade the spikes flying across their path, but she knew she had to try.

"Okay," she began. "I'm going to take everyone across one at a time." Without waiting for a volunteer, she reached out and took Neela's hand, pulling her around Kevin. In the night-vision goggles, Neela's monochrome black on black was now white on white. Her mass of curly hair looked like a Santa Claus wig on steroids, and her eyes, rimmed in real life with heavy black liner, were huge and sparkly. Persey couldn't tell if she was crying or if the sparkling was just an aftereffect of the goggles.

"What do we do about those flying spikes?" Neela asked.

Persey wasn't entirely sure. If she saw one coming, she and Neela might have time to flatten against the bridge before they were impaled. *Might.* It was a chance she had to take. "When I say duck, duck. Ready?"

Neela squeezed Persey's hand. "I trust you."

"Of course she's taking the lame one first," Mackenzie cried. "The. Fuck."

"I'm *not* lame," Neela said, bristling. It took all of Persey's self-restraint not to push Mackenzie into the pit and be done with her.

"No, you're not. Come on."

The plank felt surprisingly firm beneath Persey's feet. A little wiggly as Neela joined, but not enough to make her lose her balance. She walked slowly, purposefully, Neela's hand still clasped in hers. The bridge wasn't particularly long, but Persey wasn't taking any chances. She kept her eyes glued to the far wall, which had shot the initial spike, praying she'd have enough warning to dodge the projectile.

They weren't even a quarter of the way across when the barrage began.

The first spikes came in a cluster. Four of them, aimed at the beginning of the bridge, behind where Neela now stood.

"Don't move!" Persey said, holding Neela's hand firm. "They're behind you."

She froze, holding her breath, as the spikes whizzed past. From the distance, it looked as if they'd all been shot at once, but as they struck the wall, they did so with a distinct rhythm. *One-two. Three-four.*

Persey started moving again, wondering why the spikes had been so poorly aimed, when she saw another set of green dots streaking toward them. Closer this time.

"Move!" Persey cried, tugging on Neela's arm. They stumbled together, Persey's eyes fixed on the wooden beam beneath her feet, which was now sagging so close to the spikes on the ground that she could see their gleamingly sharp tips. Neela's balanced wavered, but she regained her footing, following closely behind Persey. They just cleared the spikes that went racing by Neela so closely that if her hair had been blown backward in the nonexistent breeze one of the spikes would have soared right through it.

Once again, they hit the wall with the same, distinct rhythm: *one-two, three-four.*

"Hurry up!" Mackenzie screamed. "What if those spikes get shot at us, huh? We can't even see."

Not that Persey needed Mackenzie's reminder to keep moving. After the last near miss, she didn't so much as pause after the spikes hit. She and Neela kept moving forward as quickly as they could safely manage, but they were far enough away that when the third blast was unleashed, they struck the wall harmlessly behind Neela. *One-two, three-four.*

Persey could see the other side now as they began to climb upward on the sagging plank. She just had to deposit Neela safely, then do this four more times. Easy, right? The spikes seemed to be meant as an incentive to keep moving more than anything. If it was the same on the way back, then she had this one—

"Get down!" Riot shouted. "Now!"

"What?" Persey turned her head. Riot, who couldn't see his hand in front of his face, was waving his arm wildly over his head as if to get her attention. Why would they stop now, when the spike blasts were just driving them toward the far side?

"GET. DOWN," he repeated.

Before she could even process how she and Neela were supposed to "get down" on an unstable piece of wood hardly a foot wide, she saw the danger. Tiny little green points of light on the far wall. At least fifty of them, all in a row.

She tugged at Neela's hand while she flattened herself on the wooden plank. "What's happening?" Neela cried, awkwardly groping for the beam with her free hand. Persey wrapped her arm around Neela's head, pushing it down onto the wood as she tucked her own face into Neela's cascading hair. A row of spikes the width of the entire room flew above them, followed by another identical wave, striking the wall one after another, *one-two.*

Without Riot's warning, both she and Neela would now be pincushions.

"Holy fajita!" Neela cried. Even in the face of death, curse words escaped her.

"Hey!" Riot called. "You guys okay?"

"How did you know?" Persey unwrapped strands of Neela's curls from her night-vision goggles as she sat upright.

"The rhythm," Riot explained, sounding relieved that they were still alive. "It's an Elizabethan rhyme scheme. ABAB CDCD EFEF GG."

The library call numbers. Now they made sense.

"I just assumed the GG part would be cataclysmic," he continued. "Was I right?"

So right.

"Get to the other side before it starts again," Kevin instructed, as if Persey or Neela needed to be told. They were almost all the way across before the rhyme scheme of lethal projectiles began again. *One-two, three-four. One-two, three-four. One-two, three-four. ONE-TWO.*

They made it safely to the other side before the final couplet, and Persey positioned Neela with her back to the wall, safely out of harm's way. "Stay here."

"I will do so until you return," Neela said. She sounded out of breath. "And try to relocate my heart from the unfortunate migration it has made to my throat. Ha-ha."

Persey made it halfway back before she had to hit the deck to avoid another volley. The spikes were striking the wall in the same place as previous rounds, bouncing off each other and clanking down to the spike-lined floor, which meant Persey also had to keep an eye on the ricochets, but she made it back to the group safely, this time taking Mackenzie's hand. Not for girl solidarity or because she thought the guys would be chivalrous, but because she couldn't stand listening to her whine anymore.

"Do what I tell you to do," Persey said, trying to sound like she was in control. "Understand?" Mackenzie didn't have a good track record when it came to taking Persey seriously, and this kind of command would have touched Mackenzie off a few hours ago, but to her credit, Mackenzie just nodded, and despite the nagging fear that Persey might be holding hands with a killer, they both made it safely to the other side.

Riot was next, and when Persey took his hand, she felt his thumb graze over the back of her own. It was the last thing she should have been thinking of, but her stomach fluttered, and for one fleeting moment, she thought of what it must be like to have someone in your life—anyone else—who cared about you.

Persey half expected to find Wes and Kevin engaged in a blind-man's fistfight when she returned, arguing over who would go next. The countdown clock was at 378 seconds, or about six minutes if Persey's crappy math skills could handle basic division, which meant she had time to get both of them out, even with the now-predictable spike volleys, but instead of the expected altercation, she found Kevin leaning back against the wall, arms folded across his chest, über-casual.

"I'll go last," he announced.

"Really?" she blurted out.

Wes answered for him. "Yes, really." He inched his way toward her, one hand trailing against the wall. Even through night-vision goggles, he looked awful. The sheen of perspiration on his face glistened in green light. His hair was stringy and matted down, like he'd been running a sweaty hand through it repeatedly, and his eyes were puffy. She wondered if he'd been smoking more of his special weed while he waited.

She tried not to cringe when she took Wes's moist hand.

They started across the plank at the same deliberate, steady pace

Persey had used for the others, but Wes wasn't content to move that slowly. "Hurry up," he growled in her ear.

One-two. Three-four.

"The wooden plank isn't very sturdy," Persey said, refusing to be bullied. "We'll make it halfway before the first big barrage, and you'll have plenty of time to get down and avoid—"

He shoved her. "Move. Faster."

Persey stumbled, hand down to the wooden beam for support, and just barely avoided a headfirst fall into the spike pit below. "Cut it out!" she yelled, trying to yank her hand free from his. If he wanted to run blindly in the darkness, he could go right ahead. But she wasn't going with him.

One-two. Three-four.

"What's wrong?" Neela cried. "Persey, are you okay?"

Before she could answer, she felt a hand smack her head. Then another. Wes was groping for her goggles.

"Fuck you!" she yelled, trying to fend him off. She dropped to her knees, gripping the plank with one hand and shielding her face with the other. If he managed to get them off her head, the rest of them were probably dead. Wes wasn't exactly looking out for anyone but himself.

"Give them to me!" he roared.

"Wes, if you hurt her, I swear to God I'll kill you." Riot's anger was sweet but impotent.

One-two. Three-four. Closer. Right behind them.

Despite the fact that Wes was a cheat, an asshole, and a selfish douchebag, Persey couldn't just let him die. She reached back and tugged on his pant leg. "Get down. Now! Or you're going to get—"

Persey wasn't sure exactly what happened first. She felt the denim of

Wes's jeans slip from her fingers, as if he'd yanked his leg away from her. She heard a scream. Felt the air move above her as two dozen metal spikes shot across the room. Felt their impact. But also, another. A juicy thud was the best way to describe it.

"Persey!" Neela and Riot cried simultaneously. "Are you okay? What's happening?"

"I'm okay." Her voice was breathless. "I'm okay."

"What about Wes?" Mackenzie's voice was significantly calmer than it had been in the last half hour.

Persey raised her head and looked around. The sight that greeted her made her wish she hadn't.

Wes's body was almost directly beneath the bridge, faceup, eyes still open. Persey could see the spikes impaled through his body: arms and legs, abdomen, throat. He was still twitching.

She felt the world spin. The green-hued image of Wes's death throes circling her field of vision as if she was on a carousel set to ludicrous speed. She staggered, unsure of where the bridge was, or the ceiling, or anything else. Just as she thought she was about to pitch forward, she felt an arm around her waist, pulling her upright.

"I've got you," Kevin said, his lips close to her ear, saving her for the second time that day. "I've got you."

THIRTY-SEVEN

I'VE GOT TO TALK TO MY DAD.

Intellectually, Persey knew that the voice inside her head was 100 percent right. It had been years since Persey had had a conversation with her father that hadn't ended (hell, *began*) badly. Even innocuous topics like the weather or the traffic coming home from work turned somehow into a scathing commentary.

Rain in the forecast? Better not use that as an excuse for staying home from school.

Traffic? Took me an extra hour to get home, so I spent that time on the phone with the headmaster trying to convince him not to kick you out of school.

Meat loaf for dinner? I should start charging you for these meals. You're clearly too used to freeloading.

Persey did actually remember the last kind, loving conversation she had with her dad. She was in the sixth grade and had just experienced the most embarrassing moment of her young life when she managed to get her period for the first time in gym class, bleeding through her gray cotton gym shorts with such ferocity that it looked like she'd just slaughtered a chicken in the locker room.

The mortification had been enhanced by the fact that one of the boys—a fiendish little prepubescent piece of shit named Cosimo with bad teeth and a monobrow who loved nothing more than to point out everyone else's weaknesses in some kind of subconscious effort to distract people from his own—was the first person to see her. If it had been one of the girls, there might have been a moment of empathy while they hurried her back into the locker room to find a tampon and a change of clothes, but no. She got Cosimo. Who promptly pointed out the growing spot of red on the back of her pants and yelled as loud as he could that Persey was a vampire who peed blood.

By the time the driver got Persey home, she was in tears. Her mom had gone to bed with one of her migraines, but her dad was in the kitchen.

"What happened?" he asked the moment he saw her. She clutched a clear plastic bag with her soiled gym clothes and waddled into the kitchen, the enormous old-fashioned maxipad between her legs making it difficult to walk.

"I . . ." She sniffled. Should she tell him? "I just . . ."

His eyes drifted to the bag, and she saw understanding wash over his face. "I see."

She'd been half hoping he wouldn't say anything—sympathy and comfort weren't really her dad's strong suits—and just let her retreat to her room in silent mortification, but instead, her dad sat down on one of the barstools next to the kitchen counter and folded his hands in his lap.

"I'm so sorry this happened while your mom is, um, indisposed, but I just want you to know that this is totally normal and it happens to all girls at some point in their lives, and one day, you'll be able to look back on this and laugh. I promise."

It hadn't exactly been a hug and a shoulder to cry on, but there had been a gentleness about her dad at that moment, something she'd rarely seen before and never since, and his little speech soothed her. Calmed her.

And she never did talk to her mom about it.

Persey almost wished she could forget that episode, even though it was one of the few nice memories she had of her father. Somehow, recalling that moment was like salt in the wound of their relationship, and every time she thought of it, her entire body would clench up, preparing for the pain she knew was coming.

Unfortunately, it was this very memory, combined with the conversation she'd had the week before with her brother, that gave her even the smallest bit of hope that she would be able to talk to him. To make him understand that going to college would be a waste of money, and lay out the plan she'd come up with instead: the Peace Corps. She'd be able to help people who needed it, see more of the world than the upper-class community she was raised in, and gain skills that would help her in whatever career came next. *See, Dad? I'm not freeloading. I have a plan!*

She just needed her parents' support for the two years of her service, and then they could be done with her if that's what they wanted. But by then, Persey planned to have proven to them that she wasn't useless or lazy or all the other horrible adjectives her dad had used for her over the years. By then, she was going to earn his respect.

And if not? She still had her West Valley theater crash pad.

Cold comfort.

It had taken Persey six whole days to find the right time (and gather enough courage) to talk to her dad. Things had been hectic at work and her parents hadn't been around much, but when she'd gotten home from rehearsal to find that dinner had already been prepped on the table in covered dishes, Persey had decided to take the opportunity to discuss her plan with her parents.

The first warning sign Persey should have heeded was her mom's intoxication level. The heavy clank of a glass bottle going into the recycling bin meant that an entire chardonnay had been poured, another already taking its place in the tabletop cooler sleeve. Considering that the sun wasn't even down yet, this was a bad sign.

The second warning came from their housekeeper, in the form of her absence. During family dinner nights, she usually stayed until the meal was cleared, but tonight she was already gone, which meant one of two things: either Persey's dad had dismissed her early because he was in a mood and didn't want any witnesses, or he'd already managed to insult her and she'd left in a huff, swearing never (temporarily) to return.

Either of these two signs should have given Persey pause, but whether from a desperate need to get it over with or the deep-seated knowledge that her plan wasn't going to work anyway, Persey plowed ahead, entering the dining room for pot roast, arugula salad, and to secure her future happiness.

"Hi, Mom!" she said with more perk than she thought herself capable of.

"Dahr-ling!" Her mom reached one hand out to her daughter, the other firmly grasping her wineglass, and grinned like a sleepy infant. "I've missed you so."

Neither of us has gone anywhere. Persey took the outstretched hand and kissed it and, just for a moment, wondered if her mom thought it was her son who had joined them for dinner.

"Dad," Persey said in a friendly, matter-of-fact way. No superfluous emotion. That's the kind of greeting he appreciated.

True to his form over the last year, Persey's dad ignored her. He held his phone in one hand, tabbing through pages with his thumb while he absently stabbed at a stray potato on his plate. His meal was two-thirds consumed already, despite the fact that Persey was five minutes early for dinner. His timing, she guessed, was intentional.

"You must be hungry, dahr-ling," her mom said, gesturing to the poppy-red Le Creuset pot in the middle of the table. "You need to eat, eat, eat!"

You should take your own advice. Her mom's plate was spotlessly clean. "You first, Mom."

She waved Persey off, whipping her head back and forth with the motion. For a moment, Persey thought she might keel over. "I ate at the office."

"When?"

"Earlier?"

Persey didn't miss the inflection at the end. "Are you not sure when you ate last? Mom, I'm worried about you."

"Imfine." All one word, slurred together.

"But—"

"Your mother said she's fine," her dad said, sharp but not a yell. "Let it go."

Persey took a deep, silent breath. He'd spoken to her. Broken the seal. It was practically an invitation to have a conversation.

"Okay," she said, trying to sound cheerful in the face of her mom's raging alcoholism. "I'm glad we're having a family dinner tonight because there's something I've been wanting to talk to you about."

"We already changed the will." Her dad didn't even look at her. "So don't bother begging."

His coldness was a slap in the face. She was used to his temper, his ability to hold a grudge, the lightning-quick flashes of anger and rage, but this disgust? This total detachment? This was new.

"I'm not asking you to change your mind," she said. "Because I know you won't."

"Good."

"But I wanted you to know that I do have a plan for after I graduate."

"Gra-du-ate," her mom said, languid and slow. "Columbia."

Ugh. "No, Mom. That's my brother. I'm still in high school."

"And not going to college," her dad said.

This was not going the way she'd hoped. "No, but honestly, Dad, it would be a waste of your money if I did, and besides, I have a plan that—"

"Don't care."

"That I think will be good for all of us. It will allow me to find my purpose and—"

"Don't care."

"And help those in need—"

"Still don't care."

"And . . . and give back all that I've been given."

"Are you done?"

Persey started, flustered. She hadn't even told them what the plan was. "No, I mean . . ."

"Because this is me not caring."

"Dad, the Peace Corps—"

"DON'T CARE."

And that was it. Years of being beaten down, denigrated, ignored, and yelled at finally boiled over. Persey's well-practiced calm vanished, replaced by the one thing she'd apparently inherited from her father: a white-hot temper.

"Oh yeah?" she said, rocketing to her feet. "You don't care about me? Really? I didn't hear you the first three million times you told me that."

Her dad flushed. "How *dare* you speak—"

"No, how dare *you*, Dad." It was the first time she'd ever interrupted him, which left her dad momentarily speechless and allowed Persey's semi of rage to keep on trucking. "I've spent my entire life trying to earn your respect. I know you think I'm lazy and useless, but I'm not. I've tried so hard at school. Twice as hard as my brother. But everything came easily for him and hard for me. And now he's off burning through your money while he runs away from a missing-persons investigation, and I'm just asking you to let me join the Peace Corps for two years. Which will cost you like a fraction of what you're paying for him right now."

"My poor baby." Her mom was crying now, drowning her tears in more wine, but Persey wasn't sure who the tears were for—her or her brother.

"Don't talk about your brother like that," her dad barked. "He's worth more than you'll ever be."

Persey snorted. "Yeah, more in legal fees."

Her dad kicked the chair out from behind him as he rose to his feet. "Say another word and you'll—"

"Regret it? Please. I'm already out of this family, and unless you want the press crawling all over you for turning your sixteen-year-old daughter out in the cold, you can't actually make my life any more of a hell than it already is. So you can hero-worship your son all you want, but don't pretend like we don't know the truth."

"Which is?"

"I saw him that day. I caught him stealing. And he told me last week that you're cutting him off."

"WHAT?" Only, the wailing question didn't come from her father; it came from her mom.

"He just needs to come home," her dad said, placating his wife. "I'm just trying to force him to go back to school."

Persey laughed. "He's not coming back to you, Daddy. He's running from the law, remember? Or don't you know why you had to pay for all those lawyers?"

Her dad clenched his teeth. "Shut. Up."

"Lawyers?" Persey's mom said, her voice breathless. "Is our son in trouble?"

You have no idea, Mom.

"He'll be fine," her dad said, though the words lacked his characteristic conviction. "He'll be home soon."

"No, he won't." For the first time in her life, Persey had the upper hand in a conversation with her father, and she let the power go to her head. "He's found someone. A girl. They're planning to get married."

The next wail her mom let out sounded like a wounded animal. "Nooo! My baby. He can't!"

"Look what you've done." Her dad turned on Persey viciously, spitting the words through clenched teeth. "Get out of here. Out of this house."

But Persey stood her ground. "No. I'm going to my room."

"My baby, my baby, he's leaving me," her mom sobbed.

"You're going to regret this," her dad said. His voice shook with rage. "You're no longer my daughter."

Fine with me. Persey turned toward the door.

"Don't you walk away from me without a word!"

Persey spun around, eyes narrowed. Usually her father wanted her to stay quiet, and now he wanted her to talk? "How about this? I FUCKING HATE YOU AND I WISH YOU WERE DEAD!"

Finally. The words she'd spoken silently in her head a thousand times. They exploded from her, taking all the rage and anger and resentment with them. She didn't wait for him to respond, but stomped out of the kitchen, ignoring her father's face, red with rage, and her mother's painful wailing from the sofa.

By the time she got to her room, Persey was pale and trembling, the bravado gone, and she was left with the cold, barren realization of what her life would now be.

What have I done?

THIRTY-EIGHT

THE LIGHTS WERE ALREADY ON INSIDE THE NEW ROOM BY the time Persey followed Kevin inside, and she had to yank the night-vision goggles off her head to keep from blinding herself. The pain that shot through her eyes from front to back momentarily wiped away the image of Wes's impaled body. But as she dropped the goggles to the ground from her trembling hand, Wes's death and all the emotions that came with it flooded through her—the horror, the fear, and the guilt.

"I . . . I don't know what happened," Persey began. Even though no one had asked, she felt the need to explain. "He was trying to get the goggles from me and I told him to get down and then . . . then . . . I don't know. I guess he fell?"

"It's not your fault," Kevin said.

"Isn't it?" B.J., Arlo, Shaun—those deaths might not have directly been her fault, but Wes? That one was on her. She'd been in charge, she'd been the leader, and yes, he'd attacked her, but she'd let him die.

The cost of this stupid competition was getting steeper every moment.

Total (hopeless) silence had fallen among the Escape-Capades All-Star competitors. No one commented on the iron maiden. No one pointed fingers or took jabs at one another. Neela crouched on the floor, back against the wall, head in her hands. Riot kept obsessively running his hand over the top of his flat hair, Mohawk long collapsed, and Kevin paced back and forth, head bowed in thought. Even Mackenzie had forgotten her relentless pursuit of Kevin: she stood with her back to them, arms wrapped around her waist as if giving herself a hug.

Wes hadn't exactly been universally (at all) liked, but his was the first death that had occurred since they all realized their connections to Escape-Capades, the first death since they understood that they were being hunted. Persey knew what they were all thinking: *If we couldn't prevent his death when we knew it was coming, what chance do any of us have?*

I wish I knew.

Kevin was the first to break the silence, his voice so jarring, Persey actually jumped.

"We have to assume that one of us is meant to die in each room."

"If that's supposed to make us feel better," Riot said, "I think you're doing it wrong."

"No one's after *you*," Mackenzie said, back still to them. Persey couldn't see the look on her face, but the bitterness in her voice said it all. "You have no connection to this awful place."

"I'm a witness," Kevin said. "Persey and me both. I doubt we're supposed to get out of here alive. So if we all work together, maybe we can—"

"Work together?" Mackenzie spun around, index finger pointed at Persey. "This is *her* fault. She was supposed to be leading us through that challenge, and now Wes is dead. I'm not working with her at all."

"I didn't kill him," Persey said, fighting back her very real sense of guilt over Wes's death.

"It's not your fault," Kevin said.

Isn't it?

Kevin inhaled deeply. "We can't all turn on each other, okay?"

Neela lifted her head from her knees. "You're forgetting that one of us is still a killer."

Kevin opened his mouth to respond, then snapped it shut. Neela had a point. One of them had bludgeoned B.J. and poisoned Shaun. Hell, maybe one of them had even been responsible for Arlo's death somehow. *Except we were all down in the Cavethedral then. . . .*

Persey sucked in a sharp, gasping breath as she pictured the moment of Arlo's death. "Oh my God!"

"What?" Neela said. "What's wrong?"

Images came flashing into Persey's brain at a rapid clip. Wes wandering back to the iMac after sulking in the back of the Boyz Distrikt loft. Wes slapping Shaun on the shoulder in the Cavethedral, a moment that Persey had registered because it was so out of character. The fact that Wes was the only one upstairs with Arlo when she died.

"Wes."

"Still dead," Riot said. Then added with a glance at Mackenzie: "No special effects there."

But that wasn't what Persey meant. "When we were in Boyz Distrikt, gathered around the TV while Kevin played *Mortal Kombat,* Wes got pissed and left the group. He stayed in the back corner until we were all fixated on the iMac."

Neela sucked in a breath. "He wasn't with us when B.J. was killed."

"Exactly!" Persey said. "And Arlo . . . Wes was the only one left upstairs with her. If he intentionally moved while she was sliding down the pole, it would have caused the trapdoor to snap shut—"

"Snapping *her,*" Kevin said, completing the thought. "Holy shit, you're right. His timing would have to be perfect, but it's doable."

"And then, down in the Cavethedral, I remember Wes slapping Shaun on the back. It felt so weird at the time that it stuck in my memory."

"You think that's when he poisoned Shaun-bot?" Kevin asked.

Yes. "It's possible."

"But why would Wes be killing us off?" Riot shook his head, limp Mohawk waving like palm fronds in the desert wind. "He's clearly not out to get revenge for the Brownes' deaths since he's the one who started this mess in the first place."

"He was also desperate for money," Neela said. "Was he not?"

Persey was so glad someone else had picked up on Wes's motivation. "Yes!"

"Maybe Leah offered Wes cash to do some of the dirty work for her."

"Then killed him off?" Mackenzie sounded skeptical. "How could she be sure Wes would die back there?"

"Perse," Kevin said, touching her arm. "Did you see anything suspicious?"

Persey shook her head slowly. "Sorry."

"It might have been an accident," Riot added. "And if so, that means—"

Neela jumped to her feet, energized. "That means maybe we'll be okay! If Wes was the murderer, we might make it out of here!"

Persey watched the glimmer of hope ripple through the group. They stood straighter, raised their heads, moved with more energy. The mood was infectious: perhaps they were all going to survive after all?

"Okay, kids," Kevin said, clapping his hands like a motivational speaker. "If we're going to see the light of day, we'd better get cracking at this . . ." He turned, taking in their new challenge. "This classroom?"

Persey examined the room for the first time, and she had to agree with Kevin's assessment. This room had been dressed to look like a schoolroom.

Wooden chairs with attached desktops stood in pristinely aligned rows, all facing away from them. An open wardrobe was tucked into one corner, filled with winter coats and lunch bags as if the students who had piled into school that day were outside at recess. Inspirational posters with slogans like "Dare to Dream! Work to Achieve!" and "Play Nice, Work Hard, Stay Kind" in rainbow-colored fonts were plastered on the walls beside cubby storage bins overflowing with school supplies.

The door that must have been the exit stood adjacent to a map of the world, near the corner of the room, and it was the only item in the entire space that seemed out of place and wrong. Instead of a wooden classroom door with a window and a simple doorknob, it was a steel security door with five different numbered touch pads lined up down its center.

Lastly, beside the door and taking up the rest of the front wall of the classroom, was a classic dark green chalkboard, filled with numbers and letters in crisp white chalk.

Persey inwardly groaned. A math problem? She hoped (prayed) that she wouldn't be forced to solve for x here because if so, they were all screwed.

"Recess," Riot said. "Now I get it. This looks like a fourth-grade classroom when all the kids are outside."

Kevin walked up to one of the desks and ran his finger over the back of the wooden chair. "It's like actually the polar opposite of what I thought we'd find. Like if you looked up 'polar opposite' in an encyclopedia, there would be side-by-side photos of the Pointy Floor of Death and this."

Riot approached the door, examining its five different combination locks. "Looks like a classic escape room scenario. Find the clues to open the lock. Should be pretty basic."

"Nothing about this place has been basic," Mackenzie said, then added, "except her," with a nod toward Persey. Because even facing death, Mackenzie was unable to finish a sentence without getting a dig in. *You're making it kinda hard for me to care whether you live or die.*

Neela edged her way toward the chalkboard, slow and cautious, as if afraid the floor might fall out from under her at any moment. Which, in fairness, was an absolute possibility. But despite the danger, Neela was drawn to the mathematics like a moth to the flame. "If three-x minus y equals twelve," she read from the chalkboard, "what is the value of eight to the x power over two to the y power?"

"The answer," Kevin said quickly, "is I don't fucking know."

Neela glanced back over her shoulder and grinned at him. "Anyone mind if I try my hand at this?"

Thank God Neela was a math fiend. "Go for it," Persey said. "We'll look for any other—"

Before she could finish the sentence, a rumble rolled through the room. By now, Persey knew what that feeling meant: somewhere nearby, a motor had roared to life. "Watch out!" she cried, stepping away from the wall.

They all froze, spinning from corner to corner, waiting for one side of the classroom to sprout spikes and begin marching toward them.

Nothing moved.

"Huh," Kevin said, staring at the back wall. "Maybe the mechanism broke?"

"I can still feel the floor rumbling," Persey said. Which meant *something* was happening behind the scenes.

A low hiss whistled above the hum of the faraway motor, followed by another and another. Four small white clouds erupted from the floor, billowing up from unseen spouts.

"They're going to gas us!" Mackenzie cried. She pulled the neckline of her off-the-shoulder shirt up over her nose and mouth, muffling her voice. "It's poison or something."

Riot stepped closer to one of the clouds, which was thickening with every passing second, appearing significantly more opaque as it grew. He sniffed, then stumbled back, his body racked by a fit of coughing.

"See?" Mackenzie climbed on top of a desk, trying to stay above the white clouds.

"Not. Poison," Riot sputtered. Then he flipped the collar of his shirt up and held it over his face, just as Mackenzie had done. "Chalk dust."

Neela stared at the advancing cloud. "Standard classroom chalk is made from calcium carbonate, which is considered nontoxic, though prolonged exposure to the dust has proven to be a mild irritant and may complicate previously existing respiratory conditions."

"So it won't kill us," Kevin said.

Nonlethal chalk dust seemed like a wasted opportunity to knock off another competitor. So far, every detail of the rooms had been meticulously planned: the designer had been one step ahead of them at all times. So why this innocuous school supply? What did it signify? Or what was it meant to hide?

"Look through the desks," Persey cried as she raced to join Neela at the chalkboard. "See if you can find any other clues before we're blinded by this stuff."

Kevin set on the nearest desk while Riot headed to the exit door. Persey could just make out his figure through the thick cloud of dust as he examined the touch pads affixed to the door.

But while they were both working to find the solution, Mackenzie stood firmly on her perch, shirt still clutched around her mouth. "I'm not going anywhere until that door is open."

As much as Persey wanted to table-flip the desk with Mackenzie still on it, she didn't have time. Neela was transfixed by the chalk, probably trying to work out the mystery of its purpose when she needed to be working on a different problem altogether.

Persey grabbed Neela by both shoulders, physically turning her back to the math equation. "How fast can you solve for *x*?"

Neela blinked rapidly, refocusing as she scanned the chalkboard. "Um, a minute or two? But I have no idea what those are." She pointed to the numbered chalk dots that were scattered seemingly at random to the right of the equation.

"Leave them to me."

Neela nodded, then attacked the equation.

"Eight to the *x* over two to the *y*. Yes, definitely advanced exponent rules." She muttered to herself as she started to work out the answer. "I'll just rewrite this side of the equation, then substitute two to the three-*x* power for eight to the *x* . . ."

It was like number-and-letter salad to Persey, and while she marveled at Neela's ability to see that jumble as a sentence to be diagrammed rather than a nonsensical collection of symbols, she didn't have time to watch the magic unfold. The numbered dots presented another challenge. One they also needed to solve.

"It's like a microcosm of Y2K over here," Kevin said between coughs. His voice came from the back of the room, but the chalk was so thick, Persey couldn't see him. "*Lizzie McGuire* notepad, tattoo choker necklace, Pokémon packs, Quidditch card game. Too bad Arlo isn't here to nerdsplain how to play it."

"Dude . . ." Riot said.

"What, too soon?"

"All your jokes are too soon," Persey said, without pulling her eyes away from the chalkboard. She could still see it clearly, but even the few inches of space between her and it were now clouding over with whiteness.

"OW!" Riot yelped. Out of the corner of her eyes, Persey saw him jump away from the door. "That thing fucking electrocuted me."

"The door?" Mackenzie asked.

"The lock."

Persey joined him, peering closely at the line of number locks. "Which one?"

"Bottom." Riot shoved his fingers in his mouth like a teething infant. "I barely even laid a finger on the number pad."

A creaking hinge signaled that Kevin was searching another desk. "Any luck with those dots?"

"Then we just substitute twelve in there," Neela continued. "So it's two to the twelfth . . ."

"No idea." Persey sighed, causing the chalk cloud to ripple before her, further jumbling the dots and digits. "These numbers are all over the place. Fifty-seven, fifty-eight, fifty-nine here. But another sequence starts at three hundred and two, or four thousand and ninety-six—"

"Four thousand and ninety-six," Neela said at almost the exact same time.

Persey spun toward her. "Is that the answer?"

"Yep."

"Can't be a coincidence." Riot was right beside Persey, though she hadn't seen him approach. His fingers lightly grazed her hand, trailing down her thumb until he found the piece of chalk she held. "May I?"

"O-of course." *Why does he make me so nervous?*

Riot smiled, soft and relaxed despite the danger they all faced, as he pressed the chalk to the dot labeled "4,096." He drew a line from it to the next one in numerical order. "It's like a giant connect the dots. Four thousand and ninety-seven, ninety-eight, ninety-nine, five thousand."

The sequence ended there, with no 5,001, but the line Riot had drawn pointed directly at the second number lock from the top.

Persey waved her hand in front of her face, trying to drive away the thickening dust so she could see the door clearly. "That must be the one we're supposed to use."

"You think?" Mackenzie said. Her voice was close, and Persey realized that, despite her protests, she'd left her perch on the desk.

Neela hurried around them and stood in front of the door. "The code to open it must be four thousand and—"

"Don't!" Persey cried, snatching Neela's hand away just as she was about to punch in the first number. She thought of Riot's minor electrocution when he started messing around with the number keys, and the consequences of wrong answers in the ATM booth. What if this was the same, except pressing the wrong code might lead to something bigger than just a tiny shock?

"You're thinking it's something else?" Neela asked, eyebrows knitted together.

I'm thinking you might get killed. "Yeah."

"What else could it be?" Mackenzie asked, exasperated.

"Five thousand and one, for starters," Riot said, tapping the final connected dot with the piece of chalk. "It's next in the sequence."

"Anything else?" Persey asked.

"The crap I found in those desks was all from the year 2000," Kevin said. "Even the copyright on the *Lizzie McGuire* notepad."

"Three options," Neela said. "Which do we try?"

"I vote for the year!" Kevin said, raising his hand. "It seems like the most 'escape room–y' solution."

Mackenzie stepped up to the pad. "Don't listen to him. He's not even supposed to be here. I vote for math girl's solution."

For a moment, Persey wondered if it was Mackenzie, not Wes, who was conspiring to kill them off. "That thing is rigged to deliver an electric shock when you touch it," she said. "Riot only hit one number. What

286

happens to the person who enters an incorrect code?"

Neela leaped away from the door. "Holy cow babies! I could have died."

Persey was pretty sure that was the intention.

"Wrap some fabric around your hand," Riot suggested, rolling his sleeve down so it covered his palm. "For protection."

But Neela shook her head. "That's a capacitive-sensing screen. Like a cell phone. It'll only register if the electromagnetic field is interrupted by something conductive."

"I'm telling you—the year 2000. I've got a good feeling." Kevin turned Neela to face the door. "Try it."

"I'll do it." The words flew out of Persey's mouth before she even realized what she'd said. *What are you doing?*

"No!" Neela cried. "Kevin's right. I . . . I should be the one to do it. I solved the equation."

"Which means you've already done your part."

Persey stared at the flat, illuminated number pad. The wrong combination was probably going to fry her like a hush puppy, so she needed to choose carefully.

Four thousand and ninety-six.

Five thousand and one.

Two thousand.

"Choose carefully," Kevin said. "Please."

Right. *Carefully.* Three options. But were those all the clues this room had to offer? Or . . .

Persey thought of the rooms they'd been in so far—the office, the loft, the collection, Cavethedral. Each had details that when combined together, revealed the exit. Those details had been chosen carefully. And yet here they were in this classroom that was slowly filling with a nontoxic, annoying-but-not-lethal substance. How could it not have a purpose?

"The chalk," she said, unable to shake the feeling that it was the key to this mystery. "How could it translate into a number of some kind?"

Kevin snorted. "Maybe if we figured out how much all this chalk weighed."

"Weight!" Neela cried. "You're brilliant!"

Riot dropped his voice. "Said no one ever."

"You think we can figure out how much all this powder weighs?" Kevin asked, rubbing his reddening eyes as the dust thickened around them.

"Nope!" Persey could barely see Neela's face, but her voice sounded positively giddy. "Just one molecule."

The ATM booth. Persey's first instinct had been some sort of chemistry problem. Was that the answer now?

"Calcium carbonate," Riot said. "That's what, $CaCO_3$?"

"Yes!" Neela said, her voice froggy from the chalk. "So the weight is easy to figure out. One calcium at forty point oh seven eight." She took a quick breath, then broke into a fit of coughing as she sputtered out the rest of the formula. "One . . . carbon, which is twelve point oh one oh seven. Three oxygen at fifteen—" She sneezed, the chalk cloud billowing in front of her mouth. "Sorry. Fifteen point ninety-nine ninety-four."

Persey waved her hands in front of her face, trying to clear the air. "Thank God you have a photographic memory, or we'd all be dead."

"You're welcome," Neela said, still calculating in her brain. "Carry the one and . . . one hundred point eight six nine."

This had to be the answer.

"Argh! That's—" Mackenzie gagged on the thick dust. Even her coughs sounded exasperated. "That's not four digits!"

"Who said it had to be four?" Persey asked.

"Fine. Then you try it."

"Fine, I will."

"Okay," Kevin said on an exhale, as if giving permission. "Go for it."

Without hesitating so she couldn't change her mind, Persey typed in the first digit, letting the pad of her finger rest against the glass long enough to feel the electric shock, if it was going to come. But she didn't feel a thing.

"It's working!" Neela gasped.

Persey sure the hell hoped so. Hand trembling, she typed in the next five numbers as quickly and accurately as she could, then paused before entering the last one. *If you're wrong, this stupid door will be the last thing you ever see.* Her eyes drifted toward Kevin. She couldn't see his face through the haze, just the outline of his tall form and his small, almost-imperceptible nod of encouragement.

Now or never.

Persey held her breath and hit the nine.

THIRTY-NINE

PERSEY HAD OFTEN WONDERED WHAT IT MUST BE LIKE TO BE electrocuted. Such a punishment hadn't been deemed "cruel and unusual" in the eyes of justice departments across the country, who used electrocution as a common means of execution, but Persey had seen a documentary on television once about a man named Willie Francis, who survived the first attempt to execute him by the electric chair. He said that when the switch was thrown, his arms jolted involuntarily and his skin felt as if he was being pricked by thousands of needles all over his body.

It was with a Riot-like intellectual curiosity (fatalism) that she touched the final number on the pad, half wondering if she might discover the truth in Willie Francis's words for herself.

But instead of the sensation of transforming into a real-life voodoo doll, all Persey felt was the bolt sliding free inside the heavy door, releasing the lock. With her finger still pressed firmly against the glass pad, Persey pushed.

The door swung open.

Adrenaline still pumping blood through her ears with a thunder so deafening she couldn't even hear the people around her, Persey felt a hand on her back, a figure brushing past her arm, and then her legs were moving as she was half dragged out of the classroom.

"You okay?" Kevin asked. He held her by the elbow, supporting her weight. Once again, he'd made sure she was safely out of a dangerous situation.

Persey nodded, not entirely sure she even knew what "okay" was anymore. "Yeah."

He leaned closer to her. "Why did you volunteer as tribute back there? What if you were wrong?"

"But I wasn't."

"You could have been killed."

"But I wasn't."

Kevin's brow clouded, and once again, Persey was struck by the dichotomy of his personality: carefree and flippant one moment, deadly serious the next. "Just be careful, okay?"

Persey's smile was tight. "Okay."

Neela bounded up to Persey, hands clasped before her. "You saved me. I was so confident the correct answer was the algebraic solution, I didn't even consider other options. I would have . . . I mean, it might have been my last . . ." She heaved a steadying breath. "This is why you solved the Hidden Library: you know how to step back and assess all the options."

"It just reminded me of the ATM booth," Persey said, uncomfortable (unworthy) with any kind of praise. "The first answer that popped into my mind was the atomic number for oxygen."

"Lucky guess," Mackenzie said, tossing her hair over her shoulder.

"Not so lucky if she'd gotten deep-fried from the inside," Riot said. "It was pretty ballsy of you to put your life on the line like that."

Mackenzie grunted. "I wonder if the keypad was really even *that* lethal."

"Are there different levels of lethality?" Neela asked. "I was under the impression that dead was dead."

Mackenzie ignored her. "Maybe Riot was exaggerating."

Riot shook his electrocuted hand as if it still stung. "Or maybe you're an ungrateful hag."

"That room was meant to kill me," Neela said softly. She seemed surprisingly calm and collected.

"We don't know that," Persey lied.

"It's true." Neela's eyes drifted around the new space. "Now who is supposed to die in here?"

There was no mistaking the theme of the new room: if the giant Union Jack pinned on the wall beside a portrait of Her Majesty Queen Elizabeth II didn't tip you off, the four round tables, each set with a hand-painted teapot and saucer set, would have. It was High Tea. An English tearoom.

Was this meant for Mackenzie, Miss Royal College of Music?

As with every other room in the competition, the tearoom had been expertly appointed. A white chair sat at each table, the cushions upholstered in a mix of toile, plaid, and Victorian striped fabrics. The flowers in the little vases, which served as centerpieces, were Tudor roses, their virginal white centers offset by bloodred tips, the symbolism of which wasn't lost on Persey. The walls were papered with a garish pink floral pattern, dotted with framed needlepoints that ringed three sides of the room, and the fourth wall, which housed the flag and the queen, also held a door. It was wooden, old and rough as if it had been taken straight from a thatched cottage in the Cotswolds, but more striking than its style was its functionality. Or lack thereof. This door had no handle.

"Is it too much to hope for that the door will just swing open when we push on it?" Kevin said.

Persey ushered him forward with a sweep of her arm. "You're welcome to give it a try."

With a characteristic shrug, Kevin charged forward, lowering his shoulder at the last moment as he drove it into the wooden door.

The thud of Kevin's impact was quickly followed by a crash as he bounced off the wall, spun backward off-balance, and grabbed hold of the queen's portrait as he attempted to break his fall, carrying it with him onto the floor. The frame cracked on impact, but thankfully, there was no glass.

"Good news!" Kevin said, popping to his feet. "I wasn't electrocuted."

"Is there bad news?" Persey asked.

"Yep. It looks like this door extends down into the floor."

Mackenzie joined him, peering down at the base of the door. "You're right. It just disappears down there. That's the weirdest thing I've ever seen."

Kevin snorted. "No, it's not."

Mackenzie couldn't stop herself from flirting, even in the face of death. "You know, I could show you . . ."

"Maybe later. Right now, I'm starving." He bent over the nearest table and tried to lift the lid off the pot. "It's stuck." Then he tried to pick up the cup and saucer, also with no luck. Same with the vase of Tudor roses and a little tray that held a slip of paper. "I think they've been superglued to the table. Why would anyone do that?"

Persey wasn't sure she wanted to find out.

"Hey, there's even a check!" Kevin bent over the little tray. "Twenty-two pound fifty. That sounds expensive."

"Like thirty bucks," Mackenzie said.

"For thirty bucks, the queen better pour out herself."

Persey approached the nearest table to see the bill for herself. Unlike Kevin's, this bill was for seventeen pound even. Weird.

"These needlepoints are all poems," Neela said. She slowly ringed the room, examining each frame. "'I wandered lonely as a cloud / That floats on high o'er vales and hills / When all at once I saw a crowd / A host, of golden daffodils.'"

"Is that Coldplay?" Mackenzie asked. "Sounds like Coldplay."

"Ew, no." Riot reared back his head, offended.

"It's Wordsworth," Persey said quietly.

Riot's face lit up with admiration. "Nice."

It was the first time she'd admitted to anyone that she read poetry, let alone classic British poetry. Not the Elizabethan stuff that Riot specialized in, but the romantic poets. She loved the way they sounded when read by the English narrators in her audiobooks.

"Oh, yeah, and there are a bunch of volumes of Wordsworth piled up down here on the floor," Neela said.

Kevin clicked his tongue. "Could we all stop quoting dead men before we *become* dead men?" He sounded annoyed by the poetry.

"And women!" Neela pointed out, way too cheerfully for the sentiment as she moved to the next frame. "'For whatsoever from one place doth fall / Is with the tide unto an other brought: / For there is nothing lost, that may be found, if sought.'"

Riot was crouched beside one of the tables, checking underneath, where the tables, like the items on them, had been secured to the floor. "Edmund Spenser's *The Faerie Queene*."

"Yeah?" Neela said, crouching down. "More piled books. *The Shepheardes Calender, Complaints*."

"All Spenser."

Neela moved on to the next one. "'Better to reign in Hell, than to serve in Heaven.'"

"Milton," Riot said quickly. "*Paradise Lost*. Let me guess, the books beneath are titles like *1645 Poems* and *Samson Agonistes*?"

"Yes and yes."

"Shit." Riot stood up and raced to the nearest framed quote, moving around the room quickly. "Wordsworth, Blake, Keats, Tennyson, Shakespeare over here in this corner. All British poets."

Persey immediately realized what he was implying. This room wasn't meant for Mackenzie: it was meant for Riot.

"I wish a clock would start." Mackenzie, always the whiner, stalked toward the nearest table. "Then maybe we'd know what we're supposed to do." She tried to pull the chair away from one of the tables to sit down, but it wouldn't budge, so she slipped between it and the tabletop. "I'm tired of—"

The instant her designer jeans hit the damask cushion, the floor jolted.

The ground beneath Persey's feet jerked sharply, causing her to grab hold of the nearest table to maintain her balance. Then, as she gripped the wooden tabletop by the sides, she had a strange sensation of vertigo, an out-of-body dizziness that made it appear as if the floor was tilting downward. It wasn't until her feet began to slide against the concrete that she realized it wasn't an optical illusion.

"The floor is moving," Kevin said, stating the obvious. "That's why everything is bolted down."

Persey, Neela, and Riot were in the corner of the room farthest from the exit, while Mackenzie and Kevin were nearer the door, and while Persey's side of the room was tilting downward, Kevin and Mackenzie's corner was rising toward the ceiling, so that the floor at their end was blocking the door entirely.

"Neela!" Persey called, fighting to keep her balance as she sank down beneath the lower edge of the papered wall. Piles of books, the only thing in the room not securely fastened to the floor, toppled over and began sliding across the smooth wooden surface. "Get closer to Kevin and Mackenzie. See if we can even this out."

Without a word, Neela edged her way toward the door, sidestepping a huge volume of Shakespeare. Persey followed her, slowly, waiting to feel the room equalize. For the first few steps, she was going uphill, fighting for balance on the steeply tilted floor, but as the shift in her and Neela's weights changed the balance of the room, she felt the floor even out. Inertia slowed the books, scattering them about the room, and when Persey thought the ground had reached horizontal once more, she froze in place.

"You're at the fulcrum," Neela said. "The central balancing point between the weights on either—"

"We know what a fulcrum is!" Mackenzie snapped.

Persey stood with her knees bent, feet hip distance apart, as she tried to get a feel for the ground beneath her. She could sense the angles change as the floor moved like a Tilt-a-Whirl.

"Let me try something," Kevin said. He inched his way around to the left, hugging the wall. Immediately, Persey felt the floor shift toward him, and she had to shuffle her feet to keep from falling.

"Okay," Riot said, moving in the opposite direction to counter Kevin's weight. "The whole floor is anchored at the center, and moves according to our weight distribution. I'm not sure how that's supposed to open the door."

BZZZZZ.

"Shit!" Four of them said it in unison, all but Neela, who merely sucked in a breath.

"Now what?" she squeaked.

Kevin pointed to the Union Jack. "Look at that."

Shining through the thin fabric of the flag was a series of numbers. 263,550,198. Not a countdown, this time—it was too huge a number for that, plus it wasn't moving—but the L-shaped symbol with a line through it signaled that this was a monetary sum in British pounds.

"Two hundred and sixty-three million, five hundred and fifty thousand, one hundred and ninety-eight pounds?" Mackenzie read. "What kind of random-ass amount is that?"

Persey stared at the flag, trying to wrap her head around that huge a sum of money, when a sound caught her attention. A whir of a motor. But when Persey glanced around, she noticed with a sigh of relief that none of the four walls were closing in on them.

Then an odd glint in the corner of her vision made her look up.

Gleaming in the darkness two stories above their heads, Persey could see the pointed ends of the spikes slowly descending upon them.

FORTY

"GUYS," PERSEY SAID, HEAD TILTED BACK. SHE COULDN'T TEAR her eyes away from the ceiling. "We're in trouble."

"And that's news, how?" Mackenzie stepped forward away from the wall to get a better look. As she did, the weight distribution of the floor changed, and her corner was pushed farther toward the ceiling.

"Fuck!" Kevin cried, ducking. "You think they'd come up with something more original. Dudes, you've done spikes *to death*."

Persey groaned. His humor was literally the worst.

The roof wasn't close enough yet to prove immediately dangerous, but Persey recognized the dilemma right away. Unless their weight was evenly distributed, or they were all gathered at the dead center of the room, one side of the floor would be depressed while the other raised toward the murderous spikes.

Mackenzie froze, arms wide as if trying to keep her balance, then slowly scooted back until the floor was even again. "I thought we were done with those!"

"Thinking was your first mistake," Riot said.

"Okay, kids, we must be missing something." Kevin carefully stood upright again, hand still over his head for protection. "Everybody look around."

Persey's attention drifted to the number on the wall. 263,681,285.

Was that right?

"Neela," Persey said, hardly daring to move as she spoke lest the floor might career upward out of control. "Is that the same number that came up originally?"

Neela tilted her head to the side, lips pursed. "No." Then she closed her eyes. "Two six three, five five zero, one nine eight."

Kevin held out a thumbs-up. "Photographic memory for the win."

"Did anyone see it change?" Mackenzie asked.

"No, but . . ." Riot's voice trailed off. "Brace yourselves. I want to try something."

Persey crouched as Riot took a few tentative steps forward. That moment, the weight balance in the room changed, shifting the floor back toward the exit. The force of gravity pulled on the scattered books, pulling them down toward the dipped corner, and as everything shifted, the numbers on the readout changed as well. The pound amount shot up, accelerating as the floor angle became more precipitous, and stopped when Riot froze, balancing with the floor at a thirty-degree angle.

"So the numbers are important to opening the door, I'm guessing," he said. "But how?"

"Seems like a lot of money," Kevin said. He leaned to his left, and the tally went up seven pounds. "Mack, what's the exchange rate?"

She turned her back on him. "Don't call me Mack."

Kevin snorted. "An hour ago, you would have let me call you whatever I wanted."

"Oh my God!" Neela cried, throwing her hands up in the air. "Is this really the time and place for that? You can lick your ego wounds later; just tell us the freakity frack exchange rate!"

It was the closest Neela had come to losing her shit, and even "freakity frack" seemed practically like a swear word coming out of her mouth. Mackenzie looked startled by the outburst and dropped her snideness for a moment.

"Seventy-five cents to the dollar," she said.

"Thank you." Then Neela closed her eyes again, lips working silently. "So almost three hundred and fifty-one million dollars."

Kevin whistled. "That'd buy you a lot of escape room tickets."

"Or a lot of tea services," Riot added.

Persey looked around at the tables, all of which had been set for tea. Tea for four people. Because there were only supposed to be four of them left. Four survivors.

"I wonder . . ."

"What is it?" Kevin said, watching her closely.

"I don't know."

"We're about to get skewered from above, which means we don't have time for coyness." His eyes narrowed. "You've got an idea."

"Okay." Persey's eyes drifted to the nearest table. "There are four tables, and four of us should have survived Recess. Maybe everyone is supposed sit at a different table."

Riot nodded. "Makes sense."

Persey pointed to the center. "Neela, stand right in the middle. At the . . . whatever it's called."

"The fulcrum. Right."

The floor tilted precariously while everyone took the nearest chair. Using the oscillations of the floor, Neela found the central balance point and tried to position herself above it without adding weight to one side or the other. Once everyone was settled, the side of the floor that abutted the door shifted up about two feet, and the numbers on the wall raced up and down as people reorganized themselves, coming to a rest at 377,042,581.

Neela did the calculation without being prompted. "That's five hundred and two million, one hundred and forty-four thousand, three hundred and one."

"Means nothing to me," Kevin said. "Switch?"

They shifted chairs moving one seat clockwise, like a complicated game of musical chairs. This time the floor tilted back toward the door, but not far enough.

"Three hundred and seventy-two million," Neela began, "nine hundred and—"

"It doesn't matter," Mackenzie said, cutting her off. "We know it's not right. Keep moving."

They shifted again, and again the floor dipped toward the door. Again, not far enough.

"Neela," Riot asked as he stood up from rotation number three, "how many different permutations are there for the four of us at four tables?"

She didn't even hesitate to do the math in her head. "Twenty-four."

Persey glanced up at the ceiling, close enough now that an NBA player going for a dunk might be in mortal danger. "We don't have time to try all of them."

"The numbers must mean something," Kevin said, shifting to the next table. "But I've never seen fuck all of three hundred million or whatever dollars."

Three hundred million dollars . . . "Holy shit." She was a fucking idiot. "Neela, how much did you say the Brownes lost after the Prison Break debacle?"

Neela gasped. "Two hundred and fifty million!"

"Backward math," Kevin said, pointing at Neela. "Stat."

She was way ahead of him, eyes closed, lips working as she did the mental calculation. "One hundred and eighty-seven million, seven hundred and sixteen, two hundred and fifty pounds."

"And a partridge in a pear tree," Kevin added dryly.

The ceiling was dangerously close—another couple of minutes and Kevin and Riot, the tallest ones in the room, were going to have to crouch as they moved from table to table—and even though they suspected their target amount was correct, it was still a moving target. Neela, poised at the center, directed traffic. Persey could see her eyes flashing back and forth between the tally and the tables, watching as the numbers raced up and down.

"This is useless," Kevin panted, eying the rapidly approaching roof as they futilely switched places yet again. "We're about to be Swiss cheese, people."

"Swiss cheese?" Neela asked.

"Holey." Kevin forced a laugh at his own joke. "Man, I wish there was actual food with this. . . ." He bent forward to look at the bill on his table. "Twenty-four and a half pound tea. I'd like *something* for my last meal."

"Twenty-four pounds fifty . . ." One check had been for twenty-two fifty, another for seventeen. The one at the table where she currently sat was for twenty. Those numbers, all different, couldn't have been random. Nothing in these rooms ever was. "Guys, the numbers on the checks are all different. Maybe that's a clue to where we're supposed to sit?"

"What are the numbers?" Riot asked.

"Twenty-four, twenty-two fifty, twenty, seventeen."

"Huh," Mackenzie said. "I just turned twenty last week."

"And I'm seventeen." Persey straightened up. *Could it be that simple?*

Riot raised his hand. "Twenty-two and a half," he said. "Almost to the day."

They all turned to Kevin.

"Any chance you're twenty-four?" Persey asked.

He smiled. "That's what my ID says!"

"And I'm nineteen," Neela added. "But since apparently I wasn't supposed to survive this long, it makes sense that my age would not be represented."

Persey didn't know what was going to happen when they all took their "assigned" seats, but it wasn't as if they had much of a choice. Without further discussion, they scurried around, dodging sliding books and one another, and took their places: Kevin was nearest the door, Riot farthest way, Mackenzie and Persey in opposite corners. Neela stayed at the dead center of the room, trying to remain a neutral weight. Kevin was the last to take his seat, and then they all turned to the tally on the wall. It should have been 187,716,250 pounds, if their theory was correct.

"One hundred and eighty-two million, five hundred thousand, seven hundred and twelve," Neela read. "It didn't work."

"Fuck!" Mackenzie started to stand up. "This is pointless. We're all going to die!"

"Don't move!" Persey cried, holding up her hand. She was watching the wall near her table, where the floor wasn't perfectly perpendicular to the wall. She waved to her left. "Neela, can you shift that way?"

Neela complied with little baby steps. The tally shifted slowly, rising incremental amounts. Persey held her breath. 185 million. 186 . . . Neela froze with the tally just a few hundred pounds from their target, then shifted her weight onto her left leg. 187,716,250!

The sound of a heavy lock being thrown echoed through the tearoom; then the door swung open into the darkness beyond.

FORTY-ONE

"NOBODY MOVE!" RIOT CRIED. THE MOMENT THE DOOR WAS open, everyone had subconsciously begun to move toward it, which rocketed Riot's end of the floor upward toward the descending spikes.

Persey froze, then shifted her weight backward. Slowly the floor reached the horizontal. But the dilemma had been clearly illustrated by their collective impulse: every time one of them tried to reach the door, it would tilt someone else toward a pointy death.

"Neela should stay," Mackenzie said. "She was supposed to die last time. It's only fair."

"Um, how is that fair, exactly?" Neela asked.

"No one has to stay and get impaled," Persey said, not entirely sure how she was going to accomplish that mandate. "We just need to find something to balance the weight. Like a piece of furniture—"

"Which is all bolted down," Kevin countered.

Yeah, I know. "Or . . ." Persey cast her eyes around the room, looking for anything they could use as a counterbalance.

"The books!" Riot cried.

"Oh my God!" How could Persey have been so slow? "Of course. That's why they're here."

"Okay, but . . ." Kevin pointed up. The gleaming tips of a hundred spikes were just inches from his head now. "We need to do this quickly."

With the books scattered across the tilting tearoom, this wasn't going to be an easy task. They had to get everything piled up at Riot's end of the room to act as a counterweight to the five of them as they all tried to make it through the door. Mackenzie, shockingly, refused to help, parking herself inches from the open door to ensure that no matter what happened, she'd make it out alive.

Neela did most of the hustling. Aside from being the shortest contestant left, thus able to stand upright long after the others were forced to crouch, she was also, essentially, superfluous weight, so as she moved back and forth, to and fro, across the room, and the shift in one person's weight was easier to counterbalance than if Persey, Kevin, Neela, and Riot had all been schlepping those books around at the same time. She started with the largest volumes—Shakespeare, Byron, Tennyson—and with every additional hardcover added to Riot's corner, he and Persey were able to move a little bit closer to an escape.

"Almost there," Persey said after delivering all of *Don Juan* to the back corner. She had to crouch low, which affected her speed, and wasn't entirely sure how many more of these trips would be possible.

"We're almost there." Riot was halfway across the room at this point, Neela having long abandoned that area as the shifting fulcrum took her closer to the open door. "We're going to make it."

But Leah wasn't about to make it that easy. Almost as soon as the words left Riot's mouth, the motor that powered the ceiling roared, the intensity of the noise indicating a new level of danger, and the ceiling began to fall faster.

"Shit." Persey had an armful of books, but at this rate, there was no way she'd be able to deposit them at the other end of the room and make it to the door in time.

"Throw them!" Riot cried.

It was a good idea. They needed the weight of the books, not eBay-condition collectibles. She dropped them on the ground and with a swift series of kicks, sent the volumes careening toward the corner.

"Go!" Riot ordered, taking a few more steps toward the door.

Mackenzie and Kevin hadn't waited. They stood as close to the door as they could without actually stepping through.

Persey eyed the distance between Riot and the door. "You won't make it."

"Perhaps," Neela suggested, "if we move fast enough, Riot can outrun the acceleration of gravity. I mean, not really, but the appearance of it in this case, yes."

"It's worth a shot," Persey said, though she didn't think it would actually work.

"On three, then." Riot edged closer to the door before he even started the countdown. "One. Two. *Three.*"

The angle of the floor shifted almost as soon as Persey began to run toward the door. She immediately felt as if she was running uphill, if the hill was magically growing steeper by the second, and the open darkness of the door began to disappear. They hadn't distributed enough weight at the door end of the room to make this mad dash work.

But just as suddenly as Persey had found herself running uphill, the dynamic shifted. She'd passed the point of no balance return, and she had to lean back to keep from tumbling forward into the darkness of the open doorway.

"Son of a Shatner!" Neela cried. She lost her balance and slipped onto her butt, sliding all the way down toward the door. The faster she fell, the faster the room tilted until Persey was sure the whole floor would topple over and fall away.

"Shit!" Riot cried. Persey turned to find that he had flattened himself on the ground, his head just inches from the spikes.

"Go through the door!" Persey cried. Mackenzie, Kevin, didn't matter. They had to even out the weight or Riot was going to get skewered.

Mackenzie, thankfully, was only thinking of herself and didn't need to be told twice. She disappeared through the doorway, followed closely by Neela, who rolled rather than stepped off the Tilt-a-Whirl. The absence of their weight did the trick, and the room shifted back toward equilibrium again. But the ceiling hadn't slowed, and Riot was only able to push himself as far up as his hands and knees to continue the trek.

"You can do it," Persey said, turning to face him as she ducked into the doorway, careful to keep both feet on the tearoom floor so they didn't lose Riot altogether.

"Come on!" Kevin held out his hand as Riot frantically crawled toward them on his elbows and hips, an army trainee doing the crocodile.

"He's not going to make it," Persey said, hoping that Riot didn't hear her as she tried to guesstimate the distance left between spike and flesh.

Riot stopped crawling. "I know."

"Dude!" Kevin cried. "What are you doing?"

"I won't make it to the door in time." He rolled onto his side, eyes flying across the ceiling as it rapidly approached. "But what if I don't have to?"

"Has he gone mental?" Kevin asked.

As if in answer, Riot began to stretch his limbs in a variety of ways—one hand out before him, elbow crooked at a ninety-degree angle, a leg kicked back as if he was stretching while the other was hitched in front. Riot kept glancing back and forth between his weirdly stretched body and the lethal spikes, and just when Persey was about to look away because she couldn't handle the idea of watching his impalement in slow motion, he called out excitedly. "I've got it. This is going to work."

"What's going to work?"

Kevin clapped his hand over Persey's eyes. "Don't look. You don't want to see this."

THUD.

Then silence.

"I'm okay!" Riot's voice was excited, rapturous. Not even a hint of agony. Persey's eyes flew open, and she saw that he'd managed to contort his body so that his sinewy limbs all fit in the gaps between the spikes that were now penetrating the floor. But they'd stopped, leaving a gap of about twelve inches between ceiling and floor, crisscrossed with the metal spikes.

"Now what?" Persey asked. It was a miracle that Riot was still alive, but how long would he stay that way? Would he have to lie there until they managed to escape and summon help?

"I think I can get to you," Riot said, craning his neck in her direction. "I just need to get my shoulder around this one spike; then it's almost a straight shot."

"Really?"

"Yep. Pretty sure."

"Dude," Kevin said, repeating himself. "That is pretty badass. Do you think you could teach me how to curl my body up like a—"

But Kevin's final thought was cut off by a sickening crack. He and Persey felt the floor shudder beneath them and just had enough time to leap into the open doorway before the two pieces of the tearoom—floor and ceiling—slammed together like a giant industrial garment press.

Persey heard a scream accompanied by the crunching of 206 human bones being pulverized all at once.

And then Riot was nothing but dust.

FORTY-TWO

PERSEY CONTINUED TO STARE AT WHAT WAS LEFT OF HIGH Tea. From her vantage point on the other side of the door, she could see the seam where roof and floor had slammed together. They were totally flush, not a centimeter gap between the two. The force of the two pieces being clapped together pulverized everything. Tables, chairs, books. Riot.

He was still in there, just on the other side of this door, pinned like a pressed flower in a book but with significantly more blood and guts sprayed everywhere. Dead. Just like Wes. And Shaun. And Arlo. And B.J.

Persey couldn't save any of them, and as she slowly rested her forehead against the rough surface of the door, she wondered if there truly was no escape from all this death.

She understood why everyone had been brought to Escape-Capades that day, understood the gravity of what Riot and Wes and Mackenzie and Shaun and Arlo and even the unwitting Neela had done. But did they deserve this? Wasn't there some kind of less lethal justice that could have been doled out instead? Couldn't they have been turned over to the authorities and prosecuted for idea theft, extortion, *something*? Why wasn't justice left to the authorities?

"This shouldn't be happening," she said out loud.

"But it is," Kevin countered. He stood close behind her.

She turned to face him, tears welling up in her eyes. "Why?"

"It just is."

That's not an answer.

Kevin's face was hard-set as he stared down at her. He looked bigger than before, wider and stronger, and he stood like a wall between her and whatever lay behind him in the room. The implication was clear—he meant to protect her. But would he be able to? If push came to shove, would he let one of the others die to save Persey's life?

And could she live with that?

"I didn't do anything. I didn't. I didn't do it." Mackenzie paced in a tight circle, wringing her hands in front of her once-white shirt, like Lady Macbeth attempting to get the imaginary spots out. Her eyes were wide, hair half matted, half frizzy, and the carefully applied makeup from this morning was now smudged and smeared across her face, leaving raccoon eyes and the illusion of an off-kilter mouth. "I didn't. This isn't happening. This is all a dream. I'm stuck in a bad dream."

"Mackenzie?" Persey asked as Mackenzie passed by. "Are you okay?"

"I'll just wake up, that's what I'll do. I'll wake up and I'll be in the hotel and all of this is not real."

Kevin waved his hand in front of her face, but she didn't even flinch. "I think Mack has gone bye-bye."

"Guys," Neela said. "I don't know what the hell that thing is, but I'm scared."

"That thing?" Persey turned away from Mackenzie to face the rest of the room. It was almost entirely bare, a rarity in the Escape-Capades All-Star Competition. Instead of an incredibly detailed set, perfectly thematic and mindfully decorated down to the square inch, the space looked unfinished. Half conceived. The floors were a gleaming white tile, shined squeaky clean so that it reflected the bright overhead lights embedded in the ceiling. The walls were white to match, so unmarred that Persey assumed they had been painted that morning, perhaps not even dry. A single black dome on the ceiling housed a camera, which was mounted right in the middle of the room, as if begging to be seen and acknowledged. Not just a reminder that someone had been watching them all along, but a demand for that surveillance to be recognized.

But the walls and the tile and the camera were background noise to the star attraction in the room. Standing squarely in the middle of all that whiteness was a giant yellow tractor-looking thing, with a conveyor belt on one end and some kind of blower on the other. It looked as if it had been brought inside to do some kind of industrial construction work and just left there, forgotten.

There was one more item in the room, so small in comparison to the tractor that Persey almost didn't see it at first. A table stood directly in front of the yellow machine: simple, small, and made of a clear acrylic material, it was the perfect display for the handgun that sat squarely at its center.

Just sitting there. Waiting for someone to take it.

"Welcome to True North."

Neela jolted at the sound of the obviously male voice. "Wh-who's that?"

Persey shook her head. "No idea." They'd only heard Leah's voice today, so this was jarring.

"Who the fuck are you?" Mackenzie screamed, spinning around the room looking for someone to address. Her trance had been broken, her hope that this was all a bad dream obliterated. "Why are you doing this to us?" Her entire body shook. The raccoon eyes now looked more like leaking inkwells, her face streaked black by running mascara, dragged down her porcelain cheeks by heavy tears.

The voice paused, contemplating. *"Isn't it obvious why you're here? You've already had that conversation."*

Mackenzie sobbed uncontrollably, drool flinging from her lips with each word. "I had nothing to do with that, okay? It was all Wes. All of it."

"I don't know about the Black Widow over there," Kevin said, speaking directly to the camera, "but I'm just an innocent bystander."

"Are you?"

Kevin threw his arms up in a gesture of blamelessness. "Dude!"

Persey stepped around Kevin, whose protection she wasn't sure she wanted. She felt stupid addressing a black domed camera. It was like talking to someone in dark sunglasses—you could never tell if they were looking at you, paying attention, or even awake behind those shades. "What do you want from us?"

"Justice."

"This isn't justice!" Mackenzie screamed. "I didn't do anything wrong."

Kevin shot her a look. "Why, because you didn't actually put the Glock in Melinda Browne's hand?"

Neela crept up beside Persey, staring at the camera. Unlike Mackenzie, she was perfectly calm. Resigned, perhaps, to their fate. "I know we can't bring them back," she said. "And I know this doesn't make up for anything, but I just want you to know that I'm sorry."

"Neela," Persey said, "this isn't your fault."

"I'm the one who solved the puzzle."

"But you didn't know what you were doing."

Neela swallowed. "Does it matter? People died because of what I did.

Because I wanted to show off that I could solve the puzzle when no one else could. Because . . ." She paused, brow pinched. "Because I wanted to impress Arlo. She was cute and smart and so fajita-ing cool, and I thought maybe if I did solve her puzzle she might, like, want to meet me or something. See? I was totally selfish about the whole thing. I wasn't solving a puzzle to, like, end world hunger. It was ego. I deserve to die here."

"There!" Mackenzie pointed at Neela. "She's accepting blame. You want to punish someone? Punish the nerd."

Persey wanted to smack Mackenzie across her cowardly face, but that wouldn't solve their problem. She took Neela's hand and squeezed it. "You're not going to die here," she said under her breath, then stepped toward the camera. "What do you want, L. Browne? That's who you are, right? The child of Derrick and Melinda Browne? The sole inheritor of Escape-Capades?"

"What are you doing?" Kevin hissed. For the first time that day, he looked afraid.

She didn't stop to answer him. "You want justice for your parents' deaths? Wes, Arlo, Shaun, and Riot have already paid that price. Don't you think that's enough bloodshed for one day?"

There was a pause during which time Persey's heart thundered. Kevin's words rang in her head. *What are you doing?*

"I want the truth."

"The truth?" Did anyone even know what that was anymore?

"We haven't heard the whole story yet."

"We haven't?"

"One of you is holding back."

Persey groaned. How many more secrets in conjunction with the Brownes and the Prison Break disaster could there possibly be? "Who? Who isn't telling the truth?"

The voice on the loudspeaker paused; then instead of answering her question, he launched into what sounded like a prewritten speech.

"The piece of machinery in the middle of the room is a wood chipper, an industrial model. It can reduce an entire tree to pulp in seconds."

"I do *not* like the sound of this," Kevin said.

"It can also render a body unrecognizable. There is one person in this room who is still lying about what happened last year, but I'm not going to tell you who. That's the final puzzle—the one you need to solve in order to escape."

Persey stiffened. "Puzzle?"

"On the table, there is a Glock 29 Gen-Four Subcompact. Like the one used in the Brownes' deaths. Loaded and ready to fire. Identify the guilty party, dole out justice, and get rid of the evidence. If you get it right, I'll let the rest of you go."

"And if we get it wrong?" Kevin asked.

Again, a pause. This time Persey was pretty sure it was for dramatic effect. *"Then we keep trying."*

Time seemed to slow down. While Persey and Neela were still processing the meaning of his words—that one of them might get shot and pulverized, but it could be the wrong person and they'd have to do it all again—Mackenzie and Kevin had jumped into action. They each lunged for the gun, knocking the table over in the process. The Glock slid across the floor like a puck on ice and slammed into the wall, ricocheting off at an angle.

"You're not going to make me the scapegoat!" Mackenzie raced after the gun, reaching down as the weapon's momentum slowed, but Kevin was faster. He shoved Mackenzie from behind, sending her sprawling to the floor. As she struggled to get up, hands slipping on the slick, pristine tile, Kevin pounced on the gun.

"It's not me!" Mackenzie screamed. "I've told you everything. I admitted as much in the iron maiden, remember?"

Mackenzie must have truly believed that Kevin was about to take her out, but as he scrambled to his feet, the Glock firmly gripped in his hand, it wasn't Mackenzie he turned the weapon on.

It was Persey.

FORTY-THREE

IT WAS THE YELLING THAT THREW PERSEY OFF. NOT THAT there hadn't been plenty of yelling in Persey's house—almost entirely from her dad, though occasionally her mom yelled back—but most of it was centered around or directed at Persey, so to come home from school and hear raised voices already in progress was new.

The argument was coming from the kitchen. It filtered through the swinging double doors into the foyer, and Persey recognized the voices right away: her dad, her mom . . . and her brother.

He must have come back from Vietnam, just like their dad wanted. But judging by the volume level, it wasn't a joyous homecoming.

He was trying to get Dad to reopen the money tap. That's the only reason she could think of that would lure her brother back home. And since he was accustomed (conditioned) to using his considerable charm to get his own way, it made sense that he'd use what was left of his funds to fly home in an attempt to get more.

The old Persey would have turned upstairs, retreated to her room, and let the conversation downstairs play itself out. The outcome was practically a foregone conclusion—why witness her brother's manipulations firsthand? *But the shouting.* It was angry, stubborn. Things weren't going according to her brother's plan.

And that was worth seeing.

She crept to the kitchen door, careful to keep her body to one side of the gap between the two swinging sides so as not to give away her presence, and listened.

"I don't understand why you won't get over this," her brother said. "I'm never going back to Columbia."

"Of course you're not," her dad snapped. "They wouldn't allow you to reenroll. But I have connections at other schools. State, for example. They'd be happy to have you."

"I'm not going to State. Or anywhere. I'm getting a real-world education."

"But, darling . . ." Her mom sounded slightly less intoxicated than usual. "What kind of career do you expect to have without a college degree?"

Hadn't she made the same argument in reverse to describe Persey's future?

"Mom, you're adorable. I already know how to run this company. Why do I need a BA for that?"

"Okay, Boss. Slow down." Her dad again. Less angry, more surprised. "Your plan is to take over the family business? Just like that?" He snapped his fingers.

"No, that's *your* plan, Dad. The one you've been drilling into me for years. But what I'm saying is, why wait? Why wait until you're both too old to enjoy your retirement? You could take Mom to Fiji for a month, one of those all-inclusives she's been talking about literally since I was five."

"Yes," her mom said, "but I don't think we're—"

"And you could still be involved," her brother continued, talking faster. "Like a pitch man on TV. You would stay here and hold down the fort while I build our brand overseas."

"Which I'm *happy* to let you do," her dad said, "once you've finished your degree."

"FUCK THE DEGREE!" Her brother's fury exploded, rage propelling the words so violently out of his body that Persey could hear the globules of spit that accompanied them. "I'm not waiting four years to start living my life. Genevieve and I—"

"Don't bring her into this," her dad said. "This isn't about her."

"There is no 'her' and 'me' anymore. Only 'us.'"

There was a pause, and then a strangled gasp from Persey's mom. He must have showed them something. A wedding ring? Had he actually gotten married to his girlfriend?

"God DAMN IT!" Her dad slammed his palm down on the kitchen counter, a move which heretofore had usually (exclusively) been reserved for addressing Persey's grades. "You can't just waltz in here and demand the company business, understand? You have to earn it. You have to go to college and get your degree and then you come and work *for* the company, learning the ropes before you can even begin to think about taking over."

"And what if I don't want to?" Her brother's voice had gone eerily (ominously) calm, and though Persey wasn't even in the room, she felt a chill of dread creep down the back of her neck.

"Then I'll be forced to take drastic measures."

"Like you did with my sister? Cut me out of your will unless I do exactly what you want me to?"

A pause. "If that's what it takes, yes."

"I'm sorry, but I can't let you do that."

Then a gunshot echoed through the house.

FORTY-FOUR

PERSEY HELD HER HANDS UP BEFORE HER. AS IF THAT MIGHT *actually* stop Kevin. "What are you doing?"

"I'm trying to save our lives," Kevin said. "Those that are worth saving, at least."

Persey shook her head. "I don't understand." The bottom dropped out from her stomach, her eyes fixed on the hollow muzzle of the gun.

"Wes might have killed B.J., Arlo, and Shaun," Kevin said. "But he didn't do it randomly. He had to be working with somebody. At somebody's direction."

"Okay . . ."

"Someone who turned on him." Kevin's eyes shifted to the camera for a split second. "I'll kill her. Let the rest of us go or I'll do it."

"I see where you're going!" Mackenzie cooed happily. Thirty seconds ago she'd been willing to shoot Kevin in the head if she'd gotten her hand on that gun first, and now she had his back. Her instinct toward self-preservation was impressive. "*She* wanted Wes dead. And *she* was the one wearing the night-vision goggles in that room. Persey was the only one with the opportunity to kill him."

Was I?

"I knew you didn't solve that Hidden Library on your own," Mackenzie continued, positively gleeful. "You were on the inside the whole time. What's your real name, huh? Linda Browne? Lori Browne?"

"No," Persey said. "And just for the record, anyone who was working this from the inside would have to be completely batshit crazy to put themselves in the kind of danger we've experienced today. And I may be a lot of things, but I'm not crazy."

"Crazy might be an overstatement," Kevin said.

Mackenzie was quick to agree. As always. "Yeah. I mean, you'd have all the insider information. Know all the secrets. There'd be a thrill in it, too. Of course you were the one coming up with all those solutions today. Oh!" she said in a mocking falsetto. "A confession! That must be what we're supposed to do!" She laughed. "You knew the secret already. No one would have figured that out on their own."

I did. "That actually makes a lot of sense, but it still doesn't mean your insider is me."

"Well, it's either you or Kevin. You're the only two not connected to this Prison Break thing."

"So why not him?"

Mackenzie shrugged. "He's the one with the gun."

"Persey didn't kill Wes," Neela said. "She couldn't have."

"We don't know what happened in there," Mackenzie said. Her voice had turned slimy. "Maybe she pushed him."

"You were there, too." Persey arched an eyebrow. "Maybe *you* pushed him."

"I don't get my hands dirty."

"You sure about that?" Kevin asked.

The words weren't spoken in a flirtatious way, but Mackenzie certainly took them that way. She slid up behind Kevin and brushed her hands down the sides of his body. "I'll show you later just how dirty they can be."

"Make up your mind!" Kevin said, glancing to the camera once again. "Her or us."

And suddenly, Persey had an idea. She narrowed her eyes at Mackenzie. "I'm sure your hands are quite capable of making people do whatever you want. Like Wes?"

Mackenzie laughed. "Wes was broke and desperate."

"But not smart enough to come up with that Prison Break plan on his own."

A tiny smile broke the corners of Mackenzie's mouth. "Okay, I mean, when he told me about how he'd met B.J. while the two of them were getting drunk at his parents' casino, I *might* have planted a suggestion."

"You masterminded that plan?" Kevin asked.

"Yep."

"That's pretty hot."

Mackenzie's Achilles' heel. "You think?"

"Smart is sexy."

It took every ounce of self-control Persey had left to keep from rolling her eyes. "Just to be clear, it was you, Mackenzie, who came up with the plan to obtain confidential information on the Prison Break escape room?"

She laughed. "Well, you didn't really think it was Wes, did you?"

Kevin's eyes met Persey's. "No. I didn't." Then in one fluid motion he spun around and fired.

The bullet hit Mackenzie square in the chest, just an inch or two from her heart, and Persey could tell by the way her body hung frozen for a moment that she couldn't quite process what had happened to her. Blood spread rapidly across her white shirt, mixing with the grime and the gore already there and creating a mosaic of texture and shade that reminded Persey of a piece she'd once seen in a modern art museum.

But . . . Mackenzie mouthed rather than said; the words had no sound, just air. *But you . . .*

Persey had no idea what she was going to say. With a groan, Mackenzie collapsed onto the floor.

"Is . . . Is she . . . ?" Neela swallowed. "Dead?"

"I sincerely hope so," Kevin said. He approached Mackenzie's body, gun still gripped in his hand, and bent down, feeling for a pulse. With a sharp exhale, he leaned back on his heels, the gun dropping to the floor, forgotten. "She's dead."

"I should feel something," Neela said, her calm returning. "But I really don't. She wasn't a very nice person, and apparently, she's the reason we're here."

Kevin pushed himself to his feet. "I'm going to fire up the wood chipper, and then maybe we can all go home?"

Persey cringed. "Is that really necessary?"

"I don't make the rules." He pointed to the domed camera. "Don't worry. You ladies just chill. I'll take care of this."

He walked over to the wood chipper and began searching for an on button while Persey continued to stare at Mackenzie's body. She half expected to see her move for the gun, and despite not wanting to go anywhere near the body, she inched toward it and snagged the gun away.

A deafening roar erupted in the room, like metal grating against metal, and Persey and Neela both jerked away from the wood chipper, wedging their backs to the white wall. Persey tucked the gun into the waistband of her cargo pants before shoving her fingers into her ears, desperate to dampen the noise. She stood huddled against the wall until she felt Neela nudge her with an elbow, motioning toward the opposite side of the room. Right. They didn't want to be anywhere near that chute when the body went in. The last thing she needed was to be body-painted in Mackenzie chum.

They sidled down the wall to the opposite side of the room while Kevin returned to the body and gave them a thumbs-up before lifting Mackenzie and throwing her over his shoulder. Persey wanted to close her eyes, and yet somehow she couldn't. It was like watching news footage of a multi-car pileup: you knew it was going to end badly, but you can't look away.

Kevin was debating the best way to insert the lifeless corpse into the wood chipper, when Persey felt something. A thud against her back.

At first she thought it was Neela trying to get her attention, but a glance to her right proved that Neela was practically in the fetal position by her side, head tucked beneath her arm, refusing to watch.

She felt it again, stronger this time. And more than one. It felt like something or someone was pounding on the wall from behind them.

From the other side.

From the exit.

"Neela!" she screamed into the deafening roar. "Do you feel that?" She couldn't even hear her own voice and was pretty sure that Neela couldn't either. But her heart began to race as Kevin decided that headfirst was the way to go. Someone was outside this room trying to get inside.

Lifting with his legs, Kevin managed to flop Mackenzie's body off his shoulder and onto the short conveyor belt. It took all of five seconds for the belt to drag the corpse into the machine and then the metal grinding that filled the room shifted to a heavier, wetter sound, and instantly, a splatter of chunky red gore shot out the other end, spackling the white wall like a giant paintball pellet.

Kevin stared at the wall, nodding in appreciation of his handiwork while the wood chipper's deafening roar continued to fill the room.

Persey dashed over to the control panel and switched it off, letting out a slow breath as the gears wound down. Maybe now she'd be able to tell where that pounding was coming from.

"Tango Yankee," Kevin said with a salute.

"Huh?" Persey asked.

"It's the NATO phonetic alphabet," Neela explained. "Tango for T. Yankee for Y. Meaning, thank you. For turning off the chipper."

"What's the word for the letter L?"

"Lima."

Persey didn't even pause to offer an explanation. The word was hardly out of Neela's mouth when Persey yanked the gun from the back of her pants and pointed it straight at Kevin. "You."

Kevin stood preternaturally still. "What about me?"

"Mackenzie was right. There *was* someone working the inside, making sure that Wes did most of the dirty work before getting rid of him too."

"You think *I* work for Escape-Capades?"

Persey shook her head. "No, I think you *are* Escape-Capades."

Neela stepped behind her. "Persey, are you sure?"

"I've been a complete idiot," Persey said, holding the gun steady. "He told me his last name at the Hidden Library and at the time I thought it was kind of odd, but I couldn't put my finger on why. Kevin Lima. The international symbol for the letter *L*. Like in L. Browne." She took a step away from him, shepherding Neela behind her. "What does it stand for? Lucas? Larry?"

If Kevin had been considering a protest, he quickly decided against it. The carefree Kevin vanished, and the guy who remained was cool and calculating, an imposing figure of vengeance. "Lincoln."

"Oh my God," Neela said.

"Lincoln Browne," Persey said. "Sounds like a car model."

"Cute."

The pounding was louder, closer. She could hear voices too, shouting words that sounded very much like "Police!" and "Open up!"

She eyed the camera, hoping it was recording. She wanted a record of what happened next. "Wes killed B.J. and Arlo, and drugged Shaun. But it wasn't at Mackenzie's direction. It was at yours."

Lincoln laughed as he flashed one of his winning smiles. His overly tan skin gave him an affable-worldly-guy kind of aura that was deceptively disarming, and Persey could see how manipulative he could be. "The best part was that he didn't know it was me! I was a voice on the phone only. He had no idea I was there to get rid of him afterward."

Neela flattened herself against the wall. "Oh my fajita-ing God."

"In the Hidden Library, I was faltering. I couldn't figure out the final puzzle, and I remember you said that Persephone translated into 'bringer of death' and suddenly I knew how to solve it. Because you fed me the answer."

"Okay, yes." Lincoln grinned wider. "But you mostly figured out the rest on your own. I swear. You're pretty damn smart."

"And . . . and you wanted me to punch in the wrong code in the classroom," Neela added, anger creeping into her voice. "Because you knew what would happen."

Lincoln shrugged but didn't offer a defense.

"I think you picked me," Persey continued. "I think you'd been waiting for someone to get close to the solution so you'd be able to tag along on this competition without anyone suspecting who you were. Someone who had no connection *whatsoever* to the Brownes and Escape-Capades. So you doctored the game to make sure I'd solve it."

"Was Leah in on it, too?" Neela asked.

Lincoln shook his head. "I didn't trust anyone with my secret. She knew her script, and that was all. As soon as the competition began, she was completely locked out of the control room. Everything was automated."

The pounding was now accompanied by a buzz, which caught Lincoln's attention. "I'm guessing she's the one who called the police."

A flash of metal jutted through the pristine white of the shiny wall, and then a circular saw ripped into the stucco. The police were cutting through.

"They're coming!" Neela cried, grabbing Persey's arm. "We're going to be okay!"

"It's over, Lincoln," Persey said. *Finally.*

"Not quite."

The words were ominous and Persey tensed, but instead of racing toward her, Lincoln backed away. Toward the wood chipper.

"I get to choose how this ends," he said, pausing by the conveyor belt. "This is *my* escape room."

"Lincoln, no!"

In a flash, he had turned the machine on; the deafening roar drowned out all other attempts at speech. The police had managed to cut an L-shaped portion of the wall away and were using a battering ram on the other side to knock the rest in. Lincoln flashed Persey a smile, gave her a familiar wink; then as the police barreled through into the white room, Lincoln dove headfirst onto the conveyor belt and was gone.

FORTY-FIVE

PERSEY REMEMBERED NEELA'S HAND. IT SPENT THE BETTER part of the next hour clasped in her own, neither girl ready or willing to let go until a detective, anxious to get their stories separately, forced them apart.

She also remembered Leah's panicked, tearstained face, running back and forth getting information for whoever was asking. And Greg, still sullen in his neon lime green, leaning against a wall after his statement had been given, staring fixedly at his phone.

A veritable army of police and firefighters had descended on the Escape-Capades Headquarters. From where she sat in the glass-walled lobby, Persey noticed rows upon rows of black-and-white sedans, white-and-blue SUVs, and red trucks—a sea of spinning lights and beeping radios—parked haphazardly throughout the once-empty lot.

Between the questioning and conversations going on around her, Persey picked up the basics of what had happened since the moment Leah had ushered them into the Office Drones room six hours ago.

Six hours. They'd been inside the escape room gamut for six hours. And Persey would never be the same.

It had, apparently, taken Leah a while to figure out what was wrong. Lincoln's explanation had been correct—as soon as she tried to access the control room, she'd discovered the locked door. But with no reason to expect foul play, she assumed it was a glitch, and had gone first to her desk and then to the server room in an attempt to unlock those doors.

Soon, she realized that the system had been tampered with, at which point she called the heads of the Escape-Capades IT department and in-house security, both of whom were off on a Sunday. Forty-five minutes later, when security and IT confirmed that something really, really bad was going on, Leah had called 911.

It took the fire department a full thirty minutes to ax, cut, and saw their way through the many security doors that lead to True North, or as Persey would always remember it, the White Room. And they'd only arrived in time to save Persey and Neela.

There wasn't much left of Lincoln Browne, just a splatter on a splatter as he and Mackenzie were joined together for eternity. Persey overheard a uniformed officer say that it would take months to sort through the evidence, longer to positively ID the bodies who went through that wood chipper. At the moment, all they had were Neela's and Persey's eyewitness accounts, and the video footage from True North.

But *only* from True North. The rest, it seemed, hadn't been recorded.

Not that it mattered. True North included confessions by both Lincoln *and* Mackenzie. The room had lived up to its name—the public would now know that Derrick and Melinda Browne's deaths had been the result of an organized campaign of theft and greed. If Lincoln had been looking to avenge his parents, he had succeeded.

Persey wasn't sure how long she'd been sitting there by herself in the lobby when Neela was finally released from her questioning. She looked exhausted, escorted by a middle-aged female detective with sharp eyes and a sympathetic smile. She patted Neela on the shoulder before depositing her in the chair beside Persey.

"We'll have an officer drive you ladies back to your hotel," she said. "You're free to leave Las Vegas whenever you'd like, as long as we have contact information on both of you."

Neela simply nodded. She looked talked-out. A state that would have seemed impossible that morning.

"You okay?" Persey asked as soon as the detective was out of earshot. She might not have been able to save the others, but at least Neela was still here.

"I'm okay." She took a deep, steadying breath. "I just keep thinking that I should be one of them. One of the bodies. The 'evidence' they keep referring to. As if they weren't people. As if it shouldn't have been me."

"But it's not."

Neela turned to her. "Only because of you."

"We got lucky."

"Lucky . . ." Neela's face clouded for a moment. "It was bad luck," she said slowly, "that you ended up in all of this."

"Not entirely," Persey said. "Lincoln had been waiting for someone like me. Someone he could use."

Neela paused again, chewing at her bottom lip. "But lucky for him, I guess, that he found you just a couple of weeks before this competition."

"Yeah. Lucky."

Neela started to speak again, to ask a question, maybe, judging by the look of confusion on her face. But then she thought the better of it and clapped her mouth closed, leaving Persey to wonder what she'd been thinking.

A black-and-white pulled up in front of the main doors, and a tall young policemen with sandy-blond hair and an impressively 1970s mustache climbed out, triggering the automatic sliding doors as he strode up to the entrance. "Persephone?"

"Yes."

He nodded toward his squad car. "I'm supposed to take you to your hotel. Neela Chatterjee, your ride will be along in a sec."

Persey turned to Neela as the officer returned to his vehicle. "You're going to be okay. This is all over."

"Will I ever see you again?"

The question was so plaintive, so sad. Almost like a child who thinks Mom and Dad might not be there when they wake up in the morning. "Yeah, of course." Persey tried to sound cheerful. "I'll be in touch."

Neela nodded pensively, then threw her arms around Persey's neck and pressed their cheeks together, whispering in Persey's ear. "Take care of yourself, okay?"

"I—I will."

"Promise?"

Persey broke away from the hug. "I promise."

Persey climbed into the back of the police car and barely had a chance to close the door before the officer peeled away from the curb, lights and sirens blaring. Which seemed a little extra, considering they were leaving a crime scene, not going toward it. But whatever. He was having fun.

They drove in silence back toward downtown Las Vegas, and somewhere along the way, the lights were extinguished, the siren silenced, and the speed went from "Talladega" to "I-15" in the course of just a few miles.

By the time they got to the suburban outposts of Las Vegas, the drive felt so normal that Persey could have sworn she was just in an Uber, heading to the airport. The vibrations of the car lulled her, eyes heavy, the fatigue of the day overtaking her, and before she even realized what was happening, Persey had fallen fast asleep.

FORTY-SIX

IT WAS DARK WHEN SHE WOKE, HEAD STILL LEANING AGAINST the window of the squad car. Someone had knocked on the other side of the glass, jarring her from a blissfully dreamless sleep, and when she shook herself awake and climbed out of the car, she found that they were parked in an underground lot, as abandoned and empty as Escape-Capades had been that morning, beside a long black limousine with tinted windows.

It was unremarkable, especially in Las Vegas, where limos practically outnumbered cabs. A car that would blend in, unlike the enormous lime-green Escape-Capades Hummers. A guy stood at the rear door, holding it open for her, and without a word, Persey ducked inside.

"Can we get out of here?" she said impatiently. The driver, who looked remarkably like Greg, but without the hideous lime-green uniform, nodded and closed the rear door before taking his place behind the wheel. A few minutes later, the limousine pulled onto the brightly lit streets of Las Vegas.

Persey was not alone in the limo. Two people sat opposite her, a guy and a girl. He wore a slate-gray hooded sweatshirt, oversize and hood pulled low over his face so his features were obscured by the ceiling light that illuminated the plush, decked-out interior, and a pair of black track pants hiked up to the ankles so that Persey could see the well-manicured toes exposed by a pair of flip-flops.

A lowball glass sat in the cup holder to his right, ice cubes tinkling as Leah refilled his glass with a reddish-brown liquid at the bottom. Scotch.

Just like Dad.

Glass replenished, Leah curled up beside the guy before she tossed back his hood, exposing an unruly head of dark blond hair. And an exaggerated 1970s mustache that Leah promptly peeled away, revealing the smooth, hairless lip beneath.

As soon as his mustache was gone, he returned the favor, grabbing Leah's black-bobbed hair with both hands and giving it a vicious yank. The wig fell away; the straw-blond hair beneath was pinned into little rolled buns. Once her disguise was discarded, he took her face with both hands and kissed her deeply.

Persey averted her eyes.

"We did it," he said a full two minutes later when their tongues finally disentangled. "It worked."

"You were brilliant, babe," Leah said, stroking his cheek. "You should have been an actor."

He preened a little, as if the thought wasn't unfamiliar to him. "I quite enjoyed that, too. The theatrics, the character . . ."

The killing.

"I think I've been bitten by the acting bug," he said smiling. "Might have to try it again sometime."

Persey reached her hand to Leah. "You must be Genevieve."

"Yes!" she squealed, then held up her left hand, where a customized puzzle ring—Persey's mother's—sat on her fourth finger. "And we are sisters now! Isn't that exciting? I've always wanted a sister. Well, anyone other than Marshall." She gestured toward the driver, formerly known as Greg. "Little brothers are a pain in the ass."

"So are big brothers," Persey said.

"Oh, come on," her brother said, eyebrows raised. "You got what you wanted."

Not yet.

"And what did *you* want, huh? Revenge?"

Her brother looked at her with quizzical brows. "Yes, of course. They killed our parents."

No, they didn't.

"Why are you so pissy, huh?" Lincoln may have dropped out of college, but he still managed to sound like a frat boy. An entitled rich asshole who always got exactly what he wanted.

"You told me no one would get hurt."

The plan, as he'd told it to her over a cup of lukewarm coffee two months ago, was to use scare tactics and paranoia to extract confessions from those people who had been responsible for the "murder-suicide" of Derrick and Melinda Browne. They'd utilize the escape rooms already in development at their parents' company, which specialized in disorientating situations, to do the trick, videotaping the confessions to clear their parents' names.

He'd lied to her from the beginning. She knew that at the time. She knew more than he realized, but she'd gone along with it because her brother had something she desperately needed.

Money.

Persey's crash pad at Las Vegas's West Valley High School theater had been fine for the last few months, but scrounging for food as she tried to stretch her meager savings had proved more difficult (disgusting) than she'd anticipated. Besides, she'd be graduating in a couple of months, and then her access to the theater would be cut off. Her brother offered her something that was difficult to turn down and he knew it. But he'd promised that no one would get hurt.

Meanwhile he'd been planning this bloodbath all along.

"I said no one who was *innocent* would get hurt."

Liar.

Lincoln had been a liar his entire life, showing one face to the world while nurturing a dark, perverted secret deep within himself. Persey was probably the only person who truly understood who he was, and yet she'd allowed herself to believe this would be different.

She may not have killed all those people with her own hands, but their deaths were on her head.

Lincoln watched her carefully. "Don't be like that. You got to save your little friend back there."

Persey's eyes narrowed. "Promise me you'll leave Neela alone. She had no idea what she was doing."

"I still say she's the guiltiest of all." He met her gaze steadily, and once more, Persey recognized the bloodlust that had so terrified her that day in the guesthouse.

"Promise."

"I promise to leave her alone."

Persey didn't believe for one second that her brother was telling the truth, and she realized with a pang that Neela's life was, and would continue to be, her responsibility.

"Actually, it turned out to be a good thing you kept her alive," Lincoln said. "Two eyewitnesses instead of one."

Was he trying to placate her? Con her into letting her guard down with Neela? "Okay."

"And you're sure she doesn't suspect anything?"

Persey was careful neither to jump in too quickly with her response nor pause too long before she gave it. She thought of Neela's face as they sat in the lobby—the face of someone who realized the pieces didn't all add up—and lied to her brother. "Yes."

"Good. She'd be our only loose end, and I wouldn't want to have to snip it."

"You won't." *I won't let you.*

Persey needed to change the subject. "You went too far posing us as Laurie Strode and Michael Meyers. What if one of them had been a horror fan? They might have realized we were represented as brother and sister and put the pieces together."

Her brother laughed. "Oh, please. None of those people were going to figure that out. I was just having a little bit of fun."

"Fun?"

"So. Much. Fun!" He clapped on each word. "I don't even know what I loved the most: the staging, the trapdoor on that wood chipper, the maze of escape rooms? I mean, I know we had most of that stuff in development already, but it was a positively *inspired* idea on my part to string them all together."

There was his ego again.

"Brilliant," Genevieve said, stroking his cheek. "Amazing."

Barf.

"Or the night-vision goggles. Man, those things are a trip. Gen, you have to try them sometime."

"I'd love to!" Genevieve squealed. Which seemed to be her default mode of speaking. Turned out that Genevieve was the real actor of the bunch, playing a calm, suave businesswoman all day. She must have been very good at reading from a script.

"I'm surprised no one heard the clank when I dropped my pair in the pit," Lincoln mused.

Persey gritted her teeth. "I seem to recall a lot of screaming at the time."

He wasn't even listening, lost in his own rhapsodic replay of the afternoon. "But I think my favorite was that wood chipper. Setting it in a white room? Wow. The way the blood hit the white . . . I . . . I just . . ."

"Are you crying?" Persey asked, horrified.

He wiped his eyes. "It was beautiful."

Persey felt her stomach lurch. "It was Mackenzie's internal organs." This was her brother, her flesh and blood. Was there a piece of this bloodthirsty megalomaniac inside her as well? The thought was sickening.

"Your mess is my art."

Had he no sense of remorse for all these murders? Even the victims who were completely innocent? "Whose body did you use?" she asked. "In the wood chipper. That wasn't fake blood sprayed on top of Mackenzie."

"You know what I love?" Lincoln said. "I love that you care. About some drunk pedophile on the sex offenders list. You're a much better person than I am."

Fuck, I hope so.

"Don't worry about him. He died painlessly. And by the time the cops track down his DNA, you, Gen, Marshall, and I will be long gone."

Long gone. She was going to disappear where no one—not the police and certainly not her brother—would ever find her. She would leave Las Vegas and never come back. It might have been her hometown, where she was born and raised, and where her parents were buried, but she would never voluntarily set foot in it again. She just needed one thing first.

"Do you have it?"

"Always business. Just like Dad. You're more like him than you think."

"Take that back."

Lincoln laughed. It was genuine and disarming, and almost made her trust him. "Well, he would have been proud of you anyway. They both would."

That's when Persey snapped. "Proud of me? For what, standing by while you killed six people?"

Genevieve laughed. "Standing by? You practically ruined it today by trying to save them!"

Ugh. These two really *were* perfect for each other. She thought of Shaun's shrieks, of Mackenzie's pulverized remains, of the sound of Riot's body being squished by the collapsing ceiling. This was her fault. Their pain and suffering were on her head. "None of them deserved to die."

Her brother's head snapped up, eyes wide, nostrils flared. He looked like a bull who'd just been released into the ring. "Are you fucking kidding me? They killed Mom and Dad!"

Persey bit her lip. She wanted to tell him that she knew, that she'd been listening that afternoon in the kitchen. She wanted to ask how he'd moved their bodies to the office and made a murder-suicide look so convincing. Maybe he bribed the police. Or maybe he was just *that* brilliantly evil. Either way, she was done pretending that this whole endeavor had been one big helping of justice served instead of what it actually was: a way for her brother to appease his bloodlust.

She lowered her chin and stared Lincoln dead in the eye. "I know exactly who killed Mom and Dad."

Lincoln didn't blink, but the lines of his face tightened. *He knows I know.* Good. If there was one thing Persey wanted to take away from this horrible day, it was the knowledge that her brother was ever so slightly afraid of her.

Lincoln gave his head a shake, tossing off the tension that had descended upon him, harshing his post-kill high, and reached into a side compartment in the wall of the limo, removing a slim white envelope. "Here."

Persey's fingers trembled as she took the envelope from his outstretched hand, then tucked it into her bra strap beneath her shirt. Inside, the access codes to a bank account with ten million dollars. Her future.

"Aren't you going to look at it?"

"I trust you." She didn't, but if he hadn't given her a portion of the inheritance like he'd promised, it wasn't as if she had any recourse. "What time is my flight?"

"In two hours," Genevieve answered, pulling her phone from her bag. "You change planes in Atlanta, then Chicago, then back to Las Vegas. Similar to your flights in this morning. It'll take all of tonight into tomorrow, but it should make it difficult for anyone to trace you."

Persey nodded. *Especially since I'm buying a new ticket out of Chicago.* It wasn't just the police she was running away from. "What about you guys?"

"Marshall has a one-way ticket to Brazil. He's got a business scheme down there. Gen and I are headed back to Phu Quoc island for a little honeymoon on the beach." He slipped his arm around his wife's waist, pulling her close.

Persey didn't know much about Vietnam, but she was pretty sure it was a country with no extradition treaty.

"And then?" Lincoln continued. "I don't know. LA, I think. I rather enjoyed my time as Kevin. Maybe I'll try my hand at acting?"

"I'm sure you'd be great at that," Persey said drily.

Her brother grinned, amused. "Or maybe I'd be better suited as a producer. I did a rather good job of it today. Maybe game shows. Or competitions."

Persey didn't really care what he did as long as he did it far, far away from her, and silence descended upon them as Marshall pulled into the terminal at McCarran Airport.

"One question," Lincoln said, leaning forward so his elbows rested on his knees. "Why did you choose Persephone?"

Persey wondered if her brother even remembered that Persephone was her middle name, that she'd always felt some sort of kinship toward the kidnapped princess who spent half the year in a cage of luxury, or that she'd always hated her first name, but she wasn't about to share any of that. "I've just always liked it."

"You could have used your real name," he pressed. "No one even knows who Kimber Browne is."

Kimber, a name more suited to a cheerleader than a loner. That name was dead.

"I guess." Persey shrugged, then realized she had one more question for her brother. "Do you have a name picked out?"

His face lit up, delighted to be asked. "As a matter of fact, I do. Abe, after Abraham Lincoln. Get it?"

Ugh.

"And Bronson. It means Browne. An homage, if you will."

"Abe Bronson," Persey said committing it to memory as she opened the back door of the limo. "I'll keep an eye out for it."

He leaned forward, eyes dancing around her face. "I'm relatively sure you'll see that name again."

(NOT) THE END

ACKNOWLEDGMENTS

I'VE ALWAYS SAID THAT WRITING A NOVEL "TAKES A VILLAGE," but writing a novel right after giving birth to a child brings a whole new meaning to that phrase. Here are the people who made *#NoEscape* possible:

To my husband, John Griffin. I usually start with the professionals and end with the family, but I literally could not have written this novel without his help, taking over baby duties with our newborn son over and over and over again to give me time to write. And sleep. Well, mostly write. I couldn't do any of this without him.

To my editor, Kieran Viola. When I turned in this manuscript, I told her that this was either the greatest book I'd ever written or it was completely unreadable. She assured me it was somewhere between those extremes, and then really helped me mold this manuscript into the madcap murderfest it is.

To my agent, Ginger Clark, who definitely endured more whinging from me during the course of this book than during any other time in our long partnership. Thank you for putting up with it.

To the fabulous team at Freeform Books, whose collaborative efforts made this book shine, especially Marci Senders, Cassidy Leyendecker, David Jaffe, Guy Cunningham, Christine Saunders, Seale Ballenger,

Elke Villa, Dina Sherman, Marybeth Tregarthen, and Sara Liebling.

To my "orange" family at Curtis Brown, who have continued to kill it (see what I did there?) for me through ten novels, especially Sarah Perillo, Nicole Eisenbraun, Holly Frederick, and Madeline Tavis.

To my mother, Peggy McNeil, who came for multiple visits during my deadline push to lend a hand with the baby and make sure I got as much writing and editing time as possible.

To the entire NICU staff at Cedars-Sinai who lovingly took care of my son for forty-six agonizing days when I should have been writing this book but wasn't.

And lastly, to my son, also John, who would nap beside me while I worked and has taught me a whole new meaning of the word *love*.

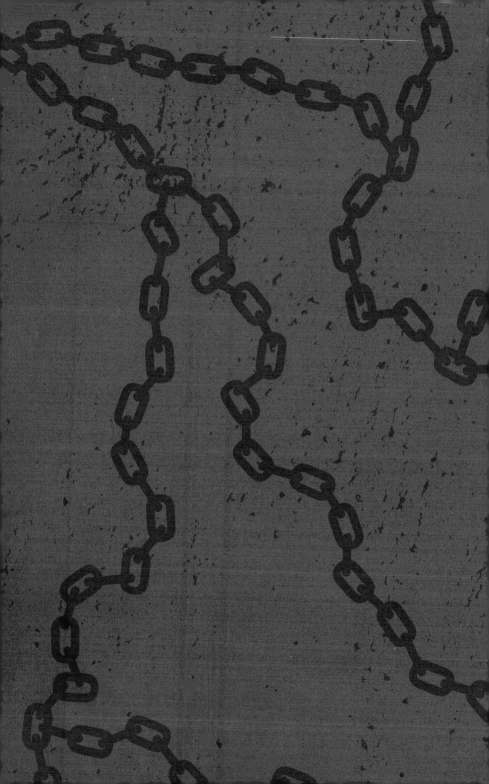